Natural Causes

by

Gary Neil Gupton

1.

The royal blue and gold of Earl's warmup suit shimmers in the sunlight streaming through the silvery bows of loblolly pine. Tall and proud in all his glory after hurdling the boundary, the cyclone fencing, between academia and adolescence, free from the sophomoric reality of Loblolly High School. Safe. Inside the boys' fortress surrounded by pine and laurel.

His best friend Chuck stumbles into the center of the pine straw clearing, gasping for breath. He tugs at the seat of his baggy jeans, rips the hole started by his awkward attempt to follow his athletic friend over the barb-topped fence. Chuck shakes his head and rolls over, submitting to his plight. Earl kicks the sole of Chuck's airward canvas high-top.

"Hey, dog, you ain't getting no belly rub."

Earl sits down on the overturned orange bucket at the edge of the clearing and sears open the Velcro side pocket of his pants. He slides out a red and white poly pouch and pulls the tab. The seal hisses, the aroma of flue-cured tobacco. Chuck perks up, eager for the treat. Earl plucks a tiny rectangular box from his slash pock, slides it open with his thumb and removes a single red-tipped wooden match. A hot commodity.

His sister Pam had supplied him with just enough matches to light the ration of tobacco cigarettes she had gotten through her connections at Viceroy College. Last year she was forced to confide in him at the Quik-Charge station. She had fumbled a suspicious pouch from her satchel, snatched it up, tucked it away and flipped out her Unicard, a slight of hand trick she hoped would distract her brother. But her furrowed brow and shifty eyes gave it away. Her brother had seen something he shouldn't have.

She slid her card into the slot, lifted the handle and plugged in the charger for their mom's electric car.

"What's that?"

"What, this?" She eases the pouch just above the rim of her satchel.
He smirks. "Yes, that."

She pinches the corner of pouch and holds it up. "This little pouch? Just a little tobacco."

"Cigarettes?" He shuffles to her side. "You know they're illegal, right?"

"Shhhee-it. You don't say?"

"We read about those in Domestic History class."

"They're not history." She plucks a brown fingerlet from the pouch. "See? This is real time."

Earl holds his palm over the cigarette. "Somebody'll see."

She brushes his hand away. "No big deal." She brings the little paper cylinder to her lips.

"You can't..."

She grins and puts the contraband back into the pouch. "Scared you, didn't I? Wouldn't want you to get arrested, brother."

"I ain't scared of that." He looks around to see if anybody is looking. "Emaw said they used to call them cancer sticks. They'll kill you."

Pam stuffs the pouch deep into her satchel and clinches it under her arm and looks up at Earl. "She's right."

"Then why use..."

"We just do." She watches the meter as the power flows into the car. "People have always used or abused something: tobacco, alcohol, prescription and over-the-counter drugs...each other."

Earl tilts his head like a confused mutt. "But they're illegal. Vaping is the safe way..."

"Those fruity e-cigs? Those little jewels might vaporize you." She frowns. "This is serious. The e-vape companies don't have to etch any warnings on the vials – like the lung-rot photos on the old cigarette packs. But those giant tobacco companies are gone. People got scared."

"Shouldn't we be?"

The meter blinks 'Full' and Pam unplugs the charger.

"Scared of the big companies that hide the truth. They deny the dangers of vaping. They lobby – pay off - the government officials blind us to the truth. Their truth is in the profits."

"But what about..."

"Yeah, we should be scared. But not of these little things. The bigger things. The giants."

"So how do we know..."

They get in the car, slide the doors closed. Pam turns to her brother. "I'm gonna tell you. My people, the Naturalists..."

"Your people?"

"My people, the club, the NUB: Naturalist Underground Bar."

"That says a lot, 'Bar'."

"It's not like that – not exactly." Pam tucks her satchel in the compartment behind Earl's seat. "We like the old ways, natural: Harvesting and curing. Picking, squeezing, and fermenting. Growing, eating organic – everything. It's all good!"

"All?"

4

"Well, not all of it. The natural ways are a lot better than those imitation vapes, a flavor for everything, to cloud our lungs and minds. Get you high; bring you down. Cure what ails you; kill you."

Pam looks left, right then left again and eases the electric car onto the thoroughfare.

Back at the fort.

"That smells so good, but you know it's illegal, right?" Chuck moves in a little closer, takes a big whiff.

"So, don't take the chance." Earl plucks the brown paper fingerlet from the pouch. Natural, organic tobacco. He puts the cigarette to his lips. It wiggles as he speaks. "You can always pull out your e-cig and vape on that. Wouldn't want you to get in trouble."

"I'm not afraid of trouble. I'm skipping school with you, aren't I? I'm *looking* for trouble, in fact." Chuck holds out his hand. "You want me to hold that while you light it?"

Earl places his thumb and forefinger at the base of the cigarette and begins the lightly tapping ritual, packing the tobacco. "For a slow burn." He holds it out to Chuck.

Chuck gingerly takes the prepped brown cigarette, fumbles it, recovers, and places it between his lips.

"Don't drop that baby! Pam would kill me if she knew I'd shared this – and worse if she knew I wasted it!"

The little brown twig wags. Chuck maintains his lip grip.

"Hold it still! I've only got one match!" Earl slides the red tip of the match along the rough worn edge of the orange bucket. A baby flame licks off the end of the wooden stick. Cupping his hands to block the breeze he offers the fire to the tip of the cigarette. It accepts the gift and glows cherry red.

"Ahhh…" Chuck inhales a sigh. It becomes a coughing fit trying to expel the hot fleck of tobacco from his esophagus, the smothering smoke from his bronchioles.

"Easy, Chuck. Don't drop that cigarette!".

The victim surrenders the smoking gun. "Worried more about your precious contraband than you are about your friend."

Chuck pulls the piccolo sized device from the fat pocket of his carpenter jeans. "I'll stick with this." He presses the button. It lights up, ready. He inhales deeply and holds it in, relishing the bubble gum flavor. A cloud of white vapor bellows out his mouth, a dragon ready to burn. A little nicotine, purified water – and a few carcinogens enter his lungs. Chuck smiles a satisfied, toxic smile and doesn't cough. "Ahhh…"

Earl blows smoke rings toward the clear blue autumn sky. Buzzards circle high above the cool green tips of the loblolly pines.

"This is as good as it gets, Chuck." Earl puffs.

"Yep." White vapor spills upward with the word.

A ring of decaying pine logs, outlying laurel, saplings, and weeds shield them within the circle – like where a UFO landed. Nothing grows through the flat, compacted layer of brown pine straw. Natural. Strangely unnatural, the orange plastic bucket sits at the edge of the circular plane.

As good as it gets.

The boys who built this fortress years ago never thought they'd grow up.

Forever.

Yep.

The woods were a sanctuary from the wilderness out yonder.

"You're 'most a man," Earl's dad had said to his sixteen-year-old son.

Puffing and thinking. Pondering everything. And nothing.

A faint whistle in Earl's earwig derails his train of thought.

"Who'd be calling me? I'm supposed to be in school."

"You'd better see. Don't mention me being with you!"

Earl touches the flesh colored bud in his left ear. The digital voice identifies Reverend Arnold.

"Hello?" Earl says.

"Earl? Reverend Arnold. I tried to get you through the school office, but they said they couldn't find you, so I thought I'd call you."

"I – I'm not feeling so good. I left school – on my way – walking home." He coughs, feeling guilty for the fib.

The Reverend worries. *He can't go home, not now.* "I need to talk with you - about something. Why don't you come by my office at church first?"

The Reverend prays. *Watch over him, Lord.*

"What's up, Reverend Arnold? I'm really feeling kind of – nauseous." *Fibber.* Earl thinks.

"You'll be OK. I'll fix you a sandwich – you'll feel better." *You're going to feel worse.* The Reverend thinks.

"Oh – okay. I'm on - on my way."

"Good. Now, don't mess around." *Lord, give me strength.*

Earl touches his earwig and ends the call.

"What's going on, Earl?" Chuck worries. *We're busted.*

"Just the Reverend. Wants me to stop by the church to see him before I go home – didn't say why."

"Want me to come with you?" *I don't want to go.*

"Nah, he'd know we were skipping school if we were together. I told him I was sick." *Fibber. Stop it!*

"OK, call me later, or come by the house. Let me know what's up."

"I think he might know I've been skipping - and want to *counsel* me, maybe save my lost soul." *Lying - and blasphemy. I'm going to hell.*

Chuck smacks him on the back. "You're not lost – you're right here." As Earl takes the cigarette from his mouth, the hot cherry pops off the end of the cigarette. It rolls and drifts down among the dried pine needles, unnoticed. Earl snuffs out the remainder of the cigarette with a pinch of his fingers and tucks it into his pouch – for later. Never waste a bit of the precious golden leaf. His sister Pam taught him well.

2.

The Gospel of Truth Church is on the north side of school, and their fort home to the south. Earl wouldn't have to pass home on the way to the church.

Thank God, the Reverend prayed.

He would have to take the long way around – several blocks – so he wouldn't pass the school and get caught skipping. Earl lopes northward keeping a city block's distance between him and school.

Chuck lumbers through the woods toward home and emerges on the green grass by the cul-de-sac at the end of their street. Two black and white police cars, blue lights bubbling, are parked in front of his house. An ambulance is backed up to the walkway, red and white lights flashing above its open rear doors. He runs, baggy jeans flapping and sagging, resistant to his stride. He stops. The commotion is not at his house, but at Earl's house next door. Earl's mom, Mrs. Cleveland, is hunched over at the edge of the yellow police tape, sobbing onto the shoulder of a man. The man is not Mr. Cleveland. It's Coach Bruce, the high school basketball coach.

Mr. Cleveland – everyone called him Cleve – lay sprawled on the gray slate patio by the pool outside the French doors at the rear of the house. Dressed in his favorite red, black and white Hawaiian shirt, baggy Bermuda shorts and flip flops. He could be relaxing, on a tropical beach. But he's dead. A bloody crimson halo, painted on the cool slate pallet, crowns his head. His eyes stare up at the house. The eerie blue light of an e-pipe glows in the palm of his lifeless left hand.

Beside the granite façade of the church office, Earl raises his fist to knock on the mahogany door. Muffled on the other side of the door another man's voice, not of the Reverend's, strikes a concerned chord in Earl.

I knew it. There's going to be trouble. Earl contemplates running away.

From the piney woods behind Loblolly High School, ominous puffs of black and white smoke.

Prelude to Earl and Chuck skipping school.

Felicity, Philly to her friends, stands behind Earl watching him fumble with his kno-pad, trying to disengage the charged battery from the power port in the back of the locker while holding the spent battery from the disabled unit in his hand. He haphazardly drops a red and white pouch on the floor by his size 14 feet. Philly bends over discreetly in her short Tartan plaid schoolgirl skirt and snatches the pouch, but just as quickly the hand above grabs her wrist.

Earl bends to her level, takes her by the shoulders, pulls her close to him and looks her squarely in the eyes.

"Hey, girl, you looking for trouble?" he asks.

Philly quick smiles; Earl loosens his grip. So close to kissing that they can feel each other's breath, they are interrupted by the loud violin music, the two-minute reminder to head to class. Earl's parents had told him stories of their high school days where obnoxious bells and buzzers sounded warnings to 'get to your place – and now!' This loud string music was irritating, because you knew the motivation behind it, but Earl would much rather be soothed into action than prodded.

"I've *found* trouble." She whispers in his ear, "You better hide that contraband."

"Oh, I'm getting rid of it. Chuck and I are cutting out as soon as the second violin plays."

Philly knows where the boys are going. Earl has taken her to their fort once. Funny how little boys used to play there, and young men still wanted to play there. A year ago, and a year younger (Philly was always a year younger than Earl), they had been walking around the 'hood – she lives a half dozen blocks away from him.

"Want to go see our old fort?"

"Where?"

"In those woods," Earl said, pointing to the pine grove at the end of the subdivision.

"Sure," she answered, suspicious.

Earl took off running through those woods as fast as he could go – not so fast that Philly couldn't keep up.

She had lost sight of him and was about to turn around and go back home when Earl jumped from behind a laurel. Philly squealed, but knew it was Earl. He took her by the hand and walked her past the laurel thicket, into a clearing, where there was nothing but a floor of pine straw and a big orange paint bucket. *He lifted her up by the shoulders stood her up on the bucket pedestal.*

"Now we see eye to eye," Earl grinned.

"You!" She pushed him. Neither of them could quite recall how it happened, but Philly started falling and fell right into Earl's arms. He leaned in to her startled, slightly parted lips, and... or did she lean in? They kissed. Eyes wide open, she pushed away from him, stumbled backwards, tipping the bucket. She turned tail and ran for home as fast as she could run. Earl stood there, mouth hanging open. Philly disappeared into the piney woods, running like a rabbit from a beagle hound. He leaned over and picked up the overturned bucked and looked down into it, as if expecting to see something – nothing was there. No one was there except him holding the bucket.

3.

The voices hushed behind the door of Reverend Arnold's office. Earl knew he had been found out.

"Earl?" The Reverend opens the dark mahogany door. "Come on in,"

A light-complexioned African-American man, deadpan expression, dressed in a business brown suit and tie, stands by the Reverend's desk in the center of the amply stocked library, half-facing Earl.

"Earl, Earl Cleveland?" the suited man asks.

The Reverend introduces them. "Earl, this is Mr. – Detective – Brown. Detective Brown, this is Earl Cleveland."

"Earl." the detective offers his hand – which Earl declines – then offers his fist.

"What's up, Reverend Arnold? Sounded like it was something important." Earl squares off with the man. "What's he doing here?" *Am I in trouble?*

"No, no, you're not in trouble, Earl. Sit down, we need to talk about something – important." The Reverend tries to reassure.

Earl sits in one of the burgundy leather armchairs by the door. The Reverend slides his chair close to Earl's. Detective Brown stands over them, his hands in his pants pockets.

"Earl, son." the detective says, a bit too familiar.

"I'm not your son."

"I'm sorry, son – Earl. Something's happened at home." He puts a hand on Earl's shoulder. Earl shrugs it off. "It's you father, and we wanted to break the news to you before you went home."

"My dad? Is he OK?" Earl knows that his dad is not OK, considering these clandestine circumstances.

Reverend Arnold lays his hands-on Earl's arm.

"Your father's dead." The officer comes directly to the point, ripping off the Band-aid. "He was at home this morning…"

"No! He was there…this morning…I left him and Mom…"

"Earl, your mother was there…" He doesn't want to say it. "She found him lying on the patio."

"Tina!" Earl suddenly realizes that his four-year-old sister might be home. "Where's Tina?"

"Tina's fine. She's with your grandmother, Ester. She wasn't home when… it happened," Reverend Arnold tries to reassure.

"When did *it* happen? What happened?"

Detective Brown cuts in. "We're not sure yet – could have been a heart attack." A usual, vague answer to an unexplained death. "He fell on the patio, hit his head."

"But he can't be…"

"I'm sorry," Detective Brown says.

Earl gets up and heads toward the door.

"Why don't you stay here for a while, Earl, until things settle down at the house," the Reverend offers.

"My Mom! What about Mom?"

"Don't worry, Earl," the Detective says. "Coach Bruce happened to be going by the house. I think he was looking for you - when you weren't in school."

"Coach?" *Why would Coach be there?* Earl wonders.

"Would you like me to take you to your grandmother's, to be with your little sister?" Detective Brown offers.

"Pam, at college – who'll let her know? I should go there…"

"No, you'll be better off with your little sister, grandmother, your mom - and Reverend Arnold. Chuck's parents have offered to drive up to Viceroy college to let your sister know."

"But, what…" Earl suddenly thinks of himself. Everyone's taken care of – but him. He's stuck here in the middle between the official and the Reverend, neither of whom he can really talk to - or not talk to.

"Son let me drive you…" the detective starts.

"You're safe here, Earl, stay…" the Reverend advises.

"No, I'm OK. I need to go…back to school…my friend Chuck, and…" he thinks, *Philly.*

"You need to…"

"Stay here…"

"I gotta go." Earl deliberately pulls his arm from Reverend Arnold's grasp. He bounds for the door, bumping hard against the end table. The door slams against the bookcase, sending books flying. Earl sprints down the hall, disappears around the corner of the church annex.

Detective Brown and Reverend Arnold, dumbfounded, admit that two middle aged men cannot possibly chase down an athletic sixteen-year-old. The detective immediately calls an officer at Earl's house to give a head's up that the boy is upset and may be heading home.

Earl's thoughts spin, running, running back to the safe place – the fort. That's where the good memories are, the serenity of the laurel, the tall pines, the insulation of the pine straw, his best buddy Chuck – and once, Philly. A little friendship, a little love, not some official's duty or a reverend's dogma. Simplicity, the way it was when he was a boy in the make-believe fort.

He stops in front of the school. Hordes of students are circling up in classroom groups and little cliques, while lovers stand against the cyclone fencing on the boarder of the school yard, spectators of the main event behind the school. Smoke, exhaled by the dark green bows at the tops of the loblolly pines, follows the south wind, in the direction of home.

"No!" Earl shouts. No one hears above the noise of the crowd. He runs through the throng of classmates, oblivious to the pushing and bumping and stumbling over running shoes, high tops, sneakers, and sandals, toward the back fence over which he had leapt so many times. The black *caution* of the yellow police tape weaves along the metal links. The royal blue and orange *Warrior* billboard towers above, watching over its Loblolly High School.

A heavily armored yellow-coated, helmeted fireman orders, "Son, you'll have to stay back."

"Where's the fire? I don't see it," Earl pleas, delirious.

"Back in the woods – brush fire - some kids' camp, or a homeless camp. Illegal smoking, probably. Now move back, son."

Earl stares deeply into the pine grove, but sees only charcoal gray pine tree trunks, nothing beyond, as was their plan when he and Chuck built the fort those years ago. Hidden, secret, forbidden except to the original settlers, the pioneers – and occasional invited guest.

A hand grabs Earl by the elbow. Normally this would incite a defensive reaction, but today, now, he is numb.

"Earl," the familiar easy voice calls. He doesn't respond to her voice nor the touch of her hand. Philly steps around him, gazes up at his face. "I'm sorry."

Earl stands staring into the pine grove, something beyond the trees. Philly leans into him and places her arms around his waist, laying her head against his overheating heart.

"It's gone." He's cold, bland.

"I'm sorry." She embraces, squeezing him tightly.

"Dad's gone." No emotion.

"What?" She tries to remain calm, for Earl, though she hasn't heard this worst news.

"Dad's dead." His voice fades.

Philly tries to read his face but cannot read the blank page. She knows there's nothing else she can do, so she clings to him, holding him up. The young man a half meter taller than she. He could lift her up and kiss her —or crush her. Here she stands, supporting Earl.

4.

"Want me to drive awhile, honey?" Mrs. Taylor asks her husband, who seems distracted, lost in his own world behind the wheel.

"What?" His thoughts fly away. Charlie had not been close friends with Cleve, but they had played golf on occasion, had family cookouts, and spoken back and forth coming and going to work and during Saturday yard work – casual stuff. Cleve seemed a hardworking man, content with his job, caring of his children, but not overly or outwardly happy or enthusiastic, but neither did he show signs that he was unhappy -or unhealthy.

"Do you want me to drive, Charlie?" Rae Taylor pulls him back to the here and now.

"For a three-hour trip? We're over halfway there, and I'm fine, Rae. Driving keeps my mind off things."

"What are you thinking?" She knows he won't tell. "How do you think Pam will take the news?"

"How? It'll devastate her. Cleve was so healthy. How could her Dad have died?" Charlie stares straight ahead.

"The Lord works in mysterious ways. But people talk. If anything is suspicious, we'll hear about it soon enough through the grapevine. Hopefully Lila will cut it before it grows," says Rae.

"So, it's official, natural causes – until there's evidence otherwise," says Charlie.

"The main concern now is for Cleve's family, the children, Pam and Earl - and especially that sweet little girl, Tina. Think she'll understand?" Rae says.

"Understand? No, all she'll know is that her daddy's not here today, or tomorrow, or the next day. She'll wake up first thing, or realize later in the day, times when Daddy would be leaving or coming to Ester's. 'Where's Daddy?' Tina will ask her. 'Daddy's not here.'" Charlie looks straight down the highway.

"It's a good thing she has her grandmother Ester. Her wisdom will help Tina get through this." Rae furrows her brow. "You know she stays with Ester more than she stays at home? Lila doesn't work – outside the home – but she's always found ways to get away from those kids. I don't know about her. When Earl was big enough to get out and play on his own, about the time we moved in – they were 9 – she just let him run, all day long in the summers, and never thought twice about where he was. He was

15

usually at our house, playing with Chuck, or they'd be off in the woods at their fort. I knew where they were; she hardly ever did." Rae shakes her head.

"Maybe you're being a little hard on her, Rae. She's just become a widow, with two children still at home. She'll need all the support she can get. The grapevine spread all those stories, some truth I suppose about Lila being treated for depression - and Lord knows what other kind of psychological disorders." Rae punches his shoulder. "Ow!" He gives her a look. "They say she's drugged up all the time – can't cope with the kids, especially."

"All I know is she dumped that little girl on grandma – probably fortunately for Tina. I know Ester thinks the world of that granddaughter. Thankfully, Chuck and Earl are buddies. Lord knows what Earl would've gotten into without Chuck," says Rae.

"And what Chuck would've gotten into without Earl. Earl did get into that little Philly girl from up the block." Charlie smiles.

"She's a real sweet girl, Charlie. She and Chuck have been really good for Earl." Rae lays a hand on Charlie's arm.

"I hope they can all keep it together – with this mess with Cleve – and not lose it like Lila has." He frowns. "All alone, I don't know who she's going to turn to."

Chuck allows a wide girth around the police line stretched across Earl's front yard. He walks slowly past the scene – of the crime? Two ladies stand on the sidewalk in front of the duplex across the street, looking, pointing, shaking their heads.

"I just can't believe it. Why would somebody *do* that?" one of the ladies says.

Chuck thinks. *Do what?*

The other lady continues. "That nice, beautiful family. Everything seemed fine. Well, except for that woman. Maybe *she* pushed him over the edge."

"To just haul off and die like that, out of nowhere. He seemed fine."

"Maybe there's a lot we didn't see – and I don't know about her. Just look at her, huddled up with that man – is that the basketball coach from the high school?"

Chuck had seen. *What is he doing here anyway? Looking for Earl?* He turns his head as he passes. Coach sees him and eyes him all the way home.

5.

Ester's four-years-old granddaughter – Tina corrects, *almost five!* - fidgets in the metal folding chair at the card table, swinging her shiny black patent leather shoes and lacy white socks underneath. She raises her miniature pink flowered china teacup, pinky out, to her lips and takes a loud pretend sip of hot tea.

"Oh, be careful, Tiny Tina, the tea is very hot." She cautions her rosy-cheeked yellow-bonneted doll boosted up by a mountain of old catalogues and magazines. Tina sits upon two 1955 brown leather Funk and Wagnall dictionaries so she can see to take tea. Tiny Tina doll, pursed porcelain lips and brightly painted baby blue eyes, stares straight across the table toward Emaw's empty seat.

Ester answers her old-fashioned black flip phone.

"Hello, this is Ester speaking.

Yes, how are you, Reverend Arnold?

Yes, yes, she's here – why?

Something's happened - to Cleve? How is he?

No, no, it can't be."

Ester begins a controlled whisper. She turns toward Tina, smiles, and then returns to her call in the kitchen.

"He was fine. How?

No, he seemed OK this morning when he dropped Tina off.

Yes, yes, I wouldn't want her anyplace else.

No, I haven't seen Earl.

He left your office. Real upset – of course.

If he comes here, I'll keep him. Yes, yes. He's a levelheaded boy. Just needs to get it straight - in his head.

No. Yes, I'll call you as soon as he shows up, Reverend.

Thank you. Alright.

Bye." She closes the flip phone.

"Emaw, come drink your tea before it gets cold, please," Tina implores. How can Emaw let a phone call interrupt teatime? Teatime is *very* important, and they must sit and have tea every afternoon, like proper ladies – that's what Emaw says.

"I'm coming, madam. Heat up my cup for me, would you, please?" Tina picks up the china tea pot and pours a spot of pretend tea in her grandmother's cup.

Ester stops at the old upright piano and picks up a photo of her Cleve when he was four or five, about Tina's age. He's holding up a toy wooden rifle in one hand, a faux coonskin cap atop his freshly bowl-cut hair, standing in front of the broken tree limb fort that he had built out back of their house.

"Whatcha looking at, Emaw?"

Ester stares into the little boy's eyes in the picture and kisses his cheek. "Oh, it's just an old photo."

"Can I see?"

Ester stands the frame on the card table beside the teapot.

Tina touches her finger on the silver frame. "Oh, I've seen that before. That's my Daddy when he was little."

"That's right." She takes Tina by the hand. "That *was* your Daddy."

6.

"You sure this is the dorm, Charlie?" Rae asks.

"See, right here on the GPS." Charlie points to the broken screen in the console of the Prius.

"Third floor? Where's the elevator?"

"Come on, old woman." He taunts and takes her hand.

Huffing and puffing up three flights of stairs, they stop and take a breathy break.

"We're not eighteen anymore, are we, old man?"

"Here we are, Room 311." Charlie exhales.

"Hers is 301, Charlie, at the far end of the hall."

"Can this room really be any further away than this?"

"Come on, Charlie, you're a young buck."

"Yes, deer." He snorts.

At the far end of the hall, Rae looks at the 301 then at Charlie. "Well, knock on the door."

"But what are we going to say to her?"

"She'll know there's something wrong, but we'll just go slow – or should we break it to her quickly?"

Before Charlie can knock, the metal dorm door swings in. A young short-haired brunette wearing a tank top, baggy blue plaid boxers and white bobby socks steps up, nonchalant as if expecting them. "May I help you?"

"Oh...um..." Charlie stammers. "...is Pam in. Pam Cleveland?"

"My roomie, Pam? No, she's not here. She went down to the NUB." The freshman hesitates. "She went out to...uh...study."

"We need to see her. We've come to take her home," says Rae.

"Home? Who are you? You're not her parents." She looks them up and down.

Charlie checks to see if his shoe is untied – or if his fly is undone.

"Charlie, we should tell her – we've got to get Pam." Rae becomes impatient.

"OK, let's start with what's *your* name?" Charlie asks.

"Stew – that's what they call me. My last name's Stewart. Don't call me Marguerite – that's my real name, but Stew suits me better." She gives her long introduction. TMI.

"OK, Stew." Rae gets to the point. "We have some rough news for Pam."

"Are her parents pulling her out of school? She's been working hard – I swear. She's just been distracted with all this experimentation – college, you know?" Still, TMI.

"Experimentation? What *kind* of experi…" Charlie starts.

"Mr. Cleveland died today." Rae gets to the point.

"My God! Died? I know he was kind of old – like you…" Stew chatters on. "But he hadn't been sick. Pam hadn't said…"

"It was sudden." Rae steps up, puts a gentle hand on Stew's arm. "I'm sorry to put you in the middle like this."

"She's my roomie, my girl." Stew gets serious. "That's what I'm here for."

"Thank you, Stew. Pam will need all the support she can get." Rae continues. "Where'd you say we can find her?"

"I shouldn't tell." She pauses. "But this is kind of an emergency, so…she's at the NUB. It's sort of a bar slash coffee shop slash study hall slash dealer in contraband," Stew elaborates.

"Contraband?" says Charlie.

"Yeah, all the *natural* stuff you guys used back in the day: tobacco, *real* coffee, fermented beverages – wine, ale, beer." Stew stops abruptly.

"We remember. They're all illegal now. Nicotine, caffeine, alcohol – the same stuff, but now prescriptions, vials, vapes, joules, e-pipes…" Charlie continues, thinking. *It's safer. Regulation, control…no more alcoholics or addicts…they say.*

Stew stops him. "Yeah, all that. But you've got to promise to be cool – if I tell you how to get there."

"*Be cool?* We used to say that *back in the day*," says Rae.

"Don't tell her I told you any of this. Pam's my girl." Stew continues. "She's a Naturalist, you know…"

"Naturalist…whatever you want to call it, it's still illegal – but I've been there." Charlie remembers, *what was illegal in our day, much worse than this.*

"You're cool. Just please don't tell her I told you anything," Stew pleads.

"Promise. Now where do we find her?" asks Rae.

"Hold on," Stew goes back inside. Shuffling papers. Slamming drawers. Searching for something. She emerges holding a brown three by five card – homemade paper.

"No GPS?" Charlie quips.

"This is the *map*. Just start here." Stew points to a spot on the card as she hands it to Charlie. "When you get to here," she points to the card again, "you'll see an old brick building with a faded *Viceroy* cigarette ad painted on its side. There's no light, but a black metal handrail leads down to the basement. That's the NUB."

"The NUB?"

"Naturalist Underground Bar."

The Taylor's park their old Toyota Prius - a hybrid first generation of eco-friendly cars. Even their old Prius looks out of place parked across the cobblestone street from the crumbling two story brick building, like a shiny new penny among the old coins Charlie collected with his son Chuck since the government's recalled 'hard money' ten years ago. Once a cigarette manufacturing plant in this college town of Old Viceroy, it shut down decades ago with the decline of tobacco use and abuse – and ultimately the outlaw of tobacco.

There was a new school of 'old school' thinkers emerging on many college campuses: the school of Naturalists, not an official school within the college, but an underground school founded on the belief in natural foods, organic and holistic medicines and herbs. The Naturalist Underground Bar was invisible from the street and only accessible to members through e-code security. If 'strangers' came upon the entrance, they'd be greeted by the smoked glass façade with etchings and stained-glass renderings of colorful produce, butterflies and birds – a beautiful frontage.

Charlie leads the way down the dark flight of stairs, holding the cold metal handrail with one hand and Rae's hand with the other. She clings to the back of his shirt collar with her other hand.

"Charlie!" Rae whispers loudly. "Can you see? I can't see."

"Wait a minute – yeah, there's a dim light down here."

Their eyes begin to adjust to the faint yellow mottled glow of the glass front.

"Is that a picture of a butterfly?" Rae whispers.

"And a bluebird? And strawberries? Is this a bar or a kindergarten classroom?" Charlie snickers. "Shh! I hear something."

A hum and a click above Charlie's head draws Rae's attention. "Charlie, look – don't look! There's a cam eye above your head!"

"If there's a cam, there's probably an audio-sensor, too, so they've – whoever 'they' are – heard us."

A button to the left of the dark solid door begins slow, rhythmic flashing, a pale, yellowish-green light.

"Press the button, Charlie," Rae says.

Before he can press the button, the door clicks and swings inward.

Inside the bar, groups of young college students sit around, reminiscent of the old soda shops - but drinking illegal wine and ale. The scene is sophisticatedly retro. Kids were reading real hardback books with paper pages, like Reverend Arnold keeps on his office, not e-books on digital pads. Some were smoking tobacco, a mild aromatic diversion, not the chain-smoking addiction of the old days of Big tobacco and opposed to the chemical vapor infusion of today's e-cigs. The NUB: Illegal. But *immoral?*

Pam greets Mrs. Taylor at the door with a hug.

"Stew tagged me that you were coming - you couldn't have gotten in otherwise," Pam says. *Something is wrong.* Making mundane conversation, she continues. "You guys look so good. It's nice of you to come all this way. You didn't have to."

"Pam," Rae holds Pam's hands in hers and studies her face, exploring the next move and reaction.

Charlie shuffles his feet and looks around the café, trying hard not to look at Pam.

"Pam, your dad would be so impressed. He was such a rebel back in the day, your grandma always said."

"What's wrong? What's happened to my dad?"

She knows. It was just like Emaw had told her about Uncle James, her dad's younger brother who had enlisted in the Army and gone to fight the war in Iraq twenty-some years ago. That week James' regular letter didn't come – no phone call, and emails were just coming of age in the military. Emaw knew something was wrong. James' high school girlfriend, Jeannie, had come over to their house, worried because she hadn't heard from him either. That same day Jeannie sat on the couch with Emaw, trying to cheer each other, talking about James' funny ways. The doorbell rang. Emaw somehow sensed, as only a mother can, that something was wrong.

Jeannie knew by reading Emaw's expression. As Emaw opened the door, two Marines in dress blues stepped up.

"Mrs. Cleveland?" one Marine spoke.

Emaw heard a thud behind her; Jeannie had fainted onto the foyer rug. The second Marine ran in to assist the fallen girlfriend of the fallen Marine. The first Marine took the mother's trembling hands into his steady white gloved hands and said the words she never wanted to hear but knew in her heart.

"I'm sorry." Rae broke the seal on the message: Dad was dead. Pam's five-foot, six-inch frame collapsed into Charlie's waiting arms. He had dreaded the moment when Pam would realize why they were there. The NUB manager, Frank, made his way across the room to help support Pam. He knew the *condolence look* on the Taylor's faces.

Frank remembered – he was just twelve – that tragic Friday night. His older sister Patty had gone to the prom all dolled up in a formal satin and lace gown, smelling of frou-frou perfume. He remembered ribbing her about displaying her cleavage, unveiled with her New Secret push-em-up bra. Patty had caught Frank and pulled his head tight against her boobs, giving him a 'noogie' with her knuckles, rubbing his hair and scalp 'til he felt the friction burn. Big sister and little brother laughed 'til tears ran, and he finally got loose. Frank playfully tossed her the matching shawl for her gown, so her shoulders wouldn't get chilled – and her Secret wouldn't show.

"Now cover those boobs!" He laughed and ran upstairs to his room as the doorbell rang. Her date, a too slick, too popular senior high brat, made his entrance wearing a designer black tuxedo with a silver flask bulging, tucked at his waist, just above his black tails.

Frank loved his big sister Patty and would have killed that arrogant prick if he found out that he'd done her wrong. But the knock at the front door at two in the morning spared Frank the life sentence of a murderer. His mom opened the door. Frank clomped down the stairs, psyched to grill his sister Patty about dirty dancing and making out. The grim-faced black and gray uniform told his mom what had happened, and her reaction showed the terribleness of that night. Mom collapsed onto her knees. The officer knelt beside her. Frank's bare knees hit the floor with a thud beside his mom. Frank searched the stern face of the highway patrolman, who was about the age his dad would have been.

"What's wrong?!"

The officer only had to say, "Your sister..." Then Frank knew what his mom already knew. Frank was sentenced to a life without his beloved sister.

Tonight, Frank was cradling Pam's head against his shoulder when she regained consciousness in a booth sitting across from the Taylor's. Frank was the bar keeper - but so much more. He knew all the club members - his brothers and sisters, he'd say – and could read their faces and body languages as they entered the bar.

Did a brother need a boost, a special fruit or veggie smoothie? Or was a sister a bit high strung in need of a mug of pale ale or a glass of sweet muscadine wine? Or just a little something to take the edge off – or put a little edge on – with a custom wrapped tobacco cigarette or extravagant imported (smuggled) Cuban cigar.

The tobacco and alcohol were, of course, illegal contraband, but the organic fruits and vegetables were even harder to get. Only commercial farms could legally grow and supply produce.

Frank pats Pam's head like he would a puppy. She rouses and tucks her hair behind her ear, out of her face. Frank reassures her, squeezing her shoulder firmly and brotherly before heading to the bar. Mrs. Taylor offers her a tissue. Pam wipes her damp, bloodshot eyes – and the drool from the corner of her mouth – and blows her nose loudly.

"Thank you," Pam speaks hoarsely.

"You're welcome." Mrs. Taylor holds out her hand, takes the spent tissue and gives her a fresh one.

Pam wipes her nose bright red and asks, "What's happened?" She sniffs. "He was fine when I saw him a couple weeks ago. How could he be..." She covers her eyes with her hands.

"Honey," Mrs. Taylor answers the unfinished question in a soothing motherly voice, "they don't really know yet. It was sudden – he was home, taking the day off, lounging around – "

"In his Hawaiian shirt?" Pam can't help but smile at that happy picture.

"Yes, he was taking it easy, out on the patio, puffing an e-cig," Mrs. Taylor starts.

"E-cig? I thought he'd quit those. I thought I'd convinced him they were no good for him." Pam puts the tissue on the table.

"I don't know, dear." Mrs. Taylor tries not to linger on the negative. "Appears he just suddenly collapsed, quietly, peacefully. Your mom found him. She needs you at home now – you and Earl. Lila always talks about how strong you are."

"We got it from Dad." Pam knows Mrs. Taylor is aware of her mother's *problems*. "Dad is – *was* a strong man." She bows her head and her stringy hair falls, veiling the pain on her face.

"Cleve was a good man." Charlie musters the words.

Pam blows her nose and manages a weak smile. "Thank you." "He liked you, Charlie – you're a good neighbor. He always liked the golf… cookouts…a good man…" she fades.

Frank returns to the booth carrying a pitcher of a dark purple elixir, slices of lime and orange floating on top.

"Is that Sangria?" Charlie asks, excited by the prospect of drinking the sweet alcoholic Mexican drink.

"Um, sure -" Frank hesitates. "-but don't tell the authorities." He raises an eyebrow and sets the dewy pitcher on the table.

"I haven't had Sangria in *forever*." Charlie says a sparkle in his eye.

"Really?" Rae tests him. "And how long is that?"

"Oh, back in the day." Many moons ago in college before the *real thing* became illegal and you could spend Spring Break in Mexico – cheap!

"It's sweet," Frank says. "It'll give you a little boost Pam. And you need to eat, too. That, and a little red wine and grain alcohol, might take the edge off."

Pam plunges her hand into the Sangria and fishes out a slice of orange from the green glass pitcher. She nibbles and sips the fruit's sweet nectar and twinge of alcohol from her fingers. Rae and Charlie give each other a look. Must be a new tradition, dipping the fingers into the pitcher of Sangria. They shrug and follow Pam's lead, pinching and kissing slices of orange and lime, relishing the memories of the simple things.

Frank announces, "I'll be right back with some more fruit, organic goat cheese and fresh baked bread – to keep up your strength."

"Dad would have loved this – if it wasn't for his diabetes and taking e-nsulin," Pam says.

The Taylor's share puzzled glances. This was the first they had heard of Cleve having diabetes and taking e-nsulin. They blow it off, respecting Cleve's privacy. He probably didn't want everyone to know that the strong man had an Achilles heel.

7.

Behind the yellow police tape in front of her house, Coach Bruce stands beside Lila, his arm around her shoulder.

"You shouldn't be here, Bruce." She says as she takes her head from his shoulder. "People will see." He keeps a close grip and pulls her closer.

"What they'll see is your son's coach comforting the family – which is why I'm here."

"I think they know." Lila eyes the two ladies across the street. They're always at home this time of day.

Chuck trudges by, his baggy jeans' bottoms scuffing on the sidewalk. *I think he knows.*

"We have cared for each other, enjoying a little bit of life. You did the best you could for your children, Lila. Cleve just didn't 'get' you – you needed more. Now he's gone. Things just happen. It was his time to go. He's in a better place," Bruce ends with clichés, like the pitiful pep talks he gives his losing teams.

"But it's so sudden. Even though I didn't love him anymore, we were part of each other's lives for over twenty years. There must have been something – now there's nothing. He's gone," says Lila.

"I'm here for you, Lila. I'll stand beside you, help you with that boy – I *am* his coach – and do what I can. People will see me as a friend of the family, a comfort at this time of loss – even though *we* know I'm more. They don't –and won't know."

Bruce thinks. *Even you don't know, Lila. It was his time. The clock was set. It was his time. Now it's our time if we can just keep those kids out. That little Philly girlfriend – should keep Earl out of our hair. And that little four-year-old girl – she's cute, but she frays your nerves. If Grandma can take her – full time – and we keep you steady on your e-meds, we'll have a sweet life together – in your house with his life insurance and pension taking care of us. I can retire and we can travel... with Cleve out of the way, naturally.*

From his front porch, Chuck glares at Coach and Mrs. Cleveland and thinks, *I don't like that man. I tried out for the basketball team and I'll admit, I wasn't too good at the tryouts, but I did try and could sit on the bench with the worst of them. He just doesn't like my style. Underneath these cool jeans and mussed hair lurks the heart of a warrior.*

Earl sees it. We're a team, always have been since we built our fort together before fourth grade.

Earl pleaded with Coach to let me on the high school basketball team, but no deal. He even told me he'd quit the team if I said so, but I couldn't let him do that. Earl's the best, the leader of the team. They'd fall apart without him. Shoot, even Coach would fall apart.

So, I sit on the back row of the bleachers with Philly, cheering Earl on, as he leads the team to another loss, because he's the only talent on the team – if only Coach had drafted me. But look at Coach now; I'm glad I didn't make his team. I would have made him lose even worse, and I'm going to beat him in this little game. Earl, I'm on your team, always. Coach, I will defeat you at your game.

Bruce looks toward Chuck's house. *That little punk, he suspects something, but knows nothing – that little SOB. He's always been a gnat flying around my face, worrying the crap out of me, wanting to play ball – but he's got no talent, no coordination, even. He can't figure anything out, connect the dots. He won't get at it. The only one who knows is me. What's in the pipe stays in the pipe – just a nicotine dose, that's all. Very few people even know Cleve was diabetic. Unfortunately for him – and fortunately for me – I knew.*

"Bruce, what are you grinning about? This is serious – I have to stay serious," Lila states. *I wasn't in love with Cleve for a long time, just hanging on to this so-called life. But I feel like I've lost Cleve, and his love, a second time. I'm sorry; I'm not sorry. I don't know how I feel. But the children, he was something to them that he wasn't to me. Cleve seemed to have lost his life a long time before he died. If I'm seen with Bruce so soon... Bruce filled a void in my life, but I don't need him. I've got the children, what's left of my family. The insurance and pension money will start coming to us soon – thanks, Cleve. God blessed you – and your family.*

"Oh, I am serious, Lila," Bruce squeezes her shoulder. She dabs her eye with a tissue, but not to dry a tear. She impishly smiles behind the paper veil. *Sure, sure, you're my hero. But you think I'll rescue you?*

8.

"Come on, Earl, let's go home," Philly implores.

"I can't go home. There's nothing there for me," Earl says flatly. *Mom hasn't been there for a long time. She's been hiding behind those e-meds for longer than I can remember, sucking on those pipes, thinking she's hidden in the bathroom, the laundry room, the garage – I saw. Dad saw. And we saw Coach, meeting Mom at the house when she thought I wasn't coming home 'til late afternoon those days – I came early. I saw. Coach is probably over there right now.'* "It's messed up!"

"Come with me, Earl, to my house. My home is always open to you – always. Come home with me, Earl," Philly pleads. She doesn't want him to be alone at this rough time especially.

The tears well in Earl's eyes as he clinches his jaw. "That's just messed up!"

Philly squeezes his hand. "Come on. Let's go," Philly commands softly.

She leads him by the hand, along the fence of the school yard, beyond the perimeter of students who don't know that someone's world has just fallen apart. The sharing of laughs, e-tags and u-videos continues, an unsympathetic, ignorant, and misunderstanding cacophony – even if they knew - except for the few kids on the fringes whose worlds have also fallen apart, unnoticed. Philly's heart is thumping as she guides Earl around the apathetic field, sharing her strength with her tall broken friend with whom she had shared her first kiss. Home is in her hand, where the heart is.

"Come on, Earl, let's go home," Philly leads.

9.

On the dark ride home, cramped in the back seat of the Taylor's old Prius, Pam barely hears the sounds of the ancient music – coming from the outdated, but still functional, MP3 player wired and plugged into the car's once modern, now antiquated stereo system. What's a CD player? She remembers seeing her dad's collection of over two hundred CD's stacked and preserved in clear plastic cases in a watertight Sterlite plastic box in the back corner of the attic. She'd taken a couple of the shiny silvery discs from their 'jewel' cases and held them up to her ears and said, 'I don't hear anything."

"Give me those! If I can ever find someone who remembers how to repair a CD player, you'll hear something, alright. The best music in the world is on these – except for that classic stuff that's still locked up in your Emaw's attic, black vinyl albums in cardboard sleeves, all decorated with art and groovy, hip musicians.

"Albums? Oh, yeah, Emaw showed me all those faded images of you as a boy in those albums she keeps on the shelf by her broken antique console tubular television. Earl is the spitting image of you when you were a boy," says Pam.

"Yeah, but – I'm not talking about photo albums! Music albums! They store music like these CD's – except with grooves – and like that new MP3 player that we got two years ago, and I guess like the micro-digitized music in your earwigs," Cleve explains to his daughter.

"And the music streamed in from somewhere out in the clouds," says Pam.

"We called it 'the cloud' – not sure of the technical term," her dad says.

"I just call it 'on', and the music comes to my earwig!" Pam says, "- and speaking of ears, can I keep a couple of these 'CD's?"

"Sure, you're being a little bit sentimental, too, huh?" Dad asks.

"Yeah, I saw this older girl in the Chic hair and aesthetics spa just last week. She had on a pair of ear discs just like these. I asked her, and she said, 'Yeah, I made these myself – from my dad's old CD collection!'" Pam says, excitedly.

"OK, you – give me those! There'll be no earrings made from these!" Dad objects.

"For now, Dad. One day I'll make my fortune in CD jewelry – 'will' me these, OK?" Pam says.

"Deal – but at least try to get the CD player fixed, OK?" says Dad.

"Groovy, Dad," Pam laughs.

"Right on, girl!" Dad beams, making a mental note to update his will to include CD's left to Pam.

Through the visor mirror Rae sees Pam, serious and far away in the dim moonlight.

"You alright, Pam?"

"Hmm? Uh, yeah, just listening to the music," says Pam.

"Want me to turn it up?" Rae asks.

"No, I'm fine. I might try to take a little nap," says Pam.

"You must be tired – it's been a lot for you," Rae says.

Pam rolls her jacket and places it against the cold plastic side wall in the back seat and snuggles her head and shoulder against it. She's not really intending to sleep, just sink into her own little world. *In a moment she's floating up the stairs to the attic, shiny silver disks orbiting around her beautiful glowing dad, like many moons, and one hanging from each ear.*

Rae raises her eyes to the mirror again and sees a faint cherubic smile on Pam's face. *She'll be OK.* She turns toward her husband admiring his handsome profile as he navigates home.

10.

Philly opens the wooden side gate leading to the privacy fenced back yard and heads to the kitchen door of her house. Earl stands for a moment, pondering Philly's invitation to come in. He had been here many times before, but always with the purpose of studying together or working on some school project or maybe picking her up to go out for a bite to eat.

"It's OK – come in," she assures him.

"I don't know . . . "

"My mom will be home about 3:30; she's on first shift." Philly says. Her mom is a nursing assistant and studying to get her nursing certification next year. It's been a struggle, a tough time for her mom – and Philly, too – but Philly has been content with preparing the meals, cleaning the house, wearing second hand - but good quality and tasteful – clothes, and working part-time in the hospital cafeteria, where she's able to see her mom on duty once in a while.

Philly looks up, literally and figuratively, to Earl as the strong one, not realizing her own strength as she takes care of her mom and herself these last five years – since her dad left. She didn't hate her dad for leaving to pursue his dreams and traveling the world; she just wishes she and Mom could have gone with him. The last she heard – he'd sent a postcard filled with tiny handwritten sentences describing his adventures working on a cruise liner in Alaska – he might be working on a fishing ship in the Bering strait for a year.

Of course, she misses him, but her dad is fading as a dad, and morphing into more of an adventure novel, a continuing saga of a 'wannabe' pioneer who never can quite make it to that ultimate peak or westernmost point. She sees that pioneer spirit a bit in Earl, too, but he's closer to the ground – grounded – right here not chasing dreams elsewhere. Philly hopes Earl will realize his dreams here or at least take her with him in search of them.

Philly finally coaxes Earl into the backyard – like trying to get a scared stray dog to eat out of your hand.

"Hungry?" she asks as she opens the storm door to go into the kitchen.

"Nah, I can't eat with this knot in my stomach," he says as he sits down on the seat of the rusty metal 'A' frame dinosaur of a swing set. The chains creak and the tubular frame sags and groans a bit as he picks up his legs, holding them straight out so his feet don't drag the sand trap underneath.

Philly still comes out in the backyard and swings on sunny days and sometimes in the middle of the night when her mom works third shift, and Philly feels too still. The rhythmic swaying back and forth, rising and falling like a quick shallow tide, soothes her and comforts her like a ten-year-old Philly rocking on her mom's lap after Dad went away and left them.

'It's OK, baby,' her mom soothed her. 'Dad still loves you – and me – from afar. It's like a fairy tale, a bedtime story: He'll come back one day riding his white horse to get his little Philly. But 'til then, I'll take care of you, baby.'

'I'll take care of you, too, Mom,' Philly would tell her as they rock, drift off and dream.

Philly stands behind Earl sitting on the swing – she'll always stand behind him – with her hands on his shoulders, in a stance as if she's pushing her mom's broken-down hybrid car.

"Uh," she grunts as her size 2 white canvas pony shoes slip in the sand. She hears a little snicker come from Earl.

"You could help a little bit," Philly prods him as he lifts his legs, so his feet clear the ground.

"There, no friction," Earl says.

"Uh – OK, you get it started, then I'll nudge you to keep you swinging," She steps back. He pulls back on the chains to start the flow of the swing. After a couple of swings, Philly comes back in and pokes him in the ribs as she gives him a little nudge. Earl hunches over in the seat laughing.

Philly says, "Gotcha!"

As Earl twists around to deflect Philly's pokes, a creak and a pop and a thud find him sprawled in the sand with chain rattled around his head. Philly jumps back with a hop and an 'Oh!' as her faces shows a worried, 'he might be hurt' look.

"Earl!" She shouts, falling onto her bare knees beside him, prepared to perform CPR, pulling the chain off him, and clinking it to the side. "You hurt? Are you alright, Earl? Speak to me!"

He opens his eyes and blinks up at her concerned face, and then… he reaches up, grabs her slender waist, and becomes 'the tickle monster!'

Sand is flying, chains are clinking, big and small feet are flailing as Philly falls on top of him, beating his chest with her plumb sized fists as the two kids giggle and roll over and back in the swing set's sand pit.

Halt. Suddenly Philly stops pounding his chest and she becomes flush, redder than her plum fists. She realizes that she's been rolling around in the sand in her short tartan schoolgirl skirt, behaving a bit unladylike. Philly rests on her naked knees beside Earl who's lying flat on his back, knees up. She leans away from him, brushing off the sand and damp hair that has stuck to her face. He loses his smile, just staring at her, admiring her innocent beauty.

I do like this girl, just a couple of kids playing together in the back yard. But what about that time, back in the woods at the fort, the day I kissed her? I scared her off that day – but she came back, but... He's thinking too much.

As he thinks that Philly is about to get up, she leans over and quick kisses his surprised mouth as sand falls from her tangled hair onto his forehead. And that's that.

She hops up on cue to her mom calling from the house, "Philly, I'm home!"

Trotting up the steps to the storm door, Philly turns, wipes the sand off and smoothes her skirt and hair, and beckons Earl to come into her home.

"I'm coming, Mom- Earl's here, too."

34

Chuck goes in the front door of his house, through the foyer, and out to the kitchen, the first place he goes every day, famished from having skipped the dreadful school lunch. On the kitchen island, the Taylor's central messaging area, a note is illuminated on the kno-pad.

Dear Chuck,
By now I'm sure you've seen the commotion next door and have heard the news that Earl's dad has died. You're a smart boy, I know, and can handle this situation better than Earl can right now. You've always been good buddies, and I'm sure he needs you. Mrs. Cleveland couldn't get up with Earl, but Reverend Arnold was calling him. Please take care of your friend in his time of need.
Love you!
Mom
Oh, your dad and I are going to get Pam at college and will be back late. There's leftover lasagna in the fridge. You know what to do. (Have Earl over and make him eat something!)

'Where is Earl?' Chuck thinks. 'He was going to Reverend Arnold's office, but I know he couldn't be there this long.

"Call Earl." Chuck touch-activated and spoke to his earwig.

An electronic musical ditty plays as the target cell is connected.

"What?" Earl replies into Chuck's ear, irritated.

"Are you OK?" Chuck asks.

"You mean since my dad died, or since I set fire to the fort?" Earl asks, sarcastically.

"Both! Where are you?" Chuck asks.

"At a friend's house," says Earl.

"You mean Philly's – cause you're not at my house, and we're your two friends," Chuck bites.

"OK, you got me," says Earl.

"Are you OK?" asks Chuck.

"Sure, I know what's going on: Dad's dead; Mom's being comforted by Coach; Tina's with Emaw; your folks are getting Pam from college. I know everything. Any more questions?" Earl says, irritated.

"Who's that, Earl?" Philly asks, in the background.

"Oh, nobody – you know it's Chuck," Earl says sarcastically.

"Well, ask him over to dinner," she commands. Company would be good to help put some distance between her and the awkwardness of having kissed Earl. *I need some backup.*

"You sure?" Earl asks her, hoping she'll say 'no'. He'd rather be with this friend right now.

"Yes, Earl. Are his parents at home?" Philly says.

"No, they went to get Pam from college," says Earl.

"Well definitely, tell him to come over," she tells Earl. "Mom is it OK if Chuck comes for dinner, too?" she calls out to her mom, who's down the hallway in her room.

"Sure, you're doing dinner, right?" her mom calls back.

"Tell him to come on over, Earl," Philly orders softly.

Regretfully, even though he needs Chuck in a different way than Philly, Earl says, "Come on, Chuck. Her mom says OK."

"Be there in five minutes," Chuck quickly RSVP's. As he's ending the call, Chuck composes a short note to his parents:

Dear Mom,

> *Gone to Philly's to hang out with her and Earl. We'll take care of him.*

> *Love you!*

> *Chuck*

Philly rattles pots and pans in the kitchen, rummaging through cabinets and slamming doors, bends over and sticks her head in the fridge, and finally comes up with a dinner plan. She's good at improvising with whatever's at hand to make a semi-gourmet meal when pressed to utilize her culinary skills.

"OK, guys, how's this menu sound: linguini with marinara sauce, fortified with organic ground round, accompanied by crisp hydroponic romaine and greenhouse ripened vine fruit with sesame seed vinaigrette?"

"Yes! Spaghetti with meat sauce and a lettuce and tomato salad -no meatballs? Sounds great!" Chuck, interpreting the menu, enthusiastically supports the chef. *Tastes a lot like the lasagna I left back home.*

"We could have meatballs, Chuck. You know how to make 'em?" Philly asks.

"Uh, sure," Chuck lies, "just add a little of this and that and roll it into little balls and throw them in the sauce, right?"

"Sounds good, Chuck – hop to it! The mixing bowl is under there. You'll have to scrounge for the rest, whatever it takes," says Philly.

Chuck stoops to the lower cabinet, grabs the clear Pyrex bowl and bangs his head on the edge of the counter on the way up. "Ow!"

"Nice shot, Chuck," Earl throws in his two cents (which is worth nothing since hard currency is no longer used). "For the next entertainment, can you do something a little softer, say a little 'soft shoe' dance on this sandy floor?"

"Oh, yeah, Earl, why don't you sweep the kitchen while I go change clothes," Philly directs, realizing that sand is still clinging to her elbow – and everything else – and starting to irritate her everywhere. Earl watches her cute little butt prance out of the kitchen in bobby socked feet. "Back in a jiff." She peeks back around the corner, "And, Chuck, start that water for the linguini – in that big pot – and Earl, would you open that big can of marinara?"

"Yes, ma'am."

"Yes, 'm."

They both salute and bow to Philly. She rolls her eyes and flips her skirt tail as she exits stage right.

As she passes her mom's room on the way to changing clothes, she untucks her blouse and drops a trail of sand. Mom notices and pops her head out the door, asking, "What have you been up to now, little Philly?" Her mom ribs her.

"Oh, just swinging – fell off into the sand. Earl saved me from the quicksand - my hero!" Philly says. She stops in the middle of the hall, halfway to her room, remembering why Earl was here. *I've got to tell Mom, but so Earl doesn't hear. He's doing so much better now, in such a good mood.* Returning to her mom's bedroom door, she sees her neatly pressing and smoothing the lavender scrub pants and flowered top, so that she can wear them again – no time for washing clothes on her schedule. Her mom heads for the shower, getting ready for her five-thirty nursing class – she's required to wear white for that.

"Mom," Philly calls.

"Yes, sweetie," Mom answers.

"I need to talk to you for a minute."

"Can you talk while I shower?"

"Sure," Philly says, thinking the shower will muffle their conversation so Earl doesn't hear and get upset again.

The shower sprays white noise and steamy water over her mom as Philly steps into the bathroom. "Ah," Philly hears her mom and sees her silhouette rinsing the dark hair flat against her head.

37

"Mom, something happened today – it's Earl," Philly begins.

Oh, it's finally happening – she and Earl. She's almost – mostly – a woman, but so young. "What happened with you and Earl?" she asks. "You can tell me."

"No, Mom, it's not that," even though Philly begins to think her mom suspects the kiss.

"What is it, then, Philly?" her mom asks, a little more seriously, but relieved it's not what she had first thought.

"This morning, Mr. Cleveland – Earl's dad – fell out on their patio – dead!" Philly says.

"What? He always seemed healthy – what happened?" her mom asks.

"They're not sure yet, but they're saying, 'natural causes'," says Philly.

"I know that you – and Chuck – are taking care of Earl. You're good friends. But how are his sisters, his mom?" Mom asks.

"They're OK. Tina's with her grandmother. Chuck's folks have gone to get Pam from school, and his mom – she's as well as she can be, taken care of," *by Coach*, Philly didn't verbalize – too much info for her mom to deal with and worry about.

"Is there anything I can do to help? Does Earl need anything? Do you need me to do anything?" Mom asks.

"No, I'm – Chuck and I – taking care of Earl, but if you hear anything at the hospital – "Philly starts to ask.

"About Earl's dad – why, or what happened?" her mom asks.

"Yeah, it's probably nothing, but Chuck has a feeling, like something's not quite right about Mr. Cleveland dying. Chuck's just very protective of Earl – and Earl of him, since they were boys," says Philly.

"OK. I'll keep my ears and eyes open. You know I think highly of Earl – and I know you do," Mom says.

Yes, I do. "Thanks, Mom. 'Love ya."

"You, too, sweetie. Now you'd better get back to dinner – before some disaster happens with those two," her mom cautions, not knowing of the fort fire disaster earlier today.

"Oh, my God! I forgot!" Philly says, loudly and frantically, as she runs to her room to change quickly into an old pair of her mom's scrubs so she can go save two boys and a dinner.

11.

Philly's mom Glenda unplugs the Prius hybrid from the garage power port and tosses her backpack onto the back seat. Her digital health monitor, comfortable nursing shoes, and her cold pack dinner are vitals. The kids had prepared of spaghetti with meat sauce and salad. *Those are some good kids.* She settles into the frayed fabric bucket seat and presses the 'start' button. "Hello. Welcome back." The Prius greets her, a bit too cheerily. The whirring commences, the instrument panel blinks 'on' and the garage door hums its opening tune. *Darn, low on gas. Hope the battery power takes me to the hospital and back – don't have time to stop.* She pulls the shifter to reverse and backs out onto the street. The closing overhead door veils the garage light.

Barely five minutes from home, Glenda worries about Philly being alone. Those long third shifts. *But tonight's an early night – class work – and I'll be home by eleven if I can get my patient reports done without problems.*

Mrs. McKenny knows my situation at home, but as my mentor and supervisor doesn't cut me any slack. 'Hang tough', she says, and I do – and so does Philly. That girl – 'most a woman – has a lot more on her plate than I had at fifteen –until I got pregnant; she takes it all in stride. She's got her dad's easygoing spirit, but she's got gumption. Responsibility. Maintaining our home while I'm in school.

My little Felicity, my goodness, my love – she's everything I could have been, if I hadn't been such a spoiled brat and... Well, those days are over, and I'm not being taken care of anymore – except by Philly. Too young. When I'm a licensed nurse, she'll be able to go to college, not have to work her little buns off, some menial job... concentrate on her studies... be somebody. My feisty little Philly gets ridden hard. But look at her – she's amazing! That boy Earl better appreciate her. I'd kill for my little girl – but she's not a little girl. She reminds me of me, wearing my old scrubs, so baggy and faded – they don't fit her. She's made to wear something else.

Be tough with that boy – 'most a man – 'cause he needs to be tough to be with you, little Philly. Don't take any junk off him, but help him. He needs you, right now. His father's gone.

"You're the best, Philly! That meal was truly gourmet." Chuck burps.

Earl rolls his eyes at Chuck and turns to Philly. "Yeah, do you and your mom eat like this all the time?"

"Oh, it was nothing, just something I whipped up – and you guys helped. We're a good team." Philly glows in her humble glory.

"We are a team." Chuck envies his two friends, so close, yet selflessly inviting him. "It's late. I better get home – before Mom and Dad get back." Big grin. "You two can be alone."

"What about Pam, Earl?" Philly asks, concerned about Pam coming home to an empty house. She can relate; she doesn't want to be left alone either.

"Yeah, but it'll be awhile, won't it, Chuck?" Earl asks, hoping he can stay with Philly a little longer – and hoping Philly hopes the same.

"Hey, Chuck." Philly has a marvelous idea. "Why don't you e-tag Earl when Pam gets home, then he won't have to be over waiting alone."

"It's OK if I'm alone at home, huh?" Chuck adds. "Where's your mom, Earl? She's not home?" Chuck suspects. Knows.

"I guess she's over at Emaw's with Tina – I don't know."

"Shouldn't you all be together?" Philly asks.

"Tomorrow. Everyone will be too tired tonight. Tina's in bed by now. Mom's probably taken some e-sedative to help her sleep, and she's zonked out. Let me know when Pam's back, okay, Chuck?" Earl says, thinking of himself – and Philly.

"Sure, buddy. I know when I'm the third wheel. I can take a hint."

"You know we love you, Chuck." Philly puckers and makes kissy noises at him.

"Yeah, love." Earl socks Chuck in the shoulder and nudges him off the couch.

Philly springs up and quick-kisses Chuck on the cheek. "G'night, Chuck. Don't forget to e-tag Earl, OK?"

"Sure thing. It'll wake you up after you fall asleep on this cushy couch."

Earl sings, "Good night, Chuck."

12.

Lila stares beyond the French doors at the dusky amber glow of the stone patio. A halo stain remains where Cleve's head had lain. Bruce had dropped her off just as the cleaning crew was leaving, after the hazmat crew had secured the area, after the police tape was pulled down and evidence of the death of Cleve was removed. His life had been erased from the spot leaving only a halo that Clorox could not bleach.

Cleve had not been alive to her for a long time, years even. The routine of getting dressed for work, with his pressed starched white shirt – always 'white collar' – simple striped tie and silver dime tie tack, worn with one of his three gray worsted wool suits. A clone of *his father*, immortalized in a photo on the mantel beside his mother, Ester.

The senior Mr. Cleveland had become a solid, reliable, consistent worker after Ester came into his life and set him on the right course. But the junior Cleve was tired, tired of the drudgery of every day, getting consistent dissatisfaction from his job, coming home yesterday, just watching, staring at Tina as she played quietly with her favorite doll, one that Cleve's mom had given her last birthday when she turned four. He had said something uncharacteristic, out of the blue as Earl got up from the breakfast table to run off to school. *I'm proud of you, son.* Earl had turned, slightly perplexed and simply said, *Later.*

When Cleve came up the hall, after brushing his teeth, he wasn't carrying his briefcase. He had changed out of his gray suit and into baggy plaid Bermuda shorts and that tacky Hawaiian shirt, royal blue with the red hibiscus flowers, the one he always wore to the cookouts with the Taylor's – and flip flops.

Lila sat there at the breakfast table, hair askew, terrycloth robe clasped tightly over her bosom, coffee cup in hand; she paused mid-sip. Cleve grabbed the day's paper from the corner of the table, slapped it on his thigh. *It's such a nice day, I think I'll take the day off, just take it easy. I'll be out on the patio.* He paused at the portrait of Pam hung on the wall by the French doors. *My little girl.* He stretched his arms a wide 'T' against the backdrop of the red, orange and yellow variegated sunrise. *Red sky in morning.*

Lila went back to the bedroom to clean up and get dressed. She flipped through the hanging clothes. *What to wear?* She had e-tagged Bruce. He had been supposed to pick her up at ten o'clock for brunch at her favorite little café in Clay Town, a walk at Lemmon Park by the river, and maybe *a little more* if there was time - and if she was *in the mood.* Bruce had to be back at school by one. Cleve had really messed up their plans staying home with *his little mid-life crisis episode.*

Cleve kicked off his flip-flops and stood on the edge of the dewy lawn, bare feet squishing in the wet green grass. A bright red cardinal landed on the top of the privacy fence, cocked its head and looked at him and fluttered down to the feeder. It chose a prime sunflower seed and flew off. Cleve fished in his deep shorts pocket and retrieved the smooth e-pipe. He smacked his lips in anticipation of that bitter-sweet tobacco vapor.

The afternoon before, he stopped by the school to see Earl's coach, who had given him a sleeve of special tobacco ampules. Coach Bruce had expressed concern about Earl's recent behavior – cutting classes – but also about the possibility that college basketball scouts were already interested in Earl. *Earl could have a bright future – starting with a full scholarship to attend State or Chapel College – if he'd just focus, not let 'the wrong element' drag him down.*

By 'wrong element' Coach had meant Chuck, who never could make the basketball team, but monopolized Earl's time and cut class with him. Coach didn't like Chuck for some unknown reason. Chuck was a good kid, just different. Cleve thought they complemented and were positive influences on each other. They had been friends for over five years, ever since the Taylor's moved next door.

Cleve agreed with Bruce about Earl's prospects. *Call me Bruce.* He chummed up and offered him an e-pipe, which Cleve accepted, though he had given up the vice. They talked about some of the highlights of Earl's season thus far, puffing their e-pipes.

"What is this I'm puffing, Bruce? Tastes like real tobacco – I remember, back in the day..."

"It's an imported e-bacc from Cuba, with natural tobacco flavor mingled with the nicotine – a rarity."

"Smooth, but bold."

"Yeah, there are some sweet things coming out of Cuba since it became a state." Bruce was proud of this novelty and his connections. "You want some to take with you? Sort of a pre-recruit, pre-draft celebratory gift?"

"That's nice, but..."

Bruce slips the gift from his desk drawer. "Here, take these."

The sleeve was full, but the seal was broken. The second ampule in the pack contained a surprise – most certainly. Their meeting had presented the opportunity Bruce had anticipated. Lila had casually revealed that Cleve had diabetes, a delicate balance between sugar and insulin. Bruce had been racking his brain to find a weapon to sever Cleve's Achilles heel. Finally, he had it in hand.

Bruce had started enhancing his team's performance this season with e-nhance, a high sugar supercharger and adrenaline booster to increase the boys' energy and stamina. The players ritually puffed it via e-pipe just prior to games. The prescription enhancer, illegal without a doctor's order for each player, really did work, boosting energy and morale, but offered no increase in basketball prowess for the guys who didn't already have talent. Earl became unstoppable, a Super Man. He took the drug but said he really didn't want or need it. Coach persisted. If the other guys used it, so would Earl – for the team.

When Cleve got home, he loosened his tie and unbuttoned his starched collar, took off his jacket, rolled up his white shirt sleeves and slipped out to the patio to relax in the evening shade. He puffed the first vial, saving the second one for the morning. Relaxed. No worries.

13.

Detective Brown

Detective Brown starts to leave Reverend Arnold's office. "Shouldn't I get a cruiser to pick him up, Reverend? I wouldn't want him to hurt himself."

"No, Earl will be OK; he'll probably be with his friend Chuck. He's usually pretty levelheaded, and Chuck helps keep him grounded."

"You know these kids. They trust you – and I'll trust you," the detective says.

"Trust in the Lord, Detective Brown. He will watch over them."

"If He needs me to help, you'll let me know, won't you Reverend?"

"I'll be listening, watching and praying."

Listening and watching, yes, but praying – for what? Detective Brown, such a good detective, always skeptical. Hard evidence. He'd get down on his knees and sift through the evidence, things overlooked – if he got a gut feeling, something didn't feel right.

Detective Brown drives to the Cleveland house, compelled to take one more look around before the seal is broken on the scene. *It just doesn't feel quite right – doesn't smell right.* Two uniformed officers sit outside the house in their super-volt electric black and white vehicle. *Wish I had one of those supercharged models like that instead of this mini-electric.*

I remember seeing photos of my grandpa posing proudly beside his black Monte Carlo SS, Regular leaded-gasoline powered, eight cylinders – now that was a car! You could hear its powerful engine say 'get out of my way, boys, the man is coming through!' Those were the days.

Grandpa was so proud of making the State Highway Patrol back then. He was quite a man, took no junk from anybody – until that night. On patrol on I-95 he pulled over a slow-moving rusty Rambler with its engine smoking, apparently having mechanical problems. As he approached the driver's side window, the strung-out punk shot directly through the window with a .38, killing Grandpa, dead on the spot – no reason. Just stoned.

If Daddy hadn't been just a boy of 10 at the time, I'm sure he'd have killed that murderer before he left the courthouse that day, sentenced to 'life' – yeah, 'life'. The sentence was 'death' when the murderer 'slipped' in the cell block showers his first week in Central Prison. They never said it wasn't an accident, but my Daddy knew. He knew the code of honor, of the men who worked with Grandpa, so proud. Daddy never said if he thought it was right or if it was wrong, but he was glad that justice was done – but it didn't bring Grandpa back. Daddy said that I got a lot of Grandpa's genes, so 'be careful, listen,' the Reverend had said. OK, I'll get on my knees, pray, trust, look and listen. I know you're up there, Grandpa.

Detective Brown approaches the black and white. He taps on the window. "Wake up!" He steps back so they see him. "Did you guys look around the house, in Mr. Cleveland's room – his personal things?"

"Uh, no sir. The coroner ruled it 'natural causes' so we didn't look any further than the body," Officer Hart says.

"That's procedure, but if you don't mind, I want to take a quick look around the house before you guys break down the scene, and the cleaning crew comes in. "Something may have been overlooked." That feeling that something wasn't quite right.

A special cleaning crew comes in, to the messiest of domestic scenes, normalizes and sanitizes everything so the family can come back to their home as quickly as possible, with bad memories erased from the surface.

"We'll be outside. Just call when you're done," says Officer Hart.

"Then again, your eyes might be helpful and see something I don't. Humor me, guys. Come inside with me," says Detective Brown.

They walk around the spot where the body had been outlined with white tape; the bloody oval where Cleve's head had hit the stone patio remains, dark crimson, unclean. Nothing else remains.

"The e-pipe was wrapped and tagged, right?" Detective Brown asks.

"Yes, sir – procedure," Officer Lowe states.

"Good," says Brown.

"The wife said he'd started puffing again – just yesterday, actually," says Officer Hart.

"Let's take a look back in the house, in the bedroom," says Brown.

The officers, feigning serious investigation, follow the detective down the hall, looking at, around and underneath tables, and a wall clock.

"OK, men, this briefcase on the bed – was it open like this when you got here to the scene?" asks Brown.

"Yes, sir, I remember – just like that," Officer Hart shares.

"Right beside the suit, tie and shirt – dress shoes on the floor, too." Officer Lowe adds his observation.

Detective Brown lifts the papers in the briefcase with the end of his pen and pulls open the side pouch with his purple gloved hand. "What's this?"

Officer Hart carefully removes the ten-centimeter-long clear plastic sleeve of ampules.

Brown holds it up to the light. "A special batch -from Cuba, see the crest and 'Cuba' etched on the side of the sleeve?"

"You don't see these Cubans very often – I never have. A shame to put 'em into evidence," says Officer Lowe.

"When the investigation closes, boys, we'll celebrate with the Cubans. Put 'em in evidence: eight special Cuban ampules in a clear sleeve," Detective Brown notes.

"So there are two gone," says Officer Hart.

"Right – check the one in the pipe that was found by the body, and see if it matches," says Brown.

"Gotcha," Hart says, "Uh, roger that." They head toward the door. "Call us when you're done here, and we'll wrap it up."

Hart and Lowe are puzzled by the further 'investigation'; the coroner had said 'natural causes'. There was no official investigation.

Detective Brown taps his earwig and calls the coroner. "Jackie? Carl Brown."

"Oh, hey, Carl – what's up? I've got your body down here on the slab – you don't need a full autopsy, do you?" Jackie asks.

"No, but I do need you to make certain of something for me," Brown says.

"What's that? Anything for you, sweetie," Jackie flirts.

"Run a complete blood workup – toxins, gases, cholesterol, sugar, iron – whatever 'complete' is."

"Sure, hon', but that's a bit more expensive – you got the budget for that? This one's supposed to be simple: natural causes."

"What's 'natural' anyway, Miss Jackie?"

"How about 'normal'?"

"What's 'normal'?" He adds. "OK, Jackie, how about anything somewhat unnatural or slightly abnormal?"

"Agreed, you'll get the whole report by day after tomorrow – sample has to go to the state lab in Oak City, and they're always swamped."

"Just let me know, OK, sweetheart?"

"Sure, sugar." Jackie says goodbye with a loud kiss into the earwig.

Carl puts his finger in his ear to scratch away the tingle from the obnoxiously loud kiss.

14.

Lila had been sitting on the couch for over an hour, her concept of time diminished, flipping through the photo album, reminiscing about life before – before what? She smiled with the happy pictures of Pam as a girl of ten, and Earl at six going on seven -but almost as tall, with bigger feet. Tina wasn't even a thought when these photos were taken of Pam and Earl. Tina would come years later – when Lila was much improved, taking her medications and continuing with the therapist.

Before what? So many years ago. Lila could not remember the tragedy. She initially stayed in the psychiatric hospital, sedated to the point of catatonic, so she wouldn't hurt herself. The guilt sandbagged her conscious mind, and the memory of what happened that morning lurked in the recesses.

I'm not alive – I don't want to be. Why? Lila would ponder as she sat on the edge of her twin bed in the dimly pale green semi-private room, staring out the wire reinforced window at the yellow light from the street lamp just around the corner of the building, filtering onto the oak tree. Light shined indirectly on Lila those dark days right after the tragedy.

Even though she *knew* what happened on that awful morning, she could not *remember*. Lila only remembered what she had been told. The psychiatrist had told her the horror story.

On the way home from dropping Pam and Earl at the elementary school, Lila had spilled a cup of hot coffee on her lap. As she looked down just for an instant, but an eternity, driving the posted 25 mph, but warp speed, on the dead-end street that never ended – thump! Silence for seconds, but hours, after her car came to a quick skid stop – then a piercing scream from outside, and inside.

A golden retriever came swishing its tail from the far side of the street as a blonde head bobbed up and down out of rhythm, in and out of sight just in front of the car's hood. As Lila opened the driver's door – it weighed a ton – and stepped onto the pavement, a terrified animal cry burst forth from the crushed metal grill – was it the golden dog's howl of pain?

"You've killed my baby! Why – why? Tina?! Tina!" the broken will of the woman cried out, screamed sorrow, anger, despair.

Lila passed the left quarter panel and rounded the shiny chrome trim of the headlight of her stalled car. The melting face of desperation looked up at Lila as the whimpering, wagging retriever, rubbed softness against

Lila's exposed leg. The golden dog. The golden blonde little girl, maybe four years old lay still at her mother's knees and the dog's curious black nose. The blood – oh, the blood! – puddled the pavement beneath the child's silken hair, washed the mother's hands crimson and streaked her face like a warrior's.

"My baby – you've killed my baby girl! Tina? Tina!" the mother cried despair, anger, sorrow. "Murderer!" Her laser eyes burned through Lila.

The doctor had told Lila, 'The little girl just sprang out from between the parallel parked cars. She was running after her dog – you couldn't have helped it.'

Lila had stopped and stood above the scene for a minute, for days, just staring devoid of external emotion, dead internal soul. She began walking a zombie march in the direction from which she had come. Driving without shoes – and the witness said she was in stocking feet when the officer pulled up beside her as the ambulance and another patrol car came to the scene.

"Ma'am, ma'am," the officer called calmly. No response. He parked his car and began walking beside her.

"Where are you going?" he asked again, soft and low as if talking to a sleep walker.

Handcuffed in the back seat of the patrol car, Lila showed no emotion.

Still catatonic, Lila made her first appearance in court three days later, her attorney and Cleve had pleaded to have her committed to a treatment facility.

Lila retreated inside herself, trying to find something, lost in a strange place without a clue how to find her way out. She remained in the facility for months without progress. The doctors resorted to electric shock therapy – a primitive treatment revived – trying to jolt her back to reality, unsuccessfully. Eventually, with the right combination of medications, Lila became cognizant, enough so she could function daily, but void of emotion and of memories of that day. She was not cured, but the doctors declared she 'no longer posed a danger to herself or others' – she never did, intentionally.

She went home to find her husband, Cleve, walking on her fragile eggshells, trying not to break them – anymore than already broken. The children had been staying with Cleve's mother, Ester, for the past three months, and they had adapted. Pam and Earl had come and visited their mother every week, at first, then every two, then once a month – Mom didn't seem to recognize them. She did know them, but she was unable to communicate her feelings to anyone, not even her own children.

For almost two years Pam and Earl stayed with Ester, learning and loving their grandmother's old ways and memories, visiting their parents Sunday afternoons. Out of the blue one Sunday afternoon, Cleve said, 'You're coming home, guys,' and they did. Lila didn't seem much different than two years previous, but Pam and Earl could tell that Dad needed them to be home with him. They would do this – for him, and for her, too, if she needed them. But she didn't seem to need anything, or anyone.

A couple of years later Lila decided that she needed someone after all, so she stopped taking the hormones, the birth control pills, feigned a lust for her husband for several weeks until she felt a new little life inside her, who would need her to care for. She decided to name her 'Tina' – not sure why, it just sounded right.

During her pregnancy, Lila had an awakening, with the new hormones pumping through her incubating body, permeating her emotion-deprived brain. She became a sensitive, emotional bombshell, giddy at times, with bouts of snapping and days of crying over old movies or nothing and sleeping. An amusement park funhouse, rollercoaster and house of horrors. The family didn't really mind these mood swings, grateful that at least she had moods.

The proverbial 'shit hit the fan' when baby Tina popped out – an easy birth for Lila, but the after birth was the beginning of a different life for her. Postpartum depression sent Lila back to the facility and to her catatonic post-tragedy self. Ester cared for the sweet new baby and, like a baby chick, Tina imprinted her grandmother. Lila's need to care might never be fulfilled.

15.

My sweet little Tina. Ester sits on the wooden stool next to the four-year-old's bed. The round milking stool with countless chips in the yellowed white paint, probably lead-based, had a comfortable fit-your-butt contour. Ester had little Cleve sit in the corner on this stool many times for major infractions of the rules – like cursing. She could hardly bare punishing Cleve for those boyhood slips of the tongue because his daddy set the bad example. If she had her way, she'd have set her husband on that low stool until his legs cramped up, his punishment for cursing.

Cleve was a good boy but rough around the edges. Cleve the man had stuck by Lila through all her troubles – never strayed, as far as she knew, probably on the road to sainthood – if he had been Catholic. This angel child, Tina, should get him through the pearly gates if nothing else would.

Tina has Cleve's face, and she's an angel, so he must be an angel, too. He'll be OK up there with his brother James, who's been waiting for him a long time. It'll be a big reunion: James, Cleve, and their daddy. I've been blessed – and still am blessed by this child – so I shouldn't be sad, shouldn't cry. They're all in a 'better place', but, God willing, I'll be able to hold off going to meet them until I get this last child raised. I don't think Tina knows it, but she's had a hard life. God, help that woman – sorry, Lord – Lila, to come back around to her senses so she can be a part of all these children's lives. They could all use a little support now that Cleve is gone. You know I don't pray much – of course You know – but keep on hearing me and listen in on those children. They're all good – you know. Teach us to pray to You, even when we're not desperate, like your Son taught: "Our Father, who art in heaven..." and she prayed the Lord's Prayer as she sat low on the stool beside Tina's angelic blond head.

16.

The storm door slams as Chuck leaves Philly's house. The closure on the door is broken; her dad never got around to fixing it. Chuck strolls down the sidewalk, in no hurry. A neighborhood dog barks and comes out of the shadows and trots along beside Chuck.

"Hey, boy." Chuck kneels and pets the black and white Border Collie.

The dog hassles, tongue hanging out then 'grins' and wags as Chuck tousles its long fur and scratches behind its ears. "Whatcha up to, Zebe?" When the neighbors got the dog as a pup four of five years ago - about the time Tina came along - the kid thought it looked like a zebra. The dog licks Chuck's hand then runs ahead of him and looks back. Chuck follows, glad for the company. A streetlight above buzzes in loud protest to its blown bulb.

Zebe stops in his tracks and starts barking, protective and wary. The figure of a man throws a shadow across the dimly lit front yard of the Cleveland's house. Zeke runs onto the lawn in front of Chuck's house triggering security light. The flood of light illuminates the man heading to the mini pickup parked of Earl's house. *Coach. What's he doing here? Back to comfort Earl's mom? What about Earl? He has not contacted or attempted to contact Earl. Coach, a bit too cozy with Earl's mom, if you ask me.*

Zebe continues backing and chases after the VW pickup as it slowly drives up the street. Chuck crouches on the lawn by the sidewalk. Coach drives slowly passed, turning his head and looking directly at him, and offering a sinister smile and a nod. The pickup accelerates then pauses and winks its red taillights, passing Philly's house up the street.

Chuck turns and runs down the sidewalk toward home, his baggy jeans swishing like a canvas sail in the wind.

Light flashes like neon around the edge of the curtains of the den picture window. Chuck pauses his Z-box. He's been playing Hugo Virtual Warrior since he got home, trying to distract himself.   *Coach   is back!* Chuck blacks out the screen, pushes off the floor and closes the window shades. He peeks around the edge of the shade, one eye closed like a pirate, trying to focus. The car lights go out. For a moment, his vision is cloudy. Someone is coming around the front of the car – not the Coach's pickup. The man has on a driver's cap, the kind Reverend Arnold often wears.

The Reverend? Kind of late for a house call. Maybe he was waiting for Coach to leave the Cleveland's. Does he know? He must know. Maybe he'll counsel her to get out of that situation with the coach. Earl and his mom deserve better!

17.

A beautiful picture of a blond angel hangs hazy in Lila's mind. The red devil keeps screaming from the dark cavern in the back, clawing at the sweet image of a little girl, pulling her into the abyss.

Lila wakes up in a sweat. She takes the e-pipe from the deep front pocket of her crimson velvet robe, along with the clear cylinder of e-script ampules. She had been hoarding the best, most potent of these during her last stay at the facility.

The third shift nurse, working a double, had been easily distracted. Lila snatched the cylinder of five e-ludsions from the pharmacart and slipped them into the elastic waistband of her hospital issued scrubs, and padded sock-footed back to her room. The nurse had inventoried the cart three times the next morning, coming up five e-ludsions short, no clue as to what happened to the e-script. The nurse had been accused of stealing the drugs; they went missing on her watch, so she was responsible. Drug-test negative, but with no excuse for the misplacement, the nurse was honorably discharged - under questionable circumstances. Her nursing license revoked, she could only practice nursing as an assistant after that. Lila heard of the nurse's misfortune, but she would have swiped even more – with no regrets. The worst kind of unrepentant, addicted criminal, selfishly satisfying the need for high, low or limbo. Lila preferred limbo, the state of neither guilt nor innocence, numb to the mental devil.

"Lila, I understand he was your husband and all, but you told me you hadn't loved him for a long time – so you don't need to get into this funk." Bruce had told Lila, his feeble attempt to comfort, unable to empathize.

Bruce had never married. The closest he had come to matrimony was getting his high school girlfriend pregnant the summer before he went off to college to become a teacher/coach. He'd been using her, and she thought she was using him. He had gotten enough money from his dad for Angie to have an abortion, but she didn't want to, couldn't do it.

Bruce had gone off to college, thinking Angie had 'taken care of it'. He would never discover that he had been deceived – and never gave 'the problem' another thought. He continued believing he had stolen her virginity - and her pride. He had escaped clean and clear – except for his soul.

He joined the fraternity at State College that had the most action, parties, beer and girls. This was a time before e-pipes became the inebriators and sexual surrogates, a time when tobacco, beer and illicit sex were legal. Bruce was glad he 'grew up' before regulations and e-chemicals replaced the real thing.

When he graduated and became a coach, advantages of the e-chems became apparent. Bruce realized that e-nhancers could be used by his student athletes without being detected. The chemicals were not detectable in routine blood and urine analyses, but changes in metabolism and bodily functions, physically and psychologically, could be seen. Authorities in athletics rarely delved into physiology and psychology because of the difficulty, time and expense of testing beyond the realms of bodily fluids.

Bruce seemed to have an infinite supply of e-nhancers, mind-altering drugs, ordinary e-cigs and pipes – and vice-friendly e-licit products. Cuba, the new state in the union, offered an easy pipeline of legal-but-underground/over sea e-products. An old fraternity brother lived down in the Keys and brought the products over from Cuba in his yacht and sent them north via ESP – Eastern States Postal. ESP detected illegal contraband using chem-sniffing and object recognition scanning, neither of which would detect this legal, though bootleg – and hermetically sealed - supply of e-products from Cuba.

"Lila, if you feel like you're going to crash again, why don't you take something? You know I have what you need – want me to get it?"

"Bruce, I'll be OK. I've got what I need," Lila had thought.

"Be careful with that prescription stuff from the hospital – it's strong. It'll kick your butt. I've got something smoother," Bruce offered.

"I have what I need, Bruce, but mostly what I need is rest. You need to go. Leave that light off when you go out, so maybe nobody sees you here so late – people will talk."

"Okay." Bruce leans in to kiss her; she turns her cheek away.

"Good night, Bruce. I'll e-tag you. Don't call me – we've got to be careful. Remember, I'm in mourning."

"Condolences." Bruce bites.

"Bye," she says tersely, shooing him out the door.

Lila inserts the tiny ampule of e-aldol into her dusty pink piccolo e-pipe and activates the vaporizer. She purses her lips around the mouthpiece and inhales deeply, holding the heavy vapors in her mouth, forcing them down into the alveoli of her lungs. Hold. Exhale slowly.

Pull them in, Lila. Another puff you'll be feeling better. Relax. Drive that red devil back into his cave.

She slips the piccolo back into her robe pocket and melts into the cushions of the couch, feeling no pain – feeling nothing at all. Slits in her eyes offer a narrow view of Pam's portrait on the wall and Tina's silver-framed photo on the end table. She had placed photos of Earl and Cleve on the white marble coffee table. Her family gathered around her – where had they been all these years? Where had she been?

She fingers the e-pipe in her pocket. *They've been locked up in here.* She rubs the pipe, her magic lamp to conjure a genie. The faces of her children and her husband rise from the vapors. *Just vapors.*

Could she feel good, at least be able to fake being happy even if her mind said she wasn't happy? The life she had with her family – which she never really had – would return.

My baby, Tina. She reaches for the photo on the end table. A red light flashes from the recesses of her mind – then retreats.

"That's right!" she says loudly. "Go back to your cave! You can't hurt *my* Tina."

Tina, my beautiful little girl. She's fine... with Cleve's mom. She'll be home soon... everything will be fine.

Tina? Tina! The voice screams in the back of her mind. Red flash. Shimmer of golden blond.

Lila plucks the device from her pocket, presses the button, and puffs frantically... sucking the vapors once more. *Hold. Hold...*

Save me from that bastard!

She lies back on the couch, closes her eyes and waits.

Nothing. I feel nothing. She begins slipping into a dreamless sleep.

Reverend Arnold presses the button. The door chimes once. Pause. Again.

Maybe she's not in.

He steps back from the door. "Nobody home. Oh, well." A dim light flickers from deep inside, a weak but present illumination through the window shear.

Someone is home – I didn't wake anyone.

Brighter light floods the foyer, trying to escape. The door opens, presenting the disheveled Lila, barefoot, robe gaping open, eyes squinting as if staring into the sun.

"Oh, good morning – or is it evening? Oh, Reverend, it's you." Lila gathers a few wits, snatches her robe closed and ties the frayed sash. "I wasn't expecting you, was I?"

"No – sorry I woke you, Mrs. Cleveland." The Reverend apologizes, yet knowing that he is obligated to be here this day – what remains of it anyway – to comfort and council the bereaved family. Tomorrow they will meet with the funeral home director – for the final *plans*, the arrangements for memorializing the passing of the mortal body. Tonight. But tonight, is for the caring of souls – of the loved one and the family of souls.

Lila Cleveland needs a Savior, Reverend Arnold prays.

"Come in." Lila invites him in. She swaggers to the living room and plops in a chair. The Reverend sits on the warm and cushy couch across from her. "I was just resting on the couch…"

The Reverend clears his throat. "Waiting for the children?"

"Children?" She hesitates. "Oh, Tina's with Ester, and Earl, Pam, uh…" – "she hesitates, uncertain.

"Pam is on her way home. She should be here shortly – with the Taylor's. They drove up to the college to get her."

"Yes, yes, of course." Lila lies, has forgotten or lost the memory - or the present. She tucks her feet underneath her, on the verge of a fetal position.

The Reverend tries to bring her back. "He must be with Chuck – or Philly. I haven't seen him since this afternoon when he stopped by the church office." *I hope he's safe with one or both. I know the Lord's watching over him – over them – but where are You, Lord? Lila seems lost. Find her, Lord – or use me to find her. Bring her back!*

The Spirit had moved him to come to the Cleveland home to begin the journey to find Lila. The dim light, triggered by the door chime, had roused Lila to unsteady feet – but she had risen, switched on another light, and opened the door to him - to Him.

Now he verbalizes the thought, "The Lord is watching over Earl."

"What about Cleve? Was He watching over him? Where's my family? Where have they gone?" She buries her face in her hands, sobbing.

The Reverend leans forward but does not got to her. "They're coming home, Lila. You and Cleve were blessed with such wonderful children." *Lord only knows how they turned out so good. The Shepherd was watching over these lambs. 'The Lord looks after fools and children', the Good Book, or somebody, said. But is Lila a fool, or are demons clawing away at her soul? Tell me, Lila. Tell me, Lord.*

"Blessed by them? Cursed by me!" Lila self-loathes when the pain-numbing drugs begin to evaporate from her mind. *I can't stand it!* She returns to the pipe every time, inhaling the numbness, exhaling the pain and the toxic fumes, her tolerance worn down by the red demon, the weak will of Lila, the will that won't allow anyone to go down that dark cavern to flush it out that bastard. She continues believing in the Will of Lila.

"Lila, you haven't cursed this family. Just think. Remember." He leans forward, tilts to his toes, to his feet, on the brink of getting up and going to her – but, no. He picks up the silver-framed picture of Tina. "This child. She is a blessing, brought here by you – and God's Will."

Lila remembers the flash of terror that came right after Tina's birth. Where did that come from? Tina could have been such a blessing to her, but instead, Tina had been a blessing to Ester.

"Look at that girl – a woman now – in that portrait." He points to the wall. "I feel that Pam blesses and influences scores of young lives at college."

Lila looks up at the photo. "I remember Pam, a little girl – and Earl as a little boy, like that photo on the coffee table – before the…" She stops.

"Before the *what*, Lila?"

"Oh, before the hospital, my first breakdown…dammit!" She catches her words. "I'm… after the…" She pauses.

"What, Lila?" The Reverend persists. "You know you can talk to me, don't you?" *Something is trying to get out of her – that demon?*

No! She shakes her head. *Shut that door! The Reverend, no one, not even God Himself can go down there… no light, no love, just terror and tragedy.*

"There's nothing to talk about, Reverend. I can't talk about it," Lila says.

"So, there's *nothing* – but what is *it*?" *Bring it out!*

"I don't know." Lila can't remember it, the *it* that broke her mind, her spirit, her will.

"Lila, would you let me pray with you?" the Reverend asks.

"Pray? I don't think I have a prayer," she says, pretending to be funny, just kidding – but she believes what she's saying.

If only she'd believe.

Lila shakes her head. "Fine." *Our Father...* she prays in her head.

Reverend Arnold gets on his knees by Lila's chair and softly but deliberately takes her hand. He closes his eyes. Lila looks at the back of his bowed head, confused by the whole prayer *thing*.

"Our Father," he begins.

The Lord's Prayer, Lila recalls.

"Thank You for these blessings – You know what and who they are – and help us to recognize them as blessings. Thank you for the life of Cleve..."

Lila chokes back a tear, tenses her hand, but doesn't pull away; the Reverend continues holding on.

"He was a blessing, this family with blessed children, and his wife, Lila; a father and husband – and much more, Lord. Please watch over Lila and these children, as I believe you are, as they face difficult times like these. Offer them strength. Lord, help us to hold the Faith, continue to Hope, and greatest of all, Lord, teach us to Love, as Your Son taught us. In His precious name we pray, Amen."

Reverend Arnold lifts his eyes. Lila's are closed muddled with tears, flushed cheeks. He moves to take his hand away, but this time Lila puts her other hand over his and won't allow him to move away.

18.

Mrs. Taylor turns softly, motherly toward Pam leaning asleep against the side panel in the back seat, hair fallen across the side of her face. "Pam, we're almost there – wake up, honey." Pam twitches and squeals a little puppy wakeup noise.

"Did you have a nice nap, sweetie?" Mrs. Taylor asks.

"Mm.".." Pam stretches and wipes the locks of hair away from her face with the back of her hand. She dabs the drool on the corner of her mouth with her sleeve. "Yeah, nice." She regains her raspy voice, rusty after the snoring spell.

She smiles, remembering her dream. *We were all dressed up.*

"You looked like you were resting so comfortably." Mrs. Taylor looks in the vanity mirror, smiling and pursing her lips before applying fresh pink rose lipstick.

Daddy had on his brown suit – not his ordinary gray one that he wears to work – and looked so handsome. He pecked Mom on the cheek as she did a last hair and makeup check in the hall mirror. She was so pretty in that spring flowered off-the-shoulder dress that I helped her pick out from Belk's, and the pearls Daddy gave her on their last anniversary. I liked the way I looked in my baby blue 'shorty' dress, even though it's a little bit girlish – and scratchy around the collar. I felt it in my sleep. Of course, Earl was uncomfortable, complaining about having to wear dress pants – too short because he was growing faster than Mom could keep up with his clothes.

We were in the fellowship hall at church, Easter Sunday. Mom and Daddy stood in the corner sipping coffee and eating shortbread cookies; Daddy's cookie broke and crumbled down his jacket collar. When Mom plunged her hand in his jacket to help retrieve the cookie, Daddy sloshed his coffee on their feet. They started giggling – and they kissed after locking eyes and becoming very still, quiet. I reached over and took Earl's hand, squeezed, and he didn't even try to pull away. Mom and Daddy were ahead of Earl and I, holding hands as we walked two by two under the wooden arch into the sanctuary.'

"Pam, want to borrow my brush?" Mrs. Taylor offers as they pull into the driveway. "Your mom's still up; the light's on." Pam takes the brush and begins frantically straightening her hair, watching her reflection in the car window, fogging from her close, warm breath.

Dreams, a long time ago. Daddy's gone; Mom's unhappy – for a long time – and maybe lost her mind. I wonder if I got those crazy genes.

"I'm sure your mom will be glad to see you, Pam." Mr. Taylor, trying to encourage. "She'll need you now – Earl and Tina, too."

"Tina – I wonder if she knows?" Pam wonders aloud.

"I'm sure Ester has her ways – like she does with everything – to help Tina through this. She's a good woman – with a sweet granddaughter, all good grandchildren," says Mrs. Taylor. "Your grandmother will be there for all three of you – your mom, too."

"Is that Reverend Arnold's car?" Mr. Taylor observes at the curb.

"I think so – he's here for you. You know we're here, too, right Pam?" Mrs. Taylor says.

Back at the Taylor's house Chuck is kicked back in his dad's comfortably worn retro leather recliner, puffing one of his dad's e-cigs. He tried to relax but remained wary and alert. The coach might come back. The kitchen is dimly lit, ambience coming from a series of old filtered LED lights mounted beneath the wall cabinets. The aroma of oregano, spicy tomatoes, garlic, and Romano cheese linger – Chuck couldn't resist eating the leftover lasagna, even after gorging himself on a mound of spaghetti and meat sauce at Philly's earlier.

A sliver of light cuts around the edge of the front window shade. Chuck kicks the recliner's footrest down, crouches low and creeps toward the window. With his eye to the slit, he peeks out. *Next door at Earl's house.* Three figures exit the car.

"Darn, they're back!" He stands and draws the last vapor before de-activating and putting the device back into its holder on the end table beside his dad's recliner.

Got to e-tag Earl!! He feigns calm and speaks clearly.. "On. Connect Earl. Tag. Start: They're home." The earwig recognizes his voice and *sends*.

Philly's disheveled strawberry blond hair is splayed across Earl's lap where she had fallen asleep soon after Chuck left. Even with his legs as they begin to numb. Legs tingling, he had rested better than he had – seemed like days. His mom's been restless lately, getting up in the middle of the night, sometimes more than a couple of times, puffing e-meds until they kick in and rock her to sleep on the couch. Her life is saturated with chemical vapors, waking her in the morning – late, after he had left for school – picking her up enough to face the retail shopping center's anonymous clerks, or to go to a seemingly endless procession of doctors' and therapists' appointments.

He realizes after the second series of vibrations that his earwig has fallen from his ear into his chest pocket.

"What?" He starts, wishing the e-tag had not come, and that Philly could remain peaceful as she is, his legs so numb he couldn't possibly stand. He does not want to stand. Philly nuzzles against his stomach, sleeping like aa puppy on his lap. Earl checks the e-tag and engages voice-back.

The monotone but not unpleasant synth-voice plays. "They're home."

"What?" Philly turns and pushes herself up on her elbow, her tender baby fat pooch peeking from underneath the hem of her loose fitting faded purple flowered scrub top. Barely awake, she catches Earl's eyes wandering to her bare stomach, and pulls the shirt down to meet her drawstring pants.

"Sorry – it's OK, just Chuck tagging. Pam's home," says Earl.

"I know. You must go. My Mom will be home soon anyway. It's late for the Taylor's getting back."."

"Wish I could just stay here. I was sleeping so soundly," says Earl.

"Maybe another time – when my mom's working third shift," Philly says, blushing, realizing what she is inviting. *But I do care for – love, maybe – him. He's a good guy, and I know I can trust him with anything – even with me sleeping on the couch with him, only thin cotton scrubs between him and me.* She smiles a slightly impish smile and bats her sleepy eyes up at Earl.

"I have to go," Earl says regretfully, not eager to see his mom, but obligated - and really missing his sister.

They walk to the front door, Philly padding barefoot behind Earl and his size fourteen basketball shoes. When he reaches the door, he turns the knob, acting as if he'll just dash out with a casual 'good night', but instead turns to face Philly. She rises to the occasion, standing on her tiptoes, wrapping her arms around Earl's neck, and pulls herself up. He leans his head down, just enough for their lips to meet. A brief pause as their lips part; they realize they have mutually kissed! *We kissed.* He smiles; she beams. They kiss again, a little longer as Earl holds her up, her toes no longer touching the floor.

He eases her down, their young bodies sliding along each other. Regretfully he says, "Good night," and they leave it at that.

19.

Mr. Taylor is poised to knock on the Cleveland's front door - instead of ringing the doorbell.

I've got it." Pam unsnaps her key from the inside her satchel, presses the hands-free button. The lock clicks, and Pam opens the door. A dim lamp light shines from the living room. "Mom?"

A pause. "We're in here." Her mom is wiping her eyes with a tissue as they enter the room. The reverend is sitting on the edge of the coffee table with a box of tissues in his hand.

Lila stands, pulls her robe sashes tight. "Pam… oh, hi Rae, Charlie, thank you so much for bringing my Pam home." Pam hesitates and steps back as her mom approaches. She is off balance when her mom hits her with a big hug.

*This is not like Mom. S*he had almost forgotten how to hug her mom. Pam performs a theatrical mama bear hug with a firm slap on the back. *I don't remember the last time Mom exuded such positive energy.*

"I'm so glad you're home, Pam, sweetie. You must be tired – it's been a very emotional day. Are you hungry?" her mom offers, the traditional Southern hospitality - food.

"I couldn't eat, Mom – some chamomile tea would be nice, though," says Pam.

"Sure, honey, I'll…" Mom starts.

Reverend Arnold volunteers, "I'll get it. You just sit down here with your daughter, Lila. You've got a lot to talk about."

"Thank you, Reverend. The kettle's on the stove and the teabags are in the canister, right there on the counter," says Lila.

"I'm sure I can handle it, Lila. You just visit," the Reverend says.

Mrs. Taylor nudges her husband. "We need to go, Charlie. Chuck's at home, probably wondering where we are."

"We'll be up for a while, Rae, if you two want to stay," says Lila.

"Thanks, Lila, but we're kind of tired, too," Rae says.

"Won't you stay for tea?" Pam asks, not ready to be alone with her mother.

"No, no, thanks."." Mrs. Taylor gives Pam a big, genuine hug. Mr. Taylor hugs Pam, too, but he is a big, awkward bear, bumping the side of her head with his own. He has never had a daughter.

Rae hugs Lila gingerly and kisses her cheek. "Let us know when you need something. I'll bring a casserole over tomorrow – don't worry about cooking."

Lila never worried about cooking; her cooking always involved frozen and micro waved, instant or ready-to-eat. "Thank you so much, Rae – for everything."

"That's what neighbors are for."." Rae reassures Lila. They had not been close for a long time – if ever.

"If you and the children need us…" Charlie starts.

"I know. Thank you both."

"Yeah, thanks, Mr., and Mrs. Cleveland." Pam says.

"Call me Rae, Pam, now that you're all grown up." She smiles.

"Thanks – Rae," Pam says for the first time. *Grown up?*

"G'night."

The Taylor's, and Reverend Arnold's vehicles are parked in front of his house. To avoid a grand entrance, Earl slinks like a panther through the Taylor's back yard, into his own. *Going through the kitchen will give me a little chill time before jumping into that fire.* He presses the button on the door handle softly, inaudibly. As he inches the storm door open, a squeaky hinge cries out.

Caught in the act.

"Earl?" the Reverend peers around the door casing.

"Uh, yeah, it's me. Hey, Reverend."." Earl feels the urge to run like the wind, as he did from the church office earlier. *Run! Run, Earl, run!* He pauses on the top step.

"Come on in, Earl. You're home. Your mom and sister are in the living room. I think the Taylor's are just leaving – it's been a long day, I know."."

"Yeah, long."." Earl is short with the Reverend, apprehensive of the lecture he's going to get.

"It's OK, Earl. I knew you'd be alright. The Lord's watching over you."

"Chuck and Philly were watching over me."

"The Lord works in mysterious ways, with different vehicles through various avenues. I knew Philly and Chuck would be there."

"How did you know I wouldn't just go off to be by myself?" Earl asks.

"Because your 'alone place' was the fort…" the Reverend starts.

"…and I know it burned down. It's my fault," Earl confesses.

"No one was hurt, fortunately. Smoking tobacco again, Earl?" the Reverend asks. "You know it's illegal."

"Naturally." Earl says. ""Those e-cigs are unnatural. Pam says they'll both kill you – got to die somehow." Earl stops short, realizing he's preaching to the preacher -- and reminding himself that his dad is dead. His eyes refuse to dam the tears, and he sits down at the kitchen table, elbows on the surface, hands over his eyes.

"It's going to be alright, son. You're feeling the way you should feel now." The Reverend rests his hand on Earl's quivering shoulder. Earl shrugs it away.

"But why'd he have to die? He wasn't sick. Just all of a sudden; just suddenly, 'Boom!' and he's gone."

"Mysterious ways, Earl, mysterious ways."

"Mysterious? Yeah, mysterious because they haven't found out…what killed him." Earl gets riled.

"Natural causes, Earl, that's what they said," the Reverend says.

"*Natural causes?* That fire in the woods was natural *causes*, too…… but I'm guilty. I am the natural cause that set the fire. I was smoking natural cigarettes.".."

"Earl, I'd say you're an effect, not a cause. Everything that's happened in your family and everything that's touched you. But you're not innocent, son. You've made choices that affected you – and those around you, too," the Reverend says.

"But I can't accept…" Earl starts.

"Right, Earl, if you don't accept every force that hits you, that's you making choices – sometimes positive, sometimes negative. That's a major thing I like about you, Earl: You don't just accept things. You're a thinking young man. The wind doesn't just blow you around like a fallen leaf – you hang on to the tree. And when you do fly, you're like a kite, grounded by a string and stabilized by a tail. But one day, sooner than you expect, you'll soar on wings like eagles. I believe that for you, Earl, and pray for you every day. The Reverend pauses. "All this may sound corny."

"Yeah, corny…" Earl wipes his tears on the back of his hand and onto his shirt then sits up, unable to stifle his boyish smile. "…but I like corn."

"I've got a whole crop of it," says the Reverend, slapping Earl on the back as he goes to the stove to answer the whistling kettle. "Teatime!"!"

the Reverend announces. "Grab those cups and teabags; I'll bring the kettle and the honey."

Tee time: time to tee off with Mom.

"Are you OK, Mom?" Pam sits by her mother on the couch, still awestruck by her mom's show of emotion.

"I feel better since having a talk with Reverend Arnold. He's really a good man. I've shied away from church for years, but maybe…" – "Lila closes her eyes.

"He's been good for Earl, too, Mom. I know I stayed away from all that religion and God stuff, but the few boys in Earl's youth group have turned out pretty good. Earl's starting to become a man," *something a sister wouldn't normally say at* her *age.*

"Yes, quite a young man," says Mom, trying to remember the years that she lost while he was a boy, when she was – lost.

"Where is he, anyway?" Pam asks, annoyed that he's not home.

"Reverend Arnold thinks he's probably with Chuck and Philly. They're all good friends, but the Reverend sees a little bit of a romance flaring between Earl and Philly. That Philly is a sweet – and smart – girl. I like her – and Chuck, too," says Lila.

"Yeah, but Chuck's going to feel like a third wheel if Earl and Philly hook up and become an item. He's Plus, he's been passed over so many times for the basketball team, but he *is* sort of clumsy," Pam says.

"He just needs a little boost, Pam, a success or two," says Lila.

"Girls at college talk about preferring guys like Chuck – smart and funny, not cocky and obnoxious. He'll be a hit when he goes to college in a couple of years – might just bring him out of his shell," Pam says.

"I was thinking, Pam, that it might be good for Earl to get away for a few days after…" Lila hesitates. "…the memorial service."

"Yeah, I've been thinking that this might be the right time to bring Earl for a visit to college. He'll be going in a couple of years, and this way he can get his feet wet, see what it's all about," Pam says.

"And you two can get re-acquainted," Lila smiles.

"We all could use some of that. You want to come, too, Mom?" Pam asks.

Lila laughs. "Sure, but I'll need to get a new look, a college wardrobe."

"Mom, you'll be fine. The grungy look is *in.*" Pam pokes her mom. *It feels awkward, but good talking with Mom. Besides, this helps avoid the elephant in the room: Dad died.*

Pam puts on a serious face.

"I don't look that bad." Lila pretends defense as she observes Pam's transformation. *Pam has come back to reality: Cleve's dead.*

Lila turns the eyeglass away from the elephant. "Where's that tea, Reverend? Having troubles? It's just boiling water, you know!"

"It's my special brewing method," the Reverend calls back. "Takes a little longer, but worth it. Want something sweet with it?"

"Surprise us," Pam answers.

"OK," the Reverend swings open the kitchen door and holds it open with his backside as he carries the kettle and honey.

"Earl!" Pam squeals and rushes over to the door. Cups and teabags fall to the carpet – cups unbroken –as Pam grabs his shoulders and gives him a big smooch on his left cheek as he turns his head to the side.

Lila is beaming. She doesn't recall this much joy and emotion in their home in a long time. *It's a shame Cleve's not here to share this. Did I say that aloud?*

Pam reiterates the thought. "It's a shame Dad's not here." Pam pauses. "We're so happy." Her eyes focus on Earl, then their mom.

"It's OK to be happy," Reverend Arnold says. "We need to celebrate Cleve's life. Just look at you all – you are His family. God blessed Cleve with you. God is proud of His creation, and Cleve, I'm sure is, too."

"Dad's dead," Earl says flatly.

"But he will be born into new life!" the Reverend exults, sloshing hot water.

Pam sits back on the couch, head in her hands, sobbing, "Dad, I love you. I love you, Dad. Why'd you have to leave now...when we're... happy?"

Lila places her arm around Pam, rocking back and forth with her. "Shh... now, now...... I miss him, too."

"Do you?" Pam sits up straight, brushes her hair from her damp face. Lila takes her arm away.

"I do. It's been so long. I still have a long way to go to get back to being the woman that Cleve loved," Lila says. "I love Cleve, but I got lost – still not found. It's been hard for me, but harder for Cleve – and you children."." Lila looks from Pam to Earl and back.

"Mom, I know; you changed. We could all see it after Tina was born – the depression. Or PTSD? You had it years before Tina, when I was a little girl – when you had the accident." Pam mentions the unmentionable.

"Accident? What accident?" Lila asks.

"You don't remember the accident, Mom?" Pam persists.

"I just remember nightmares." Red flashes, shiny gold strands, a bright light. "I don't know where they come from. They've always been in my head." Lila doesn't remember. *Remember…don't remember…*

"Let's talk about Dad, Mom."." Earl tries to lure them away from the pit; Lila is getting too close to the edge. "Pam, what do you remember about *the good old days*? I was too little to remember."

The Reverend begins to counsel. "Yes, Pam, share some of those memories; help your brother remember. Lila, you must recall those earlier, happier days? Share with us." He pleads with his eyes. *Stay with us, Lila. Don't fall into the abyss. You're doing so well.*

If the Reverend had seen her puffing that e-pipe, trying to induce happiness, or at least numbing the sadness, he would know that she was, and is, close to the edge. But she had taken the *edge* off just before his arrival he got there. He only saw the outward, haggard melancholy which she had tonight, as she had those years ago, after the *accident*.

Accident? What accident? Lila thinks.

"OK, Pam, you start. Tell us a good story," the Reverend encourages. *Please bring Lila back, Lord. Don't let her fall. Help us to help her.* He prays.

20.

Pam begins her story.

Mom just had to wear that giant orange straw hat – she called it her 'fishing hat' - since we were going out in the country to fish in Aunt Naomi's little pond. The water was practically at Aunt Naomi's back door so one had to be careful about coming down those back steps with an armload. Aunt Naomi had fallen into that pond once with a basketful of wet clothes she was taking out to hang on the line. After that she would go out the front door and walk the long way around the opposite end of the house.

Mom, Daddy, Earl and I piled out of that old dinosaur – one of those old Saturn station wagons – and started unloading our folding chairs and cooler before Aunt Naomi came out the front door, around the house the long way. On the way to greet us, she stopped at the weathered gray wood storage shed behind the house to get the cane fishing poles.

"Earl! Pam! Come help me with this!" Aunt Naomi called.

We went running and met her with big hugs around her ample legs – we were little then, and she was a big lady.

"Here, big boy." She presented Earl with a spade – for digging the earthworms for bait. The spade handle was longer than Earl was tall, so Daddy came to help. Earl carried the bucket while Aunt Naomi and I carried those long cane fishing poles.

I saw Daddy and Earl take a detour and go out behind the pump house to the grapevine where Aunt Naomi said lots of worms lived and ate her scraps – making compost fertilizer. All this time, Mom was sitting in a folding lounge chair, with her shirt off - her tube top was underneath – to get some sun on her shoulders, but not on her face. She wore that big orange hat. What an embarrassment!

I could hear Earl hollering out by the grapevine. They must've found some worms. When they got back, Daddy threaded a worm on each of our barbed hooks and tossed the cork, sinker and worm suspended from the cane pole by a shiny blue fishing line, past the green slime at the edge of the pond. Aunt Naomi said it was a good day for fishing – it was always a good day for fishing, according to her. We always caught fish.

Anyway, Earl sat down in his little chair between Daddy and Mom. Daddy always stood up to fish. Suddenly, I heard a 'plunk'; Earl squealed and dropped his fishing pole at Mom's feet. He was so excited, and Mom was so startled – she had her eyes closed and shaded by her hat – that when she grabbed for the pole, she slipped on the damp grassy bank and splashed 'ker-plash!' into the green slimy algae in the edge of the water.

I grabbed Earl. Daddy, our hero, dove into the pond and emerged from the murky brown water behind Mom – with the orange hat perched atop his head! The pond bottom was so miry that when Daddy tried to stand in the shallow water, his feet wouldn't come unstuck from the mud, and he fell backwards. Mom grabbed him and pulled him toward the bank but turned and went back out – her orange fishing hat was floating out toward the middle of the pond. "My hat!"

Earl and I were jumping up and down on the bank, me laughing hysterically and Earl crying. Mom crawled from the pond, her droopy, soggy orange hat dripping water and green algae onto her tanned shoulders and lily-white face. Earl finally started laughing – Mom and Daddy, too.

Aunt Naomi called out to us, and we all looked her way. "Smile!" she said, and she saved the moment for posterity on 35mm color film.

"Mom, which old photo album is that in – or is it digitized?" Pam asks.

"It's still in that antique album stored in my hope chest that used to belong to Aunt Naomi. I'll get it out later – that picture gets more hilarious every time I see it," Mom says.

"Good story, Pam. I just wish I remembered. I was too young," Earl says. "Mom, do you have a story that I might remember?"

"I can tell you, Earl, your dad was thinking about you and concerned for your welfare right up to the very end. Did you know he went to see your coach… about prospects for college scholarships and concerns about you, just the day before." Lila stops short, thinking about what's after *before*, and wondering why Coach Bruce had never shown such 'concern' before. Why then?

"No, Mom, he didn't tell me. Neither Dad nor Coach mentioned any scholarships – or concerns," Earl replies, agitated. "Why had nobody talked with me about it? Why didn't they let me in on all this planning of my life?"

"I don't know, honey. Maybe they just didn't want you to lose your focus – on high school," Mom tries to calm Earl. *Bruce never mentioned anything about Earl, except his irritation at his being around, when he was with me.*

"Your dad really cared about you, Earl, but had difficulty expressing it," Lila adds, thinking, 'just as I do - care, and have difficulty showing it.'

"So, the wheels were already in motion, planning for your college, Earl? That's great!" Pam encourages.

"No one had told me about the plans, though," Earl says.

"But, Earl, it's a bit Earl for you to be thinking about all this. You've got a couple of years of keeping up your studies – and grades – in high school. Dad didn't want you to lose all that, and I don't either," Mom says.

"But, Earl, like Mom and I were talking about earlier, maybe it would be good for you to come back to college with me to visit, after the…"Pam stops, realizing the next words would be the memorial *service*. *No, no, no! Dad can't be gone. Why'd he die? Who's going to help Earl – and me and Tina and Mom – with all this? This was not the time to go, Dad – we need you!*

The Reverend notices the pause and the awkward quiet in the room, and he interjects, "…after the memorial service, Pam.   You need to remember, a memorial service will help us all get through this difficult time. And Earl, you didn't know about the meeting and the plans your dad was helping draw up for you…because he cared. What is something you remember, some time you and your dad shared?"

"I do remember sometimes when I was little – I even think I remember that time at Aunt Naomi's, Pam." He looks at his sister. She had suddenly gotten quiet and introverted 'after' but rallies as Earl remembers.

"Do you remember that time, Pam, when Dad was getting ready to go on his first weeklong business trip, the first time I recall him being gone for more than a couple of days?" Earl asks.

"I remember," Pam says.

"I do, too", says Mom.

A week was just too much time for me to grasp, and Daddy wanted me to understand that even if he was far away, and I couldn't see him, I could call and he'd answer -and he would be back, Earl remembers.

He squatted down beside me, investigated my worried face, and he said, 'Let's take a walk', so of course I wanted to take a walk with him. Maybe he'd changed his mind about the trip.

He took my hand, and off we walked toward the end of the block, where the woods begin. 'Now, Earl, you wait here, and I'm going into the woods,' Daddy said.

'But, Daddy, I want to come, too,' and I started to sniffle. 'Don't cry, Earl – I'll be right back. Now you wait, and when I get out of sight, I want you to call –real loud –for me.'

'OK, but you're coming back, right?'

'Definitely - OK, I'm off.'

I squatted on my haunches, hands tucked behind my overalls' bib, rocking, watching, and listening to Daddy rustling through the undergrowth. I squinted, and when I couldn't see him –but still heard his footsteps – I called out, 'Daddy!'

'Earl! I'm still here.'

'I hear you, Daddy!'

'Good. Now I'm going into the woods a little further, and when you can't hear my footsteps anymore, you call me.'

'OK, Daddy!'

Daddy walked a minute more, and then –silence.

'Daddy? Are you there, Dad?'

'I'm here, Earl!'

'Come out, Daddy!'

'Are you OK, Earl?'

'Yeah –just come out. It's time!'

A minute later, Daddy runs out of the woods and grabs me up in his mighty arms and says, 'I'm back! Did you miss me?'

'Yeah, but I knew where you were, and that you were coming back.'

'So, you weren't afraid?'

'Maybe for a minute…'

'But when you called, I answered, right, Earl?'

I understood. When Daddy went away on that business trip, I called him the very first day. He called me the second day – I knew he would.

Earl finishes the story, adding, "But what about now?"

"Your dad may not answer now, Earl," the Reverend replies, "but he's there, 'out in those woods' or 'flying away on a trip.' Call him, Earl, and God will answer for him, for now. Always remember those good times. Your dad – and your Father – isn't far away."

Pam grins at Earl, as if holding a secret that wanted to get out. "That place in the woods – where Daddy was just out of sight –is where you built 'the fort', right?"

"…the fort that burned down," Earl adds.

Reverend Arnold reassures Earl and the entire family. "But, Earl, you know those old pines will survive the flames, the undergrowth will green again, and the place where you built the fort before, will be there still.

And, like that, the place in your heart that hurts, misses your dad, will heal, and you will rebuild."

The Reverend puts his hand on Earl's shoulder, Pam comes over and hugs him and kisses her brother's cheek, while Mom sits back in the wingback chair, relishing the love.

"I remember when I was pregnant with Tina, and your dad was so proud, anticipating a second daughter – the first daughter was, and is such a joy," Lila nods and smiles at Pam, who rolls her eyes and says, "Yeah, right."

"He doted over me so much in the last trimester, making sure I wasn't overtired, that I didn't lift anything and got enough to eat –and, yes, I ate and ate! I got huge! My ankles were like elephants'. Your dad still found it in him to compliment my beauty." Lila pats her hair and holds her chin up, properly, "He was always saying that he loved me more with each passing, pregnant day. He said I was 'glowing'; I think he was glowing more than I was."

"Did you have any cravings, Mom?" Pam asks.

"I was getting to that," Mom says, starting her pregnant story.

One night, Cleve had been sound asleep for a couple of hours, when, at maybe one o'clock in the morning, I couldn't sleep. I sat up in bed – with difficulty, a giant weight in my belly –and said, 'bananas'. Something in my brain – or my womb – was craving the yellow jungle fruit.

Tiptoeing as lightly as elephant ankles and feet could, I lumbered down the hall to the kitchen, squeaking the door as I entered.

'Bananas – shoot, no bananas!'

I started banging pots and lids as I retrieved the double boiler from the lower cabinet –with trouble and trepidation due to my belly –and commenced gathering ingredients to make a banana pudding.

Lila laughs to herself, thinking of how Ester says Tina loves banana pudding. *I started that.*

Well, with all the banging and fussing about bananas, Cleve awoke and trudged into the kitchen in his striped cotton pajamas, hair all disheveled, scratching his mussed head, eyes squinting at the light.

'What are you doing, Lila?' he muttered, sleepy and a bit perturbed.

'Bananas, Cleve, I need bananas,' she answered.

'What are you making, Lila,' he asked me.

'Isn't it obvious? Banana pudding! All I need is a bunch of ripe bananas – with just a few black freckles on the skins –not too ripe, but definitely not green.'

'So, you want me to go out for bananas?'

'Of course! The baby, our Tina, craves some bananas – and I'm making banana pudding!'

Cleve, too tired to argue, and practically sleepwalking, slips on loafers and dons his trench coat from the hall closet, and without another word jingles his keys and heads out.

'Thanks, honey –and hurry, the baby's hungry!'

Thirty minutes, an hour passed, and I finished making the custard, had the meringue fluffed, and had a layer of vanilla wafers in the clear glass casserole dish – still waiting on Cleve and bananas.

When he finally got back – he'd been all over and across town to locate the 'perfect' bananas. "Guess what?" Lila asks the kids.

"You had given up and gone back to bed, sound asleep?" Earl guesses.

"You'd made the pudding without bananas?" Pam guesses.

"Close, Pam."." *I was sitting at the kitchen table in front of an empty clear casserole dish, an empty yellow and brown vanilla wafer box, and two licked-clean bowls with remnants of custard on my chin and a dab of meringue in my hair!*

Pam, Earl and the Reverend cackle, picturing Lila sitting there – and Cleve standing in the doorway with an armload of bananas, in various stages from lime green to ink spattered spotted to smeared soot black, as Lila describes.

"He was so sweet," Lila said.

'Here are the bananas, honey.'

'That's good because Tina is still craving bananas – but I'm full of pudding!'

Cleve sat across the table from me, offering various versions of banana, which I force-fed myself – Tina was kicking me!

Your father was so patient with me when I was pregnant, and most all other times, too. Anyway, next day while he was at work, I made him a banana pudding – and only ate half of it before he came home! They all laughed again.

Earl asks, "Do we have any bananas, Mom?"

"Don't get any pudding ideas, Earl," Lila says.

21.

The Taylor's pull into the driveway. *It was silly to park at the Cleveland's and then driven one door down to get home.* "All the lights are out. Chuck must have already gone to bed." Mrs. Taylor observes.

"Kind of early for Chuck to turn in – just before eleven? He was supposed to be home, right?"

"He really didn't say, Charlie. I thought he'd be here with Earl, since Earl's not at his house yet," not knowing that Earl had slipped in the back door just as they were leaving the Cleveland's house and that Chuck and Earl had been at Philly's house most of the evening.

"I know he thinks he's *grown*, but Chuck still needs to have a little courtesy and let us know where he's going – and when he'll be home," Charlie says, agitated.

They approach the front door. A sliver of light slices the edge of the window shade by the door.

Chuck is sitting in the kitchen by the dim light above the stove. The rattle of keys startles him, and all he can think is that it might be coach. He slinks around the corner into the dining room, illuminated only by the filtered streetlight from a block away. The feeling that Chuck sensed about Coach had evolved into paranoia. Chuck anticipates the front door opening, and the confrontation that might ensue – if he doesn't stay hidden.

The door creaks and Chuck's heart races as adrenaline pumps like e-nhancer stimulation. Fight or flight? He could run back through the kitchen and escape out the back door. The foyer sensor clicks, and the doorway is flooded with white light.

"Chuck, are you home?" His mom's voice.

He exhales and sighs.

"Maybe he's asleep," his dad says. "I'll go back and check."

Chuck stands with his back against the dining room wall, taking deep breaths. Counting to himself, *eight, nine, ten* seconds, taking deeper breaths. *They don't need to know I'm scared.* He makes his grand entrance into the light.

"I'm up, Mom – just getting a snack." His voice quivers.

"Are you alright, son?" his dad asks. "We thought Earl would be here. Have you seen him?"

"Oh, we were at Philly's earlier, and then I came home; Earl should be home by now," Chuck begins to get concerned. *He should be home by now.*

"Why don't you call him, Chuck, to ease our minds," Mom suggests.

"Okay." Chuck heads back towards his room.

"Let us know, please, Chuck," says Dad.

Chuck hurries down the hall making the earwig call.

"Hey, Chuck," Earl answers. "We're still up chatting – what's up?"

"Where are you? My folks are worried."

"I'm home."

"Mom and Dad didn't see you there…" Chuck starts.

"I must've been in the kitchen with Reverend Arnold. I came in the back way." Earl explains.

"I'm glad you made it home. I was worried, too. "

"Worried, Chuck? Philly looked after me 'til you e-tagged."

"Was her mom home when you left?" Chuck asks.

"No, Chuck, but she should be by now. You're becoming quite the mother hen, Chuck."

"Somebody's got to tend the baby chicks. I was just worried that…"

"Don't worry, Chuck, the Reverend's praying over us."

The Reverend is speaking softly with Lila and Pam in the living room.

"Good, we can use all the prayers we can get," Chuck says.

"What is up with you, Chuck? Is there something you're not telling me?"

"No, no, I'm just saying – "

"As long as you're *just saying*, Chuck."

"Glad you made it home," Chuck says. *This is just a feeling about Coach, but I should keep checking on these guys, just for peace of mind, if for no other reason.* "Mom and Dad are still wondering – where you are. I'd better let them know you're home and OK," says Chuck.

"Thanks, Chuck."

"De nada."

Chuck yells down the hall. "Mom and Dad, he's home!"

"I wish he wouldn't do that, Charlie, yelling like we're out in the yard," Rae says.

"OK, Chuck!" Charlie yells back. "And don't yell in the house!"

Rae disgustedly shakes her head, "And I wonder where he gets that behavior."

"What?" Charlie doesn't get it.

After seeing Coach's pickup slowing by Philly's house earlier, Chuck calls to make certain her mom is home.

"Hey, Chuck. What's up?" Philly answers her earwig.

"Uh, nothing, just checking up on everybody. Your mom home yet?" Chuck asks.

"She's just driving up, and no, Earl's not still here, Mama Chuck." Philly snickers.

"Are you and Earl in cahoots? He just called me *mother hen* and now I'm *Mama Chuck.* I'm just trying to be responsible," Chuck puffs up.

"Our lives are in your hands, Chuck. You're going to *save* us." Philly continues ribbing him.

Chuck thinks, *I'm the only one suspicious of Coach. Don't want everyone worried; I have enough worry for everyone.*

"Never fear, Mama Chuck is here!" Chuck plays along.

"Our hero!"

"Much later, Chuck."

Philly didn't want Chuck to worry, omitting the fact he had seen Coach's VW pickup slow down in front of her house earlier. She didn't know what Coach was doing in the neighborhood and didn't want to know.

Chuck didn't want to know either, but Lila and Coach had crammed the knowledge down his throat earlier in front of Earl's house. Yellow police tape still in place, Cleve's body still warm, and Bruce and Lila in each other's arms. The scene of the crime.

There was no crime scene. 'Natural causes' is what the preliminary report stated. No evidence pointed to foul play, only people who 'had a feeling' or 'wondered about', or a couple of people who were 'looking into' just to 'make sure' that the cause of Cleve's death was 'natural'. One could assemble this picture of death with all the pieces of the puzzle, the how's and the why's, the physical and the metaphysical. One piece was missing, which the Reverend had not found: Coach Bruce

Supernatural? The Reverend may have thought. He would be talking about *God's will,* which we can't understand. *Pray,* he said. And he prayed.

22.

It's a shame, isn't it? Bruce thinks. *Cleve's weakness, his Achilles heel, that little genetic malady, diabetes, 'natural cause' of death. Me? I didn't do it – I'm innocent! The little boost Cleve got from that glucose ampule, those boosts that those boys have been puffing all season, with only a 1:10 record to show for that 'enhancement.' What have I learned from all this, this loser of a season? If the boys don't have talent, all the 'boosts' in Cuba and Mexico won't win basketball games – but it will win Lila.*

That boy of Lila's –Cleve's, too, God rest his soul –is the only talent on my team. He's going 'pro' someday – if he can just graduate high school, get recruited and go to college – with no injuries! Wouldn't that be a blessing to Lila – and me –if he made some 'pro' money? Along with that sweet pension and life insurance from Cleve – thanks, Cleve –she'd be living high on the hog with me. No more driving old VW pickups. No more coaching losing teams of pimply-faced high school boys. No more worries - thanks to my brilliance and one little e-nhance ampule. Goes to show, it's the little things that make a difference.

After Earl left, Philly's had seen the headlights shining in the window. "Mom's home!" She opened the front door, but Mom's car wasn't coming up the driveway. Disappointed, she started to close the door; then she saw the little pickup. *That's coach's truck. Wonder what he's doing out here?* The truck pulled past the house with red brake lights shining, reminding her of the eyes of a black bull she had seen on a bull fighting poster her dad had sent her.

She shook off the image of the red-eyed bull. *Coach must have gone by Earl's house concerned about his star player. That's nice. Earl could use a good male role model, now that his dad's gone.* Philly waved in the direction of the red taillights, in case the coach could see her, acknowledging his thoughtfulness.

A trusting soul Philly, seeing –or attempts to see – the goodness in people. She trusts Earl - and Chuck - earned over several years of friendship. Coach is a figure of authority and respect, up on a pedestal at school - especially to the students who have no direct contact with him. The athletes, like Earl –and even Chuck who hasn't made the team –trust Coach because he is supposed to be their leader, mentor, and role model. Many of the boys at school have no father at home, so they latch onto the first strong male figure that touches their lives, shows them the ropes, and spends some time with them.

Earl didn't need a father figure, but Coach brought him into the fold because he needed Earl on the team. Earl felt obligated to Coach in case there were college recruiters and potential scholarships, but mostly he wanted to make his dad proud. Coach knew this and played Earl with the 'Dad card'.

Philly saw Coach's loyalty to Earl. Chuck, on the other hand, had the gift of discernment, the natural ability to differentiate between right and wrong, good and evil, green and red, trite and essential. Chuck could see the ruse, but he dearly wanted to be on the team. He was completely comfortable doing things on his own, but like Earl, wanted to please his dad, make him proud. Chuck's dad had difficulty expressing his feelings, so Chuck didn't know when he'd made him proud.

23.

Wouldn't Philly love some ice cream? I know I would. On her way home from the hospital Glenda pulls off at the '24/7' convenience mart to get a couple of liters of gasoline for her old Prius hybrid and a half liter of Ben and Jerry's Chunky Monkey. Ben and Jerry's had been around since Glenda was a little girl sitting at the kitchen table, on a booster seat made of Sears catalogs sewn in a homemade patchwork bag. She and her mom ate right out of the carton – like she and Philly do.

This gasoline, $6.87 per liter, costs more than ice cream! I remember watching Daddy pump gasoline in his 'economical' Ford Focus – before the hybrids, and way before total electric. Wish I had one of those electric cars. As it stands now, between my educational supplement and Philly's part-time – bless her heart, she works so hard - we barely eat and pay for essentials.

If it weren't for the Government Fair Food Act and the State Supplement for Single Parents Enrolled in Educational Programs, I'd be running the dish sanitizer at the hospital cafeteria - no hope of getting out. When I become an RN, Philly can quit that menial labor at the hospital and concentrate on her studies – and a teenage social life. I want Philly to have so much more –but tonight, she'll have ice cream! Chunky Monkey is her favorite flavor with banana, chunks of fudge and walnuts. Well, sometimes we must compromise half weeks GOFAFA funds and a half week of pasta and sauce –no meat. I'm sure she'll throw in a salad. I love that girl!

"Philly, I'm home!" Glenda announces.

"Mom!" Philly runs to greet her at the door, hugging hard, almost toppling her over.

"No, you didn't," Philly excitedly grabs the bag of ice cream from her mom's hand. "You know I can't resist 'Chunk Monkey'. I'll get fat, and then who'll love me?"

"I will, honey –and Earl, too."

"Mom," Philly blushes.

"Oh, I know," her mom says.

She's the wise one. How did she know Earl stayed over so late? "But, Mom, we didn't do anything –just talked and watched a movie."

"What movie?" She suspects there was no movie.

"Um – we just talked, mostly. The movie wasn't any good," Philly says.

"What about Chuck? Did he stay for this bad movie?"

"OK, Mom, here's the deal. Chuck left after dinner – Oh, I saved you some spaghetti!" Attempting to derail her mom from the track of the story.

"Oh, thanks, I'll have that spaghetti." Mom then gets her back on track. "Chuck left after dinner. And then what happened?" Philly takes the brown paper bag with ice cream and trots to the kitchen. "I'll heat up the spaghetti right quick, Mom. I know you're hungry – then ice cream!"

Glenda stands in the foyer for a minute, absorbing the sweet little girl she knows, hoping she won't grow up too quickly. She drops her green canvas school bag by the door and hangs her white cardigan on the rack.

"Philly don't run away from me," halfway kidding with her daughter, the other half wanting to keep her nestled under her wing forever.

"I'm not running away, Mom. I'm right here –in the kitchen getting your dinner. It's kind of late for dinner, but you need to eat, and not just Chunky Monkey!" Philly calls, playing the mom part.

Glenda heads down the hall pulling her scrub top over her head as she goes. She puts on her white terry robe and drops her scrub pants. "I'm coming – just getting comfortable," Glenda says.

Philly is stirring the pot of leftover spaghetti on the stove. With her back to her mom, she says, "These old scrubs are about as comfortable as anything." Still making banter, attempting to distract her Mom from the pending conversation.

"So, Chuck left after dinner – and then what happened? Please, continue." Her mom sounds a little serious.

"Oh, I don't remember what movie –just something boring that we streamed in," Philly goes on, not describing her evening after Chuck left.

"So, bad boring movie, and you and Earl were enjoying stimulating conversation –for how many hours?"

Stimulating? Mom can use just the most embarrassing words. "Mom, there was nothing *stimulating.*" Philly defends her virtue, turning the conversation. "In fact, we were so bored that we fell asleep…" She stops herself. *Gotta explain that one now.*

"Asleep, huh? Where was all this 'sleeping' going on?" her mom asks.

"Mom, don't you trust me? I'm fifteen, practically a woman now," Philly gets a little defensive.

"Philly, I'm sorry. I do trust you – and Earl, I think."

"Thank you, Mom."

"Now go on with your story. You don't have to hide anything from me. I'm your mom, but also a woman –hard to believe," says her mom.

Philly sits across the table from her mom. They're just two women having a conversation.

"I was just getting so sleepy after this long day –a lot happening with Earl's dad dying and all. Filling our bellies with spaghetti just got us comfortable," Philly says.

"It's very good, Philly," Mom talking with spaghetti in her mouth.

"Thanks. Anyway, Chuck had gone, and Earl and I were on the couch, and I just lay my head in his lap –that was OK –and he stroked my hair. There's nothing wrong with that, is it, Mom?" Philly asks, seeking reassurance.

"No, Philly –it's kind of sweet," Mom smiles.

"It was like he was comforting himself –like I used to hold your old Tiny Tear doll.

"I'm glad you were there for him, Philly."

"Next thing I know, I wake up, and Earl is nodding, sound asleep with his hand still in my hair. His earwig had fallen into his shirt pocket and was vibrating against my head. Chuck was messaging that Pam and the Taylor's had gotten home. That was just a few minutes ago –and Earl went home."

"Nothing wrong about any of that, Philly."

"Well, just one more thing, Mom," Philly continues, honestly.

Glenda thinks, 'Uh, oh, here it comes,' and says, "What's that?"

"Um, right before he left, I –um, we – kissed at the front door –just a little kiss," Philly says, but thinks, *a couple*. "You know I like Earl –for a while now –and now I know he likes me."

Glenda comes around the table, hugs Philly and kisses the top of her head. "I love you, Philly. I trust you. And I want you to be happy."

"I am, Mom –here with you, and with Earl, too."

Glenda kisses Philly on top of her head and says, "OK, OK –enough mushes! Let's have some ice cream before it gets mushy!"

Philly gets big wooden mixing spoons, and she and Glenda sit opposite each other, sliding the cold tub of Chunky Monkey back and forth, eating until nothing remains but the empty tub and the licked spoons.

24.

Glenda swivels the chair at the nursing station as she enters vital data into her patients' digital files. *Decades ago, the health care industry – they used to call health care an 'industry' – decided that for the sake of efficiency and accuracy, healthcare workers would carry Individual Data Entry Devices (IDED's, now negatively referred to as 'I dead's'.) These IDED's were strapped to their waists, instantaneously recording all vitals and related data while in the patients' rooms.*

There was great dissatisfaction with this practice. Healthcare workers were paying more attention to their IDED's than to their patients. After all the digital IDED data was compared with handwritten hard copy, the IDED was found to be 20% less accurate than the handwritten and patient satisfaction was 50% lower when IDED was implemented.

Glenda meticulously converts her notes into digital data, but she is distracted by a doctor leaning on the counter talking too loudly into her earwig. Glenda peers over her work and sees the 'coroner' badge clipped to the woman's lab coat.

"Yes, yes, Carl, I sent the sample to the State Crime Lab, and like I said, the results will be back in two days.

I promise you; I've done all I can –taken all the evidence –without being invasive.

No, unless this case is labeling anything other than 'natural causes' –maybe suspicious circumstances? I can't perform an invasive autopsy. Even the blood sample I sent off is questionably legal.

Probably should have had a court order for that.

You think you can, get one 'after the fact'?

You don't think the results will be admissible, even if they incriminate?

Do what you have to do, but we both know there's something fishy about this Cleveland death."

Glenda stops short. *Cleveland. Philly asked me to listen, pay attention for anything sounding suspicious about Earl's dad. She said Chuck was kind of funny about the death, too. What could be suspicious about his death? 'Natural causes', that's what we've heard, but this –the coroner investigating his death. What if it was unnatural, someone helped him die –killed him? Earl's already starting to accept his dad's death, Philly says, but if this were murder –that would change everything –except for the fact that his dad's still dead. Earl would have to start the grieving process all over again – beginning with anger.*

What about his mother? If Cleve's death were unnatural –Oh, God, Lila would go into a tailspin, and the children would all be Ester's responsibility.

If it is unnatural and the killer is not found out, or if they find it's not natural causes and can't prove it –would the death still be treated naturally? The Cleveland's would probably fair better if the unnatural death were kept under cover –unless the culprit can be convicted and punished.

"Glenda? Miss Glenda? Where are you? Calling Nurse Glenda," another nurse intern says. "You look like you've got a lot on your mind – care to share?"

"Huh? Oh, yeah, just trying to decipher my handwriting in these notes," Glenda lies.

The intern, Rhada, rounds the counter and peeks over Glenda's shoulder at her original notes and at the computer screen. "Legible to me – you're doing everything great, actually, Glenda. You just fret too much."

Glenda steers away from hospital concerns, toward home frets. "I guess I'm really thinking about my daughter, Philly. She was at home with two boys when I left coming to the hospital."

"Two boys –are they fighting over Philly?" Rhada kids.

"Oh, no, nothing like that. The two boys –and Philly, too, actually –are best friends. That Philly, though, she's had a thing, a crush, on one of the boys, Earl, for at least a year. She won't talk about it with me, but maybe she will soon. Philly's fifteen now and 'most a woman'," Glenda shares.

"She's your girl, and if she's taken good notes, watched your example, then she'll be just fine. We've been together in nursing school since the beginning, so I know you expect only the best. Philly will be OK, Glenda," says Rhada.

"Why, thank you. I don't get too many compliments on my parenting, with Philly's teenage attitude," Glenda says.

"But she is almost a woman'," Rhada reminds.

"Oh, right. Maybe I'll try talking with her when I get home tonight," Glenda says.

"Make sure you do a lot of listening, not just talking –and woman to woman."

"You're right, Rhada. I better get this data done so I can get home to that girl."

"Remember, 'most a woman', Glenda."

"Right."

25.

Before Cleve died, he had an epiphany. He needed to step back and see the big picture of his family. He was father to an amazing daughter, Pam, who reminded him so much of himself when he was her age. *Pam is a rebel, against the system and what is wrong with it. She makes no qualms about where she stands. He knew she smoked real tobacco –none of the e-cig chemicals. Great-great grandpa, the tobacco farmer, would have been proud of her. She had a jug of musty wine fermenting in the closet of her dorm room which he had smelled when he visited her earlier in the fall – muscadines were ripe! That Pam's quite a young woman. She's going to change the world –one golden leaf and one sweet grape at a time.*

Earl is an exceptional athlete, but his spirit is what's so special about him. People are attracted to his Spirit, and the leadership he possesses. People like Earl; he likes people. He emulates, and loves, his big sister Pam. If they can stay together, like they've done over the years, through all the hurt that I couldn't protect them from, they will be an amazing sibling team. Whose genes did they get, anyway? Oh, yeah, my Mom's.

Ester has been our savior over the years, especially for Tina. Tina might be my most exceptional –not 'special', but if she was 'special', we'd love her the most –because she's been raised by the matriarch of the family, Mama Ester. Mama brought some extraordinary genes into this family! Tina got most of her genes, her nature – and her nurture.

Oh, Lila, got some raw genes from somewhere, that remained dormant until –the tragic accident. Our first years of marriage, and our first two children, were amazing! Lila was beautiful, inside, and out, and I loved her so much –why else would I marry her, right? She had other reasons, though the greatest of these is love, for marrying me. Her family was not the most nurturing. Her father was an alcoholic; her mother was submissive to an abusive alcoholic. No more needs be said –unspeakable, unmentionable things were done, and Lila was strong enough to survive. I love my family. I think I'll take a day off, start life over –again.

And he did.

26.

Detective Brown sits in his patrol car a block below the Cleveland house – near the woods that are home to Earl and Chuck's fort. He takes a bite of the gyro, dribbling the cucumber dill sauce on his crumpled day-old oxford shirt. A light shines from the foyer of the Cleveland house.

Coach, he thinks, *What the hell is he doing here?* No one else in the world sees except Detective Brown –and the neighbors, Anna, and Bette. *Why is Lila Cleveland heating it up with Coach Bruce while Cleve's body lies on a cold slab in the morgue of the hospital? Her sixteen-year-old son is with a girlfriend a few blocks away, her twenty-year-old daughter a few minutes away, and her four-year-old daughter asleep in her mothers-in-law house not ten minutes away. Lila's life is askew.*

This just ain't right. If this 'coach' and this 'mother' had any respect for Cleve - why is the coach not respecting this time of mourning? Something's not right!

Detective Brown puts down his gyro and watches as the coach makes his way by the light of the foyer to the little pickup parked by the curb. Lila cuts the lights in the foyer, and Coach drives slowly away. Coach slows, not a block from the Cleveland's. A shadow jumps into the darkness, just up from the Taylor's.

What the –? The shadow of Chuck vanishes, and a dog materializes on the sidewalk in the light, barking his tail off at the pickup passing so slowly by. *Who's that in the shadows, and why is Coach slowing down?*

Coach's pickup continues up the street, as Detective Brown keeps vigil. Half a dozen houses up, the pickup slows, red brake lights glaring. A silhouette in the doorway of the house adjacent Coach's slowing pickup. *Someone's waving at Coach. Who could that be?* The figure goes inside, and the lights go out. *This doesn't add up. So, cipher. Coach at the Cleveland's with Lila, plus the shadowy figure next door, plus the silhouette of somebody waving at Coach up the street. Something doesn't compute – or does it?*

27.

The Cleveland's are fading fast, especially Lila, understandable if any one of them knew she had taken those e-meds just before the Reverend arrived. If emotions and adrenaline hadn't naturally kicked in, she would have been laid out on the couch, dead asleep a couple of hours ago.

I'm glad I decided to come over, even so late at night, thinks the Reverend. *Sometimes I do make the right decision if I let the Spirit move me. Thank you, Lord, and continue to watch over this family. Amen.*

Lila begins leaning into Pam, as her heavy eyelids become burdensome. Pam wants to be supportive of her mother during the mourning process. Her mom to leans on her for a moment before Pam pats Lila's hand and lightly nudges her arm.

"Mom, it's time to go to be."

Lila strains to lift her eyelids. "Mm, hmm," Mom slowly sits up.

Reverend Arnold stands and announces, "Well, folks, I have outstayed my welcome, and if I stay any longer, I'll have to request a pallet to spread out on the floor."

"You are perfectly welcome to camp out here, Reverend," Pam replies. "Might as well make it a group camp –I feel like a camper here, too."

"Oh, Pam," Lila rouses a little, and gathers her robe together and tightens the sash. "You know your room is still here, like you left it when you went off to college – and Tina's room, too."

"I know, Mom, just messing with the Reverend," Pam answers, but she really means exactly what she said about feeling like a camper at home.

"Thank you for the hospitality, and for sharing your stories; I believe they helped. You all are a wonderful family, and I am blessed knowing you," the Reverend says, "especially this young man," he offers as he walks over to Earl sitting asleep in the chair, kicking his foot. Earl jumps to attention. "Come see me anytime, Earl, to talk or just grab a chair and take a nap," he goads.

Earl settles back in his seat and tries awakening, but his head keeps nodding with his sleep-weighted head.

Pam rises first and walks across the room to the Reverend as he heads for the front foyer. She catches him by his sleeve, and he turns. Pam grabs him in a Teddy bear hug, and he gives her a big daddy hug. Reverend never married nor had children of his own, but many young people in the church recognize him as a 'father' figure, though he's not Catholic. With

Dad gone, Pam quickly realizes her need for a father, and reverts to that little girl in the frilly Easter dress, hugging the 'father'. If she had been Catholic, as their mom professed as a girl up through confirmation, Pam would have said, 'Thank you, Father.'

"Thank you, Reverend Arnold; you have been especially good for my mother today. Earl needs you, too." Pam buries her face in his strong, archangelic chest.

He holds her at arm's length, his hands grasping her shoulders, and smiling with an understanding he has always possessed. "God Bless you, Pam," he says softly just for her.

Pam feels warm, as a cleansing emersion in a heated baptistery, and she says, "Bless you, Father —I mean, Reverend."

We are all the same, 'brothers —and sisters —in Christ. He smiles into the room, a farewell for the night. *Until we gather again tomorrow evening for the family visitation.*

Reverend Arnold walks the darkened sidewalk to his car parked in front of the Cleveland's. His demeanor is energetic and happy in the presence of parishioners and believers. But now he feels a weight bearing down on him, once again alone with his Maker. As he enters his car, he feels comfortable praying aloud, even though he knows that the Lord hears even his secret thoughts.

"Our Father, who art in heaven —we need your Holy Spirit here with us now. Lord, I am so thankful to have the Spirit in me to be able to minister to this ailing family. I am weak, Lord, but You are strong —thank you, Jesus," Reverend Arnold starts his car and slowly drives up the street, past the Taylor's house, toward Philly and Glenda's house.

"Lord, I see the lights in the Taylor house. Bless them, for their precious role comforting and bringing Pam home to her family. Dear Father, Rae and Charlie are good people, with a good son —You know, Lord. Chuck is one of your precious children, and he is troubled now and in need of strength and guidance with the discernment with which You have blessed him. I sense his disturbance, the feeling that he has. You know his needs. Be with him and help me —us —to help him do the right thing."

Reverend Arnold rolls by Philly's house; the lights are 'on'. "And here, Lord, You know their needs. Something anew is troubling Philly's mom, Glenda. You know her concern, trust, and love for her daughter, but something lays heavy on her Spirit —as it does on Chuck's. You know,

Lord. Protect them. Give them strength and help them ask for help from me, Your humble servant, and for the tools they need –You know, Lord."

"Guide us and protect us. Your Son, our strength, Jesus Christ, who has shown us the way, leads us through the Spirit –Your Spirit –and shows us the Way. Bring us out from 'under a bushel' with Your Light, and help us outshine the darkness, as You do tonight in these homes. I ask these things in the Name of the Father, the Son Jesus Christ, and the Holy Spirit. Amen."

28.

The warmth of Philly's head and the silkiness of her hair had soothed Earl to sleep earlier. Even the pressure on his legs as they numbed under her weight felt better than anything he had ever felt. Earl had never had a 'girlfriend' before Philly, even though some other guys of sixteen claimed 'girlfriends' even three or four years earlier. Was he a late bloomer, or was he a little more selective, waiting for the right girl?

Stories, accompanied by silly boys snickering, by so-called 'experienced' boys longing for the touch, feel and smell that bolder boys described, getting them into lathers –but not Earl. He had seen the digital 3D images displayed on the kno-pads brought to the locker room after basketball practice, but Earl had two sisters, and he was very protective of them. He couldn't say 'respect' out loud if he was to be one of the team, but he knew in his heart that when it came down to loyalty and bravery, his sisters Pam and Tina would always be his priority.

Philly had been in Earl's narrow band of close friends for several years, and was always an equal part of their force, along with Chuck. But last year, something changed; Philly developed some of those curves like the 3D images of the female form splayed and displayed by drooling adolescent boys snickering in the locker room. Philly started seeing and feeling differently about Earl, too, quickly averting her eyes whenever he glanced her way. She began paying more attention to what he said and did, hanging onto his words and movement. Oh, and with that 'accidental' kiss at the fort last year –he knew she 'liked' him!

Earl lay in his bed, exhausted from the day's emotions which had swung between sadness at his dad's death, the subsequent fire he started at the fort, which had originated with him and his dad, and the confusion and excitement generated by the Philly kisses. Earl's senses were totally exhausted. He needed to rejuvenate his mind and body but was fighting the urge to sleep.

No, I can't sleep. What's back there, in my mind? Stay awake. Philly... remember... kisses. He loses conscious thought and finds himself in a subconscious excursion to what he desires, and from what he fears...

Smoke billows up to the pine tops of their woods, obscuring the laurel thicket which had once provided camouflage. Fire had erupted from the burning cherry carelessly dropped from Earl's illegal tobacco cigarette.

He turns, expecting to see Philly standing beside him at the schoolyard fence, but she is not —only Chuck remains.

"Where's Philly?" Earl asks the bedraggled Chuck, mourning the loss of their boyhood respite, the fort. "Where's Philly?" He tries to shake Chuck from his stupor.

"Philly? Philly! Oh, my God, she's there —there!' Chuck points to the hazy silhouette in the smoky haze.

Earl sees through the smoky canopy using his superhuman dream powers of vision. Philly is standing atop the orange bucket in the middle of the fire-encompassed fort, flames spitting and grabbing at her. But no harm can come to Philly from burning or suffocation —or anything —because she is standing safely on the 'kissing bucket'.

In a 'single bound', like Super Man of the 'Underoos' he wore as a boy, Earl clears the cyclone fence and flies between charred pines and through acrid smoke, casting away all fear. Philly waits tiptoe atop the bucket as Earl swoops her up from the circled-up fort and they levitate above the danger of stifling smoke and scorching flame. Flying above subdivision houses, they descend into the sandpit of Philly's backyard swing set. Earl begins to feel the familiar safety of home, her home. Philly suddenly slips from his grip and starts sinking like a doodle bug, backwards into the sandy trap.

"Philly! Philly!" Earl calls. She reaches up from the swirling vortex of sand, but the gravity is too great, and pulls Earl down with Philly's hand in his. "Philly!"

Earl wakes, sweating, with sand from the back of his hand rubbing against his forehead.

"Philly!" He springs from his bed, still fully dressed from having passed out exhausted on the top sheet, runs through the kitchen, out the back door and sprints through neighbors' yards all the way to Philly's.

Philly had put away the spoons and thrown the empty ice cream carton into the recycling bin. Her mom went down the hall to bed, exhausted from another long day of learning, assisting nurses and motherly duties. Philly follows her mother, after turning out the lights. As she passes her mom's door says, "'Night, Mom."

Glenda replies groggily, "'Night, Philly —love you."

"You, too, Mom."

She brushes her teeth haphazardly and changes into her daddy's old red and green flannel shirt. Philly calls it her 'magic nightgown'. She imagines she's a little girl in Peter Pan, as she slides under the cool cotton sheets and snuggles under the comforter in her twin bed. Earl's tender kiss lingers on her lips like warm minty lip balm. Smiling, "Mm," she caresses her covers and drifts off into a dream.

The fog lay ominous on the ocean of Philly's dream as she looks across the massive gray deck of the cruise ship, searching for her dad. She floats on the stream of her dream, following the current to the mezzanine deck where the lights are dimmed. Like stage lights, the circular spotlight floods the man on the stage, a man in the moon.

"Dad!" calls Philly.

He hadn't known his daughter was coming aboard the Circus Cruise Line. If Philly had come while he was waiting tables, he would have come quick to serve chocolate cake, but instead he is headlining in the bright lights, center stage, singing 'Mack the Knife'.

"I'm so proud of you, Dad," Philly mouths the words watching alone from the small, red round candlelit table.

The fog begins rolling onto the stage behind her dad as the two-story black velvet curtain rips down the middle. A foghorn sounds, like the sound of a cow bellowing, and drowns out her dad's rendition of the line 'when the shark bites with his teeth, babe.' Philly reads his lips, knowing the song. Dad used to sing her the somewhat inappropriate bedtime lullaby, and she would squeal like a piglet as he made the biting shark hand sign coming in to tickle little Philly on her belly.

The fog engulfs her dad on stage, transforming him into a white hazy Shakespearean specter. The spotted lights on shore emerge as the foghorn bellows. Two red shore lights, 'the eyes of the bull' from her dad's Key West adventure, approach rapidly.

"No!" The ship is grounding –a tremendous jolt! Philly is thrown forward, across her candlelit table and onto the musty carpeted theatre floor. Her dad has vanished from the spotlight. The red lights wink from the dock of the bay, through the foggy night mist. The echo of her dad's voice singing, 'Look out, Old Macky is back', fades into the darkness behind the bull's cherry red eyes.

Earl runs the half dozen blocks, cutting through back yards, waking family dogs, and clearing several fences, frantically rushing to save Philly.

As he reaches her back yard, he comes to his senses. Heroics are not required this time. *It was a nightmare, that's all it was.*

He grasps the cool steel chain of the swing, the one he didn't break earlier. *OK, gently.* He rocks gingerly to and fro on the dew dampened plastic seat, creaking metal chain links against metal mounting bracket.

The clouds part allowing the last quarter white lunar light to illuminate the disheveled figure seated at the swing set. 'Creak. Creak-creak,' the grating friction calls out for its mate-swing, which lies coiled and broken. Earl's long legs extend and plunge his stocking feet into the cool sand depths, gathering and spewing clumps of damp sand into the air before him, like a volcano spitting lava from a middle school science project.

Tired, he wonders why he has come to Philly's back yard so late. He smiles, picturing himself falling from the other swing, Philly falling on him, frolicking in the sand and –the kiss. *Here I am, ready to be the hero, to rescue Philly.* He pines toward the window which he imagines is hers. *Save her? More likely she'll save me.* The creaking ceases as Earl slouches.

Philly wakes face down on the scratchy faded worn carpet by her bed. *Dad, I worry about you out there –sharks, shipwrecks, and red eyed bulls. You send me infrequent letters, emails, and digital images of places you've been, but where are you? Do you read my images? I still love you – not sure if Mom does. I don't blame you, but when will your adventure end? I'm so tired, Dad. Why do you haunt me so? Where are you? Come home.*

Philly hears a clink of metal on metal out back. *The wind? No, no wind. Sounds like the swing set.* She pads barefoot out of her room and down the hall toward the kitchen. "Squeak-squeak," the metallic chains on hollow steel.

She peeks around the shade in the kitchen and sees the lanky figure seated on the swing. Suddenly she recognizes the jeans, shirt, and hair of the swinger. Bursting through the rear door she remembers to cushion the broken closure so not to wake her mom. Philly runs down the steps and through the damp grass to the sand pit and the hunched figure.

"Earl!" she whisper-yells as she jumps upon his lap, arms flinging 'round him. Earl pops back, legs flying up, jolting the child's swing with a bit too much teenage force.

Earl's butt hits the cold sand with the force of a fallen tree, "Thump!"

Philly sprawls upon him, her bare feet kicking his shins.

Earl gasps, conscious of being at Philly's house with her mom just two rooms away. "What are you doing?!"

"What are *you* doing on my swing in the middle of the night?" Philly asks.

"Um, I just – "

"You just *what?*" Philly sits up, straddling Earl's torso, her hands grabbing his shirt collar, a threat.

"Don't hurt me, Philly."

"You know I'd never hurt you, Earl," she loosens her grip on his shirt collar. "I'm scared – scared you'll hurt me."

"Never, I really –care for you," Earl hesitates in saying the word 'love', which he uses sparingly.

"I – care for you, too, Earl," she stammers.

"I was just worried about you. A bad dream – seemed so real –so I came to you," Earl confesses.

"Earl, I knew if I ever needed a hero, you'd be it."

"You're just messing with me." Earl gazes up.

"No, you are the one I . . ." Philly cuts herself short.

"Me, too, I..."

Philly leans over and they kiss as he holds her tight.

"Good night, Earl, you've got to go home." Philly lingers above him as he lies in the sand.

He stands and shakes the sand off. "You're right, I have to go."

Philly pecks him on the cheek and flits inside. Through the storm door, she mouths, "Good night."

Earl smiles, waves shyly and runs to the backyard fence, bounds over like a buck, and is gone.

"My hero."

29.

Tina wakes gently each morning to the filtered sunrise beaming into her bedroom of primary and secondary colors, inanimate dolls, stuffed bears, and jungle animals, brought to life by a four-year old's' imagination. Emaw is either baking sweet banana muffins or ladling pancake batter into her hot black cast iron skillet, sprinkling each imperfect circle with plump blueberries before flipping. Whatever Emaw fixes is fine with Tina.

Tina has always been such a happy child,' Ester tells her friends or her acquaintances in the supermarket. *'When she cries, and that's rare, she's either sick or hurt –or on occasion scared by a rogue Teddy bear in a nightmare (and she only has nightmares when she's feverish).'*

'What? Oh, you like her dress. Thank you,' Ester in reply to a compliment to Tina's cute outfit as they stroll down the grocery store aisle. *'I made it myself.'*

'Yes, a few people still sew.'

'You're right, the Vic-Mart has everything –but did you ever see a dress like this in the Vic-Mart?'

'No? I just buy toilet paper, underwear, and socks mostly at Vic-Mart. But see these little white socks? Oh, the shiny white patent leather shoes are from Vic-Mart, and the socks, too, but I sewed this lace on the tops –and around the edges of her panties, too.'

'No, Tina, you don't need to show her –you're a lady, remember.' At this Tina would turn bashfully and clamp down the hem of her dress.

'Thank you. She is beautiful, isn't she?'

So proud of her granddaughter. Tina is the daughter Ester never had. She only had boys, and now both are gone. One taken too young by a cruel war and the other snatched away too early of 'natural causes.'

"Good morning, Miss Sunshine!" Ester beams. Tina has just emerged barefoot wearing her long pastel flowered flannel nightgown, hugging her favorite stuffed animal de jour as she tiptoes quickly across the hardwood floor. "Go back and put some socks on your feet, sweetie. Your blueberry pancakes are almost ready," Ester sings in her wakeup birdsong voice.

Tina comes back into the kitchen wearing her thick flamingo pink slippers, hugging her 'Tiny Tears' doll which Tina named Tiny Tina. Her grandma had given her this doll. On Tina's fourth birthday Ester decided to give responsibility of 'Tiny Tears' to big girl Tina. The idea to name the doll 'Tina' had been totally Tina's. She had said, 'I'm your Tina, Emaw, and you take care of me, so now I'll take care of this Tina.' Sweet Tina. She gives life to a 'Tiny Tears' doll and new life to Ester.

Tina sets Pooh Bear in the chair closest to the counter where the honey pot is kept. Baby doll Tina is set across from Pooh. Tina tucks a napkin under the chin of each character and sits herself across from Ester. The toys come to life in Tina's eyes - and Emaw's, too. Ester always prepares mini pancakes for Tina's little friends and has them for her own breakfast after the 'children' leave the table.

"Do Tina first, Emaw." Ester walks around the table to serve her granddaughter one of the tiny silver dollar pancakes. "No, Emaw." Tina corrects in her well-mannered polite voice. "Not me, *Tina.*" She motions with her left hand. Ester serves 'Tiny Tina' two pancakes, each with a smattering of blueberries, like a chocolate chip cookie, and then serves Pooh the same.

"Pooh likes honey, remember, Emaw?" Tina reminds.

So do I. "Of course, Tina, and the rest of you like maple syrup, right?"

"Right –yes, ma'am."

God, that Tina's so good – 'ma'am', she says. Ester smiles wide as she stacks two saucer-sized pancakes in front of her. The pancakes smile back up at Tina with their blueberry dotted smile and eyes.

"Butter, please," Tina requests, and Ester spoons a bit of softened butter on top of the smiling pancake, making a melting, runny nose in the center. "And Pooh and Tina, too –please."

Ester places a big plain pancake on her own plate and sits across from Tina.

"Blessing, Emaw," Tina reminds.

"Your turn, Tina," as she grasps Tiny Tina's hand and Pooh's paw. Tina does the same, stretching her short girl arms to reach.

"Goddis great, Goddis good, four we thank him four our foods. Bow our heads, we all our fed. Give us, Lord, our daily bread, Ay men!"

"Amen!" Ester amens Tina's excellent recitation of the children's blessing, which Ester had said when she was a girl. *I wondered for a long time what 'goddis' was. 'Goddis great' and God is great!*

Tina wastes no time eating her pancakes, after Ester cuts them in bite-sized pieces and pours on the savory syrup. Tiny Tina and Pooh sit *staring* at each other across the table as Ester sips her organic tea and relishes the life she's blessed to share with Tina.

"I bet Tina is excited about going to see *her* grandma, isn't she?" Ester asks her granddaughter as they ride the ten minutes to Cleve's house; *Cleve's house.*

"*You're* her grandma, Emaw," Tina reasons.

"Well, really, Tina, she was *my* daughter before you adopted her. Now she's your daughter. You take care of her," Ester explains.

"So, you take care of me and then I'm your daughter," Tina thinks above a usual 4-year-old age level.

"We'll be at your mom's soon. Pam and Earl are there, too." Ester moves to a new subject, distracting Tina from the *daughter* debate.

Tina pulls Tiny Tina close both secure in the child's seat. Her eyes widen, and she sits up straighter as she recognizes the house she visits once a month to see her dad, and Earl, Lila and Pam when they're home. "So, I get to see Pam?"

"Yes, she's home from school for a few days. Lila –um, your mother is there, too. Won't it be good to see them all, Tina?" Ester asks the question, hoping Tina won't mention her daddy, but knowing that she will.

30.

Lila had confided in Reverend Cleveland that she didn't know how to tell Tina about Cleve's death. Lila had trusted him to help in the situation, and he had enthusiastically agreed to her request to come over a little before the 7 o'clock visitation.

"What do I say to her? Tina's not going to understand." Lila had implored the Reverend.

"Of course, she won't understand *death* – few, if any of us really do –but at four years old she'll be able to grasp *gone away*," the Reverend said.

"Yes, she understands that I went away, but she doesn't know why, except I was sick, but I came back," Lila said. "Pam goes away to college but comes back. Her daddy's not coming back."

"I know. Ester's been taking Tina to Sunday school. Easter wasn't just bunnies and eggs and candy –she got a taste of Jesus dying on the cross…"

Lila interrupts, "- but *He* came back."

"Very good, Lila, you were paying attention, too," Reverend Arnold notes, a bit sarcastically. "And one day, a long time from now, Cleve will return, too. He was a good man.

"And you can't keep a good man down," says Lila, keeping the conversation light with the Reverend.

"Exactly. Cleve didn't want to leave. He loves Tina and you all, very much – he had to go. She'll miss her daddy like she missed you."

"I'm not sure she misses me, because I'm just a curiosity, like a sideshow, not a mother. Ester's a mother to her," Lila calms down.

But just like Cleve didn't want to leave, you didn't either, Lila. Now I see you are better, though not 100%, and you can be part of Tina's life. You loved Cleve, in your way, in the way you could, and Tina loves you the way she can."

"If Cleve came back, things would be different." Lila says.

"If Cleve comes back anytime soon, we'll all see Jesus riding on that tall white horse," the Reverend gets philosophical.

"But, until then, we wait – "

"–with Tina. Her daddy's gone now, but we hope he'll be back when Jesus comes. I doubt if Tina can grasp this, but if she 'gets' Jesus at Easter, she might 'get' her daddy's death– he just won't be back in three days," the Reverend lightens up a bit.

"I know she'll be fine with Cleve's mom. Cleve turned out pretty good, although I was a challenge to him." Lila criticizes herself.

"Tina's going to be fine and so will you. Will you pray with me?"

"Yes, Reverend."

"Our heavenly Father, through the Holy Spirit, we are so thankful for Lila and her spirit of concern and love for her daughter. We know that you know what's best for Lila, Tina, and for all of us. Lord, just give us the vision to see, the patience to wait, and the courage and strength to do Thy Will, whatever it may be. Especially be with Tina, Lord, and all the family who love her. We are in Your Hands. In Jesus' name we pray, Amen."

"Thank you, Reverend."

"Don't thank me, Lila; thank *Him*."

Ester drives up. "They're here. Reverend, would you get Pam and Earl?"

"Sure, Lila. Pam! Earl!" the Reverend yells as he starts down the hall. "Tina's here!"

"I could've done that, Reverend, but thanks anyway."

Tina steps into the foyer, Pam and Earl are squatting, arms wide open for hugs. Lila stands dimly radiant behind her older daughter and son. She has not been this excited about family in a long time.

"Earl!" Tina runs into his bear hug; he has always made such a fuss every time he sees Tina. Earl seems to possess more motherly instinct than either of the Cleveland women, except for Ester. With Tiny Tina hanging down his back, Earl stands and whirls her around with squeals; Tina squeals, too. As they stop spinning, Pam wraps the siblings in a three-wheel whirl as they go around again. Lila, a bit apprehensive, finally begins clapping and bouncing on the balls of her feet like an excited cheerleader.

The three kids stop suddenly. They stare at Mom, bewildered, until Tina starts giggling; Pam and Earl join in.

"Mom?" Pam wonders at her mom's behavior - and happy demeanor.

"Mom?" Tina imitates her big sister. She squirms, and Earl sets her down on the floor. She bashfully approaches Lila who kneels on the floor, smiling with arms wide open. Tina runs to her, slapping her doll, Tiny Tina, on Lila's back as she hugs.

"This is my daughter," Tina presents Tiny Tina for her mom to hug, too.

"What's your name?" Lila gives a gentle squeeze hug to the doll.

"Tina, Mom, her name's Tina – like me, your daughter." Tina remembers the talk with Emaw from this morning.

Lila's eyes begin welling with tears and her lower lip won't resist trembling. Before the first tear rolls down her cheek, she squeezes the two Tina's and smiles through happy tears. "My Tina's – what a lucky woman I am to have not just one beautiful Tina, but two!"

Out of the blue Tina asks, "Do you have tea parties, Mom?" Tina looks back, seeking reassurance from her Emaw. *Oh, God, I hope Lila knows how to throw a tea party,* Ester thinks.

Lila wants to ask Ester; *Do you have teas parties?* Instead she answers Tina, "Of course we have tea parties." She winks at Pam.

Pam takes this wink as a hint to check the kitchen for teacups, but she remembers the unopened mini-Japanese tea set that her daddy had given her years ago after he'd taken a business trip to Japan.

She was twelve years old at the time, too old for little girl stuff anymore, and angry at her daddy for not bringing her something 'cool' like a silk kimono – or better yet, some inexpensive Japanese electronics. She had tried to accept the kid's gift graciously but was certain her daddy could tell she wasn't happy with it. When she was older Pam would refer to herself as an ungrateful, spoiled brat.

Being the thoughtful daddy that he was, Cleve wanted to make amends. This was one of those periods when Lila was in the 'hospital', so Mom wasn't around to guide her daddy –if she ever did guide him. Daddy got a young twenty-something lady at his office, Brenda, to take Pam shopping. 'Get yourself something stylish to wear, Pam,' he had said.

Brenda took the credit card and turned it over to Pam. 'You need to experience this for yourself –charging. Once you do, you'll never be the same,' Pam was a virgin credit card user.

Brenda took her to an upscale shop in Oak City's Old Oak Shopping Center that had a beautiful line of Japanese silk print blouses – 'great to wear with jeans,' Pam thought. She tried on several, but finally decided on an orange embroidered bird of paradise top, cut low in the neck. Brenda tried to talk her out of the 'low cut' style, 'because you need some cleavage to show off with that.' Pam knew she had none, even though she was starting to bud. 'These aren't anything to be ashamed of.' Pam looked down at her first year's breast growth.

'What you need is one of those 'push-em-up' bras. That'll make a little valley anyway, if not a cleavage.' Pam was embarrassed. 'You wanted to be a woman, right? You don't want little girl stuff,' Brenda said.

'Daddy must have told her about the tea set,' Pam thought.

With professional fitting assistance Pam tried one bra in the lingerie shop, "Pamela's Secrets" ('Lord have mercy!' Pam thought. 'Pam's Secrets – revealed!'). With the Japanese top and the push-em-up bra underneath, she looked in the mirror. 'I look much bustier –from an AA to a B!'

When she got home, she dressed in jeans and the new orange Japanese silk top – with the new enhancement underneath –and waited for Daddy to get home. Of course, he already knew, through Brenda, but was still unprepared for the transformation of his little girl.

'Ta da!' Pam jumped out as Daddy walked in the front door. Thank goodness Earl was outside playing because he would have teased her so much. It was bad enough seeing Dad's reaction: his face was beet red as he tried to smile and tell her how beautiful she looked.

'I think he was heartbroken at the loss of his little girl.'

As Pam kneels to retrieve the tea set from underneath the shelf in the bottom of her closet, she glances down her button-down shirt and studies the unrestrained twenty-year-old breasts. 'Not much progress since twelve, huh?' She buttons another button on her shirt.

Pam hurries to the kitchen and starts removing and unwrapping floral teacups, saucers, and a teapot from the original eight-year-old box. With much tinkling and clinking, she sets the table.

Tina bursts into the kitchen first, "Wow, a real tea set!" She picks up one of the pink flowered cups, which fit her four-year-old hands perfectly.

"That's beautiful –where did you get that?" Lila walks around the table to Tina.

"Oh, these came directly from Japan. Dad got..." Pam stops short, remembering Dad was gone, and Tina does not know yet.

"Daddy got these? Wow! Where is he? Is he going to have tea with us?" Tina asks excitedly.

"Daddy got these for my birthday when I was twelve," Pam answers, short and direct.

"These are the same size as the ones at home, Tina. Your *mom* got those for your last birthday," Ester says.

"I don't remember," Tina says, honestly not remembering the gift from Lila's because her mom was not there at the time. She sent the gift. "Where's Daddy?"

Reverend Arnold enters the kitchen, standing back and observing. "Hi, Tina."

"Hi, Reverend, where's my daddy?"

"He's not here, Tina."

"Is he hiding? Is this a surprise?" Tina asks.

Reverend Arnold hopes and seeks an answer from Lila or Ester. "Your daddy's gone to heaven, honey" Ester begins.

"-to be with Jesus," the Reverend adds.

"But Jesus died on a cross," Tina remembers Sunday school.

"That's right, Tina. Your daddy died, too," the Reverend says.

"But Jesus came back. When's my daddy coming back?"

"It'll be a long time, Tina —years and years —when Jesus comes back." the Reverend answers.

"Your daddy has gone to heaven to be with his brother James, and with his daddy. They died a long time before you were born," Ester says.

"They're all waiting for Jesus." Reverend Arnold adds.

"We all miss your daddy now," Lila says.

"We do," Pam adds.

"We do," Earl agrees.

"Everyone who knew your daddy is going to miss him, Tina," says the Reverend.

Tina swings the mood a hundred and eighty degrees. "I miss Daddy. Can we have a tea party now?" Reverend Arnold thinks, *Out of the mouths of babes.*

"Yes, Tina, let's have a tea party," Pam takes her hand. "And Earl, grab that stool and pull up to the table -you, too, Reverend. It's teatime!"

"1, 2, 3, 4 –is there enough for all of us –and Tiny Tina, too?" Tina asks.

"I know there is, Tina. There's room enough for everyone at the table," Reverend Arnold says. *Bless these cookies and this tea, the body, and the blood of Christ, Amen.*

31.

Lila, Ester, and the Reverend agree that Tina should not be at the visitation. She will stay with her Sunday school teacher and a few other children whose parents are visiting the Cleveland house. Some adults may be wrought with grief, and Tina won't understand why; there's nothing to cry about. She'll miss her daddy but wait 'til he comes back with Jesus. What a day it will be!

Pam finds that silk blouse from her twelfth birthday, and it still fits, so she feels it's appropriate to wear. It brings back good memories of her daddy. He would be so embarrassed, again, by his little girl and her slightly larger bust. The push-em-up bra gives her the appearance of being the young woman that she has become.

Earl wears his basketball jersey and school letter. Dad would be so proud of him. "This is all about Dad, right?" Earl confides to Pam when she sees what he's wearing, and he sees what she's wearing. "If only Mom would tone it down –or pick it up a notch," Earl told Pam.
"She should wear that orange straw hat!" Pam and Earl burst out laughing.
"She's dressing like tonight's the funeral –that's tomorrow," Earl notes.

Lila saw the way Earl and Pam were dressed and overheard their conversation. *What should I wear?* She thumbed through her closet racks. *Cleve always likes this outfit: the black cigarette pants, the red silk blouse, but no straw hat –the orange would clash; flats, not pumps, though he said I was sexy in those pumps.*

Ester had a pantsuit appropriate for every occasion. Her collection of pantsuits went back forty years, but she said they were 'timeless', well-tailored and sturdy polyester. Besides, she had no time to sew her own clothes with Tina outgrowing an outfit before the season was hardly over.
But what about Tina and the memorial service? She may not understand, but shouldn't she be allowed to mourn with the rest of us? None of us will be forced to stare at a corpse. The adults are mature enough to accept that Cleve is dead without being subjected to seeing, touching, or kissing the cold, dead empty shell of what once was my son. That's not him.

105

No, Cleve will become ashes at the crematorium –ashes to ashes, dust to dust. Some people don't like the thought of burning the body, but if –when –we rise from the dead on judgment day, isn't God just as able to restore us from ashes as he is to breathe life back into a rotten, wormy corpse? I'll have to discuss this all with Reverend Arnold.

"Tina, honey, come and let me see your dress for tomorrow," Ester calls, *the dress for your daddy's funeral.*

Tina stumbles into Ester's room, the royal blue dress halfway over her head and her belly button dimpling above her white frilly lace panties. "I'm stuck! Help, Emaw!"

Ester catches Tina in a hug, giving her a 'zerbit' on her bare belly. (A 'zerbit' is a family tradition, a kiss in which you blow onto the bare skin with wet lips, making the resultant 'zerbit' sound, akin to the sound of a bullfrog.) Pulling the dress down over Tina's golden hair, the four-year-old squeals, and dances around in bare feet, trying to escape the tickle.

"Emaw," Tina stamps her foot, "I could've stuff-a-katydid!"

"But I rescued you darling, and you didn't 'suffocate'."

"Emaw, how do you 'stuff a katydid' anyway? Is that what you did when you fixed my bear?" Tina asks, seriously.

"*Suffocate* is when you can't breathe…"

"I could breathe, but I felt stuffed' in that dress."

"How does it feel now, completely in the dress?" Ester asks.

"Feels good, except my tummy is wet where you 'zerbited' me," Tina pats her stomach.

"You look beautiful. Come close so I can smooth you out a bit."

Tina comes closer, patting and smoothing her dress. Ester squats and kisses Tina on the cheek and smooches her lips tight and wet onto Tina's flushed cheek and proceeds to give her a 'mega-zerbit'. Tina squeals, ducks away from Emaw, and runs down the hallway to her room, pulling the dress back over her head as she goes.

"Emaw, I'm stuffed again!"

"Coming, sweetie."

"I'm not ready, Earl," Philly calls out from her room as she hears Earl come in through the kitchen. "What are you wearing tonight? I just don't know how to dress for this." *What am I saying, 'for this'? It's the family visitation –the night before his dad's memorial service.*

She comes down the hall. Earl is standing in the kitchen doorway wearing his blue and orange basketball warm-ups and orange high tops.

"This was Dad's favorite suit on me." Earl holds out his arms, makes a 360-degree turn modeling his attire for Philly. "You could wear that cute plaid skirt that I like so much," he grins.

Shaking her head, "No, no, no, Earl."

"Or if you're comfortable, and I know you are, you could wear what you're wearing, your mom's hand-me-down scrubs."

"Earl, you're no help!"

"Why don't you go put something on and come back down the hall and model for me?"

"Are you serious?" Philly smirks, highlighting her dimples.

"Sure. Don't you trust my judgment –on such an important matter?" He opens his arms wide inviting Philly to come in but she turns and flits back to her room.

"I'll be back in a flash. You'd better be ready."

"I'm ready," Earl grabs a chair from the kitchen, turns it around backwards and straddles it, his arms crossed over its back, resting his head on his hands, patiently staring toward Philly's room.

In her room Philly begins flipping through her closet, which contains only one 'new' outfit, the short skirt Earl mentioned. *No way.* Money has been tight for so long; new clothes have not been an option. Even the 'new' skirt Earl likes so much came from the thrift store. *How about this one a sundress, but the flowers are nice – they'll go with our school colors.*

Philly slips out of her scrub top but leaves the pants on. *This does look nice. I must have worn it only a few times, Easter, or the spring dance. This qualifies as a special occasion.*

She trots down the hall, barefoot, and stops midway under a recessed light. Exaggerating a model, she turns, twirls, poses, passes, and pauses with her back to Earl giving him an unintentional sexy look, batting her eyes like Betty Davis.

"Wow, that's perfect, Philly! Except you need to wear shoes –and ditch the scrub pants," he says, standing by the chair with his hands on his hips.

"But it's a little cool out –I'll need to wear a sweater," she says, being practical and a bit embarrassed at wearing the spring sundress.

"Hey, why don't you wear my letter jacket? It's really warm –a little large for you, but warm, and the school colors match your flowers."

Earl is being so nice, unwittingly offering Philly a symbol of 'going steady', an ancient courtship rite –the Letter Jacket!

Oh, my God! Philly is on the verge of jumping up and down and squealing, but she merely grins ear to ear. "You think it'll be warm enough, or not too much?" she says. *I'm his girlfriend!* Smiling even bigger.

"Don't you want to see me model some more?"

"No, unless you just want to strut the runway a few times, without the matching scrub pants." Earl smiles impishly.

"Oh." Philly turns her back to Earl, discretely undoes the drawstring and lets the loose cotton garment drop to the floor around her feet. She steps out of the crumpled pants and kicks them toward her room. As she turns, Earl's mouth is hanging open starting to drool. *Oh, no, did I do something a little too sexy? Where does this stuff come from?* The blossoming fifteen-year-old asks herself.

"Wow," Earl stands statuesque at the opposite end of the hall.

"Why don't you go home and get that jacket? I'll be ready when you come back."

Taking one longer look at his girl, he says, "Wow," in disbelief, thinking *Philly is really my girlfriend.*

I'd better cool this off a little before Earl blows a gasket. Whew!

Earl stumbles over his chair, picks it up and parks it in the kitchen before tripping over his high-top laces as he heads out the back door. *Now, what was I going home to get?*

32.

Reverend Arnold parks just past the Taylor's house, considerate of the visitors who will be coming to the Cleveland's. For as far back as he can remember he's been considerate, a gentleman opening doors for ladies, saying *yes, ma'am* and *yes, sir, please, thank you*, and not speaking or going out of turn. Natural inclinations toward being a counselor, a minister.

Of course, he was not infallible, and on occasion as a teenager growth hormones and testosterone had taken the forefront. 'Arnie' was quite a handsome young man, polite and meek, adored by his female teachers who set him on a pedestal, whenever the opportunity arose, as the model male. These occasions were always an embarrassment to 'Arnie.' He didn't want to be so nice, just 'one of the guys.'

One of Arnie's moments of teenage shame commenced when his childhood girlfriend, Bobbie, invited him to her fifteenth birthday party at Bubble Gum's Skate and Arcade. Bobbie beamed with excitement when Arnie said 'yes' to her verbal invitation as Bobbie's giggling girlfriends witnessed the affirmation. Arnie never suspected that Bobbie had a crush on him. They'd been seat buddies all through elementary and middle school because his last name was 'Arnold' and hers 'Aber'. She always sat in the desk directly in front of him, except last year in eighth grade when the teacher, Mrs. Frazier, had seated the class in reverse alphabetical order. That was Bobbie's opportunity to stare at the back of his head for a change and develop that crush.

Arnie was a late bloomer, some might even say a little slow, developmentally. He paid scant attention to the opposite sex, and even less to sex. 'Sex' was a trailer park boy's stories about riding on the back of his bike's banana seat holding onto the straight blond-haired, year-older girl next door, a 'tom boy' who had developed nice 'knockers'. The stories seemed rather contrived to him, and besides, he and Bobbie had no qualms about 'playing doctor' when they first had play dates as five-year old at her house. Arnie had thought of becoming a doctor after those days. She didn't have any knockers at five years old, but since he and Bobbie had a few healthy rolls of fat on their young bodies, they both had little 'boobies' –no big deal.

Ten years later, at age fifteen and in ninth grade, Bobbie had 'blossomed' as most girls, except for a few skinny ones who'd been so cute in elementary school. Arnie had a crush on one of those cute, Becca, now in high school but still skinny, with the addition of a padded bra. Becca had known since third grade in Mrs. Brewer's class that Arnie had a crush on her. Crush? Arnie thought he was 'in love'. Becca knew she was the hottest thing since 'Malibu Barbie', so she had all but ignored sweet and chunky Arnie.

When Becca realized that Bobbie and her girlfriends were so excited about Arnie coming to the party, she thought, 'I'd like some of that action' –in a mean way. She called Arnie at home.

'Arnie, a girl's on the phone for you!' his mom had called out. He believed Becca must have been heaven sent.

'Are you going to Bobbie's party?' Becca asked.

'Um, yeah.'

'Well, I was wondering...' She tossed the bait, 'if you'd want to go with me.'

'Yeah, sure!' Arnie bites without hesitation.

'Great.' Becca knew he'd take the bait. 'Pick me up at 6:30."

'OK, I'll be there. Thanks." He hung up, having no idea where Becca lived –but mom would find out.

Mom drove Arnie to pick up Becca, she turned down the gravel road where his 'worldly' friend with the banana seat bike lived, in the Grove Way Trailer Court. Arnie knew his 'dream girl' couldn't be the one in his friend's story, the one with the knockers who straddled the banana seat, because Becca had perfectly molded petite foam rubber boobies. Arnie had formed a bad impression of Grove Way, because of the stories. Becca was different.

Arnie got out and opened the rear door of the forest green Subaru wagon for Becca. She wore black tights under a short black skinny skirt and a fuzzy red mock turtleneck sweater on top. She slides the seat about half-way - she barely allows enough room for Arnie to get in beside her. She pats the seat with her hand for him to sit.

'Don't I look nice, Arnie?'

'Yeah, you do,' his words came out falsetto.

Arnie squeezed in beside her and shut the door. Becca pressed her bony hip against his so hard he thought he might have a bruise later. Arnie's vision of this ideal girl was fading as they left the trailer park's gravel and hit the asphalt. His mom slung gravel and squealed tires as they 'got a grit' onto the hard surface road.

'Sorry, not used to the gravel,' his mom grinned, "My first time 'getting a grit'.

110

As the car approached the front of Bubble Gum's a couple dozen of his classmates had gathered. The party was at seven, and since most arrived Earl, the doors had not yet opened. Bobbie and her mom, big brother Jim, and a couple of her closest friends were inside putting the finishing touches on the decorations.

Arnie and Becca waited in the car at the curb until Bobbie came out the front door, and Becca commanded, 'Let's go.' She practically shoved Arnie out the car door, and when he regained his footing, Becca was clinging to his right arm, wearing a glossy red lipstick grin, and fluttering jet black mascara eyelashes. He hadn't noticed, until this moment, that she looked sort of like a clown, or a mime. Arnie looked up, and there was Bobbie, staring as if through to his soul. He felt like a clown, the dark frowning horrid one who scares the children and gives them nightmares. Arnie investigated Bobbie's shattering face as giant tears bubbled up from her erupting molten heart.

Arnie suddenly realized: Bobbie had invited him to be her date for her birthday - not as her friend. He had broken their date, her heart –and their friendship. Becca released her crablike grip on his arm and stepped ahead of him, laughing, and oozing into her slimy band of black tight wearing 'friends'. Arnie mouthed 'I'm sorry' across the sidewalk to Bobbie as a tear fell down his cheek. Bobbie turned and ran inside where her mom held her and wiped the tears. Her two friends and her brother glared at him through the tinted glass. Arnie got in his mom's car, still waiting, and drove away with his head, and his heart, in his hands. 'I'm sorry,' he cried a flood of sorry anguish.

33.

The Reverend falters in front of the Taylor's house. Chuck is coming down the steps, sees Reverend Arnold and stops. Chuck had not intended to walk with anyone to Earl's because he wanted to be the first person there. He hated coming into any party after the crowd had already established. Chuck would rather arrive Earl, scope out a vantage point where he can see everything, and have a convenient exit –just in case.

"Hey, Chuck, want to walk me down to the Cleveland's?" The Reverend tries to sound casual and spontaneous, but he had really been waiting for this opportunity to talk with Chuck –for a little secondhand counseling for Earl. If he could get to Philly also, he would have another angle at Earl.

Darn, I wanted to get there first to see Earl. "Sure, Reverend Arnold."

"You look rather dapper, Chuck, in your gray slacks and navy blazer. What, no tie?" The Reverend ribs Chuck.

Maybe I should go back inside and change into my sweats. Instead he explains about his lack of tie. "Neither of my dress shirts –I only have two –would button at the collar, so that's what made the crucial tie decision."

"Chuck, I think the Cleveland's will be very impressed with your efforts. As for me, this gray suit is what I always wear on business occasions; sorry, this in not really 'business', but I am the Reverend."

As Chuck steps up to the front door, the Reverend notices the black and white high-tops Chuck is wearing –unlaced. *They do sort of go with the outfit.* Chuck enters the house without ringing or knocking –just like he's home. The Cleveland's home has been his second home since Chuck and Earl became best friends over six years ago.

"Come on in Chuck; you know you're at home. You, too, Reverend," Lila says, meeting them halfway across the living room with open arms.

"Pam's almost ready." Lila calls out, "Pam! Chuck and Reverend Arnold are here!"

"Just the way I would have called her, Lila," The Reverend laughs.

As Lila excuses herself to go to the kitchen, she calls back to Chuck, "Your mom and dad are in here."

Chuck's mom peaks out the kitchen door. "Come give us a hand, dear." The Taylor's have come early to arrange the table with hors d'oeuvres and silverware and plates. Mrs. Taylor pops out the door and hands Chuck a platter of little cucumber and butter finger sandwiches, Lila's favorite. Mr. Taylor pops open a bottle of chardonnay and merlot, both acceptable and legal for religious purposes: communion. He puts them on the sideboard, with the chardonnay in an ice bucket.

"Oh, hey, Reverend," says Mr. Taylor.

"Hey, Charlie, can I help with anything?"

"No, we've got it under control, now that Chuck's here," as he nudges Chuck toward the kitchen. "Thanks for bringing him, Reverend," says Charlie.

Chuck enters the kitchen and asks Mrs. Cleveland, "Where's Earl? Is he still getting dressed?"

"No, Chuck, he just left to go back to Philly's. He had his letter jacket in his hand," Lila says. "You look so handsome in your blazer, Chuck. Earl decided he'd go casual and wear... "she stammers, "what his dad liked to see him wear –his basketball warm-ups, right before a game." She can't look at Chuck or anyone else in the kitchen as her eyes moisten. *I'm not going to cry.*

Darn it, Earl, you're all casual while I'm confined in these tight slacks and stuffy blazer –but at least spared the tie!

The Taylor's and Lila flit back and forth from the kitchen to the dining room as the serving area takes shape. Reverend Arnold strolls around the living room and notices an eight by ten portrait of Cleve hung above a card table at the far end of the room. He approaches the memorial and sees another photo of the entire Cleveland family, taken over four years ago when Tina was a baby. Lila had an anxious, haunted look on her face as if she might hand Tina off like a football to Cleve and take off running. The whole family looked more worried in that photo; even Tina was red-faced and wailing, as if she knew more than the others knew –but only vicariously through Lila.

Happy photos: Earl in his first basketball uniform; Pam wearing her bird of paradise silk blouse from her twelfth birthday; and Tina as a two year old with the gloriously frilly pink dress that Ester had sewn; all set on the card table under the gaze of Cleve's portrait. The happiest photo was the 5x7 that Aunt Naomi snapped at her pond when Earl was just a little fellow, Pam was learning to fish, and Cleve and Lila still knew how to play. *Look at Lila's orange straw hat on Cleve's head!* Reverend Arnold chuckles. *Hopefully, Lila and the children will return to this happiness.*

"They kicked me out of the kitchen, Reverend," Lila says. "Are you getting lonesome out here?" She suddenly realizes he's standing before the memorial to Cleve. "I put that portrait of Cleve up there. Pam saw it and started rambling in the old photos and pulled some more family shots. She said he'd be lonesome up there all by himself, so this is what we have, a shrine."

"I think Pam knows what'll help with the healing, don't you, Lila?" The Reverends studies her face as she shifts her gaze from one photo to the next. Suddenly he becomes conscious of gawking at Lila's attire. *Where have I seen this outfit? Somewhere...it's so familiar.*

Lila becomes self-conscious and steps back from the memorial. "Don't I look nice, Reverend Arnold?"

He hears Becca from his boyhood saying 'Arnie'. Bobbie...sorry. "Lila?"

"What, Reverend?"

"Oh, sorry, beg pardon, I was going to say how lovely you look – almost as lovely as in the photo from the pond," the Reverend brushes the 'Becca' memory aside.

"Why, thank you. This was, I believe, Cleve's favorite outfit. He said I looked sophisticated and reminded him of Audrey Hepburn – or was it Katharine?"

"Yes, I see it," the Reverend says. He thinks, *Becca. I never forgave her –or myself for hurting Bobbie. Maybe that ordeal kept me from marrying all these years. I wonder where Bobbie is now. Bet she's a beauty. Hope her husband appreciates her. Hope she's happy,* Arnie thinks. *You scare me sometimes, Lila,* Reverend Arnold thinks.

"Pam suggested I wear the orange straw hat, but it's out of season – and clashes with my red blouse," she laughs.

"So, Lila, how are you?" the Reverend gets serious.

"I'm OK, really." She turns her head from him.

"Really, you can tell me, Lila. It's just you and your minister. As they say, 'What's said to your minister stays with your minister' –or was there something about Las Vegas?"

"I feel..." She hesitates. "Guilty. I feel guilty, that's how I feel," she lets down her guard, and the dam of tears breaks.

"Guilty about what, Lila?" He puts his arm around her shoulders. "You don't need to feel guilty about anything."

"You just don't know, Reverend," Lila says, thinking of her affair with Bruce.

"Tell me, Lila, if it'll lighten your burden. Let me carry some. Let Him carry some," the Reverend attempts to comfort.

Lila is silent and thinks –and thinks. "Cleve and I weren't as close as we appeared to people."

"Lila, people notice things. I could see that you weren't *the happy couple*," he says.

"He worked, or wasn't home, all the time. He avoided me, and I…" She stops short.

"You weren't that young vivacious couple you were when the kids were little, but…" He pauses.

"And we hadn't been since Tina was born, and I…"

"I know, Lila, you had to get some help, and you did."

"But I got some *help* that I should not have. I had been going out with another m…" She stops as Pam pops around the corner unexpectedly.

"Mom, how do I look?"

"I remember that silk blouse, from your twelfth birthday," Lila says.

"Dad's co-worker, Brenda, helped me pick it out." Pam reminds her mom.

"It is beautiful, Pam. You've kept it nicely -from your twelfth birthday?" The Reverend compliments, trying to draw fire away from Lila.

"I don't think I've worn it since that year, but I remember Dad made such a big deal over it, and how I was a 'young lady'," Pam remembers that first bra, too, and how the boys looked at her differently.

"You do look beautiful, Pam," her mom compliments.

"Thank you," Pam replies, politely short.

The front door opens, and Ester enters wearing her classic yellow polyester pant suit. *That orange hat would really look good with that outfit, Emaw*, Pam thinks.

"Emaw!" Pam runs, greeting her with a kiss for each rouged cheek.

"Let me just look at you, my little Pam," Ester holds her by the shoulders, at arms' length. "You're becoming such a beautiful young lady –like your grandmother," Ester kids. "You've got some good genes, girl!"

"Thank you, Emaw, this is my best pair of jeans," Pam plays on the words.

"Don't you think Pam favors me, Reverend Arnold?" Lila asks, smiling, framing her face with her hands.

"Um– "the Reverend is cut off.

"I look like my dad," Pam politely protests.

"I just meant – "Lila cuts in, but her comment is intercepted by Earl and Philly entering the front door. Chuck pops out from the kitchen.

"Hey, boys and girls!" Chuck greets his buds.

"Whassup, Chuck!" Philly calls back.

"Wow, you look great in that dress –and that jacket, too. How'd you end up with that?" Chuck pokes Earl.

"Hey, hey!" Earl defends.

"Look at the jacket, Pam!" Philly boasts, modeling with a twirl.

"Earl's going steady!" Pam hugs little Philly around the big, puffy vinyl and wool letter jacket.

Earl is pleased but puzzled. *What's with the jacket? She just needed something over her shoulders to keep her warm. Now, she's in the house and–* his thoughts are interrupted.

Reverend Arnold interjects, "I remember in my day those letter jackets were like gold. The guys worked hard playing ball, and the gals worked hard at getting the guys to win games and pledge their love through their jackets."

"Sounds sexist to me," Pam protests. "What about the 'gals' who played sports? Were the guys after them to the get into their letter jackets?"

"The gals didn't get letter jackets, but they had trophies and awards –and recognition from the school," Reverend Arnold says.

"Wasn't there something called *Title 9* back then, playing sports teams more equal for boys and girls?" Pam asks, demonstrating her US History 101 knowledge.

"You're right, Pam," the Reverend agrees, "but a few things remained sacred, like separate locker rooms and showers –and letter jackets."

"Isn't it getting warm in here." Philly decides there's been enough jacket talk and starts to remove Earl's. Earl steps up behind Philly and helps her remove the jacket –a gentleman.

"Now that's the young gentleman right there, Philly," the Reverend compliments Earl. "I'd bet he opens doors for his lady, too, am I right?"

"Not really that much yet," says Philly. "We just started this romance thing," she smiles shyly at Earl.

"Yeah, we were just pals, only a week ago, and now..." Earl looks directly at Philly.

"Now I guess I'm his girlfriend." Philly sidles up to Earl and he takes her hand. She flashes her eyes at him, desiring a kiss, but Earl is not comfortable with such public displays -yet. He squeezes her hand, and she understands.

"So, I'm the lone pal now, huh?" Chuck says.

"You know we're all still pals," Earl says.

Philly offers him a furrowed brow, puzzled. *I'm still a pal?*

"Except now Philly's my number one pal –*and* girlfriend." Earl makes the save.

Lila adds, "And Chuck, you're the designated chaperone for these two."

"Yes," Ester agrees.

"Great, I feel even more like a third wheel," Chuck says.

Earl and Philly give each other a look and make a dash toward Chuck. "Group hug!" Earl reaches around Chuck's shoulder and gives him a *noogie* on the back of his head. Embarrassing Chuck, and Earl even more so, Philly smooches Chuck on one cheek while Earl *zerbits* him on the other.

"Help, I'm being smothered!" Chuck yells.

"With love, Chuck, with love," Reverend Arnold chuckles.

"Chuck," Mrs. Taylor calls from the kitchen door, "can you come help me for a minute."

"Sure, Mom," Chuck says.

"You're lucky she saved you," Earl says.

"Yeah, this time, Chuck," Philly teases.

"I've got my eyes on you two," Chuck points two fingers toward his eyes, then back and forth toward Earl and Philly. "Remember, I'm the chaperone. Somebody's got to be responsible around here."

In the kitchen Mr. Taylor says, "You've got some good friends there, Chuck."

"You sure do, Chuck," Mrs. Taylor agrees. "Just remember that things might be a little different now, so give them some space –but still chaperone."

"Oh, Rae, that Earl's a responsible young man, right Chuck?" his father asks.

"Definitely, Dad," Chuck agrees. *In some areas he's more responsible. Earl's dad has just died, so he's not thinking quite straight. I hope he knows what he's doing by going steady with Philly. It's kind of quick, but he needs someone closer than me now. He needs me to be objective, see what he can't grasp right now: my suspicions about Coach and Earl's mom. Earl doesn't need to think about anything more that'll bring him down. He needs balance, and Philly and I are giving him that, each in his –or her – way.*

"What'd you need me for, Mom?" Chuck asks.

"I see some of Earl's basketball teammates coming through the backyard. You know them, Chuck; why don't you bring them in through the kitchen," Mom suggests.

"They're all wearing their basketball warm-ups! Am I the only guy here who's not representing the team, wearing the colors? Even Philly's got the letter jacket! I could've come casual, too," Chuck removes his navy blazer and unbuttons another button on his shirt.

"But you look so nice, Chuck," his mom observes.

"I understand, son." Mr. Taylor agrees with his son. "*This* tie is coming off, pronto."

"Oh, you boys. Remember why we're here, to support our neighbors and friends in the loss of their father, husband and son. Try not to be too irreverent. In fact, Charlie, why don't you go talk with the Reverend," Mrs. Taylor says.

"Son, I think you've gotten me in trouble."

"Sorry, Dad," Chuck spears a Swedish meatball from the crock pot and dashes out the back door.

"What's up, guys?" Chuck runs into the huddle in the center of the backyard.

"Hey, Chuck, where're your warm-ups?" asks Buddy.

"I'm not on the team, Buddy, you know that," says Chuck.

"You should be," says Hank, who's the official benchwarmer on the team. "You could do what I do –you'd be great at it!"

"If I'd only kissed some more Coach Bruce butt, I'd be golden," Chuck puckers at Hank.

Hank's a goof-off, always kidding around and being inappropriate – more so than Chuck. He turns his back to Chuck, drops his warm-up pants and *moons him.*

"Hey, my mom's in the kitchen! Be civilized!" Chuck chides. He can just imagine his mom catching an eyeful of Hank's hairy butt as she glances out the window –and getting a good laugh. *Those boys,* she'd say.

"Yeah, Hank!" Spuddy, the shortest guy on the team joins in.

As the team files through the kitchen Mrs. Taylor grabs Chuck and gives him a big sloppy kiss on the cheek, likely for the embarrassing effect.

"Mom!" Chuck protests in a whiny tone.

"Anyone else?" Mrs. Taylor chases them out of the kitchen.

Hank is bringing up the rear, and she pops him on the bum with a damp kitchen towel.

"Ow!" screeched Hank.

"Keep your pants up, Hank," Mrs. Taylor advises.

"Yes, ma'am," he slinks out to catch up with the team.

Earl releases Philly's hand, and she joins Ester and Pam. The boys huddle around Earl chanting familiar but indiscernible phrases of brotherhood and sympathy for the loss of his father. Earl knows. The seven-foot center kneels to be on the level with the five-foot guard. Chuck and Hank stand on the outer rim of the circle, helping hold it together. Earl's head begins to quiver as he remembers and sheds silent tears that some say a man should not shed –but it's OK. All hands reach across to Earl and pull him into the center of the circle.

Reverend Arnold and Charlie stand close by and can't help but see the unbroken circle. The Reverend slowly approaches the circle, and Charlie joins him. The two men become the outermost ring of the circle, like an old whitewall tire, accessorizing from Cleve's generation. Reverend Arnold begins a prayer for the mourning.

"Our Father, who art in heaven, Your name is Holy and lifted above all. We are but small men in a boundless universe yet bounded by You. Your child, Lord, this young man encircled by his brothers, feels a tremendous weight on him now, but I know that You have sent these young men to help carry the load. His family hurts now, and they need each other and each of us who desire to be here for them. Help each of us to be the light that this family needs. 'This little light of mine,' Lord, 'I'm gonna let it shine.' Your light is here this night and whenever we dare to look and see, and even be the light that You have made us. You know our every thought and need before we say it, pray it, so help us to understand that, even without a spoken word, You know.

Thank You for the Spirit that resides in this team and is shared by them. Help us to remember that we are all on the same team, Your Team. 'Lead us not into temptation and deliver us from evil. For thine is the Kingdom, the Power, and the Glory, Forever. Amen."

34.

The young men form a circle and put their hands atop Earl's, in the center, and Chuck shouts, in an older man's voice, "Together we stand," and the others of the team shout in, "divided we fall; all for one, and one for all!" The circle evolves into a group hug around Earl.

Reverend Arnold and Charlie fade away from the huddle. Coach Bruce enters through the front door. *Too bad he missed his team -and the Spirit, but it's good of him to show up.*

Instead of going to Earl, the star of his team, Bruce homes in on Lila standing across the room. He makes a beeline toward her, unaware of the Reverend, Charlie, and the team.

Coach should step in as a role model that he's supposed to be to Earl and the boys. He's missing something, or am I missing something?

Lila, startled by Bruce's presence, sloshes her merlot on her red silk blouse –the blouse that Cleve had liked so much.

Lila hisses, grabbing her napkin and Rae's, blotting frantically at the silk. "Good thing it's red -but it will still leave a dark spot."

"I'll get some club soda, Lila. Maybe that'll help," says Rae as she retreats to the kitchen, leaving Lila alone with Bruce approaching.

"Bruce, what are you doing here?" Lila whispers.

"I'm here officially to comfort and offer support to Earl, my star player," says Coach. "Unofficially I'm here to comfort you, Lila."

"Well, don't hang around me; people will wonder."

The doorbell rings and the Reverend greets the two ladies from across the street, Anna and Bette, the neighbors who had seen Bruce and Lila on the morning of Cleve's death. He shakes hands warmly with Anna, as Bette focuses on Lila and the coach across the living room.

"Lila appears occupied at the moment," says the Reverend, "but Ester and Pam are there by the table with Philly. You know Philly, don't you?" He escorts the ladies toward the dining table.

"Oh, yes, we've seen her with Earl and Chuck."

"Philly and Earl are an item now, didn't you know?" asks the Reverend.

"That's so sweet."

"Help yourselves to a bite to eat and drink –there's communion wine, if you like."

"Thank you, Reverend, we'll just go on over and speak with the girls."

The Reverend wanders casually across the room to Lila and Bruce. A gentleman, the Reverend believes that appearances are important, so he doesn't want the widow standing with a single man. *But I was alone with Lila last night, counseling and comforting her. That's different. I was doing my job if you can call ministering a job –it's a calling. I enjoyed her company, though, and I'm a single man, but it's different.* He reasons. *I just flat out do not trust that man, Bruce. Is it just a feeling or is the Spirit moving me?* Reverend Arnold quickens his step towards Coach Bruce and Lila standing too close for appearances. Bruce seems aggressive and Lila is looks bothered.

"Hello, Bruce, so glad you could come," the Reverend says, trying not to sound sarcastic, but Lila hears it in his voice. Bruce doesn't catch it.

"I had to be here, Reverend, for *my team*," Bruce boasts.

Bruce thinks he owns that team. The only reason they call him 'Coach' is because that's his official title. The boys are a better team without him. I just felt the Spirit moving in them, and Bruce is as far away from that Spirit as he can be while still in the same room. Accidental? I think not, Lord. I'm listening, Lord, watching and waiting for your guidance.

"I'm sure that Earl and the rest of the guys here appreciate it, Coach," the Reverend says, "and the family, too." He notices Lila retreating into herself, far from where she was last night.

Lila had forgotten about the red wine that spilled on her blouse when Rae returns from the kitchen carrying a liter bottle of club soda in one hand and a cluster of white paper towels in the other. Rae gets extremely focused when she has a mission such as this merlot emergency.

"Here, Lila, dab this on the spot and blot it with these," Rae holds the materials out to Lila.

"Oh, I –um," Lila is clearly disturbed by Bruce's presence.

"Why don't we go out to the kitchen and do this, Lila, and leave these two men to talk men stuff," Rae suggests as she grasps Lila by the arm and leads her gently. "We'll just be a few minutes."

"Lila needs a woman's touch now, don't you think, Bruce?" Reverend asks.

She needs a touch, alright, the strong touch of a real man like me, huh, Cleve? "Yeah, woman's touch," Bruce says. *I need that woman's touch.*

"Earl needs a man's guidance and strength now. How do you think he's doing?" the Reverend asks.

"Oh, Earl," Coach looks across the room at the group of boys, "he's alright, a tough young man."

"Yes, but he's hurting now, finally letting himself grieve, a little, with the support of his teammates, his friends. They're a good group of young men, don't you think, Coach?" the Reverend asks.

"Yeah, but not good basketball players, except for Earl, my star player." Bruce cuts down his own team. "Maybe we'll have a better team next year, eh, Reverend?"

"Yes, maybe a better team next year," the Reverend says and thinks *If you're gone next year.* "They are good boys. They've got heart, Spirit," he adds.

"Earl's tough," Bruce says.

"Tough, but he needs positive role models, now that his dad's gone," the Reverend adds.

"Yeah, I'm his coach. They look up to me."

The Reverend raises his eyebrows. *You really believe that — that these boys look up to you? They look up to Earl, and I believe to God the Almighty. From what I hear through Chuck, and what I observe, these young men think you're a joke –a bad joke.*

"Right, Coach, 'look up'," the Reverend repeats the words of the coach. *The coach needs to 'look up' to God –before it's too late.*

"Well, Coach, since the huddle has broken over there, you should take that walk and speak some words of encouragement –a pep talk, if you will –to your star Earl," the Reverend says. *He could give Coach a shove in that direction to 'encourage' him –or provoke him. If I weren't a gentleman.* He recalls the Good Book, *a time for peace, a time for war... Just tell me what time it is, Lord, and I'll be there.*

Bruce glances at the kitchen door where Rae had taken Lila. He desires some one-on-one time with Lila. *I'll get back to her.* He walks away from the Reverend without saying a word more.

"God bless you, Bruce," the Reverend calls to him, already halfway across the room.

"Oh, you too, Reverend," Bruce says over his shoulder as an afterthought. He walks the room, not blessed at all, just agitated with Lila.

As Coach approaches the team of young men, Freddy, the center, turns to face him. The team follows suit, one by one. Chuck, who had been facing Earl, turns last and squares off between Earl and Coach.

"Good of you to show up," Chuck speaks first. *You know I saw you leaving Earl's house last night, visiting his mom, alone and creepy. You're a snake, Coach, slithering up to the garden before the body's cold, but even death is not as cold as you.*

"Sure is nice of you all to wear your team warm-ups to support Earl -all except Chuck. Where's your... "the coach starts.

"You know I'm not on *your* team, Coach," Chuck retorts, "but I'm on *their* team."

"Sorry, Chuck, not this year, but maybe you'll get on my team next season," says Coach.

"Next season may be our best ever, Coach," says Chuck. *Because you won't be there, I foresee.*

Coach brushes Chuck aside with his open hand, readied to shake Earl's hand. "I'm sorry for your loss, son, I know it's tough losing a dad."

When Bruce was ten years old, his dad had left him and his mom. As far as Bruce knew, his dad was still alive –or maybe dead, he didn't care. He was dead to him anyway since that day he left young Bruce and his mom to fend for themselves in that government subsidized apartment on the other side of the tracks. Bruce knew these big bratty boys knew nothing of the hard times he'd known. He'd been working after school when he was in high school –no time for sport.

Right after he graduated in the top twenty percent of his class, he'd left home to fulfill his obligation, signed four weeks beforehand. Bruce had been old enough, eighteen, to join the Army without his mom's permission, but she would have gladly given it. She was wasting away as an associate at the Vic-Mart, drinking and smoking any excess from her measly paycheck, and Bruce was tired. He'd promised to send her money every month, and he fulfilled that obligation.

He fulfilled his obligation with the U.S. Army, too, uneventfully, tucking away most of his pay –the Army provided room and board –to buy a brand new red 1995 Mustang convertible Cobra. When he got out of that Army stink hole, he was going to State College on the government's 'nickel' while living high on the hog on his Army savings, driving his *chick magnet* car.

In college he rarely thought of high school, but occasionally the girl that he got pregnant came back to reinforce his haughty view of himself. *She meant nothing to me, that gold digger. Why'd she get pregnant anyway? There were birth control pills; she could have prevented it. But, no, she tried to trap me. 'Ain't no way! I'm outa here! It's your responsibility, not mine. I'm just a war hero going to college. Yeah, right, 'war hero'. Go back home to your family; I'm not your family. It's yours, your fault. What did you expect? You're not Catholic, so get rid of 'it'!*

But she didn't, and his genes, his seed, were out there somewhere. He left the Army, finished college, got a degree, and became a high school coach with an inflated ego.

Your life ain't so hard, son. "I'm here for you, son. You're going far, get that college scholarship, and I'll be here. You're my star, Earl. When you're gone on to bigger and better things, I'll be moving on, too. Thanks to you, I'll get better offers than this…" thinking first of saying, *stinking hole,* but instead, "…small town steppingstone. I've done just about all I can do here. When you've graduated, it'll be time for another generation to take over."

"You saw my dad the day before…" Earl couldn't say 'he died.' "Day before yesterday, Coach. Why'd he come see you at school?"

Bruce didn't know that Earl knew about their meeting. *It was a legit' meeting.* "Oh," Bruce says, "I just wanted to talk about Cleve's young man, and his bright future." He moves to put his arm around Earl's shoulder, but Earl shrugs him off.

"My grades weren't that great lately, and I've 'missed' a little school. Are you sure it wasn't about that?" Earl asks.

"That came up, but mainly I just wanted to tell him how proud I was of you," Coach says, *'…and to seal my future with Lila.'* "Your dad had a special place in his heart for you, Earl," he says. *…and a weakness that made it easy for me to get him out of the way.*

"He was proud of me?" Earl asks, getting a quiver in his voice, a dampness in his eye.

I must be amazing to bring out the tears in this kid. Bruce says, "Of course, you were his hope for the future of the Cleveland's." *Cleve had no hope for his future.* "Lila can be proud of Cleve and you –all his children," *…and me, for making us a reality and a future.*

Coach roughly puts an arm around Earl's shoulders and jostles him like a drunken cowboy who's found a stranger at the bar to be his friend and buy him a drink. "We're all proud of you, especially your dad." *I hope Lila will be proud to get rid of you soon so she and I can travel and live the good life and shine Cleve's tarnished nickel.*

124

Bruce scans the room. "I don't see your mom. I wanted to express my condolences."

"Oh, she's in the kitchen."

"Excuse me, son. I'm here for you," Coach shakes Earl's hand. *She's there for me.*

Bruce bulldozes his way across the room to the kitchen door, which he pushes open like a scene at the saloon of a spaghetti western -at high noon. The swinging door bumps hard against the side of the refrigerator as he makes his impromptu grand entrance. *Surprise, Lila!*

"Bruce!" Lila is still holding white paper towels against her red silk blouse where the merlot had spilled. "What're you doing in here?" she asks, startled and apprehensive, even though she knows it's Bruce now –or possibly because it is Bruce. *He's changed a lot since we started –started what? Or has the excitement and intrigue of running around with another man changed into fear of this man who wanted to break up our marriage? He doesn't need to break us up now because Cleve is...gone.*

Bruce presses his body against Lila, pinning her against the kitchen sink, where cold water is trickling into a spent coffee cup.

"I just wanted to see you alone one more time before –the memorial," Bruce continues pressing against her, grinding her hips into the cabinet wood, "to express my condolences."

"You shouldn't be here. Somebody might see us together, alone. Gossip is already floating around. The neighbors across the street saw."

"Saw what?" Bruce asks. "Saw the coach of their neighbor's son comforting his mother right after her husband's death, when there was no one else to comfort her?"

"Appearances, Bruce, people's perspectives don't always –usually don't –match reality. In this case, though, some of the rumors match," Lila says.

"Match what?" Bruce pushes Lila's shoulders back. She leans backwards over the sink, but not quite far enough to avoid his slobbery kiss on her cheek as she turns her head. "Match what, Lila?" he says as he pushes harder against her black pants and slides his hand under her blotted blouse.

"Bruce, stop!" She smacks his hand away. "This is not the place or the time!"

"When is, then?" Bruce holds her shoulders and stares her in the face, up close, close enough to see the real Bruce.

"Not now -and when I say it is," she calms, gaining control mentally.

The swinging door bangs open, Bruce steps back quickly, and Lila resumes blotting over her breast. Rae stops just inside the door, letting it swing closed. She doesn't speak but stands with an orange silk top draped over her arm.

"Yes, Lila, I am so sorry for your loss. If there is anything I can do, any time or any place, please don't hesitate," Bruce throws out some lines, to fill the silence and hopefully distracting Rae from whatever she saw erroneously. "If Earl needs me, I can be his coach or whatever he needs."

He steps forward and reaches out and hug Lila, friendly and pretentiously, but Lila stands tall, puts her hand in front of her and deflects the hug.

"Thank you, Bruce, you just don't know." The usual end of the sentence is '*how much I appreciate that.*'

Rae thinks, *I think I do know, Lila.*

"Yes, that's sweet of you, Bruce," Rae says while focusing on Lila, averting her eyes from Bruce.

"Well, I'll leave you two ladies." He exits quickly glancing over his shoulder at Lila, hoping to reassure himself –and intimidate her.

"Are you OK, Lila?" asks Rae.

"Oh, I just break down crying sometimes. I must look a mess," Lila says.

"You're all *mussed*." Rae perceived correctly what had been happening with Bruce.

Lila lets the paper towels slip from her hands and begins quickly wiping and patting her silk blouse, just like her little daughter Tina would wipe and pat the frilly dresses that Ester had made.

"Never mind that, Lila," Rae walks to the swinging door, latches it, and pulls the shades over the windows. "I brought you a fresh blouse –and here." She hands Lila a lipstick, some tissues and mascara. "There is an orange straw hat in the top of the closet that matches the orange silk blouse, but I thought that might be a bit much."

Lila smiles, thinking of the orange hat and that fishing trip so long ago at Aunt Naomi's. She peels the damp red blouse over her head. "Did you see the photo on the table, the one with Cleve wearing my old orange hat?"

"I did, Lila," Rae fluffs the orange blouse and starts it over Lila's head, like a mother dressing her little girl. "It's a beautiful picture."

"Yes, it is," Lila remembers vividly.

"It's good to see you smile, Lila," says Rae. "Now, here." She hands a tarnished silver mirror to Lila. "Fix your eyes and put some orange lipstick on that smile."

Forget Bruce. He's evil-incarnate.

Lila continues smiling, caught in another dimension, with her family, long ago.

Bruce is heading straight for the front door. The Reverend calls after him. "Bruce are you heading out?"

"Yeah, Coach." Chuck calls from the group of players. "Leaving so soon?"

Bruce is snared, but briefly. He's slippery as an eel, hard to hold onto. *Won't you let me out of here? I've done what I came for, now I'm going.* "It's a school day tomorrow, boys."

"The service is at 11:00 am -if you can make it, Bruce. I know Earl's teammates will want to be there. You've been a blessing to them," the Reverend doesn't usually lie, but maybe just to get a rise out of Bruce.

"It's my job, Reverend, just like yours is a job," he replies, his comparison baffling all within earshot. "I'm just glad I can share my gift."

God help us all if he shares his gift.

"So, Buddy," Chuck asks, "how's the coach been doing? Teaching you a lot? Helping you grow as a player –as a person?"

"Ha! Hell no!" Buddy laughs. "We're lucky to see him at practice. No, take that back, we're lucky to not see him at practice usually. Earl is our captain; he leads us, gives us tips, shows us how."

"What does Coach –I use the term *Coach* loosely –do when he's there?" asks Chuck.

"Lately he's been pushing these e-nhancers," Buddy reaches into his warm-up pocket and pulls out a red and yellow cylinder and shakes it lightly by his side. "Yeah, I hear the clicking –only two ampules left for this week."

"Two left for the week?" Chuck asks.

"Yeah, one e-nhancer a day to keep us going, 'give us energy and stamina', Coach says," Buddy answers.

"Are these legal?"

"Sure, they're legal, but you're supposed to have a prescription to take them," Buddy says.

"-and a medical or pharmaceutical license to dispense them. I'm sure Coach has neither," says Chuck.

"He says they're safe, and we're all taking them, except Earl, who doesn't like this artificial stuff –doesn't need it if he eats and lives right," says Buddy,

"Where does he get so many? For the whole team he'd need over fifty of these a week," Chuck notes.

"Coach mentioned something about a pharmaceutical company in Mexico. I don't think they're as regulated there, even with their modern drug plant controlled by the government. Coach gave us a little lesson on Mexican history and economics. They used to smuggle illegal drugs into the US, but now they just ship legal pharmaceuticals along with fruit, produce and cheap electronics," Buddy shows he's been paying attention in class.

"So, all this stuff, these drugs they send from Mexico to Coach and anybody else with an international Unicard is legal –until it's distributed illegally?"

"I guess," Buddy backs off the intellect.

"Don't flash those ampules around like they were candy. You don't have a prescription, so those e-scripts are illegal. Be careful, Buddy, and make sure the other guys do, too," Chuck warns.

"OK, Chuck."

"And I wish the team would quit using them," says Chuck. "E-nhancers don't seem to be helping you all, anyway."

"Hey, we're losing, but at least we're enthused about it," Buddy laughs.

35.

The neighbors from across the street, Anna, and Bette, approach the group of three: Ester, Pam, and Philly.

"I guess you two were right there the day Cleve died?" Ester says. "Lila is fortunate to have neighbors like you two –and the Taylor's right next door."

"We came right out when we realized what was going on – ambulance and police got there first," Anna says.

"I'm sure Lila appreciates the comfort you gave her," says Ester.

The two neighbors were nice -and even nicer if you wanted the scoop on something, especially something juicy. Ester knew they would know everything that happened that day at Cleve's, from the time the police and ambulance arrived until the time the yellow police tape was removed.

Bette begins the tale. "Well, Ester, we were coming over, but before we got to the street, someone else had arrived –giving comfort."

"Yes, a man was already here," says Anna.

"We thought it was Reverend Arnold at first, but then we recognized the man," says Bette.

This piques Pam interest. "Well, who was it?"

"It was Coach Bruce," announces Anna.

"Oh, he was probably trying to find Earl," Philly jumps in.

"Yes, I'm sure the coach came by as soon as he found out about Cleve," Ester reasons.

"Maybe he was just trying to find Earl. Probably one of those days when Earl got out of school early." Philly knows for certain that Earl and Chuck were cutting class.

"Certainly, Bruce is a very concerned, caring person, especially when it comes to his team," Ester says.

"Coach Bruce seemed to be caring and comforting Lila a lot that morning. He must have been a close friend of the whole family." says Bette.

"Yes, Coach was a rock that morning, with Lila leaning on him," Anna adds with a bit of sarcasm.

"Earl never really talked much about the coach," Philly says. "Really, the only talk I heard of Coach was from Chuck, and he didn't care much for the coach."

"Why's that?" asks Pam.

"First of all, I guess the main reason was that Chuck could never make the team, not even manager or towel boy. Coach didn't seem too concerned about Chuck. Just the opposite," says Philly. "Chuck could have really used some encouragement from another adult."

"And you think Coach should have done that?" Ester asks.

"Earl has always been a strong figure in Chuck's life. Ever since Chuck moved here when he was a boy, he's been friends with Earl. The three of us are good friends," Philly says.

"-and Coach?" Ester asks.

"Chuck just wanted to be on the same team as Earl. They've been a great two-man team and Earl's been bringing him into the team, unofficially, which has been great for Chuck," says Philly.

"-and good for you and Earl, too, since you might be his 'girlfriend' now," adds Pam.

Philly blushes. "Um, yes," she spies Earl across the room. Coincidentally, he's reciprocating. "Excuse me, ladies, I need to –get something to drink."

"Thirsty, huh?" Pam asks.

Philly smiles, bashful and rosy, and heads toward the dining table. As if on cue, Earl meets her at the table, but clumsily bumps her elbow as she opens a bottle of spring water. Cold water sloshes down the front of her sundress, but Earl reacts quickly and steadies Philly's hand before the whole bottle spills.

"Earl!" Philly jumps back, a bit shocked by the chilly water.

"Darn! Sorry, Philly, I was just – "

"It's OK, Earl," says Philly. She and Earl place the half liter bottle on the table, his hand wrapped around hers.

"Here's a napkin –I'll go get a towel from the kitchen," Earl says nervously as he lets go of her hand.

Philly turns her back to the table and nonchalantly scans the room. When she thinks no one will see, she swishes her flowered dress and glides to the kitchen door and softly pushes it open. Earl has left a couple of cabinet doors open and has his hand in the drawer by the sink, pulling out a white bar towel, snapping it unfolded. He sees Philly smiling shyly, slyly before him like she's the *fox* and he's the *hen*.

"Got the towel," Earl says, holding the limp towel at arm's length between him and Philly.

"Thank you." She grasps one end of the white towel while Earl hangs on to the other.

Earl lets go and Philly daintily blots the front of her dress, properly like dabbing the corners of her mouth at a fine restaurant.

"Sorry, Philly." Earl looks past Philly toward the kitchen door.

"It's just a little spring water on cotton, Earl. No damage done," Philly says, shifting her focus back and forth between Earl and the back door.

She grabs Earl by the sleeve of his warm-up jacket and makes a dash toward the back door and pulling him along behind her. He resists initially, not knowing what this wild Philly is doing. Realizing he's been snared, Earl surrenders and bounds out the back door with her. As soon as the door clicks closed, Philly stops short and turns, facing Earl. He stops just short of tackling Philly.

"What are you doing, you crazy Philly?"

She grabs him by the collar, pulls herself up, close to his bewildered face, and says, "It's cold, so shut up and kiss me." Earl warms her with his arms. They kiss.

Inside the living room Ester says, "I wonder where that Philly went?"

"I don't know," Pam says. *I don't see Earl either. I know where she is –wherever Earl is!*

"Excuse us, ladies," Anna says, "but we're feeling a little thirsty. If there's anything we can do, Pam, Ester, you know we're right across the street."

"We're so sorry about Cleve. He was one of the good ones," Bette adds. "He's going to be missed."

"Thank you, ladies," Ester says, "you're such good neighbors."

The neighbors scope out the room as they go. Anna peeks into the kitchen, hoping to catch the young lovers, but she's disappointed –no Earl or Philly. She turns back to Bette, shakes her head 'no' and shrugs.

"They must be in a dark corner somewhere," says Bette.

"Let's be mysterious and toast the sweet young lovers with a glass of red wine," Anna suggests.

"Let's," agrees Bette.

"How are you holding up, Pam?" Ester asks.

"It's sunken in pretty quickly with me, Emaw. I loved –love –Dad, and miss him, but I've missed him for a long time now," says Pam.

"Since you've been away at school?" Ester asks.

"But not just in body, but in spirit," Pam says.

"What do you mean, Pam?"

"Oh, he just never has seemed happy –since years ago, really. Mom was so troubled, and Dad put more and more energy into her. He had little left for us, and even less for himself. I miss the dad that we loved, the one who showed us that he loved us," Pam says.

"So how was your mom taking your dad's –lack of presence?" asks Ester.

"You know, Dad had tolerated and tried to understand Mom's 'condition', but when she became aware of his 'problem', she thought he was rejecting her. It was all about her. Mom was not remembering all of her bad times when Dad had tried to help, understand and still love her," says Pam. "Mom thought Dad didn't love her anymore and seemed to give up on 'them'."

"Sounds like the blind leading the blind at that point. He had tried to see –and she covered her eyes," Ester says.

"I love my mom, but I think she broke Dad's spirit –and his heart – and that's what killed him," Pam accuses.

"No, Pam! Don't blame you mom," but Ester knows her oldest granddaughter is wise beyond her years –an *old soul*. "She's not been well."

"Well?" Pam raises her voice. "Mom's not been *well* since Tina was born. Did she blame Tina? Mom rejected her youngest daughter as soon as she was born! Tina's innocent. Mom's guilty! She pushed Dad's heart too hard, until it just could not take it anymore. She might not have laid hands on him and killed him, but she may as well have."

"Stop it, Pam!" Ester demands. "I loved - love Cleve as much as you. He was –is –my child! But he died of *natural causes.* No one killed him."

"Natural cause: broken heart. Isn't it all the same?" Pam concludes, running down the hall to her room.

The Reverend has overheard some of the angry accusations, and quickly approaches Ester. Putting his hand on her forearm, he comforts, "Is there anything I can do, Ester?"

Ester touches the Reverend's hand that's laid so gently upon her arm. "Thank you, Reverend Arnold, but she's my granddaughter. I need to go to her."

"You're a good, strong woman, Ester and I'm sure Pam will come away stronger after this, too." he says.

"I hope she learns to use the genes and good sense that God gave her, because mine are fading," Ester smiles and respectfully pulls her hand from his. She walks the down the hallway holding her head high for her granddaughter's sake.

The neighbors, Anna and Bette, huddle in the corner of the living room, adjacent Cleve's shrine.   They swirl their merlot, watching the crimson legs of the communion wine form and fade down the sides of the wine glass.

"Bette, what is your honest opinion of this situation between Lila and Coach?" Anna asks.

"My honest opinion? I give nothing but honest opinions," says Bette.

"Well, what is that, Bette?"

"Just a minute," Bette savors the last drop of oaky, plummy red wine with a neat finish. She smacks her lips. "Would you like another?"

"Sure, Bette, twist my arm," says Anna.

The neighbors walk arm-in-arm to the sideboard where they find an open green bottle and a corked bottle of the same. Anna tips the open bottle over Bette's empty glass, and a single shimmering drop creeps from the bottle neck and dives into the thirsty vessel. Anna sets the empty down, grabs the unopened bottle, and takes aim with the corkscrew, fixing to pierce the intact black foil and twist into the cork. Charlie Taylor approaches and disarms the neighbor.

"May I?" Charlie offers as he takes the bottle and corkscrew.

"Yes, sir, you have spared Anna a world of anguish," Bette says, "and saved me from watching her uncorked anger."

"Glad to be of service, ladies," Charlie says.

He pierces the foil cover and twists the curly steel into the corked bottle of 2023 Communion merlot. He flips the two arms of the corkscrew down, prying the cork to the surface with a loud 'pop' as the vacuum releases.

The neighbors think, *Charlie sure is sexy about opening a bottle of wine.* Anna speaks for them both as she says, "Charlie, you look like you've been practicing your screw –I mean uncorking. Will you be available later –to assist with another bottle?"

"Ladies, you just call on your neighbor Charlie, and he'll come running," Charlie says with impish grin.

"We'll keep you in mind for all our corkscrew needs," says Bette.

"Oh, I almost forgot," and Charlie tips the bottle over one glass and then the other, filling each to three quarters twisting the bottle professionally with a trick of the wrist after each pour, catching the drip.

"Merci," says Anna. "Mercy," says Bette. They both raise their glasses to him as he walks over to the dining room table. The Rev has christened his cocktail plate with two Swedish meatballs and a cauliflower floret dipped in buttermilk ranch dip.

Anna and Bette become noticeably louder after their double doses of wine and are within earshot of the Reverend and Charlie.

"That's sure a nice man," says Anna, "and his son Chuck is quite the young man, too."

"Yes, and Chuck's probably fortunate not to be on Bruce's basketball team," says Bette.

"Earl is becoming the young gentleman, too. Cleve did a good job of raising him. Lucky coach hasn't influenced his character," says Anna.

"I think Coach could ruin somebody. If I knew all the history on that man, I'd run him out of town with a pitchfork and a torch." Bette wipes her mouth with the back of her hand.

"If people had seen what we saw the day Cleve died, they'd think twice about the coach, too. I mean, Cleve was still laid out dead on his patio, and Coach was pawing all over the widow." Anna shakes her head, takes a long drink of wine blots the red on her white napkin.

"Funny thing, Lila didn't seem to mind until she thought we were watching." Bette runs her tongue over her lips to get the last drop of wine.

"People will talk. I wonder if anyone has seen us drinking and carrying on at this party –I mean this 'visitation'. Nobody's ever seen us drinking. We're always in the house when we imbibe," says Anna.

"Mm-hmm. Do you remember seeing Lila, on several occasions, slinking down to the intersection, and Bruce picking her up?"

"I sure do. We were on the front porch, just like the day Cleve died." Anna agrees. They set their empty glasses on the table.

The Reverend plucks a Swedish meatball from its toothpick and licks the sauce from his fingers. "These are good," he mumbles, mouth full.

"Rae's special recipe," says Charlie.

The Reverend overhears a portion of the neighbors' conversation. "Did you hear what the neighbors just said –about Lila and Bruce?" He clears his throat.

"I'm sorry to say that I've been eavesdropping on their whole conversation." Charlie confesses. "Lord, forgive me."

"If you sincerely ask for forgiveness, you will receive it." the Reverend assures him, "but if a person commits the same sin, say adultery," alluding to the aforementioned neighbors' conversation, "time after time without regret, I don't believe he –or she -is forgiven.

"But what about *grace*, Reverend?" Charlie asks.

"Grace has been offered to us, through Jesus Christ's sacrifice on the cross, free for the taking. If we want grace, it's there. But if we want sins of the flesh and don't seek God's grace, we won't receive it," the Reverend preaches.

"Grace sounds complicated," Charlie says.

"Sounds complicated, if we make it that way, but it's really simple," says the Reverend.

"Without saying any names, you know who I mean, can either one receives grace without the other receiving it?" asks Charlie.

"Charlie, I've spoken with both parties, and the woman seems to be moving closer to grace," says the Reverend, "but I fear that the man is riding down the wrong road not seeking grace."

"The man…sounds like he's trying to recruit people to his side -the sinful side, wouldn't you say, Reverend?" Charlie asks.

"He may be trying, but he's messing with some strong souls in Earl and Chuck, just a couple on the same team with the good guys. And there's the second string, you and I and some others, waiting on the bench 'til Our Coach calls us in to relieve the weary," the Reverend says.

"Our Coach?" asks Charlie.

"J.C.," says the Reverend, "Our Coach the Shepherd, the Inventor of the game, the Referee and God the Almighty."

"Put me in, Coach!" says Charlie.

"Amen, son! Are you ready to play?" asks the Reverend.

"I'm not worthy, but I'm ready," says Charlie.

"Hey, Charlie, we're ready for another bottle of red," the neighbor Anna calls over.

"Yes, ready!" Bette agrees.

"Love thy neighbor," the Reverend tells Charlie.

"-as thyself," Charlie completes the quote. "I think I'll have another glass with the neighbors."

"I'm right there with you, Charlie," says the Reverend.

36.

Rae emerges from the kitchen first and holds the door open. Lila makes an entrance wearing her tangerine silk blouse, lipstick, freshened face, and hair. Lila pauses and poses, 'Rockettes' style –sans feathers and sequins –wearing her black cigarette pants and flats with the citrus blouse. Reverend Arnold is mesmerized by Lila's transformation. Bruce had brought Lila's spirit down, but Rae had performed a miracle, reincarnating Lila to new life, Reverend believes.

Pam grins, "Wow, Mom, you look awesome!" which the Reverend had thought, but thought inappropriate for a clergyman, to say.

Lila smiles, purses her lips in kiss mode, reverses her original pose and does a wave-point in Pam's direction, Marilyn Monroe-esque.

"Something's missing. Where's the orange straw hat?" Pam points to the old family photo in which Cleve had worn the hat.

Rae mouths something to Pam, who catches her meaning and runs down the hall. Lila looks over her shoulder at Rae, who shrugs her shoulders. A minute later, Pam prances up the hall wearing the infamous orange straw hat, comes up behind Ester and holds it like a halo over her grandma's head. Pam arrives at her destination, Lila, who turns her back to the 'audience' and presses the hat to her heart. She makes a dramatic turn, facing her 'fans' wearing the wide-brimmed hat cockeyed left as she winks with her right eye. Pam flanks Lila's left, Rae her right. They acknowledge Lila with a wave of the hand gesture, 'Vanna White' style of yesteryear's 'Wheel' television game, center stage as she bows and removes her hat with a sweep across the floor. She returns the hat to her head, poses like a movie star on the red carpet and throws a series of kisses to her adoring fans.

OK, the Reverend thinks, *this is a celebration of life,* so he steps up and begins to slowly applause, joined by Charlie with subsequent 'bravo's'.

The neighbors chide in, a bit slurred from their communion with the wine, tapping their stemmed glasses with clear plastic forks. "I did say 'party', right Bette?"

"You did, and you were correct," They clink their glasses together in toast mode.

The basketball team, sans Chuck, gives a few short 'whoops' then polite applause as they huddle. Chuck is absent and Earl and Philly are AWOL also.

"Hey, Reverend," Charlie nudges him, "did you see Chuck, Earl and Philly slip out?"

Still applauding Lila, the Reverend says, "The new couple went out to the kitchen a while ago –I assume they slipped out the back. They should have returned by now."

"There's Earl's letter jacket," Charlie motions toward the chair by the hall closet. "Philly couldn't have gone far without something on her shoulders. Have you seen Chuck?"

"He and Buddy were talking, and then Chuck vanished. Maybe check with Buddy," says the Reverend. "Oh, and Earl will find some way to keep Philly warm." He winks.

"I'll look out back. If those love birds are back there, maybe they can tell us where Chuck went," says Charlie.

"Have this in hand, just in case you find a chilly young Philly," the Reverend says picking up the letter jacket and handing it to Charlie.

The girls –Rae, Lila, and Pam –are giggling by the dining table as Charlie sidles up to Rae. "Nice floor show, girls."

"Thanks, Charlie," Lila says. "These two make pretty good production assistants."

"Mom's quite an entertainer," says Pam. "She should have been in show business –a Rockette!"

"You look like you're trying to slip backstage, Charlie. 'Got a pass?" Rae nudges Charlie.

"Yeah, right –no, just going out to check if Earl and Philly are under cover of darkness in the backyard," says Charlie.

"Make a little noise on your way to give the little love birds a 'heads up' if they're nesting out there," says Rae, grinning and winking at Pam.

"Yeah, that Earl better take good care of little Philly," says Pam.

"Earl's a good boy, a gentleman," says Lila, "like his Dad."

"You're right, Mom –and he's a good brother," says Pam, putting her arm around her mom.

"Are you still planning to take Earl to college with you for a little getaway –some brother-sister time?" Lila asks.

"Yeah, this weekend –after the memorial," says Pam.

"That'll be good for you both. I'm going to spend some time with Tina and Ester," Lila says. "I need some quality time with Tina. Ester has been her grandmother and her mother for too long."

"Oh, Lila, I'm not her mother," says Ester. "I've just been filling in until you're ready." She takes Lila by the hand.

"I think –hope –that I'm ready, Ester."

137

"You're closer than ever to being Tina's mother –and mine and Earl's, too, Mom," says Pam.

"Thank you, Pam. I hope you're right. I'm really trying," says Lila. "Pam, you've been almost a mother to Earl."

"Big sister, Mom, big sister," says Pam.

"You are a good big sister, Pam," Rae adds.

"Why, thank you, Mrs. Taylor –Rae. By the way, since you think I've done such a good job as Earl's big sister, I was thinking maybe Chuck could come to college with me and Earl this weekend. What do you think?" Pam asks.

"That's a great idea! Chuck can give Earl some male companionship, and it'll be a good time to reinforce their friendship. Now that Earl has a girlfriend, I think Chuck may be feeling like 'the third wheel'," says Rae.

"Yeah," says Pam, "and Philly needs to maintain her independence, not cling to a boy so much –not that I think she's clingy. Philly has just fallen so hard for Earl –and he for her –so quickly. She just needs to remember to take care of Philly, boyfriend or not, letter jacket or not." Pam is protective of Earl –he's her brother –but protective of Philly because Pam likes her, empathizes, and doesn't want her to get hurt. Fifteen and sixteen-year-olds are vulnerable to hurts, Pam remembers.

When Pam was a freshman in high school, a senior boy named Frances had told a friend of hers, Michelle, that he thought Pam was cute. When Pam got the message, she was ecstatic that a senior liked her.

In most high schools, senior boys have preyed on pretty freshmen girls –because of their seniority. Frances remembered when he was a freshman and had a crush on a freshman girl that he had known since third grade. He didn't stand a chance at getting her because those pompous senior boys always took the freshman girls. Frances had vowed that when he became a senior, he would get his turn at those sweet naïve freshman girls.

Raised in the home of a gentle father, Pam never suspected that all men were not gentlemen like her dad. The time of the 'affair' was prom season; their first date culminated in the senior prom. Prom night was an occasion when guys dressed like gentlemen or dudes, and gals either dressed like princesses or prostitutes. Frances played the part of a dude, not a gentleman, and wanted Princess Pam to play the part of a prostitute.

The day of the prom, Frances and his buds connected with somebody's cousin who had an uncle in Appalachia who made apple brandy, bootlegged from the Blue Ridge. The 'cousin connection' imported enough brandy to fill all the cool seniors' flasks, plus enough for their cool dads.

Frances drank a lot of courage before the prom. He didn't know Pam, except that she was 'cute'. Prom night she looked hot in her fair princess gown, and Frances' inhibitions were diminished by the alcohol. After the prom, the last dance, Pam knew she shouldn't ride with Frances, but he was an experienced driver, and the drive was short.

"You missed my street, "Pam had told Frances, figuring he was just drunk enough to lose his bearings.

Frances didn't say a word, but his perfect teeth grinned like a wily fox –or was it a possum? -beneath his drunken red nose. He turned onto the gravel road that circled the backside of Solace Park where Pam had played when she was a little girl.

"I need to go home," Pam said sternly.

He said, "Just a little while." He parked the car and killed the lights.

"Now!" she demanded.

As Frances slid across the hard-plastic center console of his sporty coupe, putting a hurting on his butt, Pam realized that she was in a predicament. He grabbed the hem of her pretty pink princess dress now Pam was getting out the passenger door. She slammed the door against the top of his hard head, barely avoiding amputating the tips of three of his fingers and a thumb as her dress caught in the door.

'Call us if you need us,' her father had said as they walked to Frances' car before leaving to go to the prom. Frances acted the part of a gentleman holding the car door for Cleve's princess. 'Have a good time.' The latter entreaty to 'have a good time' had been achieved up to about the middle of the night, when Frances had tipped the tipsy scale and become blatantly drunk. The former comment by her father to 'call us if you need us' was about to happen unbeknownst the unconscious sloshed senior, sprawled across the two front seats.

Pam reached inside her dainty pink satin clutch and felt her e-cell emergency device –right beside her e-mace cartridge -and squeezed the button firmly in the 'call a friend' mode. This night her designated 'friend' was Dad whose mode she had programmed immediately after he said, 'call us if you need us'. When her dad received the message, he would instantaneously get coordinates and directions to Pam's location, which he could forward the police patrol closest to his daughter.

Within two minutes the police cruiser arrived. They patrolled Solace Park regularly, keeping crime to a minimum. A barrage of bright LED spots flooded Frances' red car, highlighting the pretty pink princess as she stood snared by satin fabric in the passenger door, calmly brushing her hair.

"Ma'am, a 'Mr. Cleveland' forwarded your emergency message to us, and you're our pinpoint location. Are you alright?" the officer asked.

"I'm fine now, officer," Pam said calmly.

"What's your name, miss, and what are you doing out here this late? Been to the prom?" the officer asked, knowing that, of course, she had been to the prom –from her attire.

"I'm Pam Cleveland. My dad sent for you. He said for me to call if I needed him, so here you are," said Pam, putting her brush away and wrapping her shawl snuggly around her shoulders.

Another car pulled up beside Frances' red ride. Dad got out, slammed the driver's door and ran around the red coupe to Pam. "Are you OK, sweetie?"

"Good, except my dress is caught in the door," Pam said as she tightened her grip on the dress, which still wouldn't release from its snare.

"How'd this happen, Pam?" her dad asked.

"Take a look in the car, Dad," Pam said, and one of the police officers shined a light through the passenger door glass. "He's how this happened!" Pam grit her teeth and pointed in the direction of the prostrate Frances, who was snuggled next to the passenger door handle, the pink satin and crinoline fabric of Pam's dress still in his hand caressed to his cheek.

"What the –I'll kill that drunken punk!" Dad yelled.

"I'm OK, Dad. He just got a little drunk and – "

"-and what, Pam? Did he try something on you? I know how these older boys are. I should have never let you -"

"Calm down and move away from the car, sir," the officer commanded. "We'll handle the drunk."

"Well, 'handle' getting my daughter out of that stinking drunk's hand. Did he touch you, Pam? I'll kill – "

"No, Dad, he just grabbed – "

"Grabbed? I'll kill the – "Dad started.

"Frances is just stupid drunk. I'm through with seniors –so *mature*! They're just after one thing," Pam said.

"One thing -what was he after? I'll kill the – "

"Not a hand, Dad. He didn't lay a hand on me. I'm not sure if he's passed out or knocked out. I hit his head pretty hard with that door," Pam said.

"I hope you brained the b- "Dad said.

"We'll handle him, Mr. Cleveland, Pam. Drunken driving, open container of illegal substance –alcohol, and assault on a female –Miss Cleveland, if you'll press charges," the second officer said.

"You put him in jail or I'll – "Mr. Cleveland started.

"We have this, sir. Do you want to file a formal complaint, Miss Cleveland, and press charges?"

"No, I don't think so. Frances' worst crime is being arrogant," Pam said.

"Pam!" her dad exclaims.

"Well, Dad, you were going to kill him. I'm just filling in the blanks for you," Pam said.

"You can take your daughter home now, Mr. Cleveland, if she's not pressing assault charges," the officer said.

"I'll take her home, officer, as soon as you get that grabby bastard's hands off my daughter's dress and free her from his car and any other connection –ever –with my little girl," said Dad.

"I'm not a little girl, Dad," Pam said.

"If Frances did anything – "

"I said he didn't touch me, Dad. I'm fine, except for a little damage to my pride. I'm still *your* little girl, always will be," Pam said.

"Let's go home, Pam."

"OK, Dad. Thanks for rescuing me."

"My princess," Dad said.

"But not a little girl, I'm 'most a woman –I'm fifteen."

"Always keep me as your *'Call a Friend'*, and I'll come running, no matter where or when," Dad said.

"You're my hero, Dad," Pam lays her head on her Dad's shoulder as he hugs her and walks her to his car.

"Cuff this boy and drag his sorry ass out of this car," one officer said to the other. "I guess we'll have to take him by the ER for that lump on his flat head."

"Girl gave him a good whack, didn't she?"

"We need more girls like her. She could give my daughter a few pointers."

"Concussion, maybe, son -you're lucky we didn't turn you over to the Cleveland's."

"Maybe we should have. They'd have tamed this young buck."

"There'd be antlers hanging on the wall in their den."

"Heh, heh –move your sorry hide, son. Get in that car before I change my mind and turn you over to that girl's daddy."

Frances moaned as he tumbled into the back seat of the cruiser.

37.

Earl holds Philly tight as they swing on the old metal glider rocker in the Cleveland's back yard. The moon slips behind a charcoal gray cloud. Philly snuggles under the warm-up jacket and against Earl's chilled shoulder. She's comfortable, but she knows Earl must be getting cold since he so gallantly relinquished his warm-up jacket to her bare shoulders, leaving his arms exposed to the chill air.

Trying not to damage Earl's male ego, she lies, "Earl, I'm cold," knowing full well that it's him who is cold, not she.

Earl's teeth chatter, "It's nice out, don't you think –just a little cool." He squeezes as close as possible to Philly.

"No, Earl, it's a bit too cool out. Maybe we should go back inside," Philly says.

Not wanting to give up his spot beside Philly, Earl tries convincing her to stay. "Maybe I could go back inside and get my letter jacket for you."

Tempting thinks Philly. "I'd like to stay out here with you."

"Then it's settled. You wait here and I'll be right back," says Earl.

Suddenly the back-door creaks open. Mr. Taylor emerges, startling the two love birds. "Hey, you guys, we were wondering where you went," says Charlie.

"Uh, we've been right here, just sitting, talking," Earl says.

"Yeah, sitting and talking," Philly agrees.

"I thought, if you were out here, that you might be a little cool, Philly, so I brought you Earl's letter jacket," says Charlie.

Yay! It's cold as – out here. "Thanks, Mr. Taylor, you're right on time."

"Yeah, I was just coming in to get that. You must have read my mind," says Earl.

Charlie thinks, *I've been there –don't want to leave that sweet young thing, huh, Earl?* "Just had a hunch –the Reverend and I just wondered where you went. Have you seen Chuck?"

"No, the last I saw he was with the team talking to Buddy," says Earl. "Haven't seen him since then."

Chuck goes in the side door of his house into the garage. He can't see where he is going, he's left the lights off -so no one knows he's there.

The shelves and lawn mower give him frames of reference as he feels for the toolbox on the worktable by the mud room door.

What tools will I need to break in –a screwdriver? Pliers? He feels his way through the toolbox drawers. *OK, that's it, plus my pocketknife,* the Buck knife that belonged to his great-great grandfather, a carpenter. Still wearing his semi-formal clothes - for warmth, not for style – he slides the screwdriver in one blazer pocket and the pliers into the other. He feels the familiar deer antler handle of the Buck in his left pocket.

He stumbles over the mower deck –Chuck is clumsy whether wearing suit or baggy jeans. *OK, out of here without breaking my neck.*

He exits by the side door and slinks around the back of the house, avoiding any traffic on the street between his and the Cleveland house. *Safe -just got to avoid attracting attention on the way to the school.* He walks deliberately, quickly, but doesn't run. Staying in the shadows, he dodges the streetlights. It takes twice the normal time to reach the school -four times the rate it takes when he and Earl run 'double time' to get the heck out and cut class.

A peach colored security light floods the rear of the gym, challenging Chuck to 'jimmy' the door lock quickly enough to avoid the security guard's 'watchful' eyes –yeah, right. Those professionals are just driving around drinking coffee and eating Krispy Kreme doughnuts, regularly stopping for naps. *No security issues.*

Hugging the brick wall, he makes his way along the side of the building to the lighted back entrance. A padlock and heavy steel chain are laced through the handles of the doors. *Darn.* He sees the windows adjacent the door –*plan B.*

Chuck clings to the brick wall and eases around the corner of the building and notices one of the windows flipped open a tad; the coach had not secured it. *Thanks, Coach.* He opens the window, removes his jacket, rolls it compactly and drops it through. Grabbing the ledge, which is some four feet off the ground, he pulls up, "Umph! Not quite." He scrounges around the side of the building and finds an empty twenty-liter paint bucket, apparently left there for this occasion.

While grunting the last inches through the window, Chuck catches the seat of his pants on the latch, ripping the seam open. *Wasn't going to wear these again anyway.*

His eyes adjust to the dim fluorescent light filtering through from the hall. Coach always deadbolts his door, so there's no exit without a key.

Must be a fire code violation, but in case of fire the only one getting burned is the coach.

Chuck gropes his way around the dark side of Coach's desk and opens the middle drawer. "Ah ha," Chuck feels the shape of a thumb sized LED flashlight, takes it from the drawer and clicks the button. "Crap!" he snaps the blinding beam to the floor behind the desk. *Why don't I just send up a flare?* Temporarily blinded, his night vision is gone; he can only see the lighted areas.

He rummages through the drawer further: whistle, gum, pens, paperclips, miscellaneous pad and receipts, condom. *Condom, at school? What the hell is Coach doing with a condom at school? Don't want to think about it.* He excuses himself for thinking 'hell', but thinks, *The coach's sins must be worse than my cussing.*

He closes the middle drawer and tries the bottom drawer on the right. *Locked.* He finds the other drawer unlocked, but contains only envelops, paper and a couple of preprinted tests. *Coach still likes to waste paper.*

Now, for some more breaking after entering. He unrolls his jacket and takes the screwdriver from its pocket. The clumsy flat head isn't going to work. He had glimpsed a brass key in the top drawer; he feels around the front edge and discovers a single stubby brass key. *This might be the thing.* He tries the key in the bottom drawer lock. *Ta da!*

Let's see what's worthy of Coach locking up. Chuck flips quickly through the thin file folders –more wasted paper. *Ever hear of digital files, Coach?* In the last folder in the back of the drawer, he feels the bulkiness of something besides paper. Lifting the folder carefully, so as not to disturb its contents, he sees the label: 'e'.

Chuck makes himself comfortable in Coach's gel padded swivel chair. *Nice and cushy.* He settles his butt, which had become a bit cool from the unexpected ventilation in the seat of his slacks. As he opens the folder on the cluttered desktop, a vial rolls out and comes to rest against a black ink pen. The pen's logo, *Figure 8 Motel' in Clay Town*, a small town less than thirty minutes away. Chuck pockets the pen. *Thief,* he thinks, self-accusatory.

He scrutinizes the vial between his thumb and forefinger: 'e-cig *Cubano.' Nothing but the finest Cuban tobacco nectar for Coach.* Chuck slips it into his jacket pocket alongside the pen.

The clanking of a heavy metal door echoes from down the cavernous hall. Chuck clicks off the flashlight, closes and tucks the folder under his arm, and slides out of the chair onto the floor under the desk, his knees to his chest. *Stupid! What if he comes in here?* He cowers lower. A rattle of the doorknob puts Chuck on the brink of peeing his slacks. The light shining through the door glass swoops across the walls of the office, shadow images like a buzzard circling its dead carrion. Footsteps gradually soften down the hall, telltale that the rattle and beam were from the security guard. *Did I pee myself?* He checks. *No worries.*

Chuck crawls from under the desk and sits in the coach's chair. He puts the fat folder on top of the desk, opens it carefully so that no more vials escape. Inside the folder he finds a sleeve of prescription vials with tiny green and red flag logos. *Hecho en Mexico* is stamped adjacent the flag. *Lot #003... Use by 03/15/2025. Caution: Federal law prohibits transfer of this drug to any person other than the patient for whom prescribed.* Printed above the small blue letters in larger black font:
e-nhancer.

I heard Earl and some of the guys talking about this. It's prescription, so how is Coach dispensing this stuff to the team? Earl doesn't need it –he only tried it once –but some of the other guys thought it enhanced their performances. It may have speeded them up, but it didn't give them skills. He smiles.

The sleeve has been opened and the stopper is lying loose in the crease of the folder; he caps the sleeve. Stapled to the top of the folder is a business card with the name 'Jorge Camino' at the top followed by a cell #, and email and business address in Key West, Florida.

Footsteps begin their long slow march from the far end of the hall outside the office. Chuck fumbles with the folder and rips the business card off along with a little piece of the manila paper, tucks the sleeve and card into the back pocket of his torn slacks and stuffs the folder back into the file. He closes the file drawer hard with a thump. He locks it, but clumsily drops the key on the floor and accidentally kicks it under the desk. He bends over trying to retrieve it. *Never mind –gotta go!*

Coach had decided to stop by the gym after spending a little time at home fuming over a few bootleg apple brandies. *Those kids up at that Cleveland girl's college know how to get the good stuff up in the mountains. And that Burley tobacco leaf they grow and cure in the Appalachian hills is almost –but not quite –as good as Cuban, but at least it's local and fresh. A shame when the government made this stuff illegal. Illegal can be legal if it's done right –and vice versa,* referring to the 'e-drugs' he's been acquiring through his Key West-Mexican connection.

Still wobbly from the hooch, Bruce swaggers down the hall like a drunken cowboy from the saloon slowly making his way to his office.

"Hey, Ponderosa, that you?" Bruce calls out thinking he had heard the security guard at the other end of the hall. No answer. He sees the flick of light, on and off inside his office and he scuffles faster down the hall.

Chuck grunts, his stomach pressing against the windowsill, as he slides out the window of Coach's office. "Umph!" He hits the bucket and then the ground outside, brushes off and slams the window closed.

Chuck had heard the rattle and clinking of keys as Coach fumbled to hit the keyhole. The keys had hit the floor just as Chuck shut the window. He runs clear around back of the gym and stops to catch his breath at the corner before stepping into the peach glow of the parking lot.

Suddenly a bright white spotlight hits Chuck square in the eyes, blinding him. "Stop! Put your hands up and put them up against the brick wall. Spread your legs apart –and don't move!"

Chuck freezes and then obeys the voice. *Busted! Breaking, entering and larceny -I'm going to jail.* He leans against the brick, waiting for the man to frisk and cuff him. That doesn't happen.

"Chuck Taylor, is that you, son?" Chuck has heard the voice somewhere before.

"Uh, yes, sir," Chuck's voice breaks.

"OK, you can put your hands down and step away from the wall."

The spotlight goes out as Chuck turns toward the man.

"I'm Detective Brown. We have not met, but I've met your friend Earl. I've been following you tonight since you left the Cleveland's. How is Earl?"

"He seems pretty good." Chuck hesitates. "Some of the team were at his house. Earl got a lot of support from us."

"How's Coach?" Detective Brown asks.

"Um, he was OK when I saw him at Earl's." *Coach is never OK. He's the same old egotistical ass…*

"Seen Coach since then?"

"No."

"Thought maybe you had a meeting with him at his office," Brown says.

"No, I – "Chuck stammers.

"Get in the car, son, before Coach comes out and wants to press charges –breaking and entering, right?"

Chuck thinks, *-and larceny.*

"You can sit up front, Chuck. You're not under arrest."

"But, I – "

"Just get in the car before I change my mind and arrest you."

"Yes, sir." Chuck gets in the passenger side up front.

"Buckle up."

"Where are we going, the police station?" Chuck asks.

"The Taylor house," Detective Brown answers.

"Please, Detective Brown, don't tell my folks. It'll kill my mom. Can't I do some community service –pick up some trash, or something?" Chuck pleads.

"I'm just taking you home, Chuck. We can talk on the way and before you go in your house. Mr. and Mrs. Taylor will never hear about your criminal history from me," says Brown.

"But you said I wasn't arrested. I'll have a record?"

"Lighten up, son, I was just kidding. You're still stressed from the coach's office."

"I –I guess so."

As they drive away from the school, the lights in Coach Bruce's office come on. The inebriated coach stumbles, bumps the corner of his desk and sits back in his swivel chair, leaning on the verge of flipping over backwards. *My throne.* He smiles, arms crossed over his puffed chest. He scans his *kingdom;* something under the desk catches his eye. Swiveling forward he topples onto his knees in front of the drawers.

"What's this?" He reaches for the brassy, coin-sized piece underneath the bottom drawer. He picks it up, fumbles, and then grasps it solidly in his fist. Still on his knees, he opens his fist and examines the object in his palm.

"My file key –what's this doing out?" He hoists himself up by the side arm of his chair. It rolls back and he hits the floor hard, catching his weight with his free hand. "Dammit!"

He struggles with his swiveling chair, grabs the edge of the desk and grunts his way up. He picks up the key and inserts it in the keyhole.

The file folders are all pushed back tight in the back of the drawer. Properly spacing the folders, he notices the tear in the back folder.

"What the -?" He squishes all the manila folders to the front of the drawer except for the one labeled 'e'. The folder is ripped.

"Why would -?" He pulls the folder out of its holder; the sleeve of e-nhancers is missing.

Who would break in and steal something as worthless as a sleeve of stimulus drugs? They're not expensive –if you can get them on the streets. That's the problem, access to these legal prescriptions. Just got to have connections. He realizes the rips in the manila folder are where his smuggling associate's business card was attached.

If anybody calls 'El Camino' without being referred, there could be trouble for him –but especially for me. I've got to find out who stole this stuff. Call the cops? No, what the thief took was illegal in my possession. Hire a private detective? No, I can narrow it down to some student in the school, or even in my class –or on my team, or close to the team. Coach knew, with a high probability. *Chuck Taylor, that clumsy slob. I've got to give him credit, though, because he got in and out of here without getting caught –by security, me or by the seat of his pants.*

"So, Chuck, what did you pinch from Coach's office?" Detective Brown asks as they ride toward the Taylor's house.

"Some little things, nothing of value -I just wanted him to know that he's vulnerable, can't hide things."

"I could tell by the bulge in your back pocket that you're carrying something. Would you like to turn it over to me, or would you rather I frisked you?"

"Uh, but it's something…that's going to get Coach in trouble." Chuck says reluctantly.

"All the more reason to turn it over, son. My job is to find trouble – and bring it to justice."

"It's just a hunch, a feeling, and some words through the grapevine that make me believe Coach is – "Chuck hesitates.

"Coach is what?"

"Coach is dispensing drugs –legal drugs, but illegally prescribed to the guys on the team."

"Performance enhancing drugs?"

"How did you know?"

"I didn't know, until you told me, Chuck. Those are the usual drugs dispensed by coaches."

"There's something else, I don't know exactly for sure, but Coach is involved with Earl's mom."

"What do you mean *involved*?"

"I'm not sure, but I've seen them together, and there's talk –the neighbors."

"We'll get all this sorted out, but for now, turn over what's in your pocket."

Chuck pulls the sleeve of e-nhancers, single vial of Cuban tobacco nectar and the business card from his pocket, and hands them over to Detective Brown as they pull into the Taylor driveway.

38.

Earl sees Philly home and stands before her at the threshold of her front door.

"Are you OK, Earl?"

"I'm just –tired. The memorial service is in the morning and - I don't know. I think Mom, Pam, Tina and Emaw need me to be strong. Dad would want me to be the strong one –the man of the family."

"You *are* strong, Earl, but you're not alone. Pam and your grandmother are there for you and Tina. You're all there for each other. With all the trouble you've had to deal with in the past…"

"My mom, you mean."

"Yeah, but she seems better than in a long time," says Philly.

"I know, but in the past, she's been OK, almost back to normal, whatever 'normal' is, then she goes 'round the bend and crashes again. I'm afraid." He stops.

Philly begins. "It's OK to be afraid, and sad –and confused. Even though your dad's gone, his spirit is still here with you." Philly says.

"I do feel him –in here." Earl beats his fist over his hurting heart.

Philly hugs him hard, and he lightly pats her back, which comforts his heart. Earl quivers against her. Philly thinks, *He's like a giant to me, but giants and heroes have their weaknesses. Maybe I'm his weakness.*

"Philly," Earl sniffs. She looks up into his red, tearing face, "would you sit beside me at the service tomorrow? If you don't want to, I understand, but I feel…"

"Of course, Earl." she says. "I will sit, stand, go with you –whatever you need," she assures him. Her commitment is much stronger and higher than the orange bucket that held her to kiss him that first time at the fort. And the warmth of his letter jacket wrapped around her strengthens *her*.

"I'll be there with you, Earl, wherever you are. Hold my hand, lean on me, cry on my shoulder," she says.

Earl loosens his hug. Philly stands on the threshold. He leans in. She pecks him quickly on the cheek and steps inside.

"Good night, Earl. See you tomorrow." She smiles.

39.

Ester sits on the wooden stool by Tina's bed watching her sleep peacefully. *Tomorrow may be hard for her, seeing people who loved Cleve who are crying, or wailing in some cases. Her father has been a steady fixture since Tina was born, but he's been more like a friend of the family for all her almost five years. Pain has been only a short distance away, the closest of which was inside the womb of her mother. Tina doesn't realize the distant pain that her mom has, taunted and tormented by something unknown to her. Tina, the same name as the four-year girl killed in the tragic accident years ago.*

Tina, you're a special soul, bringing so much joy to me, a miracle that would not have happened were it not for the death of another. The other Tina - and the other mother - torment your mother. They were accidentally the source of Lila's pain and anguish. A stronger person would have felt the guilt but not allowed it to affect her husband, two children and the 'you' who were yet unborn.

"Wake up, sunshine." Ester sings to Tina.

Tina squirms and grunts like a newborn pup, kicking her feet at the covers hanging on to the blanket tucked under her chin. Ester scoots Tina over and squeezes onto the narrow space at the edge of the twin bed.

"What if we both just stay in bed today?" Ester asks. "We can get up later and make cookies and have a tea party."

"But, Emaw, what about the memory service you told me we were going to this morning?" Tina doesn't forget anything, so the family must be careful what they say around her.

"Oh, yes, you're right, Tina. Thank you for reminding me. If it weren't for your memory, I wouldn't have a memory." *Ah, the memories that I have because you've been here with me. If no other good comes of Lila's break downs, having this child negates all the bad.*

"You can get a memory when we go to the memory service, Emaw. Who else is going?"

"Your mom, Earl and Pam, Reverend Arnold, Chuck –a lot of people will be there."

"Will Daddy be there? He needs some memory, too," says Tina.

"Yes, Tina, your daddy will be there, too, but you won't see him."

"He doesn't need to be hiding. Daddy needs to come out and get some memory, too, Emaw," Tina insists. "I'm going to get my memory at the memory service, and you can have some more of mine."

"Honey, you're all the memory I need, but I do have a lot of memories of your daddy, so I guess I should share them." Ester begins. "When your daddy was about your age…"

"Four -almost five!" Tina announces, waving her five fingers before Ester.

"That's right, Tina, and your daddy was smart as a whip, just like you."

"Smart as a whip –like whip cream?"

"Um, sweet and good as whip cream, just like you," Ester goes with the whip.

"Can we make some to go with our cookies, after the memory service?"

"Of course, sweetie –now, back to when your daddy was a little boy…"

"I'm not a boy; I'm a girl!" Tina protests.

"All girl –but you've got a lot of your daddy's spunk in you," says Ester.

"I've got *spunk* in me? What's spunk? Do we need to go to the 'peed trisha', Emaw?"

"No, honey, you're OK. 'Spunk' is a way you act, like when you get stubborn and mad and stamp your foot that you don't want to do something."

"So, when I get mad, I've got spunk?" Tina asks.

"Yes, but also when you get excited and want to go play with the bigger kids because you think you're as big as they are, that's spunk." Ester says, giving Tina a big juicy smooch on the cheek.

"I got spunk because I have a tea party with a big girl like you?" asks Tina.

"You've got spunk when you get up out of this bed and wash your face and get dressed." Ester quickly pulls the covers off Tina and tickles her into a laughing frenzy. "Spunky!"

40.

"Do you really think I need to wear a tie, Dad? Last night Earl and the guys wore their uniforms." Chuck has the royal blue silk tie draped, unknotted around his neck.

"Today's different, son," says Mr. Taylor. "Earl will be wearing a suit, and we should be respectful of the family. You look handsome in that navy suit."

"Well, I hope I'm not the only guy dressed up –again," says Chuck.

"If you are, Chuck, I'm sure the ladies will be impressed. You'll at least look like a gentleman." His dad winks.

"OK, OK." Chuck heads back to his room for the neck tying endeavor. *Didn't they used to have clip-on ties? One Fathers' Day I even found one for Dad that zipped up –great idea!* He fumbles, loops, twists, un-loops, re-twists, end-over-knot, back through, under and over and through. *What an ordeal! Before next formal occasion, I'm going to find modern tie technology.*

He gets the tie done in a rather unstylish large knot, but it works. Kicking around the bottom of his closet. He finds the dark shoes he thinks will look with his navy suit. "Yes," he exhales as he pulls the shiny black high-top basketball shoes from the bottom of the closet, sits on the edge of his unmade bed, and slides the dark shoes over his white-socked feet.

Knock 'em dead –no disrespect intended –you handsome devil! Chuck gives a suave sideways smile to himself in the mirror.

"Chuck! Charlie! Are you ready to go?" Rae calls.

"Yes, mom!" Chuck sprints down the hall wearing his Sky Ball basketball shoes, laced instead of unlaced –formal occasion.

"Coming, dear," Charlie exits the bathroom, remembering to zip-check as he comes down the hall.

Rae leads the way out the front door, Charlie follows her, and Chuck quietly slides in the back seat, sporting his bulbous necktie knot and his shiny black high-tops.

They ride in the car on the way to the church, Mom asks, "Who dropped you off last night, Chuck?"

"Oh, sorry, I didn't mean to wake you." Chuck evades the question.

"You know I don't get to sleep 'til you get home, son. I was wide awake, listening to your father's snoring and for the front door to open," Mom says. "So, who dropped you off last night, one of the guys from the team?"

"One of the guys," Chuck begins a story. *She's going to find out somehow. I probably should tell her, maybe leaving out a few minor details.* "Well, I was walking past the school, when this cop –police officer –pulls up beside me and asks what I'm doing, where I'm going, where I live –all those questions."

"What were you doing," Mom asks, "out by the school at that hour?"

"I was," Chuck thinks quickly, not exactly lying, "getting something from the gym –for Earl."

"How were you going to get in the gym at that time of night?" Mom asks. Dad is scrutinizing their entire exchange.

"The security guard was there," he says honestly, leaving out the 'hiding from the security guard' part.

"So, did you get what Earl needed?" Dad chimes in.

"Yeah, got it," Chuck says abruptly, remembering the possibly important items he turned over to Detective Brown.

"So, who brought you home?" asks Mom.

"The officer was nice enough to bring me home." *And super nice not to arrest me.*

"Did that officer have a name, Chuck?" his dad asks.

"*Detective* Brown."

Detective Brown had come by the Taylor house the day Cleve died, asking Charlie and Rae a few *routine* questions, 'just for the record', he'd told them.

"Anything out of the ordinary?" he asked.

"Nothing –just that Cleve usually would have been at work instead of being at home that morning," Charlie had told the detective.

"Oh," Rae had volunteered, not really thinking it significant, "Coach Bruce came by the Cleveland's house right after the ambulance and police arrived."

"What's unusual about that, Mrs. Taylor?" Detective Brown asked.

"Not unusual, except I hadn't seen Coach Bruce at the Cleveland house before," Rae answered.

That same day, after leaving the Taylor house, Detective Brown had gone across the street to question the neighbors, Anna, and Bette.

Everyone has a different of perspective. Detective Brown believes in investigating 'natural causes' and 'suspicious circumstances' from all angles. One angle may show a friend of the family coming in to support

155

them, while another may reveal an acquaintance 'putting on appearances' as if he were truly a friend, but not. A look from inside a person, say Lila Cleveland or Coach Bruce, might get to the heart of the matter, the 'why', the guilt or the hateful deceit. These neighbors don't miss a thing.

Detective Brown had buzzed Unit A of the garden duplex first. Most traditional neighborhoods did not have duplexes like theirs, but Anna and Bette jointly owned the lot. The two ladies are sisters but have different last names; one or both may have been married previously. They were 'joined at the hip', whether they were sisters or not.

Anna opens the front door. "May I help you, young man?"

"Good afternoon, Ms. Anna, I'm Detective Brown of the Pine Wood Police Department." I'd like to ask you a few questions –just routine – concerning the sudden death of your neighbor, Mr. Cleveland."

"Sure, come in. We saw the whole thing, from what we could see from this side of the street," Anna says.

As Brown crosses the threshold, he enters the neighbors' world: a mirrored disco ball suspended from the ceiling in the center of the great room scattering stardust memories all around; a chrome framed Saturday Night Fever movie poster, complete with John Travolta in dance pose; an orange beanbag chair in the far corner with a golden smoked glass swag suspended above it; a glowing purple erupting lava lamp atop a small bookcase; and ultimately a dinner-plate-sized "Have a nice day!" smiley face above the kitchen counter. Detective Brown had entered Goofy World, like a Florida vacation with the kids, stepping into a historical and hysterical world of half a century ago: The 1970's.

"Wow." Detective Brown reflexively utters the expletive as he scans the room, wide eyed. "I mean, you have a nice place." He stands mesmerized by the tiny white stars of light emanating from the mirrored disco ball, peppering the ceiling, walls, and floor.

"Thank you. Have a seat Mr. –I mean Detective –Brown," Anna says pleasantly.

"Rowr!" the Sylvester cat, black and white like it's 70's celluloid cartoon animation, objects to Detective Brown sitting on him, if not for his quick feline reflexes.

"Sylvester, go sit on your window seat, and don't mess with Tweetie," she says as the little yellow bird chirps on his tiny swing in the wire cage above the window seat." Anna opens the blinds so the critters can see outside. "Sorry, Detective."

"No problem. We have a dog and a cat at home," he lies, attempting commonality with the neighbor, but really only having a dog –he's allergic to cats. *This won't take long.* He reaches into his jacket pocket for a vial of allergy snuff. He sniffs the medicine up his nose and squeezes his nostrils closed, holds, then breathes.

"Got a cold?"

"I'll be fine, thank you."

"I'll get some hot tea." Anna glides to the open kitchen of the great room and clanks a copper kettle onto the avocado green enameled electric stovetop. "Just a minute, Detective; this'll make you feel much better." She pops off the top off a tangerine-colored ceramic canister containing her own special herbal tea blend.

Detective Brown stands in awe of the hodge-podge of knick-knacks: little ceramic kitten statues, dance contest trophies, artificial silk flower arrangements and movie, music, and political campaign memorabilia on shelves and attached to the walls and ceiling. The jiggle of a metal knob on the door of the wall dividing the two duplexes. The door opens and in pops Bette from next door. The door-on-a-door opens 'in' to Bette's side and opens 'in' to Anna's unit, like adjoining hotel rooms in an old Holiday Inn. *Maybe this really is Goofy Land.*

After the first steep drop on the neighbors' 70's spacey mountain roller coaster Detective Brown settles back on the couch with his cup of Anna's herbal tea. It almost instantly settles his allergy symptoms and his stomach. *What are the special ingredients in this 'herbal' tea –and are they legal?*

Anna sits on the end of the couch opposite the detective, while Bette situates in the antique cane bottom chair pulled up to the edge of the coffee table, closer to Detective Brown. Bette had made a cup of tea for herself and returned to the living room with her cup and saucer and a plate of shortbread cookies, which she called 'teacakes'.

"Now, Detective Brown what might we do for you?" Bette extends the plate of teacakes to him. He accepts two.

"Yes, Detective Brown, you said you had some 'routine' questions to ask us concerning the death of Mr. Cleveland across the street," Anna says.

"Yes, ma'am, just wanted to ask what you might know of the Cleveland's, anything out of the ordinary or amiss this morning," Brown says.

"Like I said, our view was from this side of the street, and we couldn't see anything going on in the back of the house, where Lila found Cleve," Anna says.

"I understand. So, you knew Lila had found Cleve?" says Brown.

"She came out to meet the ambulance when it arrived, about nine o'clock I guess, and no one else ever came out after that," Bette says.

"No, no one else came out. Lila came back out in a few minutes – maybe fifteen –bawling her eyes out, extremely upset," Anna says.

"Did you go over and check on her?" asks the detective.

"We started to," says Bette, "but before we got to our curb a big man, Coach Bruce, came up and almost tripped over his feet to get to Lila."

"Are you sure it was Coach Bruce?" Brown asks.

"Looked like him to us –we talked about it –with him being the size of Coach, wearing the school jacket," Anna says.

"We've seen him in the neighborhood before, parked down the street in the circle, the cul-de-sac, standing by his VW pickup waiting and puffing on an e-cig," Bette says.

"What was he waiting for?" asks Detective Brown.

"We thought he might be there to pick up his star player, Earl Cleveland, but turned out not," says Anna.

"No, not Earl," Bette agrees, "but his mother Lila."

"Yes, Lila goes walking down the block, casually like she's just taking a walk," says Anna.

"And then she steps it up a bit when she gets to Coach's pickup and he flings the door open –without getting out -for her to hop in," says Bette.

"Seems like a gentleman would have gotten out and held the door open for a lady," Anna says.

"They ride off together. That's all," Bette says.

"We saw it several times before," says Anna.

"OK, ladies," Detective Brown finishes logging the data in his knopad, "Now, back to this morning when you saw Coach Bruce running over to Lila, when she was crying."

"He bumped into her, hard, almost making them both fall, but Coach Bruce caught her in a big grizzly hug," says Anna.

"How did she seem, glad to see him? Still upset –or more so? How did the situation look from your perspective?" Brown asks.

"Lila looked kind of startled at first," Bette says, "but then she started to get all serious, concerned, but not crying hard like she had been."

"Yes, Coach seemed to affect her mood. He had his arm around her shoulder, and then her waist –but she shook him off and said something serious to him. I couldn't tell what," Anna says. "Lila looked back toward us and said something else –I don't know what –to the coach. He didn't put his arm around her again after that," Bette says.

The two ladies look at each other and nod their heads as Detective Brown logs more notes.

"Anything else, ladies?" asks Brown.

"That's about it," Anna says.

Detective Brown sets his empty cup and saucer on the coffee table, Bette picks it up and offers, "Would you like another cup, detective?"

"No, thank you. The tea was excellent. *I feel really good.* Those teacakes just melt in your mouth."

"Why, thank you, Detective Brown, that's my grandmother's recipe which has been passed down through the generations since her family came to America some three hundred years ago," Bette says.

"Yes, her grandmother's teacakes," replies Anna. "These China teacups came over on a ship from England with my family about two hundred years ago."

"And when the teacups and teacakes and my special tea come together," says Anna, "there's something special."

"Well, it's been nice having tea and teacakes with you ladies." Detective Brown stands to leave. "You have been most hospitable sharing your view of this morning's tragic event."

"We've enjoyed having you, detective. If we can be of any further assistance, please call on us again," Anna says.

"Yes, please do," Bette agrees.

41.

Philly's mom, Glenda, gets out of bed at 9:30 am still wearing her nursing assistant scrubs from her third shift, 11 pm to 7 am. She feels as if she wears that uniform all the time –and she does, though the color and pattern vary, making her appearance slightly different from day to day.

The color of the cotton scrubs changes daily. Scrub tops, smocks, could be purchased from the Uniform Supply Store –or online –in dozens of different patterns including spring flowers, butterflies, songbirds, and smiley faces. Sometimes Glenda wished she could just wear plain white like her grandmother had worn as a registered nurse. Those uniforms were starched and pressed with the classic Florence Nightingale cap on top. Patients 'knew' you were a nurse. Simpler times, that's what they were, and much more professional than wearing cartoon characters on your back.

The shoes she wore reminded Glenda of her grandfather's collection of clown pictures framed in his study, so many years ago. That was a good thing, the goofy clown shoes reminding of her O'pa. She smiled putting on her funny bulbous shoes with sweet memories of O'pa.

Glenda was exhausted the day or two before her one day off per week. Her daughter, Felicity –her little Philly – tries to do so much at home so her mom can rest for the scarce time they have together at home. Philly works hard away from home, too, most weeks going to work at the hospital cafeteria three days for four hours after school. When Philly works the dinner shift at the hospital, she and Glenda get glimpses of each other, and the occasional word or smile –or hand touch or hug. One day, soon, Glenda will be a licensed nurse, an LPN, and Philly can be a teenager for a few years. Glenda had missed those teenage years, marrying, getting pregnant –not in that order -and having baby Philly, to escape her parents' home and all the 'stuff' there.

Glenda scratches her squirrelly blond head and scuffs her footies down the hall to the bathroom. The door is ajar an inch reflecting light from the makeup mirror into her squinty eyes. She bumps the door lightly with her hip.

"Philly, 'that you in there?" Glenda asks in her scratchy morning voice as she opens the door a few more inches, shielding her eyes from the harsh light.

"Yes, Mom, I just showered and washed my hair –getting ready to go to Earl's dad's memorial service," Philly answers from behind the shower curtain.

"That's today? I'm sorry, honey, I didn't know what day it was –or when the memorial was."

"It's OK, Mom. What are you doing up? You need more than a couple hours sleep. Go on back to bed," Philly says as she twists the towel around her wet hair and steps out of the shower. Tucking the large bath towel securely at armpit level, she turns to see that her mom has dropped her scrub pants to her ankles and is sitting on the toilet. Squinting from the glare Glenda sees Philly smirking at her.

"What? I had to pee," her mom says in a hoarse, half-awake voice.

"Excuse me, Mom." Philly takes the towel off her head and shakes her hair loose.

"What time's the service, honey?"

"Eleven o'clock, but Earl asked me to sit with him, so I need to be at his house in less than an hour." Philly combs her frizzed damp hair into smooth, silken strands.

"I should come," says Glenda as she steps out of her crumpled scrub pants, struggling to remove the purple flowered smock over her head. Philly frees her mom from the makeshift straight jacket and picks up her pants from the tile floor.

"Mom, why don't you go back to bed? You need some sleep." Her mom steps into the shower, pulls the curtain and steam begins to rise.

"I'll just take a quick shower –to wake me up a little so we can talk while you get ready."

"OK, but please promise me you'll go back to bed when I leave."

"I will, I will. So, what are you wearing?"

Philly hesitates, "Earl's sister Pam loaned me a dress. We're close to the same size, but the shoes are going to torture me."

"They're such a nice family. Pam's sweet to let you borrow"– her mom stops short, and Philly hears her sniffle a bit.

"Mom, it's OK."

"One day I'll be able to buy you nice clothes." Her mom blows her nose into her wet washcloth.

"I have plenty nice things, Mom. This is just a formal occasion, and I don't make 'formal' a habit," says Philly, disinterested in 'nice things.'

"If I'd had time, I'm sure I could have found a nice dress at the Vintage Store," Philly adds.

161

"But, I…"

"Mom, I love you, and it's OK. It's no big deal. Don't worry. Earl likes me in anything I wear," Philly says.

"Especially, I bet, in that cute little skirt you wore the other day." Glenda teases as she shuts off the shower.

"Mom!" Philly sings, embarrassed.

"Would you just throw me a towel, girl," Mom requests. Philly tosses the damp towel, which she had used to dry her own hair, over the shower curtain rod. "How about a dry one, please, smart girl."

Philly retrieves a fluffy dry white towel from the cabinet and tosses it over to her mom.

"Much better."

42.

"That was nice of you to loan Philly a dress," Lila says as she walks past Pam's bedroom.

"I think she'll look beautiful in the one I picked, and I know Earl will like it," Pam says, purposefully loud enough for her brother to hear.

Earl combs his hair back using a dab of the pomade that his dad always used. *It smells like Dad.* He inhales the fresh smell of pine on his hands.

"I can hear you, Pam!" Earl speaks loudly, echoing off the tiled bathroom walls.

"Well? It's a little short for my taste, but Philly likes short dresses. She'll need to wear some pearls or something with that low neckline. What do you think, bro?" Pam describes, knowing it'll get a rise out of Earl.

"Sounds like she'll wear it much better than you, sis. She's a bit younger than you, but more *developed.*" Earl attempts to get a rise out of Pam.

"Hey, maybe so, but I know how to use what I've got. Push 'em up!" Pam retorts.

"OK, you two!" Mom calls from the end of the hall.

"Sorry, Mom." says Earl, "She started it."

"I guess I did, being your elder," Pam says.

"I'm both your elders. Now, quit," Mom steps out her bedroom door. "Pam, you said Philly needs a necklace to wear with that dress. Here's a strand of pink pearl's your dad gave me years ago."

Pam is jealous that her mom would let Philly wear those, but she walks back to her mom's room to get them.

"I'll give these to Earl to put on his girlfriend, if he's not too nervous touching Philly's bare neck." says Pam.

"Let me get my hands around your neck and see how nervous you are!" Earl yells.

"Ooo, I'm a'scared." says Pam as she takes the pearls from her mom.

"Oh, and Pam," her mom pretends to suddenly remember something, "these white pearls, a double strand, will go nicely with your dress." She holds them in front of her, draped over both hands. "Your dad gave me these for our last anniversary. They're yours now."

Pam steps forward, taking the luminescent strands laced through her mom's trembling fingers, and hugs her mom. She turns her back to her mom, pulling her straight hair off her neck; Lila drapes the pearls around her daughter's neck and fastens the gold clasp on the fuzzy nape of her neck. Mother and daughter both trickle tears of joy.

"I miss Dad," Pam quivers in Mom's arms.

"I do, too. I really do, too," Mom squeezes her daughter even tighter. "Cleve deserved so much better than me."

"Mom, you couldn't help... "Pam pauses, "the way you were. He knew you were ill."

"God, I'm so sorry for all I've put you through. If I could go back and change, get Cleve back..." Lila says, crying harder, breaking down.

Pam holds her mother. "He knew you loved him, and he had the patience of Job, with you and all of us," Pam steps back and looks square at her mom.

"I love Cleve, always will," Lila says. "I hope he's forgiven me. I hope you all forgive me for being so –bad."

"You are not bad," Earl interjects. "You had no control over your head, your hurt and all that. Please, Mom, we love you. We never gave up on you, never. Yeah, you've been ill, but not 'bad', and you're better now. Stay well, Mom."

"Whatever has happened - or will happen –no matter what, I still and always will love you, Pam and Earl –and Tina." Mom wipes a tear from her eye.

Reverend Arnold strolls through the cemetery reading the names off the cold granite tombstones. *Henry Cleveland, Ester's husband, was the last of the family to be buried in this clay ground over twenty years ago.*

This is the one, Reverend Arnold unwraps the brown package from underneath his arm and sets the marble plaque in front of the columbarium cubicle reserved for Cleve. "Henry Earl Cleveland, Jr.," the inscription on the marble plate which will seal the urn in its cubicle. "A darned shame," he says as he re-wraps the marble. *Too young, but he left a sweet legacy, his children. God, help me to be there for Earl, and the family, but especially guide me to be a source of strength they no longer have. I know I'm not a 'father', but a pastor, a 'reverend' who will be what You want me to be to this family. Amen.*

As the prelude music plays softly through the speakers in the corners of the ceiling of the sanctuary, Charlie, Rae and Chuck Taylor walk down the center aisle, led by an usher wearing a charcoal gray suit, a striped gray, white and black tie, and white gloves. The usher stops at the second row from the front and, with hand motions like a traffic cop in the old cities – sans the whistle –directs the Taylor family to the opposite end of the pew. Chuck sits first; he likes the seat on the outer isle just in case he needs to make a quick exit.

Chuck scopes out the sanctuary, bobbing his head to the upbeat music from the 1980's, requested by the Cleveland family in Cleve's honor. Mr. Taylor plays it in the car every time Chuck rides with him. His dad is bobbing his head to the music and strumming in time with the beat. Mom catches Dad in the act and slaps him on the leg, audibly. Dad stops bobbing and strumming; Chuck gives him a nod and a smirk.

At the front of the sanctuary to the left of the podium is an 8x10 brass framed color portrait of Cleve, set with several small family photos clustered around him. White lilies and yellow roses frame the shrine to Cleve, but a small bouquet of yellow and purple violas tied loosely with a purple ribbon catches Chuck's eye. He knows that little centerpiece was picked and made special by Tina, with a little help from Ester with the ribbon.

The pair of ushers, with olive hued skin and black hair slicked back are dressed exactly alike in charcoal gray suit, striped gray and white tie, and white gloves. They alternate escorting small families of three and four, white haired couples, silver and blue haired ladies wearing stylish 1950's hats with flowers of muted colors of the rainbow and fascinators with feathers, and an ancient white haired lady hunched over from scoliosis wearing all black accessorized with a veiled black fascinator.

Most of the congregation has come to this 11:00 am memorial service, in addition to townspeople, neighbors (including Anna and Bette) and a few of Earl and Pam's high school teachers, the principal and guidance counselor - and finally Coach Bruce. The school faculty is seated on the pew with the Taylor's; Coach enters first and sits beside Charlie Taylor.

Charlie politely nods at Coach Bruce, the other teachers and faculty as they stand online and then sit in sync on the pew beside him. Rae leans forward, smiles and nods acknowledging her son's teachers. Chuck stares straight ahead, refusing to make eye contact with the coach.

Chuck dislikes the coach even more after *finding* the evidence Detective Brown confiscated. What is the connection between this *evidence* and Chuck's suspicion about coach? Is Coach here at the memorial *for show* only? Coach wasn't close to Earl, but what about to Mrs. Cleveland?

Mrs. Taylor derails Chuck's train of thought, patting his leg and whispering that some of his teachers and principal are here from school. "OK, OK," he whispers as he self-consciously leans forward and looks down the pew.

His science teacher, Mrs. Pettit, leans forward and demurely waves at him. Chuck waves back and smiles. He likes her because she piqued his curiosity in science and encouraged him to investigate things, to analyze causes and effects –what makes stuff happen and why. Ms. Pettit inspired him to get to the root of problems, to be curious and follow his instincts – like searching for evidence and clues in Coach Bruce's office last night. She wouldn't encourage breaking, entering and larceny, but she would understand why he had to do it –in a scientific sort of way.

He leans back in his seat and looks down the back of the long wooden pew. Coach is glaring at him, stone faced. *Could he know? How could he know that I was the one who broke into his office last night?* Coach smiles a slight, sly knowing smile, nods and averts his gaze from Chuck and toward Cleve's memorial table.

That cinches it. Coach is hiding something and suspects I've found it. This thought gives Chuck a boost of bravado; he glares at the side of Coach's head.

The music transitions to more religious tones of 'Amazing Grace' and 'Faith of Our Fathers' as the Cleveland family enters the sanctuary. Many heads are reluctant to turn and look as the family comes down the center aisle, but others are compelled to gawk. The ushers walk in cadence, one in front of the eldest male of the family, Earl, and the other bringing up the rear behind Ester and Tina. Lila is the center of the procession. Pam, Earl, and Philly break time with the ushers and quickly slide to the end of the pew. Earl sits down in front of Chuck, who places his hand on his friend's shoulder. Pam and Philly, on either side of Earl, turn and acknowledge the Taylor's. Lila stares intently at Cleve's memorial. Ester hustles Tina, wearing her frilly royal blue dress with white lace, along the pew to her seat beside her mother.

"But, Emaw, can't I take my Tiny Tina back out to the swings. She doesn't like it in the car by herself," Tina says.

"Shh," Ester whispers, "She'll miss us, sweetie, but we'll go out in a little while," softly reassuring her granddaughter.

"Daddy -that's my daddy up there!" Tina's attention flits as she stands and points at the portrait in the memorial.

"That's right," Ester hugs Tina and sets her on her lap, scrunching closer to Lila. "Remember what we said that your daddy's gone away and can't be here?"

"Yes, Emaw, it's nice they put a picture of Daddy for our memory," says Tina.

"Yes, Tina, this is the *memory service.*"

Tina relaxes in her Emaw's lap.

Ester nudges Tina a little closer to Lila, hoping for a little mother-daughter bonding.

Lila smiles and pats Tina on her white tights-clad leg, straightening the hem of her beautiful dress. "You look so pretty, dear."

"Emaw made this dress," Tina lifts the white lacy hem of the royal blue dress for Lila to see.

"She's very good, your Emaw. We're so lucky to have her," Lila whispers to Tina and smiles at Ester.

Pam leans her right shoulder against her 'big' little brother as he sits at attention, a head taller than the others but scared as a lost boy, holding Philly's hand to his right. Of the three Cleveland children, Earl had spent the most time with Cleve over the past couple of years. With Pam away at college and Tina living with Ester, Earl has seen his dad seeking escape through his work, becoming a workaholic –and getting further away from his son.

Earl flashes back to the morning his dad died. *Dad had seemed so laid back, with a twinkle in his eye and a lilt in his voice as if he were genuinely happy that morning. What was different that day? Did Dad have a premonition that this was it, that he had to enjoy these minutes with his son? How could Dad be so happy and at ease one moment, and his heart fail the next. Was his death 'natural' –or supernatural?*

Philly notices Earl slipping away in his thoughts, so she squeezes his hand firmly; Pam instinctively nudges her brother's shoulder. They bring him back. Philly feels his presence as he puts his shaky hand on her stockinged thigh, and she places her smaller hand atop his. Pam gives her brother a *look*. Philly smiles at her. *The touch is OK.*

What is *not* OK is happening down the pew past the Taylor's. Chuck's blood begins to boil as he watches Coach leaning forward, touching Lila's shoulder with his hand as he breathes something close to her ear. Lila lurches forward in her seat and turns to see Bruce too close behind her, smiling that same sinister smile he had shown Chuck moments earlier.

Earl, Pam, and Philly are unaware of this quiet altercation, but Ester, Charlie and Chuck have seen. Ester pulls Tina tighter to her bosom as she clenches her jaw and turns toward Bruce.

"Excuse me," stifled as a whisper yet commanding and not meant as an apology. Ester means *business*; the fox doesn't want to mess with the Cleveland's while Emaw's watching the henhouse. Coach rears back in his seat as if Ester had slapped his jaw.

Charlie Taylor clenches his fists, mulling whether to pummel Bruce in the church sanctuary. Chuck's suspicions are becoming affirmed.

His dad is not a violent or quick-tempered man, but Chuck recalls an incident as a four-year-old boy –probably his first memory. Chuck can easily conjure up the memories of that trip to the mall, just he and Dad.

His dad had finally found a parking space a mile away from the store. Or so it seemed to a four-year-old. They were shopping for a Christmas gift for his mom. While crossing the parking lot they'd almost been hit by two cars, blaring horns and screeching tires. His dad had waved his fist and said some words that Chuck would find out later shouldn't be uttered in Mom's presence. Reaching the curb, with their lives intact, his dad was holding Chuck's hand. Chuck wanted to do it himself, walk alone the long ten yards to the store's automatic doors, so Dad let go of his hand to give his son a little taste of independence.

Dad stood at the curb and watched proudly, his little man braving the great chasm between him and the store. As Chuck marched the 'no man's land' toward the entrance, a couple of careless boys, old and big enough to be men, came down the sidewalk, laughing and shoving each other. His dad hurried toward Chuck to pluck him from the big boys' drunken path. One of the boys, a big-gutted oaf, got off balance and bumped Chuck, sending him sprawling to the concrete sidewalk.

"Hey!" Charlie yelled in a powerful voice.

"Oh, sorry, man." The smaller of the two teenagers bent over to pick up the loudly crying Chuck who had scraped his hands.

"Don't touch him!" Charlie barked. "Chuck, it'll be alright. Come over here." Chuck stopped crying, wiped his face with his sleeve and dusted off his size 4 jeans.

"We were just…" the big boy started an excuse.

"Just nothing! You ran over my boy here and knocked him down." Dad's 'father' voice raised.

"But we..." The other boy stood, in a challenging stance, beside the first.

"But? But both of you better just get your butts out of here!" Charlie stood as tall as a giant; Chuck stood as tall as a four-year-old could –behind his dad.

The boys started looking like they might 'do' something, but as Chuck stood behind his dad, which he vowed from that day forward that he would do, his dad's clenched fists turned from red to purple. Dad stepped one foot toward the hoodlums and commanded, "Get out of here – get!" And the boys 'got'.

"You OK, son?" Dad asked as he squat down beside his son.

"Yes, Dad, I'm fine."

"Yes, you are, son. Yes, you are. Thanks for backing me up," Dad said proudly.

"Anytime, Dad," the little boy promised.

Rae put her hand on Charlie's arm, sensing the mounting tension. His right arm relaxes to her touch, but his left hemisphere adjacent Coach Bruce remains taut, surging with adrenaline –ready for fight, not flight.

Bruce feels the strengths of Ester and Charlie surrounding him and backs down like a cornered possum. But he knows that no civil person would confront him at a memorial service, and he grins like a possum.

Reverend Arnold enters the side door of the sanctuary. Wearing his usual pastoral attire, he approaches the Cleveland family in the first pew. Starting at the end of the row where Earl and Philly sit close together holding hands, the Reverend leans in and takes their hands in his and whispers a few words of sympathy, love, and encouragement.

He repeats the personal greetings with Pam, she nods and squeezes his hand. He moves down the row to offer his comfort to Lila, the widow. He lingers with Lila. Reverend Arnold nods and speaks, his mouth close to her face, with messages and thoughts shared between him, her, and God. He hugs her; she lingers in his grasp until he nods and gently pulls away. Pam leans in and squeezes Lila's arm, laying her head against her mom's shoulder.

Tina scoots off Ester's lap as the Reverend leans over and comes down to a child's level. The little girl takes hold around his neck, and he lifts her into a big hug. Tina wraps her white leggings around the Reverend's sides, her shiny patent leather shoes dangling around his waist, perched on his hip like a baby gorilla clinging to its mother. Tina whispers a loud and airy, "My Daddy." She points to the portrait at the front of the sanctuary. Sobs emanate from children's mothers throughout the congregation. The entire Cleveland family starts crying –except Ester. Ester maintains the strength of a matriarch. Silent tears trickle down her cheeks, which she quickly blots away with a tissue. The Reverend kisses Tina on her cheek, whispering *love* in her ear, releasing her into Ester's –and God's -care.

"It's OK, Emaw." Tina comforts her grandmother, touching her elder rouged cheek. "You having memories?"

Ester squeezes Tina tight and whispers, loudly, "Yes, sweetie, memories."

"Me, too," Tina nuzzles her head to her grandmother's bosom like a puppy, snug in a warm basket with its mother and the other pups.

Reverend Arnold walks to the podium at the head of the sanctuary breaking stride momentarily by Cleve's memorial table. Head down he grips the sides of the heavy honey oak podium like Moses grasping the stone tablets before his people.

"Let us pray."

"Our heavenly Father who watches over us with all His power and majesty, we give our thanks to You today for the soul of this good man Cleve. We thank you for the life that You gave him and for the gifts that You gave him to share with us and this beautiful family, for the love they share and the love they miss, now that Cleve is no longer with them –in body. Let them be comforted, dear Lord, by the memories…"

Tina whispers, as the four-year-old in excited remembrance. Ester hears, "Memories."

"…the memories of the good times, the memories of the hard times that You saw them through. We pray that you will be with these children, children who are becoming adults and children who play and pray and remember. Comfort this woman, Lila, who needs You now and has needed comfort in her trials, but is making it through the hard times, remembering good times, and longing for better times.

Lord, we pray that you will be a comfort to Cleve's mother Ester as she shares the love with her grandchildren, love that she gave so freely to her children.

Cleve was our brother, their father, her husband, her son, a child of God whose soul is now, and always has been, comforted by You.

We thank You, Lord, for the memories of our loved ones.

In the words of Psalm 25, David sang, 'To you, O Lord, I lift up my soul; in you I trust, O my God.'

In Jesus' name we pray, Amen."

The prayer hush lingers, then Reverend Arnold remembers the next verses from Psalms, saying to himself, *Do not let me be put to shame, nor let my enemies' triumph over me. No one whose hope is in You will ever be put to shame, but they will be put to shame who are treacherous without excuse.* Bruce comes to mind: *treacherous.*

The Reverend watched from the wings Lila's reaction to something Bruce said. *What did he say? What had he done?* He had heard the rumors –were they just rumors? –from the neighbors, and Chuck was suspicions.

Detective Brown had come early and slid into the back-pew before the service began. He's an observer, likes to sit back in the corners, on the fringes, watching the behavior of people in the mall, the bars –and in the church on this occasion. Behavior's like the sweet gestures of young lovers and Tina's whispered *memories.* And the fiery stares between Chuck and Bruce. Light and dark faces of humanity are reflected here in this *sanctuary.* The tensions sparking between Lila and Bruce and Charlie Taylor short circuit the memorial service, while concern from Detective Brown and the love from Reverend Arnold bring the power, the *sanctuary* back to the church.

Sanctuary? If evil can slither into the house of God, can anywhere be safe from the serpent?

The Reverend enlightens the congregation with memories of Cleve and the service closes with a short prayer.

"May the Peace of our Lord and Savior Jesus Christ be with you as you go and *Be of Good Courage* for He is with you always. Amen."

Courage. Chuck thinks as he stands with the congregation. His eyes follow the Cleveland's as the usher leads the family out the doors to the left of the podium. Ester and Tina exit first. Earl turns to follow Pam. Chuck puts his hand on Earl's shoulder. Pam puts her hand over Chuck's and squeezes while Philly hangs onto Earl's coattail.

"Thank you." Pam whispers to Chuck.

The usher closes the white wood paneled door behind the family.

Coach Bruce quickly steps up the aisle and exits the back-double doors before they can be propped open for the congregation. Detective Brown slips out the corner door at the end of the pew just as quickly, but more stealthily, than the coach. Chuck heads up the side aisle, having the strategic advantage of the aisle seat and exits the same door as Detective Brown. Chuck is startled when Detective Brown turns around the corner and grabs him, immobilizing Chuck's arms behind his back.

"What the…" Chuck blurts out within earshot of the congregation leaving the sanctuary.

"Keep it down, Chuck," Detective Brown barks.

"You!" Chuck grunts back, his arms aching as he struggles.

"Don't struggle, you'll hurt yourself"

Knowing he can't escape, Chuck relaxes a bit. "Are you going to arrest me now?"

"No, unless you refuse to go home with your parents," Detective Brown gives the ultimatum. "Where were you going in such a hurry?"

"You know where I was going, the same place you were going," Chuck says.

"I have it under control, Chuck. You know that he's probably figured out that it was you who broke into his office, don't you?"

"*Be of Good Courage* is what the Reverend said. I *be*," says Chuck.

"Well, I *be* here to back up your courage. Now go home with your parents. I'll let you know when I need you."

"Did you find out anything from that stuff that I found?"

"I will do my job, son. You just *be* at peace, or I might have to bring out the *rod and the staff* to *comfort you.*" He releases his hold but steers Chuck back down the aisle toward the Taylor's.

"Yes, sir." Chuck heavily sighs relief at his release.

"Just remember, *He is with you always*," says Brown. "Can I get an *Amen?*"

"Amen." Chuck grumbles away.

43.

Bruce reaches his rusty VW pickup parked on the fringe of the church's pervious paved parking lot before anyone else has a chance to leave. From the opposite side of the lot, Detective Brown hears Bruce's pounding fists like a war drum on the plastic roof of the vehicle. Coach spins across the parking lot and exits, dangerously fast. Detective Brown follows him from an unobtrusive distance.

He's either going to the school gym or a bar.

Bruce drives down on Main Street, exiting the city limits, and continues driving a couple kilometers to the business district just before the interstate highway. The sign beckons 'Highway Rest.' Bruce parks in front while Detective Brown parks in a spot concealed between the bar and the old hotel.

The two men have never met, but Bruce may have seen Detective Brown at the Cleveland house that morning. Doubtful of Bruce's powers of observation, or memory, Detective Brown casually walks into the little building. Bruce is already seated on a chrome stool at the counter inside, his e-pipe laid out, ready for an ampule from the dispenser. He spins the 3D rolodex virtual menu with his index finger, reaches his favorite alcohol delivery brand. A picture of a Wild Turkey brand is displayed on the 3D screen. The ampule pops up from the counter chute and releases the device only after Bruce waves his Unicard in front of the scanner.

Bruce loads the ampule into the end of his e-pipe as Detective Brown sits on the stool to his left. Bruce begins taking long slow draws on his pipe.

"I'm new to this, friend," the detective saddles up to Bruce. "How do I order if I don't have a pipe?"

Bruce pauses and points to the 3D menu. Without speaking, Bruce spins the menu until an image of a pipe, with a tube attached, appears. "Thanks," says Detective Brown.

The detective goes through the process of 3D ordering, and immediately a clear poly mouthpiece pops up from a chute on the counter. He selects the turkey logo, per Bruce's lead. After waving his Unicard at the scanner, the mouthpiece is released, but remains attached to a clear poly tube –like an umbilical cord. Detective Brown takes a puff. *Not quite like a shot of the real thing from twenty years ago, but probably more potent. I better go slow.*

With his ID still on the counter in front of him, Detective Brown slips his official detective shield beside it so Coach Bruce can see. Coach twitches his eyebrows, recognizing the enforcement *creds.*

"What do you want?" Coach asks, immediately perturbed.

"Just need to ask you a few questions, Coach Bruce."

"Shoot, Detective Brown," Bruce speaks confidently, with an edge of cockiness, as if he knows the detective, but only just now reading the name from the ID.

"Where were you Wednesday morning, Coach Bruce?"

"School," Bruce answers shortly.

"Anywhere else?"

"Hmm –oh, yeah, I went over to the Cleveland's house," feigning suddenly remembering.

"And did you know that Mr. Cleveland died that morning?" Detective Brown asks.

"Yeah, I got there that morning looking for Earl Cleveland, my star basketball player, he wasn't at school."

"And what did you find when you got there?"

"There was an ambulance, stretcher, I presumed it was Cleve because Lila –uh, Mrs. Cleveland –was beside the stretcher, crying hysterically," Coach says.

"Did you see Earl?"

"Since he wasn't out there with Lila –um, his mom –I figured he wasn't home," Bruce says, correcting himself sounding too familiar with 'Lila'.

"So, what happened after you saw Mrs. Cleveland 'crying hysterically'?"

"The sheet was covering Cleve on the stretcher, so that's probably why Lila –Mrs. Cleveland –was so torn up."

"Was anyone else there?"

"The usual: the EMT's with the ambulance, two police officers – uniformed."

"Anything else?"

"Of course, I went to…Mrs. Cleveland, and tried to console her, but she couldn't be consoled. Oh, and the two ladies from across the street were watching. They seemed kind of funny, suspicious, to me."

"*Funny* in what way?"

"They looked like they were coming over, but they changed their minds, I guess, and stayed tight together on their side of the street," Bruce says.

"Had you ever met those ladies?"

"No, not before the gathering at the Cleveland's last night –and we didn't speak."

"What about Mrs. Cleveland? Did she stay out and talk with you, or did she go back inside?" Brown asks.

"She didn't need anyone, like I told you, so we said our 'goodbyes.' I gave her a hug and she went inside. The two ladies were still standing by the curb when I left," Bruce says.

Bruce draws long and hard on his pipe, holding the vapors in his lungs to get the full effects of the Wild Turkey. Detective Brown takes a few short puffs, trying to stymie the inebriating effect –since he's on duty. Bruce pops the empty ampule from his pipe and orders another from the e-menu.

"Don't care for the Wild Turkey, Brown?" asks Bruce in a familiar sort of way.

"On duty, Bruce," says Detective Brown, "and I prefer *Jack* brand when I do alcohol."

"How about set me up with another Wild Turkey since I've put up with your questioning. This e-tap cuts me off after two vapor shots, but you could get me one on your Unicard -how about it, Brown?" Coach asks.

"You'll have to wait 'til you get home, Bruce. I can't contribute to the delinquency of a driver."

"My driving skills were impaired long before I had any alcohol," says Bruce.

Detective Brown recalls Bruce's driving from the church parking lot. "One more thing before I go –did you see Mr. Cleveland in the days just before his death?"

"Yeah, I saw him the day before. Came to my office to talk about Earl, college scouts recruiting him, grade –school stuff. We had a nice talk –nice guy," says Bruce.

"I hear he *was* a nice guy," says Brown.

"Changing the subject, let me ask you, detective, have you heard of any break-ins around the school area, last few days?" Bruce asks.

No other break-ins besides the one at Coach's office. Could the coach have found out that Chuck was there –and he, himself, was there?

Maybe the security guard spotted his car or Chuck getting in the car with him.

"No, haven't heard of any –why?" Detective Brown lies.

"Somebody came into my office through the window last night. My fault, I left the window open –too easy. Nothing taken, that I could tell," Bruce lies, "so I didn't report it. Just some kid poking around, I guess," Bruce says.

"So, why'd you ask?"

"Just curious if this was a single hit, or a spree," says Bruce.

"Do me and your neighbors a favor and if there's a break-in, report it –call the police. If there were others, we might be able to piece them together and find out who did it," says Brown.

"Will do, detective." *I'll get the punk who broke in before he puts the pieces together about Cleve.*

"Thanks for your cooperation. You're not half as bad as they say you are, Bruce," the detective jokes.

"Not *half* as bad, but *as bad* as they say?" Bruce laughs. "Sure, you won't spot me that extra Wild Turkey?"

"Good night, Coach," Detective Brown exits reading the sign, '*Airstream.*' *Appropriate name for a place streaming vapors. Wonder if they do oxygen shots?*

44.

Glenda arrives her usual fifteen minutes early. She stows her lunch in the staff refrigerator behind the data station. Philly has been preparing lunch for as long as she can remember. The first being peanut butter and jelly when Philly was ten years old, progressing to bologna and mayo sandwiches and now, fresh salad, fruit, yogurt, and leftovers -when any remained. Not merely the meal, but the thoughtfulness in preparing it, made Glenda feel she was living *not by bread alo*ne, but by love.

Changing catheters and disposing of waste products drained from patients' weary orifices were not mundane tasks for Glenda. She empathized with her patients. She would brush the snow-white hair of the ninety-two-year-old lady, Tempie, who couldn't open her eyes nor speak to express her pleasure and gratitude but drooled and wiggled her least arthritic finger.

The seventy-five-year-old red-turned-cotton top Irish American, Ray, told Glenda funny stories and made her laugh while she changed his catheter. A debilitating infection had sentenced him to daily humility and brought humanity in the person of Glenda. Even though the tasks were cold, noxious, and sometimes painful to the patient, and for Glenda, the *cotton-top* had continued sharing his wisdom throughout the procedures. He told his newly adopted nursing assistant, 'It's the presence, not the presents,' as he had reminded his children every Christmas. 'I'm just glad you're here, Glenda. You are my present that makes all this bearable.' He cried when he was finally discharged. Glenda wept happy tears as the hospital volunteer wheeled Ray down the hall to his waiting family. He was a Ray of hope for Glenda.

Philly, at once complex and complicated, understood things in their simplest forms and brought them down to earth. Glenda wondered where Philly had gotten her gifts. After working in the hospital, discovering her own gifts, she realized they shared their tendencies for caring and empathy. *At the age of fifteen, Philly has become what took me almost twice her lifetime to realize.*

Glenda wipes the old man's brow and combs his sparse silky hair across his pink scalp. She grasps his hand and says, "Now you call me when you need anything, Mr. Murphy," knowing that he was too proud to ask for anything. "I'll be back in a few minutes." And she would be. With patient 'loads' –she despised that term –so low, she could offer more physical contact to the people she served. One personal visit per hour with each of her four patients was a lot of work but rewarding for both the patient and for Glenda. Would she love her job even more when she becomes a licensed nurse, or was CNA work the most rewarding she would ever have? *Yes, this is as good as it gets,* but she couldn't keep this pace forever. That's for the young twenty-year old's getting their feet wet and loving the heart of nursing –or despising the grunt work and leaving the field.

Philly could be happy doing any kind of work. She has so much love and enthusiasm for life. Something special is awaiting my little girl; she can make anything special. God how I love that girl.

This tuna salad is scrumptious. How does she do it? Glenda takes a bite of the sandwich, followed by a celery stick. She could go down to the cafeteria, but since Philly's not working these last few days, no reason to. Glenda has a little stool in the corner of the nurses' data station, with an old gray metal two drawer filing cabinet as her dinner table, draped with a red and white checkerboard napkin Philly had packed. *Ten minutes, I'll take ten minutes -can't leave my patients too long.*

The coroner, Dr. Limedge, comes to the nursing station counter and pages Detective Brown. The detective had come to the hospital to meet the doctor, but she'd left her earwig down in the morgue. "Can't keep playing this cat and mouse game," Glenda hears her say.

Glenda covers her mouth and mumbles through a mouthful of tuna sandwich and celery, "No."

Dr. Limedge stands at the counter shaking her head as she reviews the lab results on the pink sheet of paper. The in-house phone buzzes and she answers it.

"Yes, third floor nursing station. You're on your way up the elevator? See you in…" The elevator doors open.

"It's about time, Carl. Got your lab results." She rustles and waves the pink paper as Detective Brown walks from the elevator.

"I might need an interpreter for this, Jackie," Detective Brown says, clucking his tongue and shaking his head as he slides the paper closer to her. They lean on the counter elbow to elbow as Jackie taps her pen on the paper.

"I'll translate for you anytime." She nudges him with her elbow, flirting. "Just tell me what language you want, and I'll do it."

"How about English, not 'lab-speak'? What the heck are all the numbers, decimals, and percentages? Is this science or math?" Carl nudges her back.

"Science *and* math, rookie." What do you want to know?"

"Everything. Start at the top."

She begins reading off numbers and percentages, high and low levels of each gas, element, mineral and electrolyte. She speaks in a monotone up to a point, when Glenda overhears Detective Brown raising his voice in surprise.

"That's awful high, isn't it?" Brown asks.

"It's way above the maximum acceptable level for a healthy man his age," the coroner explains.

"What about for a diabetic who had nothing to eat that morning before his death?" the detective asks.

"Mr. Cleveland was diabetic?"

Glenda perks up when she hears the name. *Why are they checking all this now? Did he die of something other than natural causes?*

"Yes, he was diabetic," Carl says. "He tried to keep it quiet –didn't want people knowing about his 'weakness' –so he told only a few people close to him."

"This much sugar would maybe throw a healthy person into a diabetic coma, but these levels would likely kill a diabetic." Dr. Limedge says.

Kill? Glenda chokes a little on the bread crust. The coroner looks over, realizing that the CNA has been there all along.

Detective Brown takes something from his pocket and lays it on the pink lab sheet. The ampule sits harmlessly until the detective asks in a hushed voice, "Would something like this deliver the dosage for that?"

Jackie holds the ampule between her thumb and index finger and examines it closely through her golden rimmed reading glasses: "e-nhance." She raises her eyebrows as she continues reading the microscopic information.

"This is prescription strength, that much sugar could kick start a horse –or *kill a diabetic.*"

Glenda strains to hear more of the conversation but cannot get beyond *kill.*

"OK, Jackie, I have to go. Can I keep this copy?" Carl asks.

"Sure, it's a copy, but legal with my signature on it –see?" Jackie points to her signature. "By the way, where'd you get that ampule?"

"Privileged info." He slips it back in his pocket. "The story will be out soon enough."

"Bet it'll be a *sweet* story," Jackie says.

"Bye, sugar." Carl heads down the hall towards the stairwell exit. *Something's funny about Mr. Cleveland's death? 'They' said 'natural causes' before, but this isn't natural. He's cremated to ashes now. Who'd want to kill Mr. Cleveland?*

Glenda tucks her lunch bag away. *What would this mean to Earl and his family? Should it mean anything? This kind of revelation could push Lila over the edge. She doesn't need to go there again. Earl, Pam, and Tina could really use their mother back home. Lord, watch over this mess.* Glenda prays a little prayer.

Detective Brown knows it's too late to gather the evidence to ask a judge for a warrant. It's after five o'clock on Friday. And the evidence is all circumstantial anyway. He needs something else, a false move, or misstep by the one and only suspect. All Carl can do is sit tight and stay on Coach Bruce's tail for the weekend.

45.

Exhaustion has settled in at the Cleveland's after this emotional day. Most don't feel like eating, but Philly, the natural caregiver, is preparing a magnificent Italian pizza. Comfort food for the family. She has discovered their amply stocked pantry and refrigerator: Mozzarella, cheddar, and parmesan cheeses; pepperoni, Italian sausage, and baked ham; garlic, onions, mushrooms, and green bell peppers; bread flour, yeast, and olive oil. *Yes!* Philly grins as she rummages through the kitchen for hidden ingredients like a five-year-old searching for Easter eggs.

"Need any help finding anything?" Lila calls to Philly from the living room.

"No –um, I might need a hand. Would you send in Earl?" He probably has no idea how to get around in his own kitchen, but she can guide him.

Earl pushes open the swinging doors and puffs out his chest, superhero fashion, wearing his gray sweats and white socks. Everyone is casual this evening, relaxing from the formality of the memorial service. Philly is casual now, sporting her mom's hand-me-down scrubs.

She arranges mixing bowls, measuring cups and spoons, pizza pans and stones and all the ingredients in extreme military fashion. She doesn't really need Earl's assistance -only his audience -but starts asking questions to include him on the process.

"Earl, would you hop up on that stool and get me that big mixing bowl? This one's not big enough to make all this dough." She sweetly sings.

"Sure, Philly, I'd do anything for you." Earl winks and two-steps up the stool. He grabs the wooden bowl, starts to wobble; Philly grabs the back of his thigh.

"Nice butt." She giggles.

Earl steadies himself. "Excuse me, madam, but your hand is on my derriere."

"Hey, I just saved your professional basketball career –and maybe your life," Philly gives him a pinch before unhanding his thigh.

"You two alright in there?" Lila calls out from the living room.

Pam follows with, "Yeah, need any help?"

"I'm available, too." Chuck pipes in.

"You guys," Philly calls back, "I'm perfectly competent... and Earl's my sous chef, taking up my slack."

181

"Sure, you don't want us to pull Earl back? He may be more trouble than he's worth," says Pam.

"I got it, Pam," Earl calls back.

"Keep an eye on his derriere, Philly," Pam says.

"Hey, who's been listening at the door –Chuck?" Philly yells.

"Just keeping Earl on his toes, Philly. Protecting your honor," Chuck snickers.

"I don't know about you guarding anyone's honor, Chuck," Pam says.

Chuck looks at Pam who's sitting on the opposite end of the couch. *I know she's just ribbing me, but sometimes I just wish she'd take me a bit more seriously. Not that I have some sort of complex, but I would just like a little respect -like Earl gets. Pam has always been nice. She's four years older than me, but I'm not that little boy I was when we met; I'm sixteen years old - 'most a man. She did ask me to go with her and Earl to college this weekend.* He did not want to admit it to anyone, but he had a crush on Pam since he was ten and she was a blossoming fourteen-year-old.

Pam says, "Chuck, calling Chuck -come back to earth. Where are you?"

"Just thinking –I do that, you know," Chuck challenges Pam.

"I have always known, you're a very thoughtful person." Pam says.

"Why, thank you," Chuck says politely. "I will attempt to guard your honor this weekend Pam. With Earl and me as your personal bodyguards, you will have nothing to fear!"

"My life's in your hands, Chuck."

I know she's just kidding, but 'I will do my best to do my duty', as we Boy Scouts say –or used to say. I will prove myself and show her –and Earl, that I can be the star, the hero when called on.

"You can count on me," Chuck stands at attention.

"OK, but one thing – "

"What?"

"Please don't wear those baggy carpenter pants to college this weekend." Pam pleads. "They don't flatter your form."

"What do you suggest I wear, Pam, to *flatter my form?*" *What's wrong with my carpenter pants?*

"Let me take a look at your wardrobe –if you'd like."

Yes, I'd like. Chuck thinks and says, "You'd really help me *style and accessorize?*"

"Just let me see what the possibilities are –after dinner?" Pam says.

182

"You want to come over after dinner?" Chuck asks.

"Sure. We're leaving early in the morning, so we'll have a full day - before the nightlife. I need to dress you up like a college man."

"I trust you."

"*Trust me?* That could be your downfall, Chuck," Pam says.

Ester and Tina are sitting Indian style at the coffee table sipping tea using Pam's revived Japanese teacups. Lila approaches their game, not a game for Tina, but a growing stage for a young lady going on five years old.

Tina carefully sets her pink-flowered porcelain cup on its matching saucer then lifts the teapot to pour the magical tea.

"Care for more tea, Emaw?" Tina asks properly.

"Yes, please." She sets the cup so Tina may pour. "Thank you, dear."

"You're welcome."

"Lila, would you like to join the ladies for a cup of tea –and biscuits?" asks Ester. Lila is standing at the end of the coffee table hoping for an invitation.

"That would be lovely, Ester. Is there enough tea for me, Tina?"

"Why of course, Mother," Tina says, putting on airs. She pours a cup for Lila and places it on the table as Lila kneels at the end of the table. "Would you like a delicious biscuit, Mother?"

"Yes, thank you." Lila takes a shortbread from the small plate in Tina's hand.

"But Mother we're sitting *crisscross apple sauce* at this tea," Tina says, using the sitting term she had learned from Ms. Lilith in her Sunday school class.

"What we used to call *Indian style*." Emaw brings Lila up to date.

Lila shifts uncomfortably to the cross-legged position, bumping her shin on the table edge. Grunting all the way to the floor, she lifts her teacup from its saucer shaking so much the porcelain pair rattles like chattering teeth from a chill.

"Mother let me show you how." Tina lifts the dainty cup with her right hand, pinky finger pointed out, and takes a sip with a 'sippy' noise. "See?"

Lila carefully mimics Tina's tea technique, to the grinning delight of her daughter. Then she sits up straight and takes a bite of the biscuit.

"These biscuits are tasty, Tina. Did you bake these?" Lila asks.

"I helped Emaw cut and bake them."

"She's a big help in the kitchen," Ester beams. "Hey, Tina, I have an idea. Why don't we ask your mom to come for a sleepover?"

"Yeah, we could have a big girl tea party at the card table –with Tiny Tina!" says Tina excitedly. "And we could bake cookies and play dress up and – "

"So, Mom is invited?" Ester asks.

"Definitely -want to come over to Emaw's house -Mom?" Tina hesitates a bit, not used to the term of endearment. Ester is extremely proud of Tina's manners. *She's such a good girl.*

Lila swallows and blinks her eyes, brimming with motherly tears. She truly wants to be a mother to Tina, though she lacks the confidence – and she doesn't want to try replacing Ester. Ester has something that comes naturally, for which Lila can only strive to get back, that maternal instinct.

"I would love to be your guest for a sleepover," Lila says, longing to reach out and hug her daughter, but fearful and tearful.

Tina sets down her teacup, hops up and smoothes her dress as she stands beside Lila. Observing the slivers of tears sliding down her mother's cheeks, Tina says, "Don't be sad. It's happy!" and hugs her mother around the neck. Lila cannot resist kissing the sweetness of Tina's lily petal cheek.

"I am so happy, Tina! You make me happy, my sweet girl," Lila says.

"Emaw, you put the dishes away, and I'll help Mom pack her sleepover bag, OK?" Tina delegates and organizes –like her big sister, Pam –and Philly.

"Sounds like the plan, Tina," Ester says.

Tina stands back arms' length from her mother and offers her hands, "Come on, I'll help you up!"

Lila struggles off the floor, holding Tina by one hand, pushing off the coffee table with the other. She stretches and shakes the stiffness out of each leg. Tina pulls and leads her toward the bedroom.

"Come on, Mom, let's pack your bag and go to Emaw's!"

"What is that wonderful aroma, Philly?" Ester asks.

"That's her gourmet pizza, Emaw," Earl says.

"I wouldn't call it *gourmet*," says Philly. "It's more like a garbage pizza."

"One gal's garbage is another girl's gourmet," Ester says.

Pam comes in the kitchen where Philly is threshing the large wooden bowl of mixed greens, red onions, tomatoes, and a medley of other fresh and salvaged veggies from the fridge. Philly, not accustomed to such a well-stocked kitchen, is overwhelmed by the volume of old brown vegetables which she must cull in her mission to concoct a fresh salad. At home she would never allow food to go to waste, and her mom appreciated Philly's conscientious and thrift management of their household, especially the food budget. Philly and her mom had talked about how her talents and abilities could take her to pinnacles as a restaurant manager or chef. Philly imagines herself playing the roles tonight as she offers the salad tongs to Pam and dons oven mitts to retrieve the hot pizzas.

"Shall I serve the salad?" Pam asks, totally willing to help Philly fulfill this dinner endeavor. "This is marvelous, Philly. How'd you learn to do all this?"

Philly doesn't remember how or when the cooking and household management began. She only knows her mom had taught her a few basics, and she got better with trial and error. There were loads of cooking errors in the process. Philly was her own teacher, home schooling herself in the kitchen through time and experience.

"Oh, it's just a thing," Philly says.

"A big 'thing', Philly. I'm impressed. I know that you impress my brother with your cooking, too," says Pam.

"He's very impressionable," Philly bats her eyelashes at Pam, sharing some unsaid secret.

"Chef Felicity's fabulous *sah-lahd*." Pam sings, dances, and flutters around the table, twirling once and twice as Tina, wide eyed and grinning, claps, and wiggles in her chair. She serves salad beginning with Ester's plate, then Lila's. Pam says, "Oh, I'm *offering* salad, but *no one may refuse*." She raises her eyebrows at Chuck.

Philly bursts from the kitchen carrying a giant pizza in her mittened hands. "Voila! Philly makes a pizza, too!" with a cheesy Italian accent.

Earl tags behind, a bit less confident than his girlfriend, but following her cheesy lead, "A pizza here, a pizza there!" They place a pizza on a trivet at each end of the dining table.

"What kind of pizza?" Chuck asks.

"What kind do you like?" Philly asks back.

"Italian sausage, olives –but no anchovies," says Chuck.

"Yes, yes, and no to those, Chuck. Most anything else you name would be a *yes* –garbage pizzas!"

"Ew!" says Tina as she crinkles her nose, a 'yuk' face.

"Yours is special, Miss Tina," Philly says. "I knew you didn't take any *garbage*, so I made you a whirligig pizza."

Ester emerges from the kitchen carrying a much smaller eight-inch personal pizza with only sauce and cheese, topped with a spinning pin wheel –a whirligig.

Tina smiles, sits back in her seat as Ester places the custom pizza on the large dinner plate before her.

"Philly, Ester, you're going to spoil that child," Lila says.

"She will never spoil, Lila," Ester says. "Tina will stay fresh as a daisy and sweet as a lamb."

Lila marvels at the happiness nurtured by Ester. But sadness overtakes her suddenly, but only for a moment, before peace returns to her.

"Thank you, Ester, for Tina –and for Cleve," Lila says. "You've been very good to us."

Ester places a hand on Lila's shoulder as she stands, and watches Tina break a piece of crust from the edge of her pizza and dip it in her cup of milk.

Philly taps her water glass with her spoon to get the family's attention.

"Let's say a little blessing before we eat," Philly says.

Tina is the first to respond by putting down her pizza crust. She knows the drill from Ms. Lilith's Sunday School. She bows her head and closes her eyes and peeks through squinted eyes at Philly.

"Earl, would you do the honors?" Philly squeezes his fingers.

Earl sits at the head of the table, his mother, grandmother, and little sister grace the opposite end. Memories of the Cleveland family at some point many years ago gathering like this, with a father who carved the turkey, a mother who laughed and flitted about the table doling out heaping spoonful's of green English peas and dollops of creamy mashed potatoes on her children's plates.

"Earl?" Philly brings him back.

"Oh." He clears his throat. "Let's all join hands." He suggests something his family had never done.

Philly squeezes Earl's hand again and beams up at him, so happy to be here. Ester and Lila take Tina's small outstretched hands. Chuck pokes Earl's arm and reluctantly offers his young manly hand to another young man. Pam giggles. Chuck grasps Pam's more mature college sophomoric hand, a bit too tightly, and she kicks his leg underneath the table.

"Ow!" Chuck yelps.

"Fair play," says Pam.

"When are we going to pray?" Tina *unbows* her head and opens her eyes toward Ester.

"Any minute, sweetie. Earl's letting the Spirit move him," and Ester winks at Philly. Philly blushes and looks down at her plate.

"Let us pray," says Earl as his hand holding Chuck's begins to feel clammy. "Dear Lord, we thank You for all our many blessings, together this night. Thank You for the family that's here, and" –he swallows a lump in his throat –"our dad, who can't be here" –he swallows again –"but is with us always, and with You now."

Lila's grip pulses in Tina and Pam's hands as she stifles a tear and sobs. Tina and Ester sit firmly, unemotional, but for different reasons. Tina doesn't understand, but Ester understands all too well, but must be the strong one.

Feeling Pam's slight trembling weep, Chuck firmly grasps her hand, and she feels his strength. She opens her eyes and catches Chuck peeking; he reddens and looks down bashfully. *It's fine*, she thinks as she gives his hand a little squeeze of confirmation.

"Thank You, Lord, for friends." Chuck jostles Earl's hand.

"Thank You for this scrumptious pizza and salad -and the hands that prepared it." Earl says, squeezing Philly's hand.

"Be with us. Bless this food to the nourishment and strength of our bodies. Guide us and protect us as we go. In Jesus' name we pray, Amen." Earl gives a little tug and squeeze to his friends' hands and opens his eyes. "Let's eat!"

"Philly, you've outdone yourself. This is the best pizza I've ever eaten," Lila says as she hands her crusts to Tina who knows crusts are perfect for dunking in milk.

"Thank you," Tina continues to dunk.

Unaccustomed to so much praise, Philly starts to feel overwhelmed. She has never required a lot of praise; self-motivation is her way. Mom's so busy that she forgets to say 'thank you' many times, but Philly knows her mother, her love is appreciation enough. Her dad, absent a third of Philly's fifteen years, always heaps on the praise in his regular, though infrequent letters.

"Cooking for you all has been a pleasure. I love your kitchen! Happy to prepare something more gourmet than pizza anytime –a more formal affair." Philly rises from her chair and starts gathering empty plates. "Earl,

I could use a little help." he doesn't really need his help, only his companionship.

Earl starts stacking salad bowls and carrying them to the kitchen. He follows Philly, so closely that he narrowly misses being hit by the swinging door.

"Right behind you, Philly," he says balancing bowls.

Lila turns to Pam. "So, you think you can handle these two young bucks this weekend at college?"

"I know I can keep reins on brother Earl, but this young buck Chuck –not so sure about him." Pam wink-smiles at Chuck.

"I think Earl and I will be taking care of Pam, Mrs. Cleveland," Chuck says. "The wild weekends she's told Earl about– "Pam cuts him off.

"I exaggerate, Chuck, to make it sound adventurous and daring because mostly what we do is boring –studying, learning volumes of pertinent knowledge." Pam lays it on heavy to counterweight the *wild weekend* comment.

"I'm sure this weekend will be a learning experience for all three of you," Lila says.

"Mm-hmm." Pam again looks at Chuck.

Chuck says, "You want my parents to give us a ride to college?"

"That old Prius will be packed with the five of you." Lila says. "Pam, I've been considering. How do you feel about driving your dad's car?"

Pam almost falls off her chair. "Driving Dad's car?" she parrots.

"Yes, the car's just sitting, parked, serving no purpose. I'm changing the registration, putting the title in your name, Pam," Lila says.

"You mean Dad's little blue electric is mine?"

"Yes, Pam, I trust you. You're responsible. You've living on your own for two years already."

"Mom!" Pam teeters toward her mom, gently hugging and kissing the side of her neck.

Lila wraps her arms around her daughter, flooded with memories of hugs gone by.

"You can trust me, Mom."

"I always have. I'm sorry I haven't shown you more trust and love."

"Mom, we always knew you were here, and yet far away in your thoughts. I think you're here to stay now, Mom. You're doing great.

"Wish your dad was here. He never lost hope that I'd be whole again; all those visits with me at the hospital kept me from falling into the abyss. Your dad, I love him. He loves you. We always will." Lila holds Pam at arms' length absorbing the image of her grown up daughter as tears pool in both their eyes, ready to trickle over.

"I love you, Mom. The car is just a thing," says Pam.

"-but a thing from your dad. He would have given you the world if he had it to give. God, I miss him –so much. I'm sorry…" Lila fades, regretting her marital betrayal, dragged away by Bruce when she was vulnerable.

The guilt presses on her mind. *I pushed him to the limits, the pressure was too much for his heart. Cleve had such a big heart. If I hadn't betrayed him, would he be home with his family today? We need you, Cleve! What happened? You were the strong one. I broke your heart. I killed you! I drove a stake right into your chest, bursting your heart. I killed you! I was too weak to resist –that devil! Please, forgive me, Cleve. Forgive me Pam, Earl, especially Tina - and Ester.*

"Mom," Pam caresses Lila's hands which are shaking, "it's going to be OK. I'm here. We're all here and love you so much. Please, stay with us; don't go away again. We are here, Mom."

Pam's dark mascara streaks like war paint. Lila feels like she's still fighting that battle. *Don't let me go down to defeat. Pick me up, Lord. Help me be strong. Defeat this devil, this trickster who fooled me. Damn him!*

"Thank you, Pam. You are my strength, my hope, my sunshine," Lila says.

"Don't cry, Mom," Tina interjects. "We're going to Emaw's and have a tea party and sleep over. I already got your bag packed. It'll be fun –and no crying!"

"That's right, Lila. It'll be good for you to get out of this house. Tina's excited about you coming for a visit. She's the best medicine for the blues, or anything else that ails you," says Ester.

"Blue is one of my favorite colors!" Tina says.

"And it looks good on you, too," Lila says. "I'll just go wash my face and grab my bag, and I'll be ready to go."

"I'll come carry your bag for you, Mom!" Tina says.

"Come on!" Lila holds out her hand and they head down the hall.

"Philly, this was such a lovely meal," Ester says. "Can you all handle the cleanup without us three ladies?"

"No problem," says Philly. Pam and Chuck are going over to the Taylor's to 'coordinate' Chuck's wardrobe for the weekend. *When they're out of the way, Earl and I can take care of the rest.* She smiles slyly.

189

"You young folk be good," Ester says. "Come on, gals!" she calls down the hall. "Let's go to the 'doll house'," she laughs. "It's a sleepover!" Ester is as excited as a girl having a slumber party with her girlfriends.

After Ester and the girls leave, Pam walks over to Chuck, the only one seated at the dining table, and socks him in the upper arm.

"Ow!" Chuck exaggerates, but really feeling the knot cinching in his triceps. "What was that for?"

"Got your attention, didn't it?" asks Pam.

"Yeah, what do you want then?" he asks.

"I'm on a mission, Chuck, to get you out of those baggy jeans..." Pam blushes realizing what she's just implied. "And into some more *collegiate* wear."

"Oh, yeah," Chuck says, as sharp as a tack and catching what Pam had just said. *She wants me.*

"Philly, Earl, what's going on in there?" Pam yells, attempting to change the subject with Chuck. She hears a metal pan clang to the floor.

Earl, red-faced and guilty, rushes through the door. "Nothing, what's all the yelling? You just about scared us to death!"

"You look guilty, Earl," says Chuck. "Y'all keeping your hands on the table?"

"Yes, Chuck!" Philly yells from the kitchen, washing pans and pots in the sink. *Except Earl just came up behind me and put his hand around on my stomach –startled me, and I dropped a pizza pan.*

"What do you want, Pam?" Earl is irritated.

"Just wanted to know if you and Philly can handle the clean-up," Pam says.

"Well, since Philly's handled most everything else" Earl hesitates, thinking he may have just offered some teasing ammunition to Chuck and Pam. "I'll help her with the rest."

"OK, bro, you handle her, and I'll handle Chuck," Pam says, also open to comical ridicule. "We're going over to Chuck's house –right, Chuck? –and get him *prim and proper* for college. You know what I mean?"

"Um-hmm." A bit puzzled Earl cocks his head to the side and lifts his eyebrows at Chuck before smiling mischievously.

"The guy needs help, Earl," Pam says.

"Thanks, Pam," Chuck says sarcastically.

"You know what I mean, Chuck –nothing personal," Pam says.

"I know what you mean. Help me, Pam." *I was hoping for the 'personal'.*

"You going to miss me, brother?" Pam asks.

"Always –love ya," says Earl as he shoos them out the door.

"Hold on, hold on, bro. We're going out the back way to speak to Philly who's slaving away in the kitchen while you're out here working your jaws," says Pam. "Come on, Chuck." She grabs him by the sleeve and pulls him toward the kitchen door.

"Philly, I know my brother Earl is very capable," says Pam. "Just give him some commands, and he'll do what you want. Shoot, just give him some treats, and he'll do what you want - he's so smitten with you."

Earl looks at the floor and blushes, walks over to the rinsing sink, and takes the freshly washed pot from Philly. She slathers his left 'catching' hand with soap bubbles, handing him the clean pot; her hand lingers. He blushes again. *Should I really be alone with Philly? She excites me so! Got to restrain myself. She's so young. Come to think of it, I'm so young –too young.*

"We'll be fine, Pam," Philly says.

"I'm going to trust you both to finish washing the dishes –and keep it clean," Pam says, teasing a bit. "Make sure he stays in line, Philly."

"I'm in line, Pam," says Earl. "Chuck, you keep Pam in line –don't let her get you out of those jeans."

Chuck chuckles.

"He's in capable hands, Earl," says Pam. "By the time I get done bringing him up to fashion code, he'll be a regular 'big man on campus'."

"You guys," Philly Prods, "get out of here!"

"Should we expect you back home tonight, sis?" Earl asks.

"Earl, I'm just helping the guy out, and we'll be heading out early in the morning. Philly, please don't keep Earl up too late. You'll have him back in a couple of days. Remember, 'Absence makes the heart grow fonder'." says Pam.

"I'll be *fonder* of you if you're *absent*, sis."

"Done," Pam grabs Chucks hand and leads him out the back door.

What am I doing with this young buck? Pam thinks. They switch hands, and Chuck is now leading her through the back yards to his house. The wooden privacy gate slams shut as Chuck continues to lead. *He seems more 'in charge' than usual.*

I've got to take charge, Chuck thinks.

But he's four years younger than I am –the same age as my little brother Earl. She feels hand squeezing hers and pulling her to the Taylor's back door.

"Mom, Dad, I'm home!" Chuck yells. He releases Pam's hand as they enter the mudroom by the kitchen.

"Chuck, it's about time you're home!" His mom shouts from the bedroom. "If you take a shower, don't leave your dirty underwear and stinky socks on the floor!" His mom yells to Chuck, unaware he has a visitor. Pam snickers.

"Mom, I have a visitor!" Chuck yells, heading down the hall toward his room. His parents' room is at the end of the hall.

"Visitor? Who?" Mrs. Taylor sticks her head through the gap in the bedroom door. "Oh, hey, Pam. What're you two up to?"

"Hi, Mrs. Taylor," Pam says shyly, embarrassed that she's going to a boy's –young man's –room right beside his parents' bedroom. She's re-thinking this whole idea of helping Chuck with his wardrobe. Knowing he's had a crush on her for years; why is she initiating this awkwardness? Maybe it's some sort of psychological thing, like one of those Freudian complexes where the son is in love with his mother or the daughter is in love with the father - or some such weird configuration. Is Pam fixating on her brother's best friend, or is Philly her brother's 'best friend' now in which case Pam's not fixating on her? She's so confused! Who is this young man who used to be Earl's childhood playmate?

"Oh, as long as it's you, Pam. We're not used to Chuck bringing girls to his room so it's OK –just you –but, Chuck, keep it down. Your father's asleep, and he can be grumpy, you know, when he's woken." Mrs. Taylor speaks softly.

Just Pam, huh? Pam thinks. *Pam's not just a 'girl' he's bringing to his room. Pam's twenty years old, a young woman, and Chuck's never had a 'woman' in his room before. Pam's dangerous –and wants to 'get him out of those baggy jeans.* She giggles.

"Wouldn't be funny if Dad woke up, though," Chuck tells Pam, assuming she's giggling about what his mom said. "We'll keep it down, Mom. Goodnight."

"Goodnight. Good to see you, Pam. What're you doing here anyway? Chuck doesn't need a babysitter," Mrs. Taylor laughs.

"Not funny, Mom," says Chuck.

"Just helping Chuck with his college attire for the weekend," says Pam.

"Yes, Pam, he does need help," his mom says. "Do you need a ride back to school? We'd be glad to – "

192

"No, no thank you. You won't believe it, but Mom gave me Dad's car to drive. I'm an independent woman!" Pam says.

"Congratulations, Pam. I still can hardly believe it; you're just a little girl, our little Pam from next door. You can't be in college, driving your own car, taking these two boys off for a wild weekend," Mrs. Taylor says.

"We little boys will be taking care of Pam, I'm sure, Mom. All those college guys will be after her, and I –we –will be guarding her honor," Chuck says.

"Honor?" says Pam.

"Yes, your honor," says Chuck. "I will defend your honor 'til the end, Princess Pam."

"You're so noble, Chuck," his mom says. "Now, Pam, don't let him do something silly or foolish at your college, but if he –or you all –get in trouble, you know that the Taylor's will bail you out," Mrs. Taylor kids.

"Thanks, Mom," says Chuck.

"Thanks, Mrs. Taylor. I have your number on my person –just in case," Pam says.

"Goodnight, Mom," Chuck says.

"Goodnight, Chuck, Pam."

"Princess?" Pam whispers loudly to Chuck after his mom ducks into her room.

"Yes, your highness," Chuck bow's meekly.

"Your highness? Princess? This is not some fairy tale, Chuck –this is real. Now, take me to you room," Pam demands.

"Yes, ma'am –I mean, Pam," Chuck says meekly.

"That's right, I'm Pam. I'm not your Mama's little girl neighbor. I'm not my brother's big sister. I am Pam! Get it, Chuck?"

"Yes, ma'am –yes Pam, I get it. You're just so…so intimidating," Chuck fades, embarrassed and fearful.

"Never fear, Chuck, I'm here. Now, take those baggy jeans off –in the bathroom –and put these normal jeans on," Pam orders.

"Yes, ma'…Pam, whatever you say. I need some coed advice," Chuck says. He goes into his bathroom, closes the door, and unzips the metal zipper of his baggy jeans very loudly.

"I can hear you in there, Chuck. Just unzip, zip and come on back out here," says Pam.

These jeans sure are tight, thinks Chuck, *constricting me –I can't breathe!* "Here I come!" Chuck says as he steps out of the bathroom before Pam.

"Mm hmm –turn around –mm hmm, nice, Chuck. The college girls will be all over that cute butt," says Pam as she motions for him to turn around again. "Mm hmm," she studies him.

"I have a good mind also," Chuck says, putting his index finger to his temple. "I'm not just a pretty face."

"I wasn't checking out your face, Chuck," Pam grins impishly ogling him up, down and back again.

"Yeah, you're just after one thing and you can't have it."

Chuck's too young, four years younger than me, but I know some seniors at college dating freshmen girls. That age difference seems 'normal', in that case, but when the girl – the woman –is a senior dating a freshman guy, seems unnatural to many people. Pam has never put much weight on people's opinions of her private life –which is private, hers. *Let them talk.*

"Here," Pam holds out a stark white T-shirt she found in his dresser drawer.

"What are you doing going through my drawers, Pam?" asks Chuck.

"Oh, just getting my jollies fingering through your intimate things," says Pam.

"Stay out of my drawers, alright?" asks Chuck.

"You're so sensitive, Chuck," Pam says. *I can't believe he still has that wallet sized school picture tucked away at the bottom of his drawer when I was thirteen. That was right after the Taylor's moved here, and Chuck was shy. I gave him a smile and a photo. It's so sweet of him to hang on to that.*

I hope she didn't find her old school picture while she was rummaging through my drawers. She'll think I'm a pervert hanging on to a photo of a thirteen-year-old –and keeping it in my underwear drawer! She was cute then –even cuter now.

"You going to try on that T-shirt, Chuck?" she asks.

"Yeah, yeah," Chuck, without thinking too much about self-consciousness, pulls off his extra-large plaid button down and hands it to Pam as he flips and re-flips the T-shirt to find the tag.

Pam stands gawking, just long enough for him to notice.

"What?" He pulls the clinging T-shirt over his head.

"Um, nothing, Chuck. You been working out?" asks Pam.

"Some - stop studying my pecs!" says Chuck.

Pam ignores the *pecs* request and continues staring at his clingy cotton covered chest.

"Now you need a jacket over the T. What do you have in your closet?" She opens the closet door and begins flipping through the hangers. "What about this?" she holds out a half-faded blue denim jacket.

"I haven't worn that in a while –not sure it'll still fit," Chuck says, taking the jacket off the plastic hanger and putting an arm through the hole. "A little snug," says Chuck.

"Turn around. Let me see the back," Pam states. "A bit snug, but it accentuates your shoulders." She puts her hands-on top of his shoulders and turns him around to face her. She steps back and examines him head to toe and back again. "You dress up good if I do say so myself. Look in the mirror." She closes the closet door, presenting the full-length mirror.

"Hey, who is that?" Chuck sees himself newly packaged.

Pam stands behind him, places her hands on his shoulders again and peers around him at their reflection.

"You're packaged better than any man I've seen at college," Pam says. "Get you to college tomorrow and you may decide to stay -after all those sophomores take a gander at you."

"Aw, come on, Pam. I'll be right by your side this weekend, taking lessons from my elder."

She socks him in the shoulder.

46.

"Whew! Just about does it, huh, Philly?" Earl asks.

"Whew? You don't mean this little dinner party has you worn out, do you, Earl?" Philly asks.

"Oh, no, this was nothing compared to running a marathon," says Earl.

"You've never run a marathon, Earl,"

"–but, I could. Did you ever cook for this many people before, Philly?"

"No, it's either cooking for two –me and Mom –or cooking for one of us at a time."

"Speaking of 'time', we have a little before your mom gets home. Anyway, you shouldn't be home alone."

"Are you inviting me to stay awhile, Earl? I'm not sure how it'll look to the neighbors, unchaperoned," Philly says.

"How about I chaperone you, and you chaperone me. We're two responsible adults, right?" Earl asks.

"We're teenagers, Earl, but I trust you. Do you trust me?"

"I don't know. Earlier I turned my back on you in the kitchen, and you grabbed my butt!"

"No, you misunderstood! I was rescuing you from a fatal fall! You'll know it when I grab your butt –for sure!" Philly chases him from the kitchen.

"You'll never catch this butt, little Philly!" Earl circles the dining room table, shuffling chairs, and dives for the couch with Philly on his heels.

"Caught you!" Philly says as she straddles Earl's back. She grabs the collar of his shirt with one hand, like reins on a horse and shouts, "Giddy up!" as she slaps his rump with the other hand.

"Ahh! Help, help! She's gone mad! Abuse!" Earl yells with silly boy giggles between syllables.

Philly stops riding and calmly says, "Woe, boy." Settle down. Easy, easy now," using horse riding lingo.

Earl awkwardly rolls over onto his back, poking Philly with his bony elbow and shoulder blade, bumping a knobby knee into her back.

"Mph!" Earl exclaims as Philly sits and bounces once on his belly. "I...can't...breathe."

"Can't breathe? I know CPR! Check the scene. Is it safe? No, but I'll save you anyway - or I'll try," Philly says and places her lips firmly over Earl's and pinches his nose shut.

"Mph!" Earl breaks his lip free and says, "You trying to suffocate me?" He sends Philly sprawling to the opposite end of the couch. "I'll show you some basic CPR!"

Earl kneels by the couch and places his left hand under the back of Philly's head, wild tangles of her hair intertwining with his fingers. She quiets takes a shallow breath as Earl firmly but tenderly grasps her left shoulder with his right hand and leans in, lifting her pursed trembling lips to his own.

The kiss lingers for maybe thirty - or sixty - seconds as Earl caresses Philly's shoulder and massages the back of her head like a toddler in his highchair playing in his spaghetti.

What now? His heart is racing, and hers is fluttering as she begins to kick her feet. She breaks the suction between their lips and gasps.

"I need some air –you're taking my breath," Philly pants.

Earl straightens up, his hand still cradling her head, and says, "You mean I *take your breath away*?" He grins.

"Yeah, yeah, *take my breath away* –suffocation, to be more precise," Philly says, unable to stifle a smile. She sits up, *crisscross apple sauce* style as they say in pre-school, and Earl up off his knees and sits beside her on the couch.

"Are you going to miss me?" Philly asks.

"I'll be gone less than two days," Earl says.

"But will you miss me?"

It's really been such a short time –less than a week –that we've been going steady, girlfriend/boyfriend –whatever it's called. Only a week ago we were 'just friends' –hadn't really given her much thought when we were apart. What's different? Oh, yeah, the kisses and hugs and handholding and the fact that it is now spoken and in the open for everyone to see. Will I miss her now?

"You're thinking too hard about this, Earl. Maybe you won't miss me. Am I your *girlfriend*?" she asks, straight faced with a quivery voice and trembling lower lip.

Earl takes a few moments to think. He bursts out with, "Yes, I'm going to miss you. You're my *girlfriend*!"

Philly leans into Earl's shoulder, puts her slender arms around his neck, and kisses him hard. She latches onto his lips and neck and holds on tight. Minutes pass. Philly has wriggled onto Earl's lap.

Things involuntarily happen when one is a sixteen-year-old, almost a man. Earl reaches inside their embrace and places a nervous clammy hand over Philly's blossoming breast. She feels an awkward *situation* rising from Earl's lap, and she jumps away like a scared rabbit. She lands on the coffee table, pulls at her shirt, and checks the drawstring of her pants.

"What are you doing?!" Philly exclaims.

Earl, still on the couch, is embarrassed and holding a throw pillow over his lap. His face, a shade redder than hers, has a *caught in the cookie jar* expression, mouth gaping. Eat the cookies or put them back?

"Doing? Uh, just –I'm sorry. I couldn't help it." Earl stumbles. "It just -"

"Your hand was on my breast. Was that involuntary?" Philly asks.

"No, I –you were –I was –we were kissing and –I don't know. I just did it. I'm sorry, Philly." Earl stumbles into an apology.

"And what were you doing in your lap? Felt like something moving in…your pocket…" Philly fades, suddenly recalling some facts from Health class.

"I couldn't –it just –I'm sorry." Earl continues to apologize but not knowing how.

"It's OK, Earl, we need to go a little slower. I didn't know you'd– "

Earl jumps in, "I didn't try, you know, it just popped…"

"Earl, things like that just happen, but before you touch me anywhere –anywhere private –ask me, OK?"

"OK, Philly." He hangs his head meekly as he remains on the couch, pillow over his lap.

Philly tips lightly over to Earl and pecks him on his reddened cheek.

Earl walks Philly home after eleven. Her mom should be home by now. She latches onto his arm as he escorts her around the side of her house to the kitchen, where light emanates through the curtain sheers. He is trying to be the gentleman, restrain his hormonal responses. Earl walks deliberately, hands to his sides marching like a good soldier. Philly still clings to his arm, sensing Earl's timidity initiated by his earlier embarrassment.

I think I love him, and one day I'll be woman enough to say, 'Yes,' but we're both teenagers now, too young.

As they approach the light at the back door, Philly stops, and spins Earl around to face her.

"Earl, look at me. Neither of us is ready for that –but, kiss me," Philly entreats.

"But, I –you –we – "Earl hesitates.

Philly pulls him down to her face level, and he kisses her - or she kisses him. Her eyes are closed, but his are open, thinking of the first time they kissed at the fort. She remembers, too, and knows now that she kissed him; he remembers that he kissed her. Who was to blame? He closes his eyes and presses her to himself, but not too tightly or for too long. Philly rests her ear against Earl's chest and hears his heart pounding. She'll have to check his heart rate with her earwig when they're close, to assure he's not getting overly *excited.*

"Your mom's sitting at the kitchen table," Earl says. "We'd better go inside."

"She can be our chaperone," says Philly. Earl blushes by the warm glow of the kitchen light.

Earl opens the storm door for Philly.

"Hey, Mom," Philly hurries to the table and kisses her on the cheek.

"Hey, Philly, Earl. What are you guys doing out so late?"

"We cooked dinner for the family at Earl's house."

"Philly prepared a gourmet feast of homemade pizza and salad. I just helped clean up, mostly," Earl says.

"He's learning, Mom. One day he'll be my sous chef." says Philly, grabbing Earl by the arm.

"Your *sweet* chef?" Glenda laughs.

"That, too," Philly squeezes Earl tighter.

"Shouldn't you sweeties be saying your goodnights?"

"Yeah, I guess so," Philly says downheartedly. "He's leaving with Pam –and Chuck –Earl in the morning.

"You're right," says Earl. "Oh, we brought you some of that delicious pizza. I'd bet it's great cold, too, or you can re-heat it." He hands Glenda the reusable grocery bag as he shifts nervously foot to foot.

"Thank you. Like I said, you're sweeties. I was just thinking about feeding this growling stomach," says Glenda. "Ahh, the aroma –smells so good."

"Bon Appetit," Earl says.

"Philly, would you heat this in the oven. I'm going to put on my jammies. Don't get it too hot, now, Philly," Glenda glances at Philly and Earl's reddening face.

"Goodnight," Earl says.

"Goodnight, Earl. I'll just be five minutes, Philly –five minutes, that's all. Have a nice weekend, Earl."

"OK, Mom, five minutes."

"And counting," Glenda says. "On your mark; get set; go!" as she starts the oven timer and flees the room.

Earl stares at the digital numbers ticking off the clock. Time goes so quickly. Why does it have to be measured?

"Go!" Philly starts, jumps, and wraps her arms around Earl's neck and locks lips with his so quickly that he stumbles against the chair, knocking it loudly against the table.

"You guys OK in there?" her mom yells from the bedroom at the other end of the house.

Philly is laughing so hard she has difficulty answering. Earl whispers loudly, "Shh. Shh. Philly, answer your mom." They regain their composure leaning against the oven.

"Everything's OK, Mom! Nothing's broken!"

"Three and a half minutes," Philly reads the timer.

Earl's butt rests against the oven. "It's getting hot."

"Oh, sorry, Earl, I didn't mean to get you all hot and bothered again."

Earl begins blushing again. "No, no, I'm fine. It's the stove –getting hot."

As Philly starts kissing him again, Earl purposefully thinks of playing basketball, dribbling, shooting –to distract his involuntary responses. *It's working,* he thinks, but realizes he is fingering the dimple in the small of Philly's back. *Time! time out!* H tries thinking of basketball again.

Philly unlocks lips and glances at the timer: one minute and forty-seven seconds. *Cooling off.*

Getting hot, Earl thinks. "Philly, I – "

"I know, we need to cool down. You're – "

"No, it's not…" Earl stops himself. *Yes, it's that,* he thinks but says, "not that. The oven's getting got!" He pushes off the oven, bumps Philly who knocks a chair against the table again.

"You guys!" her mom shouts. "Time's just about up!"

"Yes, Mom, he's going!"

Forty-five seconds. Philly leads Earl by the hand to the door.

"I'm going to miss you, Earl."

"I'm missing you already, Philly." Earl's heart rate comes back down to normal.

With a quick sweet kiss, they lower their arms, lose their embrace, and lock eyes until Earl disappears from the back-porch light.

The five-minute buzzer sounds, and Philly slides the pizza slices onto the oven grate with a cookie sheet below to catch any drippings –she detests cleaning the oven. After setting the timer for ten minutes at 350 degrees she takes a plate from the cabinet by the window and stares at the backyard's empty swing set.

She pictures herself swinging, pushed by her daddy. girl. Like summer vacation they swing high and sprawl in the sand underneath, Daddy in his red and yellow Hawaiian *Jams* and red tank shirt, Philly in her one-piece bathing suit with the frill around the waist. At six years old she was in love with her daddy, just like most little girls at that age. Mom was probably jealous. They didn't want her to be, and Mom unselfishly allowed plenty Daddy-Philly time. Somehow, she knew that this was only for a short time –and before long, her dad would go on an adventure on his own. *I miss you, Daddy. Isn't it about time for a letter –or an e-message, even?*

"What's out there?" Her mom had been standing in the doorway for a couple of minutes, basking in the happy glow of her daughter. *This is Mom-Philly time, much different than six-year-old Daddy-Philly time, but a time of blossoming and becoming a young woman. Your dad has his own world out there, somewhere, but my world is here with you. This is the better of the two.* Her mom smiles.

"Oh, just an old swing set. Earl's gone," Philly says forlornly, "but he'll be back –in a couple days." 'Will Daddy come back? It's been –how long?' she thinks.

"You miss him already, don't you?" Glenda asks. *I missed your daddy for years, and I still miss him. It's like he's MIA, but he sends letters and messages out to his daughter. I've never told her that I've gotten letters from him, too, but only a couple each year. He seems the same, except more alive, even though he's not here in the flesh. A time came, not long before he left, when I thought I had lost him, his spirit. I hope he's gotten his spirit back. Philly and I need him –to make three. Your little Philly's 'most a woman now. Her spirit is starting to fly. Your spirits need to meet. She needs you. I need...*

"Yes, Mom," says Philly and repeats, "Yes, Mom," bringing her mom back.

"You and Earl are getting pretty close. He seems like a gentleman, Philly. Is he good to you –all the time?"

"Yes, Mom, he's sweet and kind and thoughtful –a gentleman."

"I know you've kissed –heard you banging around the kitchen," Glenda says.

"Mom." Philly opens the oven door as the timer buzzes. "It's hot." She shuts the oven off.

"Hot, good –how about you, Philly?" asks Mom.

"I'm comfortable –a little warm, but…" Philly stops short, catching her mom's allusion. "Mom," she sings.

"I know you and Earl are fifteen and sixteen, so there's lots going on up there in your head –and in your body."

Philly puts the pizza in front of her mom and sits across the table from her. "Mom, we're alright."

"Has anything happened –besides kissing and hugging?"

Philly searches her mom's face trying to read her thoughts. When she can't, she decides to open her heart to her mom about what happened tonight.

"Mom, Earl and I had a little awkward moment tonight," Philly says.

"You can tell me anything, Philly. I was fifteen once," and Glenda remembers all too well the 'awkward' moments and the pregnancy scare when her high school boyfriend graduated and went off to college.

"We were just horsing around, getting a little physical," Philly says. "Physical?"

"Not like that," says Philly, thinking, *Not yet anyway.*

"Go on."

"Well, this and that and I ended up on his lap, and we were kissing and…" Philly hesitates, uncomfortable telling the rest of the story. She realizes how Earl had felt in his embarrassment.

"And? You can tell me, Philly. Are you OK?" asks Mom.

"Yeah, I'm fine, but Earl got a little…"

"Amorous?"

"I guess you could say that. Anyway, we were kissing –a long time –and Earl slipped his hand up my shirt. "Philly look down at the tabletop, embarrassed.

"And what did you do?" Mom asks, already remembering her first boyfriend trying to *feel her up* the first time.

"Oh, I jumped off his lap, but…"

"What happened? He didn't…"

"No, he was embarrassed -apologized all over the place, but…"

"But what?" asks Mom.

"Uh, while I was on his lap, I felt a –something in his pocket and…"

Glenda put her hand across the table and took hold of Philly's, smiling and encouraging her, "It's OK."

"I didn't know what, at first, then when Earl grabbed a throw pillow and put it over his –lap, then I remembered Health class."

Earl was *happy to see you* as they say." Mom tries to lighten the embarrassment for Philly.

"Mom," Philly sings, "I know what *it* was, and Earl was so ashamed and apologetic, and we had a little talk about touching and courtesy and all that. He understands. I understand."

"You're 'most a woman, Philly, and you've got a head on your shoulders that took me a lot longer to develop," Mom says.

"Thanks, Mom, and I came up with a way to tell when he's starting to get so 'happy'," Philly says.

"Tell me. This may be the secret that all women need to hear." She releases Philly's hand to take a bite of pizza.

"My idea is, when we're close, I just put my earwig to his chest and listen for an elevated heart rate. If it's too high, I know he's beginning to get a little *too happy*, and we remind each other that we're not ready for *that* yet," says Philly.

"Good method," says Mom, and thinks, *Should work better than the 'rhythm method'.*

"Thanks, Mom. We're talking and understanding each other more and more," says Philly.

"Young love is wonderful," her mom says, thinking, *Old love, too.* "Do you think you *love* Earl?"

"I think, maybe I do. We're taking it a little slower."

"You know you can tell me anything, don't you?" Mom says, but thinking, *There'll be that time when she won't tell me something, I'm sure, but she's on the verge of being a woman. I understand.*

"Yes, Mom." Philly goes around the table and kisses her mom on the cheek, causing a pizza sauce smear on both of their faces.

Glenda wipes the sauce off Philly's cheek and licks it off her finger. "Sweet! I love you, Philly, and not just because you're a great cook."

"I love you, too, Mom, and I'll be your personal chef always!"

47.

Pam takes the short cut through the Taylor's back yard. Sitting on the back steps by the kitchen, an owl hoots as it perches in the tall pine behind the house. Her heart strings are out of tune with her twenty-year-old wisdom. *I am so confused. Why am I attracted to a boy –really a young man –so much younger than myself? In high school the age difference between freshman and senior was no big deal, and the popular boys could have their 'pick' of freshman girls. The freshman girls longed for it, the senior boys expected it, and the sophomores and juniors learned to accept the male pecking order and the 'biggest rooster' theory.*

In college the same pecking order applied, but if an older girl, young woman, stepped out of line and pursued the younger male, she would be labeled a 'cougar'. But I'm a sophomore, he's a sophomore in high school. Is she an immature twenty-year-old, or is he mature beyond his sixteen years?

My younger brother is more mature. He seems to have gotten older during the past week, and little Philly is mature beyond her fifteen years. She has been growing up, taking on family responsibilities with her mom, especially since her dad left a long time ago. Earl and Philly have that in common: they both lost their dads. Is Philly subconsciously trying to fill a void in her life with Earl? Am I trying to fill the void that Dad left –with Chuck? Did I take Psychology 101 too seriously? And as Earl's gotten close to Philly and further from me, there's another void for me to fill –with Chuck. Am I backtracking, getting younger? Since I came home from school, I've felt more like a little girl than a young woman. What's wrong with me?

Pam missed a big part of growing up, her childhood years. Her mom was sick and, in the hospital, or either not mentally 'with it', for so long, and her dad had time for nothing but work –and worrying about Lila and his neglected motherless children. Things –life –would be so much different now if 'the tragedy' had never happened. Tina probably would not have been born, and Ester wouldn't be playing such a big part in their lives.

Mom, Dad, son, and daughter needed time to bond –to love, work and play in a tighter knit. In reality, each member of the family has gone his own way: Tina's gone to Ester; Earl's becoming a man and gone to Philly; Pam's gone to college –and maybe to Chuck; Dad's dead, gone to heaven; Mom is torn between a new life with Tina and Ester –or going back to the crazy dark place.

A terrifying screech, flapping of wings, and a flurry of feathers - and a scream from Pam. The patiently hooting owl has ripped its talons into the flesh of the unsuspecting cottontail rabbit who had been nibbling the broadleaf weeds in the back yard.

"Oh, God!" Pam screams to the darkness as the beating wings carry the night bird and its prey back to its perch just as Earl rounds the corner of the house.

"Earl, Earl!" Pam cries and runs to meet him for a *save me* hug.

"Pam, I'm here. I just saw –wow! You look like you just woke up from a nightmare, sis. Are you OK? I'm here."

"Thank God you're here. I might lose my mind if you weren't." She trembles in his saving arms.

Earl holds his sister and flashes back to his Mom getting sick, losing her mind. "Don't even think that, Pam. Nature can be so cruel." *It's been so cruel to Mom. Stay with me, sis.* "But owls and rabbits got to eat, right?"

"But do they have to eat each other, right here in front of an audience? It's like the lions fighting and ripping men's flesh in the Coliseum; I'd never have gotten a ticket for that horror show either," Pam says.

"Your big brother's here to protect you."

"Correction: little brother, but bigger than me," Pam says.

"Noted," Earl gives his sister a bear hug.

"Oomph," Pam grunts. Earl loosens his grip. "You're going to love me to death."

"Speaking of love –and death –how do you think Mom's holding up, Pam?" Earl asks. "You think she's better off now with Tina and Ester?"

"She seems a bit too at ease, like she's holding something back since Dad…." Pam can't say *since Dad died.* "It'll be good for her to spend time with Tina - with Ester modeling the 'mother and little girl' thing –but I don't know if Mom's *better off.*"

"You think she could go back to… where she was? She's been there too many times, getting better and then going back down," Earl says.

"Yeah, all we can do is be here for her, encourage her and hope for the best," says Pam.

"-and pray." Earl says.

"Where did that prayer come from at dinner anyway?" Pam asks.

"I guess Reverend Arnold may have rubbed off on me."

"I'd better be praying for you –and especially Philly –since you two are *going steady,* brother."

"We're being good - trying," says Earl.

"Trying to be good? Are you succeeding? You had better be good to that Philly. She's a good girl," says Pam.

"I am, I am. It's just –sometimes –well, I –she –we," Earl stammers.

"I know, Earl; you don't have to say. I was your age –just a few years ago –and sometimes now I feel the same things again, like the clocks have been turned back," Pam gets all wise on her brother.

"You mean you had human feelings?" Earl prods.

"Hey, I can be a beast –like a bird of prey –with you, little rabbit, if you push my primal backyard buttons," Pam returns in jest. "But yes, I'm human, with all those feelings, big-little brother."

"It's hard to hold those animals, those feelings. I'm just human – 'most a man –so sometimes things just come up and – "Earl starts.

"Hold on, big-little brother, I don't need all the details –I know what you mean. Just remember, be sensitive to Philly. She's wise and mature, but also vulnerable since having a 'man' in her life is new. Her dad's been gone for a long time," says Pam.

"I know, and she lets me know when I make mistakes," he says.

"Just remember those mistakes, brother, and don't let them happen again."

"OK, OK."

"And remember another thing: I like Philly, and if you hurt her, I'll kick your tall skinny butt, comprende?"

"I understand, sis. Now you remember: Chuck's my friend, and I'll squeeze you like I'm a 'booger bear' if you hurt him." Earl grabs her in a bear hug.

"What? You don't know –I mean, yeah, I like Chuck – but he's like a little brother - like you." Pam fails to explain.

"And he's almost a man too, little-big sister, and he sees that you're 'most… a woman. Chuck's a good guy. Don't hurt him, Pam."

"I don't know what you're talking about."

"Mm hmm, and how do his jeans fit, sis?"

"Um, he's going to be dressed to kill. All the sophomore girls are going to swoon over him," Pam says.

"One already has," Earl squeezes Pam one more time in his bear hug and kisses her on the head before letting go.

Changing the subject Pam says, "We'd better get packed to go. Chuck's coming over Earl."

"Is he coming Earl to help you pick out your clothes?" asks Earl.

"Shut up." She socks him in the gut and runs inside the house.

Tufts of bunny down swirl in the back corner of the yard.

48.

Jaundiced light creeps over the spines of dark clothbound books alphabetically ordered by author's last name in stacked bookcases. Alabaster light is glowing beneath the emerald green shade of the reading lamp. The King James Olde English scripture reflects in his eyes as he studies the Word.

He closes his eyes and rubs them with his fists attempting to squeeze any drop of moisture from weary tear ducts to soothe his tired dry eyes. The hour just past eleven o'clock, but his usual study time extends to at least one o'clock, sometimes up to three in the morning.

"A cup of Earl Grey tea is what I need. What do you think, Bessie?" he asks his tea kettle and twists the knob of the hot plate behind his desk. The element crackles and hums electric heat, as the shiny copper-bottomed kettle patiently awaits the boiling so she can whistle, 'Teatime!' The Reverend rights a Wedgwood China teacup onto its matching saucer with pink flowers, green leaves, and a gold rim.

His mother had given him a set of four cups and saucers, and matching teapot, before he left home to attend seminary in Oak Forest. She was proud of his 'calling' but knew she'd rarely see him because of the ministry; his taking these mementos from home would somehow bring her peace. She had been right. She died suddenly of a brain hemorrhage midway his first year at seminary.

The kettle began to quiver and whistle as the Reverend put the tea leaves into the teapot basket. A loud, impatient whistle spewed from the kettle's spout. He shut off the hotplate and poured the scalding water over the tea leaves in his mother's teapot.

Orange and rusty brown swirls begin transforming the hot water into tea and he places the china lid onto the flowered pot. Three minutes and the tea is ready to pour.

"Would you care for a cup? He asks himself. "Thank you, don't mind if I do."

"Mother?" He pours one cup and a second for her memory.

Philly goes right to bed after their mother-daughter talk. Glenda, still wired from her hospital experience and the disturbing tidbit shared by the coroner and the detective, stays up and makes a cup of tea for herself.

She grabs a 'flow-thru' single serving teabag from the box in the cabinet to the right of the microwave. Setting her *I heart Mom* mug, ¾ full of filtered de-ionized water, in the microwave, she presses the *mug* button and waits the few seconds for the water to boil. She plops the tea bag into the mug, holding the string by the paper logo end tab, bobs it up and down in the steaming water. She ravages the pantry for cookies.

"Yes! Lemon drop shortbread cookies!" She takes the recyclable brown bag down, pulling its seams apart as she goes to the counter where her tea continues to steep. "Just two, Glenda," and she takes four cookies. "Ha!" She bobs the teabag a couple more times. She wraps the string around the bag as it sets on her teaspoon, squeezing out the last tea drops.

"Good night." She clicks off the light and pads down the hall to her room. She eats the second of the four cookies and places the remaining two with her 'heart' mug on the bedside table. Peeling off her top and dropping her pants, she leaves them on the floor where they fall. She grabs an oversized T-shirt that belonged to her husband, sniffs it, and throws it on the floor by her work scrubs. Rummaging through her underwear-socks drawer she retrieves a clean T-shirt that had never belonged to anyone but her, Glenda.

She fluffs her pillows against the headboard, grabs the latest issue of Cosmo and her tea mug off the nightstand, leans back in bed and sips. "Hot!" she hisses at the scalding tea and grabs a lemon cookie to dunk.

Flipping, flipping, looking –she closes the magazine. *This is no good, hanging onto this information, even though I was eavesdropping. I couldn't help it. What should I do? Who can I talk to?* She dunks the last cookie and sips the now lukewarm tea.

Killed him –that's what they said -but who? If the killer has not been caught, he –or she –is still out there. What will he do? What can I do? Lord, I need some advice. Help me.

She furrows her brow while sipping the cool tea. She reads, "I heart Mom." She smiles. "I heart you, too, Philly." She slaps the glossy magazine down on the table and knocks off the little white Gideon New Testament that she received when she graduated from the Certified Nursing Assistant program. She picks up the mini-Bible and pushes the Cosmo on the floor.

"The New Testament," she says. *Now when did I read this? Who reads this?* Immediately she remembers softly, "Reverend Arnold."

She's not a *regular* in church, but it's common knowledge that Reverend Arnold is a night owl. *Maybe it's a good time to call him. He knows Earl, I'm sure; he did the memorial service for Cleve. He'd want to know. Call him, Glenda. Call the Reverend.*

A bit of honey, that's all I need to charge me up for a little bit longer. The Reverend drizzles a golden micro-ribbon of honey into his cup, and softly asks, "Honey, Mother?"

The phone rings. "Mother!" He drops the silver teaspoon into the cup, splashing the droplets across the tea tray.

It's ringing. Glenda hears a second ring, a third. *Maybe he's not in. If he is, maybe this is a bad idea, calling him and laying another burden on him. He doesn't need this.* She moves to hang up.

"Hello, this is Reverend Arnold." A moment of silence passes. "Hello?"

"Oh, hi, Reverend, sorry to bother you this late, but – "

"It's no problem, dear. Everyone knows I'm a night owl. And to whom am I speaking?" asks the Reverend.

"This is Glenda, Philly's mom."

"Oh, yes, that Philly is quite a girl. Nothing's wrong, I hope?"

"Philly? No, she's fine. Better than fine, in fact. She's practically giddy since she and Earl Cleveland became 'steady'."

"Yes, I saw the letter jacket she was wearing at the Cleveland visitation. It's such a tragedy, Cleve's sudden death. That family's been through hard times. Earl really deserves good things –like your Philly. He needs someone he can talk to, like your daughter."

"They're good for each other. I just wish she could stay my little girl for a while longer," says Glenda.

"I understand," he says. *I've never had children, one of the things I regret.* "They grow up so quickly these days. You sure there are no issues with Philly and Earl –like sex?"

"No, no," says Glenda, embarrassed to even think the subject with the Reverend. "Philly and I had a pleasant –well, uncomfortable, a little – talk earlier tonight, about such things." She can't say *sex*. She's remained chaste since her husband left, repressing, and denying 'it' existed.

"Do you think maybe I should talk with Earl?"

"I don't think – "Glenda hesitates, "You know, that might be a good idea, since his dad is gone. Yes, I do think he could use a man's ear and guidance at such a tough period –father gone, new girlfriend and the whole teenage thing."

"I'll give him a call, Glenda –or better yet, I'll stop by his house."

"Oh, Philly says Earl's going away Saturday and coming back Sunday –with Chuck, to do a weekend at college with Pam," says Glenda.

"That sounds like a great idea, with everything that's been going on. Pam's a good sister, a smart girl –quite the young lady," the Reverend says.

"Yes," says Glenda. *With this news about Cleve's death – 'killed' - they might be safer away 'til the killer is caught. Hard to believe that a killer's somewhere close by.*

"Glenda –you still with me?" the Reverend says after the long pause. "I'm forgetting -was there something else you needed to talk about?" *My tea is getting cold.*

She hesitates telling the Reverend the news. *Is there anything he can really do? Is he the one I should tell?* "Yes, there was something I overheard at the hospital. I know I shouldn't be eavesdropping –is that a sin? –but since I have it in my craw, I've got to cough it up."

Obviously, something is disturbing her, and she needs to tell someone, but am I the one? Maybe we should defer to a Higher Power. "You sound like you're full of guilt over eavesdropping, but if you truly want forgiveness for that –or anything -you are forgiven –Grace!"

"Thank you, Reverend, but the thing I heard is laying heavy on my soul."

"Would you like to ease your burden? I can try to help, and He can definitely help, Glenda."

"Yes, Reverend."

"Let it out, Glenda, let it go."

"This is it." She takes a deep breath. "Detective Brown came up to the third floor at the hospital to meet the coroner. I was taking my lunch break at the time –at the nurses' station."

"I know Detective Brown. He came by my office the day Cleve died –to help break the news to Earl. Go on," says the Reverend.

"Anyway, they were discussing lab results –I couldn't hear everything –and they said 'Cleve', and something about his being diabetic – "

The Reverend interrupts, "Diabetic? Didn't know that."

"A lot of people –most people –didn't know," Glenda says. "The coroner said the sugar levels were extremely high, and for a person who hadn't eaten breakfast, something was fishy."

"Hmm, diabetic and high sugar," he thinks aloud.

"But it got weird when Detective Brown took a little thing –I think he said 'ampule' of 'e-nhancer' -from his pocket and showed it to the coroner, and something about it will 'kick start a horse' or 'kill a diabetic' –" she says.

"Getting a little technical and medical for me –except the 'horse' part. You're a nurse…"

"A CNA – will be nurse in the near future." Glenda corrects. "When the coroner read the sugar content of that ampule it about floored her! 'This could kill a healthy person, let alone a person with diabetes.' 'Kill', that's what I heard - sounds likely that someone killed Cleve!"

"Lord, have mercy!"

"So, I think that you, me, the coroner and Detective Brown are the only ones with this information now –and the killer." Glenda's voice tremors.

"We need to *not* tell anyone else, Glenda. I will talk with the detective, but not mention your name."

"Thank you, it's a relief to get that off my chest, Reverend, but I'm still worried."

"Try not to worry, Glenda, and just stay alert like you have been. The Cleveland family is covered this weekend: Lila is with Ester and Tina at Ester's house; Pam and Earl are with Chuck at Pam's college.

"Maybe he –the killer –has left town," Glenda hopes.

"Unless he - the killer - knows someone else has evidence he's probably still around, doing what he always does," says the Reverend.

"But that's what scares me, 'What he always does'! He's a killer, Reverend –that's what he does!" Glenda worries.

"Don't panic, Glenda, just be alert and stay safe, and if you need anything call me. If you sense danger, call the police; Detective Brown must be on the case."

"You're in my cell speed dial Reverend Arnold."

"You're in my prayers, Glenda. Oh, and call on Him before you call anyone else."

"Thank you, Reverend."

They close their phones. Reverend Arnold prays. Glenda worries and cries and then prays. The Reverend heats the teapot for a fresh cup.

"Oh, Mother," he thinks aloud.

"Oh, Philly," Glenda thinks aloud. She heads down the hall and peeks into Philly's room. "Angel," she whispers.

Detective Brown has been sitting in his car a block down from the house; Bruce got home around nine o'clock. Friday night and there's not much action here. Eleven o'clock and the lights go out. 'Bedtime,' thinks Detective Brown, "this must be his regular 'lights out' time. Good, I can go home.'

Bruce watches through the shades as Detective Brown drives away. *Two nights in a row he knows it's lights out at eleven.* He checks the automatic timer on the inside security panel. "Lights out, Detective Brown," "Lights out." He smiles, furrowing his eyebrows and slapping the wall hard with his hand.

Detective Brown drives away. *With the Cleveland's out of the house and Chuck gone away for the weekend, too, things should be calm. Just watch the Coach tomorrow night 'til bedtime, and I'm off Sunday.* "Thank God!"

49.

"Good morning, sunshine." An angelic voice calls to Chuck. He opens his eyes partially to see the vision of an angel with golden light crowning her head. He smiles like a cherub and snuggles under the warm covers.

"Hey, sunshine!" Earl shouts, bright lights beaming, bombarding Chuck's cocoon with fists, elbows, and knees. Pam pounces. "Flesh pile!" Chuck covers his face with the sheet, flimsy protection from this Earl morning assault.

"I give! I give up!" Chuck shouts, not terrified, but a little peeved.

Earl holds him down; Pam gets close to Chuck's covered head and whispers sweetly, "Time to rise and shine, sweetheart."

Chuck succumbs. He whispers back to Pam, "I never thought I'd get you into my bed."

Earl defends his sister's honor. He puts a wet finger in Chuck's ear. "How's that for a wet, sloppy one, buddy?"

"You're my hero, Earl!" Pam says.

Earl pulls the covers off the bed like a magician doing a magic trick, revealing Chuck in the buff. Chuck hides the 'rabbit' with his cupped slight of hands.

"Hey!" Chuck yells, grabbing at the sheet with one hand, covering the 'rabbit' with the other.

"Oops," says Earl, nonchalantly.

Pam gasps and turns away, but immediately starts laughing uncontrollably.

"Give me that!" Chuck grabs the covers and wraps up like a Greek in a toga. "And what's so funny, Pam?"

Pam turns to him and uncovers her eyes. "Toga party tonight, Chuck?"

Chuck shuffles toward the bathroom, stumbles over the end of his 'toga' and slams the door behind.

Mrs. Taylor had played along with Earl and Pam's prank, but with all the ruckus down the hall calls, "Everything alright in there?"

"Sure, Mrs. Taylor." Earl says.

"Yeah, Mom, we're fine," says Chuck, muffled behind the bathroom door.

"Yeah, Chuck's fine," sings Pam, beginning to chuckle.

"Shut up!" says Chuck. They hear the spray of the shower.

"Too much?' asks Earl.

"Too much." Pam says bent over laughing.

Pam drives her dad's car, confident in her new, responsible role as chauffeur. Earl sits up front in the passenger seat, knees touching the dash. Chuck is scrunched up behind Pam, clothes and bags mounded beside him, even less comfortable than in the middle seat on Budget Air.

"In this democracy," Chuck pronounces, "how did I get relegated to the back seat of pain?"

Laughing, Earl starts, "Because you have the shortest . . ."

Pam cuts him off, "-legs, the shortest legs."

"Yeah, legs," Earl says, looking back at Chuck.

"Short, but fast," Chuck says.

"Yeah, fast like a rabbit," Earl raises his eyebrows, Chuck has fallen into that 'rabbit' hole.

Chuck bows his head down toward the floorboard, "No, no, no..." beyond embarrassment.

Pam is tired of teasing Chuck, so she introduces a new topic. She really likes Chuck and realizes how embarrassed they made him in his room earlier. *Cruel, but funny.* She smiles in the rearview mirror and catches Chuck looking at her. *He is sweet, and cute, too.*

"So, guys, I have a couple of ideas for tonight. First, we'll go to the Naturalists' Café for food, the best you ever tasted –and healthiest –and 'refreshments. I know you like that real tobacco I've been bringing you, Earl," says Pam.

"Yes, love it! What do you think, Chuck?" says Earl.

"I'll try it again –if it's OK with you, Pam," Chuck says.

"Sure, Chuck, there are lots of new things for you to try here, some legal, others 'illegal', but not immoral," Pam says. *Confidence, that's what you need, Chuck. I'll try to help you with that.*

"Pam, I trust you –not sure about Earl," says Chuck.

"I've got your back, Chuck. Yours, too, little sis," says Earl.

"*Big sis* to *you*, little bro."

Pam rides around the closest parking lot to her dorm but finds it full. Anyway, to park there she must have a valid parking decal for her dad's car;

she drives two blocks further and pulls into a large, unpaved grassy field marked 'overflow parking'.

Chuck scans the haphazard row of parked cars for an empty spot. "Isn't there some 'visitor' parking closer to the dorm?"

"Yes, Chuck, but we're not 'visitors'," she says.

"We are!" her brother interjects.

"I'd get a sticker so we could park in the dorm lot, but the offices are closed on weekends."

"There's a spot!" Chuck yells, pointing like a bird dog.

"Great. We're only half a mile from the dorm." Earl shakes his head and rolls his eyes.

"Perfect," says Pam, "wide enough so no one puts dings and scratches my new car."

"Dad's car." Earl remembers somberly.

"Our car, little brother."

"Parking way out here in the boonies –that's some way to treat your guests," Chuck says.

"Guests –you think you're my guests?" Pam asks.

"We are, aren't we, Pammy?" Chuck asks, grinning like a Cheshire cat.

"I brought you both to be my pack mules, my cheap labor. And call me 'Ms. Cleveland', Charles and Earl."

"You won't get away with this, Pam –uh, Ms. Cleveland," Chuck says.

"I already have, Charles. You're captive for the weekend, at my mercy –Bwa ha ha!" she laughs fiendishly.

"You are loco, sis."

"Where are the campus police when you need them?" Chuck kids.

"OK, guys, grab a load of stuff, and don't make me take out my whip. Hop to it!" Pam orders.

"Yes'm."

"Yes, ma'am."

Pam swipes her wristband past the sensor at the right side of the dorm's side entrance. The dorm is locked even during daylight hours -to keep undesirables out. She's sure Chuck and Earl qualify as 'desirables' so she holds the metal security door open for them.

"Up the stairs –only three flights," Pam points.

"Didn't they have elevators in the 19th century?" Chuck asks.

"They did, Charles, but this was a trade school, for people learning to work, and humping up and down the stairs was just a part of the discipline," Pam informs.

"Discipline," Earl repeats. "Ever heard of discipline, Chuck?"

"Yes, Earl, discipline is what's required to tolerate you and Pam."

"You'd better hump your butts up those stairs, or I'll show you some discipline! Where's my whip?" Pam threatens.

"Three!" Chuck pants, reading the big red number at the top of the third flight.

"Very good, Charles." Earl stands by the door waiting for Pam, followed by Chuck, to reach the top of the stairs. Earl, the most athletic of the three, breathes normally after the three flights, while Pam pants heavily after pulling Chuck up the last flight.

"I do have the heaviest load," Chuck justifies his 'last place' position.

"You're doing good, Chuck –I mean, Charles," Pam says. "Now shuffle down the hall - last door on the left."

Chuck steps into the hall and squints as he calls, "Hello, hello down there!" and waits for the echo.

"Go; get down the hall, Charles! I know CPR, so don't worry, I'll revive you when you get to the room –if you get to the room," says Pam, adding, "If you're good."

"I'd do anything to have you do CPR on me," Chuck grins.

"I might die from nausea before we get there," Earl says.

"Oh, almost forgot: Men on the hall!" Pam yells as they make their way to the room.

A petite blonde, wet hair slicked back, wearing only a towel wrapped around her torso barely concealing her butt, traipses out the hall bathroom door.

Pam nods toward the hall mate who got the warning a bit late.

"Oh, hi, Pam! Who are your friends? They're cute. Are they legal?" the young coed skips over to the 'visitors'.

"Toni –we call her 'Tiny' –let me introduce my little brother, Earl. He's not so little. And this is his friend –our friend –Charles. We call him 'Chuck'. Guys, this is Toni," Pam introduces.

"Nice to meet you. Please, call me 'Tiny'. Need I explain?" She tips barefoot around the two guys, scanning foot to fanny to face. "Fess up, Pam. Are they legal?"

"Definitely," says Pam. *Barely.*

"Hmm," Tiny raises her dark eyebrows and winks at Chuck, then at Earl. "Maybe I'll see you out tonight." She pads down the hall, her towel flitting a 'peek-a-boo' of her bottom. "Bye, boys," she smiles and bats her bright, blue eyes.

"OK, gentlemen –and I use the term loosely," Pam says, "pick up your drooling tongues and pop your eyes back in."

Chuck and Earl return to reality. "Mm, hmm," Pam hears them moan as they cross the threshold into her room.

"This is it, folks, home sweet hole-in-the-wall," she says with a nostalgic 'Vanna White' sweep of the hand across the expanse of the room.

"Wow! It's so, so – "Earl starts.

"Small," says Chuck.

"Compact, efficient, economical," Pam says.

"Where's your roomie, sis?"

"She's out –home for the weekend. Lucky for you –one of you –that she said we can use her bed. I brought extra twin sheets; she wouldn't want a naked teenager –Chuck –messing up her sheets, unless she's in there with him."

"Hey, I wouldn't sleep 'au natural' here!" Chuck defends.

"Darn right you're not!" Pam confirms.

"Wait a minute. Who says Chuck gets the bed anyway?" Earl asks.

"We'll flip for it," says Pam. "Flip!" She pushes Earl onto the bed, which creaks and groans.

"Hey!" Earl yells.

"Hey, not fair!" Chuck protests.

"Sorry, Chuck, you've got the floor since your number three in the pecking order - unless Earl wants to share."

"Oh, no!" Earl objects.

"And you'd better not break the bed, bro," Pam says.

She throws the sheet set on top of Earl as he struggles to get off the dwarfed bed. She drops the extra bedroll on the floor at Chuck's feet and says, "Pick your spot, Chuck. See how spacious your bed is?" She waves her hand.

"Grr." Chuck picks up the bedroll.

Pam slaps him on the butt. "Nice jeans, Chuck."

"Okay, Pam, behave yourself." Earl barks. "You, Chuck, stay off the furniture," he glances over at Pam's bed, "like a good dog."

Chuck growls and snaps at both.

50.

"It's just you and me, Philly," says Glenda. She has the whole day off - with payback coming at eleven tonight when she works a third shift. Glenda can't get used to the shift rotations. The daylight hours she always wants to spend with Philly, especially since Philly now has a boyfriend taking up her free time. Today will be their day.

"Yeah, I know. I miss Earl already," says Philly.

"You don't have to sound so excited about having to spend the day with your old Mom. It's not like I get to have more than a little mother-daughter time every day, for more than a few minutes around the kitchen table anyway."

"Mom, slow down, today is yours and mine. How about we start off with a walk around the 'hood? It'll do us both good," Philly says.

"You're right, sweetie. I've almost forgotten the neighborhood around me, coming and going all the time," says Glenda. "Remind me, Philly."

"Come on, get your shoes on and we'll parade the 'hood. Let's give them something to talk about, you and me styling our scrubs on the streets," Philly says.

Glenda dons her walking shoes, not her work clogs, for a change. *They feel funny, confining. Oh, that's what they call 'support?'* The back-door slams and she runs through the kitchen to meet Philly in the back yard.

"God, what a beautiful, sunny autumn day -no jacket required!" Philly says loudly, looks up at the sky and spins around, arms outstretched.

"Race you!" Her mom stomps around the corner of the house.

"You always beat me, Mom!" Philly takes off her.

When Glenda reaches the street, she stops, winded and feeling a little older than she did just a few minutes before. She bends over and puts her hands on her knees as Philly comes up behind her and pops her Mom's butt.

"Now, don't start beating me," Mom says between breaths. She straightens up and Philly puts her arm around her mom's waist.

"Let's go!" Philly says. "We'll take it slow at first and work up to a trot."

"No trotting!" Glenda pleads.

"Where do you want to walk?"

"You're the leader, Philly. Wherever you go, I'll follow."

They walk lively down the block, passing houses unfamiliar to Glenda, but everyday sites to Philly. Glenda feels good, out in the sunshine, just hanging out with her daughter. She takes Philly's hand as they cross the street, instinctively like she had done so many times with her little girl, Felicity. Philly beams at her mom and begins skipping mid-street. *My little girl.*

Philly pulls her hand, "Come on!"

Always eager and ready to go, that little Philly. "Where are you taking me?"

"You'll see," Philly says. "Not much further."

They come to a house where two ladies are sitting out on the front porch; Philly waves. The neighbors halt mid-rock; one timidly lifts her hand and waves, followed by the other lady.

"Earl's neighbors," Philly acknowledges the ladies. Then the Cleveland house across the street, vacant and still today. "Chuck lives there," she points to the next house.

"So, you're very familiar with this end of the street, huh?" she grins at Philly.

"You know I am, Mom, but I want to show you something down there at the end of the cul-de-sac."

When they reach the end, Glenda sniffs the air. "Smells burnt." She gazes beyond the end of the street toward the woods.

"Yeah, some," says Philly. "On the other side, nearer the school, it's charred pretty bad."

"Is this what you wanted me to see?"

"No, come on!" Philly skips into the edge of the woods, following a well-worn path through the brush.

"Where are we going?" Mom asks.

"You'll see."

Glenda starts to fall behind a bit, so Philly slows her youthful stride so her mom can catch up. She runs another minute –and stops. Her mom catches up to her daughter who's standing at the edge of a charred clearing.

"What is it?"

"That." Philly points. In the center of the clearing, is an orange twenty-liter bucket unscathed by the recent brush fire. Philly walks across the charcoal black ground and flips the bucket, bottom up. She hops up onto the bucket's and stands tall. Glenda is clueless to the significance of this statuesque display.

"What, Philly?"

"This is where Earl kissed me - or I kissed him - for the first time," Philly closes her eyes and hugs herself tight. She opens her eyes to find her mom smiling like a teenager, but with motherly tears. Philly hops down and goes to her mom, sharing the hug.

"Thank you, Philly. You are a big girl now."

"I just wanted you to see. Love you, Mom," and they head back up the well-worn path, hand in hand. Philly feels like a woman, Glenda a teenager.

Bruce pulls away from the curb in front of the Taylor's house. The girl and the woman had just disappeared into the woods, and he circled the cul-de-sac quickly, to be gone when they came back. They couldn't know that he was following them. Seeing no sign of life, he had watched Chuck's parents leave - but no sign of Chuck.

The ladies across the street had been rocking on their porch, seeing anything and everything that passed by their perch: The Taylor's left; they waved at the little Philly girl and her mom; the VW pickup passed by and came back up the street; the other car lingered a block up the street. Detective Brown, the other car up the street, avoided the coach's detection, but nothing escaped the watchful eyes of the neighbors.

51.

Reverend Arnold, concerned that he's been 'out of the loop' about Cleve's death investigation, decides to call Detective Brown Saturday morning. He stands on the back porch of the parsonage sipping his morning tea, reveling in the glory of God's creations. Two bluebirds perch on silver twigs above the bluebird box he had strapped to the trunk of the poplar tree the previous spring. Colder weather looming in the northwest has coaxed the bright youngsters into staying close to their spring nesting place for shelter from the frigid forecast. They flit to the moist morning grass of fall to catch an errant earthworm wriggling toward the surface light. With no hungry chicks to feed, the bright blue male and duller female store the fat for the freeze. The Reverend dips the fresh scone, which the widow Robinson had baked and delivered to him fresh this morning, in his tea.

"Bless her," he says, "and all His creatures."

His phone vibrates in his robe pocket. Caller ID: Detective Brown. Funny, the Reverend was on the brink of calling him. "Detective Brown?" he answers.

"Reverend Arnold, how are you this morning?"

"Fine, it's a glorious morning, and I truly don't want to spoil it with the inevitable conversation with you," says the Reverend.

"So, you know the subject already?"

"Of course, how did you know, detective?"

"A member of your congregation, Glenda, called me late last night. She said that a friend of her daughter's had given her my number. Only teenager I gave my number to was a young man named Chuck, also a friend of Earl Cleveland," Detective Brown says.

"We seem to be chasing our tails, detective. Glenda called me late last night and mentioned your name a conversation she overheard between you and the coroner."

"So, you have the secondhand story –third hand?"

"That's too many hands –there may be a foot involved." the Reverend says, keeping the conversation light, but knowing the impending darkness of the subject.

"We're trying to keep 'the subject' hushed, or at this point down to a dull roar. I need your cooperation," the detective says.

"I'm always willing to cooperate for the good."

"I don't know if you consider me 'good', gut I'm definitely on the right side," Brown says.

"Do you know who's on the wrong side, the one who broke the commandment 'thou shalt not kill'?" Reverend Arnold asks.

"With ninety-nine percent certainty, Reverend."

"The Lord doesn't deal in percentages and probabilities, detective," the Reverend says. "It's either 'yay' or 'nay'."

"Then it's a 'yay', and I know the murderer," Detective Brown says.

"How can I be of service –in addition to prayer and counseling?".

"Besides Glenda, whom I don't believe the killer knows she knows, there are several people who do know –and he knows may know," the detective says.

"Too many 'knows', detective."

"You're right, but the fact is that Glenda's daughter, Philly, probably has knowledge of the killer through Chuck Taylor, who gave her my contact phone number from the card I gave him. Philly and Chuck are close friends with Earl, so he may know, though he might have been kept out of the loop to spare his emotional involvement, right after his father's death," Brown elaborates.

"And -?"

"Yes, there may be others who suspect," says Brown.

"Still, too many 'knows'."

"Lila Cleveland was the closest to the killer," the detective says.

"And the killer is -?" asks the Reverend.

"Not to mention his name, I'll only tell you his title: coach," says Brown.

"No surprise, I've had signals that he's no good, but I never thought this."

"Yes, this, and there are a couple more neighbors who may suspect 'him'. Of course, the Taylor's may have gathered suspicions from their son, Chuck," the detective says.

"And who else?"

"The two ladies across the street, Anna and Bette may have seen something. All these people may be in danger, Reverend."

"How can I help, detective?"

"I need you to help me stay connected."

"Oh, I have a connection with Him, and so do you," says the Reverend.

"Definitely could use your connection there, but also with this circle of people 'in the know', Reverend."

"I know that Pam and Earl Cleveland, and their neighbor and friend Chuck, are off with Pam at College until late Sunday, so we don't have to worry about them," the Reverend says.

"But Glenda and her daughter Philly are in town, plus the Taylor's and the neighbors. Lila Cleveland is staying with her little daughter and mother-in-law, so they're out of the 'hood," the detective says.

"So, Glenda and Philly are left. You want me to watch them?"

"I want you to call and check on Philly tonight. Her mom's working third shift. I'll be staking out 'his' house and tailing him if 'he' leaves. The neighbors are always there, aware of everyone's business. You can count on the Taylor's, too –they're good people," Brown says.

"Yes, Charlie seems like a good guy. We can use all the good guys we can round up, eh Detective?"

"This is not a posse - remember that. Open eyes, ears and stealth are what we need to get this guy, not 'shoot 'em up' cowboy heroes," Brown says.

"Detective, I'll provide prayer. You're in charge of this local mission project," the Reverend says.

"Many thanks, Reverend."

"Always thankful, Detective."

They close their phones. The Reverend takes a sip of tea.

Why can I never finish a cup of hot tea? He empties the cup onto the ground by the azaleas at the edge of his porch. The bluebirds fly over the hedge, and the Reverend retreats inside the parsonage to get ready to go down to the church and work on his sermon for Sunday morning. *Something about bluebirds and good neighbors and possess...* A cloud floats between his home and the sun, casting a shadow across his den.

52.

"What a beautiful morning, Lila," Ester joins her daughter-in-law on the patio with a cup of hot coffee. "Can I freshen your coffee?"

"No, thank you, this is fine. Where's our little Tina?" Lila looks beyond Ester toward the dining room.

"She's right behind me –Tina! –bringing teacakes that she and I baked this morning."

"How long have you two been up? You must've been up since the crack of dawn."

"Since it's Saturday, the crack of dawn-thirty," Ester says.

Tina dances barefoot carrying a mound of teacakes on a dinner plate. "Teacakes, Mom? They're still warm –I baked them this morning - and Emaw helped!"

"That would be lovely, Miss Tina." Lila delicately takes one, then another, from the plate.

"May I have two?" Lila asks as she takes the second teacake.

"Definitely, or four or as many as you can eat –they're delicious!" Tina beams. "Emaw, want some?"

"Maybe one," Ester says as she takes one. "I already ate a half dozen raw while we were rolling and cutting them out."

"You got a stomachache, Emaw?"

"No, I'm fine, Tina. Sit here by your mom, and I'll get you a glass of milk."

Tina slides up onto the white wrought iron chair beside her mom. "Cold!" Tina bunches her long nightgown under her bare bottom and legs.

"Here, take my seat, Tina. I've already warmed it for you," Lila gets up and pats her hand on the seat.

Tina slides off the cold chair, her gown sticking to the white latex paint and revealing her tender young legs. Lila smiles and helps Tina straighten her gown.

"Thanks, Mom, that's lots better," Tina says as she wiggles her little buns on the seat until they're toasty in her mom's stead.

Ester stands inside the door, out of sight, listening to the exchange between Tina and Lila. *Lila could be a good mother, in time, but right now Lila is learning to like herself, to treat herself well enough so the 'bad' doesn't come back. 'Do unto others as you would have them do unto you' is a wonderful thought unless she doesn't know how to treat herself. If Lila slides into that deep dark depression, does she know how she wants others to treat her? She still does not remember the disaster, the tragedy of 'that little girl'. It was an accident! In the recesses of her mind she stores that tragedy, the other Tina. Can she forgive herself, make peace with the ghosts so she can become a good mother to her Tina? God, I hope so. I'm here, Lila, to help.*

Maybe they need some bonding time. Ester steps just outside the door, "Ladies, I need to run some errands and get my hair done. Can you do without me for a couple hours?"

Tina and Emaw both see Lila's frightened 'cornered critter' look. Ester is about to change her mind about going when Tina says, "I'll take care of Mom, Emaw. I can show her how to do stuff like making tea cakes and tea, play dress up, read my story books –everything! What do you think, Mom?"

Lila hesitates, looking from Tina to Ester and back to Tina, who's grinning dimple to dimple. "You go on, Ester, we'll be alright. I'll be in competent hands with Tina."

Tina looks at her hands.

"Oh, I mean I trust you, Tina," Lila says.

"Like Emaw trusts me to cut the tea cakes and to be careful tasting the hot ones –and to wipe good after I go potty?" Tina asks.

"Yes," Lila giggles, "all of that. Do you trust me?"

"Absolutely, Mom -to do all that!"

"I think you two are in excellent hands," Ester says. Tina holds up her hands.

"See –ex'lent hands. Yours, too, Mom," Tina says as Lila puts her hands on the table.

"Excellent! Here's you milk, Tina. I trust you not to eat too many tea cakes," Ester says.

"What about me?" Lila teases.

"I don't know about you. Tina, keep an eye on her," Ester says.

Tina scrunches up her nose and closes her eyes twice, attempting to wink at her mom. "Got my eye on you, Mom."

53.

In the town of Old Viceroy, the evening sky glows red light filtering through the sparse tobacco brown leaves quivering on the century old oak trees. Pam traipses ahead of Chuck and Earl, kicking the dried leaves into a shower of late autumn glory that flutters through the air like fairies in a modern dance.

She feels like a young girl again, as she did prancing around barefoot on a warm fall day as her dad raked the stray leaves falling into their back yard faster than he could gather them up. Those were happy days' memories she tucked away in her hope chest to remind her of the good times before her mom lost her mind - the first time.

Tina, little Tina, the first Tina whose name Pam had never spoken in her mom's fragile state. Pam had seen little sister Tina dance her fairy dance at Emaw's, but never the first little Tina, who had flown away with the angels ahead of Mom, who was fleeing devils. Mom is further away from those demons now than she's ever been, but they may always lurk in the dark corner of her mind waiting to haunt her. The first little Tina would have forgiven in the same instant with the angels; the second Tina had never known anything but love from Emaw, Dad - and Mom who only came to visit.

Pam grabs a handful of leaves and tosses it above her head as she turns a somersault with the angel fairy beside her. She missteps on the landing and tumbles into a roll, leaves adorning her hair and sweater.

"You are a lunatic, you know that, don't you, Pam?" asks Earl.

Pam sits up, legs straight out in front of her, and flings more leaves above her head. Her smile is carefree, cherubic even, as she admits, "Yeah, and -?"

"I hope you don't get chiggers," Chuck says.

"You'd better hope not, because you'll have them, by the time the night is over, I may have them." says Pam nonchalantly. Chuck doesn't get the allusion - Pam's impending proximity.

"Behave, Pam," says Earl, "and Chuck is to stay off the furniture in the room."

"What?" Chuck asks, a little slow in the game.

"Keep up, Chuck, keep up, or you'll get left behind tonight," says Pam.

"OK, Pam." He reaches out a hand to assist her getting up. She bounces up like a gymnast hitting a landing off the uneven bars and lands inches from Chuck's face. Chuck grasps her shoulders, spins Pam around and begins wiping leaves off her back, picking pieces from her hair, shoulders, back, butt…"

"Whoa, Chuck!" Pam turns to face him.

"Um, I was just…trying…to help," he stammers.

"Enough helping, Chuck," says Earl.

"Thanks, Chuck." Pam gives him a peck on his flushed cheek.

"Anytime, Pam."

"Watch it, Chuck," she says.

"Yeah, Chuck," says Earl.

"Where are you taking us anyway? Is this a campus tour?" Chuck asks.

They get to the fringe parking lot and continue walking through the field, past the car and out the other side to an old warehouse area. Pam disappears around the corner of the first building.

"Where are you going, Pam?" Earl asks.

"Just keep up, guys."

In the alley between the two three-story buildings, the sun has already set, and cobblestones underfoot throw Chuck off balance. He catches himself on the 19th century brick wall. The corridor between the buildings is damp and mossy, not conducive to 'fun' that Pam had promised. A wharf rat the size of a Chihuahua scampers and thuds into a basement window at street level.

"Pam, where are we going? I don't see fun times here," says Chuck.

"Just a little further –like coming out of the Dark Forest into the poppy field on the way to the Emerald City," Pam sings like 'the good witch'.

"Yeah, but remember what happened in the poppy field?" Chuck asks.

"I'll look after you, Chuck," Pam promises.

"Right, but I don't think she's got her ruby slippers," Earl says.

"It's just around this corner, guys. We're off!"

230

54.

The barista stands wiping down the wooden bar after just bringing up a keg of ale that's been aging for months infusing oaky flavor into the brew. Patrons call him a barista, though he serves little coffee; brews organic and fair-trade roasted beans when he does pour a cup. He can't roast the beans on location, fearing the underground café might be discovered, following the aroma of the illegal product.

'Illegal' single source coffee, rich, robust and proud as opposed to the 'legal' cheap labor, pooled coffee from government sanctioned sources, the poor, demoralized factory plantations. 'More jobs are created through the factory farm system,' the regulators had said, referring to the poverty-stricken serfs in the newer, 'better' era of prosperity. Prosperity is relative. The family who grows the coffee and calls the laborers in for the harvest from their neighbors, pays the people according to their production, the kilos of ripe beans picked. All the people in this village are responsible, well-fed, clothed, healthy and happy. The 'new' system pays the workers per diem, just enough to keep them struggling for bare minimum, but living in 'modern', sanitary concrete block houses with electricity and electronic devices, all provided 'free' –but at the price of what freedom?
Frank shakes his head, unable to get past the morality: legal versus illegal. He draws a pint of ale and watches the head of foam form and rise to meet the rim of the ceramic mug. He sets the hefty mug on the bar and rests his elbows before the vessel, his chin in his hands. The line of demarcation grows sharper between amber ale in the bottom ¾ of the mug and the whipped creamy head atop, analogous to, but not akin to the divisions of natural, organic freedom and fluffed, sterile mass produced nouveau slavery.
Frank blows a flurry of foam off the top and wafts a mouthful of his craft brew. It is good.
He goes back down to the cellar to inspect the golden cured tobacco leaves. Sweet musty citrus aroma greets his nostrils as he kneels and opens the wooden footlocker stowed against the low back wall of the stable natural humidity environment under ground –underground. Frank puts his hands into the layers of football-broad supple, waxy mustard golden tobacco leaves fingering the perfectly cured smokable or chewable, commodity. It's 'in order'. He packs the leaves, enough to fill a wooden rectangular tinderbox, about the volume of a football, gets up and secures the tobacco

footlocker. On the way to the stairs he brushes the dust off an old brown glass jug, four liters of muscadine wine, aged a year and ready to drink, puts his thumb through the handle and brings the dark elixir up the wooden steps to ground level. He secures the thick oiled oak cellar door behind him.

"Contraband." He smiled and settles the jug into the crushed ice in the cooler behind the bar. He sets the dark wooden tinderbox on the bar and waves for the barmaid at the other end.

"Sally, care to chop?" he asks, referring to the leaf tobacco in the tinderbox. Some leaf tobacco is chopped for filler in pipes and hand rolled cigarettes, while other leaves are left whole for wrapping cigars.

"Sure, if I can have the first smoke."

"Deal -we'll have a pipe together as soon as we get our people served and happy."

"Speaking of our people, Frank, I was fixing to tell you, I heard our pet wharf rat bang against the window a couple minutes ago –must be somebody coming up the alley."

Frank looks at the security monitor underneath the bar. It shows four views: the alley to the side; the opposite side of the building to the south; a broad view of the steps leading down to the front door; and a view beside the front door for close-up facial recognition. Three figures, two male and one female are descending the steps at the front door.

"I can't see down here, Pam," Chuck whines. His feet feel for the steps and hands feel for the handrail and front door. "What is this? You taking us down to purgatory?"

"Close to heaven, Chuck," she says, "just you wait."

"What's that glowing by the door?" Earl asks.

"Security." Pam smiles for the camera and waves. She knows Frank is watching the monitor behind the bar.

A 'click' answers Pam's smile-wave, and the heavy door opens a centimeter. She pushes it open and goes in first, motioning for them to come. She pauses, securing the door behind them, closed and clicked. A dozen square wooden tables and chairs for four, two booths to the right, a huge mahogany bar straight ahead, and a kitchen through a swinging door behind the left end of the bar. A clean-cut athletic cut man, maybe thirty years old –maybe forty, but probably younger –stands behind the bar. A dark-haired barmaid, hair in a bun and wearing a peasant dress, sits on a stool opposite the barista.

"Wow! Olde world," Chuck observes.

"Definitely," Earl agrees.

"This is the Naturalists' Underground Bar –the NUB." Pam waves. "Hi, Frank!"

"Pam!" The waitress calls back, arms open wide as she hops off the barstool.

"Pam! Our baby has come home!" Frank rounds the end of the bar to meet Pam in the middle of the cluster of tables. Sally follows and hugs Pam who hugs Frank who hugs Sally.

"Like a family reunion," Chuck says to Earl, empathizing and feeling left out.

"Somebody else's family," Earl says to Chuck. "Mine never gets that excited, touchy-feely."

"Mine either," Chuck says.

"Hey, guys, come over here!" Pam calls. Chuck and Earl saunter over, playing it cool, hoping their covers as college dudes won't be blown.

"Frank, Sally, this is my brother, Earl, and his –our –friend, Chuck."

Sally hugs them both as if they've been friends for life. Frank shakes each guy's hand and pulls him into a guy hug with a slap on the back, and then a quick release.

"Glad you're back, Pam. I'm sorry about your dad." Frank pauses, steps back. "You look good."

"I am good!" Pam says. "Got my two escorts with me –couldn't be better." She stands between Earl and Chuck putting an arm around each. Chuck leans into Pam; Earl leans away from his sister.

"Here, sit in your booth, Pam." Frank walks them over to the booth, his hand placed in the small of Pam's back as if leading her in a dance. Chuck takes note of the gesture, discretely jealous.

"What can I get for you guys?" Frank asks.

"Since they've never been here, surprise us!" says Pam.

"Gotcha!" Frank says. "Be right back." Sally follows him to the bar.

"Now, Pam," Earl says, "I know this is where you got my tobacco – my contraband. What other illegal items do you have in store?"

"You won't be disappointed."

Chuck slides all the way to the corner in the booth; Pam scoots in close, leaving no gap between them. He wonders what kind of 'contraband' Pam could be 'into'. He had choked on Earl's tobacco when he tried it at the fort, but he didn't bring his e-pipe; Pam told him not to.

Frank comes back to the table holding a foot-long ceramic pipe. Sally steps up to the table with three new chilled half liter Mason jars held in her fingers by their rims in one hand and an old gallon jug of dark crimson liquid–almost black – in the other, condensation droplets formed on the glass surface. She places the drinking jars on the table; Chuck and Earl glance at each other, then at the jars.

"Wine?" asks Earl.

"Wine," says Pam.

"Year-old muscadine wine," Sally corrects. She tips the jug to fill each Mason jar as Frank holds a lighted match to the bowl of the long thin pipe and puffs, draws until the fire catches and the tobacco leaves hold the glow and offer up their ancient fire ritual.

Earl smiles, salivating; Chuck looks away; Pam takes charge, placing the pipe's mouthpiece firmly between her lips and draws smoothly.

"This is the best tobacco North Carolina's mountains produce, raised in camouflaged fields back in the woods –tax free and illegal. Enjoy," Frank boasts.

Pam holds the robust but sweet tobacco smoke in her mouth for a minute, releases a small volume, and says, "Ahh," pleasantly. She passes the pipe to Chuck, who takes it but hesitates.

I can do this. Hold...hold... and he exhales, accidentally blowing a smoke ring.

"Show off," Earl says as he takes the pipe from Chuck.

"That's smooth," Chuck says to Pam as she pokes him lightly in the ribs with her elbow. He reciprocates the poke.

"I usually smoke rolled tobacco, but..." Earl says and takes a puff from the sleek white ceramic pipe. "Mm," he holds and releases a whistling plume toward Chuck.

"More, more –I love it," Chuck relishes.

"I'll get you a cigar or two, Earl," Frank starts.

"-or a box!" Earl says.

"Can you set me up with a pipe and some tobacco to go?" Chuck asks.

"Anything you guys want. Just don't get caught, or if you do get caught, don't tell where you got it," Frank cautions.

"If I get caught, they'll charge me with 'contributing to the delinquency of minors," Pam teases.

"You guys aren't 'of age'? I'd have never guessed," Frank says.

"There is no 'of age' for tobacco and alcohol," Pam reminds. "We're all illegal."

"Drink to that!" Frank says, raising his jar of muscadine.

They all drink the sweet wine with no guilt, no fear, just a warm feeling.

"Ever had wine before, Chuck?" Pam asks as she tips the diminishing jug to his empty jar.

Chuck takes a pull off his new custom engraved bluebird blue ceramic pipe: 'Chuck Taylor, Naturalist'.

"I slipped a taste of my dad's own homemade wine a couple of times, but he said, 'Wait 'til you're a man, son,' after he caught me. Sipped the communion wine, but tasted like grape juice," Chuck says, taking a fresh sip from his Mason jar.

"For the kids, Chuck, that was grape juice at church," Earl informs.

"Oh, I just thought I needed to drink more to feel it," Chuck says.

Earl holds his forehead. "This muscadine is making me feel a little woozy."

"Just wait 'til you get up to go to the head –the restroom. That first step out of this booth is a 'doozy'," Pam slurs the words.

"Speaking of which," Chuck nudges her, "you might have to 'scuse me for a minute."

"OK, Chuck. Now listen closely. I'm standing up by the booth, and you put your hand on my shoulder as you step down, got it?" Pam offers him slightly inebriated guidance.

"Yes, dear." Chuck grins, squints and sways toward the table, he slides down the bench and puts one foot on the floor.

"Put your hand, Chuck," Pam directs. He braces his hand on top of her head and starts laughing. "Silly boy."

She gets tickled. "Put your other hand on my shoulder and step your other foot down." He does, and she wobbles with his drunken weight.

"I'll help," Earl offers as he sways out of the opposite booth and bumps Pam and Chuck. "Foul!"

Pam holds up her hand like she knows the answer in third grade class and calls, "Sally, we need your assistance." Sally answers the call and comes trotting over to the booth. "Sally, my wonderful, strong friend, I need –"

"Yes, you do." She takes Pam by the elbow as Frank hustles over to prop Chuck against the side of the booth and grabs Earl under the arm.

"You guys OK?" Pam asks as she leans on Sally.

"Gotta pee," Chuck slurs.

"Me, too," Earl says.

"OK, guys, hang onto my wings, we're flying to the head," Frank directs.

"The 'head' of what?" Chuck asks. "We need to go to a restroom – or out to the alley."

"Just come with me, men; I'll get you there."

"Be right back, Pam," Chuck turns his head back toward her. He misses every other step but keeps time with Earl.

"You know it's only seven o'clock, right Pam?" Sally acknowledges their Earl 'indulgence'.

"Yes, the night is young and so are we!" Pam revels.

"Oh, don't exaggerate; you're just a bit over-buzzed. Brother and friend are on the verge of drunk," Sally says. "How old did you say they are?"

"Didn't say."

"Doesn't matter, everything is legal here that's illegal out there –or vice versa," Sally says. "Most everything."

"Don't mess with the cute little contraband –he's mine." Pam girly-giggles.

"What about the tall one?" Sally explores the delinquent options.

"He's my brother –and he's tall, but 'he ain't heavy'" Pam slurs an oldie lyric from their parents' day. Pam and Sally wobble-walk around the opposite end of the bar toward the ladies' room.

Earl bumps into the door as he exits the men's room. Frank steps in front of him and gives the 'zip-it' signal with his eyes. "My bad, my bad," Earl says with a 'zip'. He'd forgotten to zip up before exiting the men's room.

"Chuck, you OK in there?" Frank asks.

"Yeah –can't a guy pee in peace?"

He emerges from the head, hands washed and dripping dry, jeans zipped, hair combed, walking a little steadier than when he entered.

"A load off, huh Chuck?" Earl asks.

"Much better."

"If you're better, Chuck, how about escorting Earl to the booth. I've got some more customers arriving," Frank says.

"Sure, boss," Chuck's agreeable. "Thanks for the lift to the head."

"No problem –now, I think that's enough muscadine wine for now. Sally will bring you some grub," Frank says.

"I am starting to get hungry." Chuck puts his arm around Earl's shoulder and walks him to the booth.

Pam emerges from the ladies' room. Sally holds her by the shoulder and stares into her face. Pam smiles and shakes her head affirmatively, walking zigzag to the booth, but landing solidly on her bench seat beside Chuck. She had watched as Chuck escorted her brother safely to the booth. *That's so nice.* She gives Chuck a silly, slightly inebriated smile and nudges him over toward the corner of the booth. She puts her hand on his knee under the table, sneaky and unnoticeable to the others –except for the bounce and surprised expression on Chuck's face. He turns to Pam, leans over and whispers something in her ear, and she removes her hand. She's a little embarrassed but still sits close to him.

"You guys, hands above the table!" Earl pokes. Pam kicks his shin. "Ow!"

"And you try not to slide under the table, Earl," says Chuck.

"You OK, little brother?" Pam asks.

"Uh! I'm great." Earl leans forward and rubs his bruised leg under the table. "I'm alert and sober now, big sis."

"Dinner is served!" Sally sachets to the booth and places large salad platters before each guest.

"Mm," Pam drools. Fresh greens, peppers, assorted colorful veggies with chicken fillets on top.

Earl stares at the mound of vegetables. "Hmm." Chuck is taken aback by the healthy offering after just consuming wine and tobacco.

"It's good food - good for you." Sally announces, noticing Chuck and Earl's hesitation. "All the veggies are organically grown, most by Frank, and the chicken is free range from the same mountain farmer that grew the tobacco -nothing artificial around here."

"Chicken fillets? What do you do with the rest of the chicken?" Earl asks skeptically.

"Chicken broth, stew, pot pie, gravy with the feet…We use everything but the crow and the cackle!" Sally says.

"This is great!" Chuck drizzles bleu cheese buttermilk dressing over the chicken and greens, tossing them with his fork.

"Thank you, Chuck," Sally says. "I know Pam loves our food. What's your thought, Earl?"

"Are you implying that I have only one thought, Sally? I have many thoughts –some deep!"

"No, no, I'm sure you do. Maybe you can tell me about them later." Sally flirts.

"Uh, yeah."

"Great –enjoy!"

The three quietly munch their salads. Even Earl starts to enjoy his meal –especially the chicken fillets.

"I forgot to ask," says Earl, "which part of the chicken does a fillet come from, the front or the back?"

"You've never seen a live chicken, have you, Earl? How about you, Chuck?" Pam asks.

"Not alive," Chuck says.

"If you want, we can come back here in the morning –when the fresh, live chickens arrive –and watch the entire process from foot to feather to finish and fillet," Pam elaborates.

Earl tries not to picture chicken carnage and changes the subject back to edible food.

"Good food, huh, sis?"

"Yes –and they're breast fillets," Pam offers.

"Speaking of which," Earl starts.

"Which, breasts or fillets?" Chuck asks.

Pam hits Chuck on his thigh with her fist.

"Well –both –no, I mean 'fillet' makes me think of Philly," Earl says.

"Philly's breasts?" Chuck snickers, with the reward of an even harder sock on his thigh. "Ow!"

"What about Philly, Earl –miss her?" Pam asks.

"Yeah, but we've been so busy I haven't really had much chance to think about her."

"She and her mom were spending the day together, right? That's a rarity, so I'm sure she's enjoying their time," says Pam, "but she misses you, too, bro."

"Probably. I don't know," Earl says, getting downhearted.

"Sure, she does! But I have big plans for us tonight!"

"Tonight, I thought this was the plan for tonight," Earl says.

"What could possibly top this?" Chuck asks.

Pam turns to Chuck and gives him a sexy, lip pursing, eye-flashing look and touches his hand underneath the table.

"What?" Chuck asks.

"Toga party!" Pam squeals.

"Toga party?" Earl asks. "Not where everyone –"

"Yes, everyone dons a sheet and gets into that Greek state of mind. Oh," she reminds herself out loud, "we're supposed to bring a keg."

"A keg –a keg of what?" Chuck asks.

"Take a look at the bar, guys," Pam says.

They look over, and Frank is hefting a wooden keg onto the bar, proudly with his product, his baby.

"Ten liters of amber ale brewed especially for us by brew master Frank. You have to order it weeks and weeks ahead of time –like at the beginning of the semester. I've had my mind on this keg all semester," Pam boasts.

"We already drank too much wine, sis," Earl notes.

"This is different –it's ale," Pam says.

"Still illegal, though, right?" Chuck asks.

"Shh –of course," Pam whispers adding, "why am I whispering? We're already practically fugitives from the law. What's a little more contraband?"

"You sound like you've done this before, sis," Earl asks.

"Not this, in particular, but I've been bringing tobacco to you, right? That makes me a smuggler," Pam acknowledges.

"So, Frank's a bootlegger, and we're the runners?" Chuck asks.

"You could say that –literally 'runners'," Pam says.

"What do you mean, Pam?" Chuck asks from the perspective of a non-athlete.

"We can't just put it in the car and unload it in front of the fraternity house. The proven mode of transport on campus, per the LRW fraternity, is Red Flyer," Pam informs.

"What's a Red Flyer? I thought you said 'roll', not 'fly'," Chuck says.

"When the president of LRW, now a senior, was a kid, his dad got word from the CEO of the Red Flyer toy company that financial troubles were inevitable, and they were going to sell the company or go out of business. His dad, nicknamed 'Red', worked his way up in Red Flyer from assembler to salesman to manager and ultimately VP and decided to stockpile product –for a rainy day. Well, the company went under as predicted, but much lighter in inventory than it could have been because 'Red' had leased a warehouse –right here in Old Viceroy. So, here we are, the next generation, still pulling and riding Red Flyers –Little Red Wagons!"

"Sounds pretty conspicuous pulling a little red wagon with a ten-liter keg on top," says Chuck.

"You're so practical and sensible, Chuck," Pam says, "But since this is a Red Flyer town, they're all over the place. It's like a rite of passage, you know, pulling an LRW –Little Red Wagon -Red Flyer."

"No, I don't know," Earl agrees with Chuck.

"OK, Miss Cleveland," Chuck addresses Pam, "how does this work?"

"I'm not your teacher, Chuck – or maybe I am," Pam retorts, "but I will demonstrate in a couple of hours. First step is to pay the tab –and for the keg; second is to go back to the dorm and take a nap, rest up for the toga party!"

Sally comes back with the tab, Pam pays, and Chuck reaches for his One Card.

"I've got this, Chuck. I'm taking care of you boys this weekend," Pam says.

"I owe you," Chuck says.

"You can pay me later, Chuck." Pam touches his hand as they slide from the booth. "Brother Earl, you've been paying me all your life."

"See you later, Pam," Sally says. "See you later, Earl –you, too, Chuck."

"She's coming with us to the party?" Earl asks.

"Yeah, we need a chaperone –and someone to ride shotgun on the little red wagon." Pam shoots Earl a sly grin.

55.

Chuck wakes up on his mat beside Pam's twin bed. He stretches and yawns and bumps somebody lying next to him on the floor.

"What are you doing down here?" asks Chuck.

Pam opens her eyes and wipes the back of her hand over her face removing the hair stuck to her cheek. She smiles hazily, lazily up at Chuck who's on his side, propped on his elbow looking down at her.

"Doing? Oh, just spooning with you, Chuck." She blinks.

"You have a bed, Pam."

"Well, you wouldn't come in with me, so I figured I'd just suffer down here on the hard floor with you, Chuck," Pam grins, sitting up 'Indian' style.

"You are incorrigible, Pam, but I'm starting to get used to it," Chuck says.

Pam rocks over to him from in her sitting position, close enough to whisper in Chuck's ear "Get used to it," and kisses his cheek.

Earl coughs pretentiously. "Excuse me; I am in the room, guys."

Pam hops up off the floor and rummages in her duffle bag. She pulls out the three large crumpled white sheets. "Ta da!" she sings. "Instant togas!"

Chuck and Earl look at each other, and then to Pam.

"While I go change into mine down the hall, you guys get dressed in here."

"Won't it look funny, jeans and shirts and all sticking out of the sheet?" Chuck asks.

"Yeah, what I want you to do, while I'm out of the room," Pam speaks like a massage therapist getting ready for a session, "is remove your clothes down to your level of comfort –whatever that might be –and help each other wrap your togas."

"That sounds a little funny, Pam," Earl says.

"You guys will get the hang of it –I'll help make you presentable when I get back. Now, hop to it!" she orders.

"I'm not sure about this 'level of comfort' –what's yours, Pam?" Chuck asks.

"Hm, let's just say I love the feel of 400 thread-count cotton on my entire body. Get the picture, Chuck?" Pam winks and clicks her tongue making a sound like calling a horse.

Chuck's mouth drops open in disbelief, astonishment on the verge of hyperventilation and gets Pam's 'picture' as she flits out the door and down the hall, her white sheet trailing behind her like a friendly ghost.

"You do know that you're not going to help me tuck my toga, don't you Chuck?" Earl informs.

Chuck closes his mouth, wipes the drool off his chin with the corner of the toga sheet, and says, "You neither." He turns his back to Earl and kicks off his shoes; Earl follows suit.

As jeans and shirts and BVD's drop and are kicked to their respective corners, Chuck says, "No peaking," as he drapes the sheet over his shoulder and begins fumbling for ends and tucks.

"You do know your sister's a lunatic, right, Earl?"

"Yeah, she comes by it honest," says Earl, thinking of their mother.

Chuck doesn't respond to Earl's comment, making light of his mom's mental illness troubles. *Maybe he could be right anyway.*

The trio steps out the side door of the dorm, visages of 19th century specters emerging from a time portal. Pam leads the way. As soon as they round the corner, the wind flutters their togas, Marilyn Monroe fashion, flashing the world with what's behind them.

"Nice bum, Chuck," Earl emphasizes the embarrassing dilemma.

"Alright, Earl," Pam calls him down, "and Chuck, I know you're ogling my perfect bum every chance you get. Thank your friend the wind."

"Yes…no…the wind…I didn't…" Chuck flutters.

"Chuck, you are a 'bum'," Earl mocks.

"But –I mean 'butt' –you couldn't help yourself, could you, Chuck?" Pam stops abruptly instigating a 'three stooges' domino effect.

"Umph," Earl bumps Chuck.

"Ahh," Chuck exhales as he grabs Pam's shoulders.

"Now I know you guys are not still intoxicated from the wine, are you?" Pam asks.

"No, we're intoxicated by you, Pam," Earl says, "right Chuck?"

"Mm, definitely." Chuck says. Pam flashes him her girly sweet smile.

"Yes, I am intoxicating, aren't I?" says Pam. "Eyes on the path, Chuck!" Chuck snaps to attention and averts his eyes from Pam's accidental exposure.

"We've got to stop by the LRW house to get their Red Flyer. You guys wait here, and I'll be right out," Pam says.

Chuck and Earl wait by the brick walled patio, fidgeting and self-conscious in only their sheets and thongs –flip flops. A brother of LRW walks by them wearing a red toga with 'LRW' white lettering on the skirt part.

"Whassup, fellas?" He casually greets and crosses the patio to the fraternity house front door.

"'sup!" Chuck says.

"You're so cool, Chuck," Earl mocks.

The breeze picks up, and they're forced to stand, backs against the wall and hands in front holding down their toga hems.

"Got it," Pam says, rattling the wagon across the brick walkway through the open gate. "For practice, Chuck, you push and Earl, you pull," as she hands off the red metal handle to her brother.

"What's your job, Pam, supervising?" Earl asks.

Pam laughs, "Of course, silly brother." She grabs the middle of her toga hem and rolls it between her legs in lady-like gesture before boarding the little red wagon.

"Umph." She squeezes her hips snuggly between the short metal railings of the meter-long wagon bed, just long enough for Pam's thonged feet to touch the front, her tail touching the tailgate.

"Oh, I see how this works," says Earl. "She's queen for a day."

"'Your majesty' to you, plebes -Now giddy up!" Pam points onward. "Pull, Earl, pull! Push –watch your hands, now Chuck." She slings her head and swishes her pony tail in his face.

The little red wagon train rolls into the alley by the Naturalists' Café. Pam directs her driver to the second ground level window, and she dismounts the red steed. The wharf rat shadows them, thumps into the window and disappears. "Creepy," Chuck murmurs.

"You guys wait here while I go up front and 'face' Frank." Pam scuffles back toward the front of the building.

Within two minutes Pam comes back around, and the window by the wagon clicks open, sans rat.

"Hi, guys!" Sally announces, peeking up at them through the open window.

"Sally! Nice seeing you again," Earl says.

"Really, I'm glad because I'm going with you all to the party, see?" Sally shrugs her toga bare shoulder up to the window. "Look, you two men have the hard part. I roll this ten liter wooden keg onto the platform through the window, and you two lift it into the wagon, got it?"

"I've got my end if you've got yours," says Earl, meeting the small wooden keg as it comes out the opening onto the steel platform at street level. "On three, Chuck: One, two, three!"

They heft the cool oaken keg onto the wagon's bed; Sally pushes an old woolen green Army blanket out the window.

"Wrap it around the keg to keep it cool - and for camouflage," says Sally. "I'll be right out!" The window clicks shut.

"I didn't remember she was coming," Earl says to Pam.

"Maybe you were too drunk to remember. Sally's coming –is that a problem, little brother?"

"No, not really, she knows I have a girlfriend, right?"

"Earl, it's not a date. We're just friends going out together to have a little fun –Philly won't mind," Pam says, trying to ease her brother.

"And we won't tell her, Earl," Chuck assures.

"Chuck, it's no big deal; no secrets." says Pam.

"Just so she knows I have a girlfriend," Earl reiterates.

Sally comes down the alley, skipping along in her thongs and toga, wearing a shiny gold headpiece.

"Nice bling, Sally!" Pam says.

I brought you one, too. My friend makes jewelry, and she whipped these up for us," Sally says. "What's with the serious face, Earl?"

"Um, well I…" Earl tries.

"Earl, he's just missing his girlfriend a little, that's all," Chuck says.

"Oh, I understand, Earl. My boyfriend is –was –in college halfway across the country, and I thought I would lonesome myself to death, but we broke up," Sally empathizes.

Great! Something to look forward to, breaking up. "I guess you would understand, but Philly and I –that's my girlfriend's name –are still together."

"They've been together for about a week," Pam says. "Philly's a sweet girl."

"She's a great young woman," Earl corrects.

"I'm sure she's wonderful –with a boyfriend like you. I'll try to behave myself. Just friends, right?" Sally says.

"Yeah, let's just all have a good time, boys and girls," Pam says playfully. "Sally, why don't you ride first?"

Sally tucks the green blanket along the sides of the keg and smoothes down the 'saddle'. Gathering her toga hem, she tucks it between her thighs and mounts the keg like it was a quarter horse.

"Try not to warm that beer with your hot bootie, Sally," Pam teases.

"No promises –I'm hot! But you know the English like it that way," Sally informs.

"You mean they like their ale or their bootie hot?" Chuck asks, joining the funning.

"Both! Now push, Chuck! Pull, Earl! Trot alongside, little Pamela!" Sally shouts orders like the first mate on a sailing ship, beginning to make movements with her hand like the director of an orchestra.

The Greek wagon train arrives at the frat house, illuminated by tiki torches around the brick patio. A sentry greets the messengers. "Halt!" He blocks the entrance to the patio garden with his gilded spear. Chuck takes the delicate hand of Princess Pam, who has ridden the 'steed' of ale for the second half of the journey and assists her in dismounting the cool horse.

"Thank you, gentle Charles," says Pam. Chuck kneels before her and kisses her hand.

Chuck bows his head. "Your majesty, I am at your disposal."

The red-headed sentry recognizes the camouflaged cargo of the Red Flyer wagon. "You may enter with your ale – and your booties."

"Thank you, kind sir. Carry on," says Pam. "Earl, hitch the wagon inside the lair, if you would, please."

Sally hops back onto the green woolly steed and rides it the remainder of the journey into the fraternity house. When they reach the keg's destination, a shallow round metal pan atop the kitchen counter, Sally presents her dainty hand to the driver, Earl. She bends ever so slightly from the waist.

"What?" asks Earl, not taking the lady's hint –or her hand.

"Assist me, please, sir, in my dismount," Sally implores.

Earl is resisting her flirtations, feigning ignorance, and remaining true to his lady Philly back home. He grips her hand firmly, as in a friendly handshake with a buddy from the team. "Dismount the horse, Sally."

"Lady Sal to you, plebe," Sally snaps.

"Oh, all right, Lady Sal, please get off the wagon so the gentleman can tap the keg," Earl corrects himself.

Earl and Chuck nestle the wooden keg in the pan of crushed ice, and one of the fraternity brothers sets a metal mixing bowl on top, brimming with ice and sprinkled with rock salt.

"Hi-tech stuff, eh?" says the brother.

A curly-headed brother crowned with laurel loudly sounds a shofar from the opposite corner of the great room.

"May I have your attention!" the president stands in the bed of the Red Flyer wagon, a brother on either side of him steadying the wheeled podium. "Our honored guest has arrived!"

Earl and Chuck are surprised to learn that the wooden keg of amber is 'it' –the honored guest. The president places the shiny golden crown, adorned with laurel and white roses, in the stainless-steel bowl of ice atop the 'honored guest'.

"Plebe!" the president raises his goblet to Earl. "Yes, Earl, younger brother to Princess Pam of the land of tobacco, wine and ale, you have the honor of tapping the keg. God's speed!"

Earl turns a deep shade of embarrassed, gradually pinking and whitening until able to approach the tap at the base of the wooden keg. Sally prods him, poking his sides and swatting his arid butt. Holding his white toga hem down in the back with one hand, Earl reaches the handle of the tap with the other. Pam receives the goblet from the president and presents it to the tap. With a nod from Pam, Earl taps the keg, quickly brimming the president's goblet.

A shout arises in the room of two dozen brothers and almost as many invited coeds. "Hoo-Ray!" and the guardian of the keg rings the tricycle bell at the kitchen counter-turned-bar.

Pam presents the goblet to the president, who wafts a mouthful. With foam clinging to his nose, lips and chin, he exhales loudly, proudly, "Ah, it is good!"

"Hoo-Ray!" shout the brothers and company.

"Strike up the band!" signaling the DJ brother to play the jams from the digital sound system.

The speakers begin thumping the music all around the room. "Bum-bump bump-bum-bum-bump…She's a brick…house...just lettin' it all hang out!" And the dance party begins.

"What is this music?" Chuck tries to shout above the music to Pam.

"What? Oh, these guys are a bit nostalgic. They like the old stuff – forty, fifty years ago –even older, from the 1960's!" Pam shouts back. She moves her hips and sways her body closer to Chuck.

"I don't know how to dance," Chuck shakes his head and speaks close to Pam's ear.

"That's the great thing about this music, a packed house, togas and ale: you don't have to know how to dance. Just move your body!" Pam puts her arms on Chuck's shoulders, facing him, close.

OK, I can do this, 'One-two-three, One-two-three,' he counts to himself as he watches his feet.

"Chuck, look at me!" Pam shouts, and he snaps his attention from his feet to her face, just in time for her lips to meet his.

He is initially stunned and then embarrassed as Pam keeps her face just centimeters from his as she leads the dance.

"What was that for?" Chuck asks, not loud enough to be heard, but Pam reads his lips.

"I like you; you should know that by now. Chuck, I like you," she says again while Chuck attempts to read her lips. *She must like me.* He grins, boyish, silly and excited.

Pam mouths the words. "Kiss me, Chuck."

Chuck parts his lips as if to say something, but instead, he steps in, his chest against hers, and kisses. The kiss is slow, and they begin swaying in time, not to the 'Brick House' jam, but to an old James Taylor tune from the seventies, 'Sweet Baby James'.

"Don't you just love J.T.?" Pam rests her head on Chuck's shoulder as he leads.

"Who?" Chuck asks, ignorant of the ancient golden music.

"Never mind, sweet baby Charles, just hold me."

Chuck and Pam have come to an understanding: She likes him. He likes her. They both like slow dancing. "James Taylor. Any relation?" Pam asks.

"Rock-a-bye Sweet Baby James…"

56.

Earl props an elbow on the bar, sipping and enjoying this newfound elixir. Sally approaches, goblet in her right hand, her toga slipping off her left shoulder, lily white skin contrasting jet-black hair. Earl gawks at her bare shoulder for an instant but must look away. *I'm being good, Philly. I am...*

"What do you think, Earl? 'Like the college life?" Sally asks.

"The ale's good," Earl says, and he takes another sip.

"Remember the wine from the café, Earl. Don't let this ale get you, too," Sally cautions. She brushes his drinking hand feather light with her free hand. Earl reacts like he's been touched by a hot match and sloshes a little ale and foam onto Sally's hand. She flits her fawn eyes at him and kisses the ale off her hand.

"What are you doing?" Earl asks.

"Oh, nothing –just finish your ale, and we'll dance."

A different genre, beach music -some call it shag –begins playing digitally in surround sound, the modern mode of vinyl in stereo. "Give me just a little more time..." the song plays. Earl relishes the last sips of ale, stalling the dance with Sally. She sets her half empty, half full, goblet on the counter.

"Come on!" Sally grabs him by the wrist and pulls him through an opening in the shagging crowd. She stops and faces Earl, beckoning him with both hands held out.

"Take my hands, Earl," she demands, but softly with a butter-melting smile.

At first, he shakes his head, 'No,' but as Sally begins shuffling her feet and spinning once to the beat of, 'just a little more time,' Earl offers his hands reluctantly with a buzzed smirk.

"Just follow me. Remember, you can't mess up, and with a couple ales in you, you can imagine you're Fred Astaire," Sally says.

"Who?" Earl asks.

Pulling Earl's right hand with her left, she sweeps her arm right and around his waist.

"Woe, we did it!" Earl says, excited about their first dance move. "Who is Fred?"

"He's just an old dancer," Sally says, turning her hips left, to the right and then straight into Earl, chest to chest –uh, her chest to his stomach –arms out as if flying like a swallow.

Sally takes him through a couple more shag moves and repeats them several times 'til the song ends. Before she can speak, a 'couples' song takes over: "Love me tender; love me true…" She steps in close, but a hand's width between them, face to face –uh, her face to his chest –and she presents the waltz stance, her right hand and elbow held up, almost her shoulder height, her left arm curved toward him, waist level. Earl stands dumb for a moment; Sally steps in, closing the gap between them to a few centimeters. She looks up at his face; he is looking sternly forward, not at her. Shifting her feet and stepping gingerly on his, he takes the hint –and the lead. He learned the basic box step when he was ten years old.

"You've done this before, huh?" Sally asks.

"Been a long time," he says.

"You're a good dancer, Earl," Sally compliments.

Elvis sings on, "for my darling, I love you…"

"Sally!" a barreling voice breaks in between them.

"Joey!" shouts Sally, startled that he is here, from halfway across the county. "What are you doing here? What do you want?"

"You, Sally! You broke up with me. That ain't happening!" Joey shouts. Her ex-boyfriend has the stocky steroidal body of a meaty steer.

"It happened, Joey, now get out of here and leave me alone!" Sally shouts.

"What's the problem –Joey?" Earl asks calmly.

"Who is this clown, Sally, your new boyfriend?" Joey asks, emphasizing 'boy'.

"I'm just a…" Earl starts to say, still calm, but getting agitated.

"Did I ask you, Bozo?" Joey snorts, angry and purple faced.

"No, but…" Earl starts again.

"Then shut up! Stay out of this! She's my girl!" Joey shouts, louder and more belligerent.

Elvis finishes his love song, "and I always will…" The music fades.

"I still want you, Sally!" Joey clinches his bulbous purple fists. Vessels pulse and bulge in his forehead, veins in his thick bullish neck strain outward, as if they might explode and blow his head from his collar.

"It is over, Joey –now get out!" Sally reddens with rage and her eyes fill with tears.

"I don't think you should…" Earl interjects a little louder into the hush after the 'tender' song.

Joey squares himself between Sally and Earl, bumping Sally hard, knocking her to the floor as he gets right up in Earl's face –uh, chest. Earl is over a head taller than Joey, but two chests thinner.

"You don't 'think'!" shouts Joey as he steps back far enough to throw a punch, which hits Earl in the gut. Earl doubles over and falls to the ground in a fetal position, struggling for breath.

Pam and Chuck have been dancing in the opposite corner of the great room by the DJ. They hear the ruckus during the music lull.

"That's Sally," Pam shouts, "and Earl!"

Chuck bulldozes his way through the crowd to the scene of the mini-Herculean wrestler standing over Earl who's balled up on the floor like a giant doodle bug. Sally is kneeling on the floor behind Joey.

"Hey!" Chuck yells, drawing Joey's attention from Earl.

Joey turns as Sally pounces from her kneeling position like a cougar toward her prey. He deflects her not-too-stealthy body with his left arm and points at Chuck with his dumpy right hand. "You're next, boy!" Joey shouts, crouching like an ape taking a dump.

Sally kneels on the hard-concrete floor beside her fallen golden crown. Chuck rises to the occasion and bounds four strong steps, gaining momentum with each, and dives shoulder first into Joey's chest, toppling them both to the floor beside Earl. Pam approaches the border of the fight as the men writhe and tumble at the edge of the bar and the keg. She hasn't seen Earl yet, but sees Chuck tangling on the floor with the stocky 'wrastler'. Just across the border Sally cowers on her knees.

"What's wrong, Sally –are you hurt? What's going on? Who's that wrestling with Chuck? Where's Earl?"

"That's my old boyfriend –and getting older by the minute! I don't know. I don't know…" Sally answers, trying to comprehend, hugging her injured leg. Pam notices the golden princess crown on the floor and places it back on Sally's flat dark locks. Sally manages a tearfully smudged smile.

Pam finally sees Earl balled up on the floor, the angry steer atop Chuck who has his arms crossed and fists over his face to keep from getting pummeled. Pam grabs the first potential weapon within reach, the stainless-steel bowl full of ice and salt water from atop the keg.

Directly behind Joey, Pam shouts, "Hey!" He stops his assault on Chuck and reels toward her. She flings the salt water, meeting Joey cold in the face, stinging and blinding.

"Ahh!" Joey shouts as he rolls off Chuck, places his palms over his eyes and doubles over. "She's blinded me!"

250

Clang! Pam crowns the top of Joey's head with the rounded bottom of the steel bowl sounding a successful mission; he rolls onto his side, like a lassoed steer.

The front gate sentry steps to the entrance and yells, "Police!"

"Save the keg!" the president yells. "To the safe place!" he orders as two plebes grab the wooden vessel and head upstairs to the special presidential closet with the false back.

"Grab that villain! says the president. Half a dozen plebes pounce upon the hulking intruder like flies on a steer turd.

"You guys go out the back!" he lowers his voice to a whisper shout as he helps Chuck lift Earl, who's breathing again, to his feet. Pam grabs Sally's arm and helps her up, and they hobble Sally and her injured ankle out the back through the kitchen.

The campus cop puts one hand up, "Stop!" and the other hand on his night stick. "Fun's over, boys and girls."

"What was Chuck thinking?" Mr. Taylor asks. He and Rae turn into the entrance to the college. An older gentleman is sitting in the dim white light of the guard house, reading an e-book. He stands and goes to the curb to meet the visitors.

"You kids are out past curfew," he smiles trying to lighten the mood as he sees the parental worry on their faces.

"Thanks, but we're over eighteen," Rae says, leaning forward in the passenger seat and giving a weak smile to the guard, who's wide awake and going strong at three o'clock in the morning.

Probably retired and insomniac, Charlie thinks but says, "Seriously, we wouldn't be here at this ungodly hour unless something was urgent."

"Kids arrested?" the guard asks.

"Yes, Mr." -his nametag shows 'Hank' –, "Hank, how did you know –they were arrested?" Rae asks.

"E-scanner, I keep up with police business on campus –live feed. Frat party got raided last night, maybe eleven o'clock. Fighting –nobody hurt badly."

Charlie hands his Unicard to the guard who leans over and rests his hand on top of the Prius.

"Yep, they got a Taylor –Charles –and a guy named Cleveland, neither of them students, but with a couple of female students."

251

"Female students?" Charlie repeats. *That's my boy.* He smiles proudly.

"And what are you smiling about, Charles?" Rae calls him 'Charles' when she's serious, suspicious.

"Oh, nothing, just glad no one was hurt badly. They're OK, right?" Charlie asks Hank, distracting Rae from the flashes of 'college days gone by' in his smile.

"Sounded like a few bruises, sprained ankle, hurt male egos –that sort of thing," says Hank.

"Thanks for putting us at ease, Hank. Where do we find the campus police station?" Rae is anxious and tired of the chit-chat; her son is sitting in jail.

"Mr. and Mrs. Taylor, just go straight ahead a couple hundred meters to the stop sign, the 'T' intersection."

"Got it," says Rae, plotting a map on her i-device. She is the navigator on this mission to free her son and his friends.

"You'll see a sign that points left, 'Campus Police'."

"Got it," says Rae, intent in her role.

"Take that left. Go a hundred meters, and it's on your right –blue and white sign, police car out front –can't miss it. Got it, darlin'?" he asks Rae.

"Got it."

"Thanks for all your help, Hank," Charlie says.

"No problem, glad to help. Oh," he hands Charlie his Unicard and a temporary parental passcard, "better put this card inside your windshield – shows you're legitimate being here."

"Thank you, Hank," Rae says with a tired smile.

"Don't be too hard on that boy, folks. They say your son was defending a lady's honor. I'd say he's sort of a hero. You don't see much of that chivalry anymore," Hank says.

As Charlie drives away from the guard house, Rae says, "What a nice man," as she glances over at Charlie, who's grinning.

That's my boy. Charlie flashes back to college.

Arrested

"You put a hurting on him, sis," says Earl. "Nice work!"

Joey sits on the far end of the long metal bench in the hall of the police station, holding a large blue ice pack on the top of his head with one hand, leaning over his knees, his other hand pressing his abdomen. Earl, Sally, Chuck and Pam sit on the opposite end of the bench, six or eight meters from Joey.

"I feel kind of bad," says Chuck, "but not as bad as he does."

"Don't feel bad, Chuck," Sally says. She sits with her back against Earl's shoulder, her legs straight out on the bench, a cold wrap on her injured ankle. "I just wish I could've gotten a piece of him," she says, clinching her fists and pushing her back hard against Earl's supportive shoulder. "You OK, Earl?"

Earl rubs his stomach. "Nothing broken, but a whopping bruise is coming, I'm sure." *My pride is bruised, mostly. Sorry, Sally.*

Pam sits quietly beside Chuck, her knees pulled up to her chest and her bare feet on the bench. She had lost her thongs in the shuffle, as they all had, but their togas are intact.

Pam was not intact. She had never gotten so enraged in her life, feeling guilty, ashamed and frightened by her own violent capabilities. Was she like Joey, that hyper-steroidal raging steer? How did she become such an animal –a monster?

Chuck feels her tenseness. "Pam?" She is rocking intensely back and forth on her tailbone, bumping her back against him with each wave. "It's going to be OK, Pam. You did what had to be done. You may have even saved me because I couldn't hold him off much longer. Don't feel bad." She continues to rock. "You're my hero, Pam."

She stops rocking. Sits. Motionless. Abruptly she begins to quiver and shake; Pam starts to come out of her rocking trance, crying, letting go. Chuck turns and wraps his arms all the way around her shoulders in a blanketing hug, his chest against her heaving back. Locking his fingers across hers as she clutches her knees, Chuck rocks Pam, soothing her with words of, "I'm right her, Pam. It's OK, now. I love you, Pam."

Pam lifts her head, straggly hair sticking to her tear-smeared face. She sniffs and snubs, wiping her eyes and nose on the corner of her toga. She turns toward Chuck; he untucks a corner of his toga and wipes Pam's face.

"Really?" Pam speaks softly.

Chuck hesitates. He can't say 'it' again right now, but he does. "You're going to get through this; we're going to be fine. I do."

"I do, too, Chuck. Thank you." Pam turns on the bench, facing Chuck. She blinks her damp reddened eyes. He wipes the remaining tears from the corners of her eyes, and presses his forehead to hers, butterfly-kissing her with his lashes.

A heavy metal door opens down the hall beside Joey. A lanky weathered black man in a gray uniform steps through. "Come on," the guard says in his soft Southern tenor voice. Broken, Joey stands slowly with the help of the tall man and lumbers out the door with him. The heavy metal latch clicks loudly closed, like a lone stone thrown against the college water tower by a rambunctious freshman.

Pam, Chuck and Earl turn to Sally, who says, "He's twenty-one, and nobody's bailing him out."

"I feel sorry for him," Pam says to Chuck. "He's got no one to love him, and that hurts more than stainless steel upside the head."

"Please don't hurt me like that," Chuck says to Pam, "either way."

57.

The Taylor's stand outside Pam's dorm in the coral glow of the 19th century streetlamp. There is no space between Pam and Chuck; their ale-stained togas cling to them. They look like twin beds pushed together stood on end with bare feet and legs sticking out from untucked sheets.

"You two are a sight to see," says Mrs. Taylor.

"A couple of jailbirds," Mr. Taylor kids.

"Sorry Mom, Dad, I just…"

"You just did what you had to do, Chuck. If it wasn't for you and Pam jumping in, Earl and the girl…"

"Sally," Pam fills in the blank for Mr. Taylor.

"Sally and Earl could have been really hurt. As it stands, that brut got his due!" Mr. Taylor punctuates.

"It's OK, Charlie," Rae says as she latches onto his elbow like he was her escort to the prom.

"Yeah, they all did what was necessary to make things right –and got arrested," Mr. Taylor says.

"'Right' except maybe for the part about smuggling ale into the frat party in the first place –illegal, by the way," says Mrs. Taylor, pointing out the obvious flaws of the heroes.

"Oh, speaking of illegal, that reminds me –I'll be right back!" Chuck says as he turns and runs to the dorm.

"What's he up to –something illegal?" Mrs. Taylor asks.

"Um, 'just a little surprise, a gift from all of us," Pam replies.

Rae and Charlie look at each other.

"Speaking of 'illegal', did the police confiscate the keg?" Pam asks.

"No, the frat brothers rescued it," says Mrs. Taylor.

"Where did you get the lowdown on what happened, Mrs. Taylor?" Pam asks.

"Oh, Earl just let it slip out," Mrs. Taylor says.

"And it sounds like a swash-buckling adventure the way he told it, too" Mr. Taylor says.

The dorm door slams, and Chuck runs down the sidewalk carrying a white bulging bundle in his arms. "Here, for you, Mom and Dad," Chuck grins.

Mr. Taylor takes the bundle, and Mrs. Taylor pulls the sheet apart at the top, and quickly conceals the 'surprise'.

"Is that what I think it is, Chuck? Don't you get us arrested!" says Mrs. Taylor.

"We thought you'd like it –a jug of muscadine wine," Pam announces.

"Yeah, we liked it a lot, so much that we…" Chuck starts.

Pam elbows him. "- so much that we couldn't not share it."

"Oh, yeah –I was –and Pam, she –almost." Chuck stammers. Pam steps on his bare foot. "Ow!"

"Chuck." She sings his name.

"Thank you, guys. We will savor it," Mr. Taylor says, putting his hand on Rae's as she clasps his arm.

"Well, we need to go," Mrs. Taylor says. "It'll be sunrise in a few hours.

"Why don't you guys ride up to Sauertown and watch the sunrise? It's only a half hour or so west of here," Pam says.

"That sounds lovely, Charlie –let's!" Rae sweetly pleads.

"I'm with you, Rae. Nap before sunrise?" Charlie suggests.

"A little wine, a little nap," the young bride Rae smiles at the rejuvenated gentleman she met in college. "Charles."

58.

9:30 Saturday evening. Bruce sits in the school maintenance micro-van two houses up from the Cleveland house. He had been parked behind the school gym since sunset, drinking bootleg whiskey to calm his nerves, puffing e-nhancer to keep alert so he doesn't fall asleep, and obsessing over the missing vials of e-drugs which were surely stolen by Chuck Taylor. The vial he gave to Cleve, the fatal sweetness, was from the stolen sleeve of e-nhancer. The partial sleeve of Cuban e-tobacco should still be in the Cleveland house. Although that sleeve contained only the tobacco product, the connection to the deadly vial remained, if not physically, eating away at Bruce's psyche.

Coach, here's the evidence –we found it! The conversation begins in Bruce's mind.

What's missing, Coach? You know what we found –missing.

We know. Cleve knows. Earl, Lila, Pam, Chuck, Philly, the Taylor's, the Reverend –they all know!

Guilty!

She made me do it, devil!

Lila's the devil!

Those kids –they'll get you, Coach.

Guilty!

She made me do it!

The evidence –it's here. Guilty!

The judge's gavel slaps the plane and ricochets off the walls inside Bruce's head. Bruce slams his fists on the steering wheel, the primal beast screeching, wanting to escape.

He's sweating, breathing hard. In the rearview mirror he sees 'it', the reflection of himself, and slicks his damp hair back with one hand and then the other.

No lights, no life at the Taylor's –must be dinner and a movie out on a Saturday night. Lila's out –at Cleve's mom's house. No one is home. The vials are there: evidence.

From his parking spot past the Taylor's house, Bruce attempts walking nonchalantly, but lumbers stiffly, like the monster that was pieced together from flesh, no longer human. *I'm invisible.* He scuffs over autumn grass, scrubs against ever deep-green waxen laurels. His mind soars like a buzzard across the Taylor's to the Cleveland's backyard. An owl screeches above his head, eying its prey. A rabbit nibbling the winter rye grass perks its velvety radar ears and bounces its white cotton ball, scampering away to the wilds out back, leaving brown pellets behind. Bruce steps on the droppings as he stops and fumbles in his front pants pocket for his father's antique hawk-bill knife.

The steel bill of the knife makes a perfect jimmy for the patio door lock, which clicks unlatched easily; Bruce slides the door smoothly open and closed on the patio where Cleve puffed his last breath. A thin light from a night light flickers underneath the kitchen door, catches his eye. As he slowly opens the swinging door, Bruce's sweaty jaundiced face reflects from the glass microwave door. *Who is that? Oh, me.* He exits the kitchen, crosses the dining room and heads down the hall. Light emanates from Lila and Cleve's bedroom. He hunkers down the hall as stealthily as he can manage.

He enters the bedroom and discovers the culprit, a night light in the bathroom. *The briefcase, where's the briefcase?* He spies the dark leather case in the corner, between the rustic armoire and the wall. He plucks the case from its lair and tosses it on the bed. It hops and flips like a kid on a trampoline -before coming to rest on the patchwork wedding ring quilt which Ester had stitched with love for Lila and Cleve twenty years ago before first child Pam was conceived.

Bruce hovers at the foot of the bed, looking over the bedspread that was made from love, for love –and spits on it. *This place, these things, that woman –all could have been mine! Ha!* He knocks over the framed wedding photo of Lila and Cleve and shatters the glass as he bulls past the dark cherry dresser on his way to the closet. He flings open the bifold doors, jarring one wheel off its track; the broken louvered door swings like a metronome out of time –then stops abruptly.

Lila is excited about spending another night, and Sunday morning, with Tina and Ester. She decides to go home and get a few essentials for another sleepover: fresh nightgown and underclothes, a change of clothes for Sunday morning. Maybe church with the girls, all dressed up, and the tea set that Cleve had given Pam, who handed it down to Tina.

Giddy as a high school girl going to a dance, Lila plays music off her old Madonna CD –from 'the day'.

"Girls just wanna have fu-un, O-Oh, girls just wanna have fun..." Lila sings and dances her fingers up and down, up and down to the beat of the music.

She pulls up the driveway, not noticing the little van parked up the street. Having never seen the van before, no alarm would have sounded.

Finally slowing down, catching her breath. *No need to rush,* Ester had told her before she left. Tina is already tucked in, kissed 'good night' by her and Emaw.

Unlocking the front door, she feels the security of being in the Cleveland home –her home. Maybe she could have a glass of that communion wine left over from the party. *It wasn't a party.* Lila frowns remembering Bruce accosting her. *The beast. He should have gotten the idea. It's over. Adios. No more Lila for you, Bruce. We had some good times.* She regrets being an adulterer, now a widow.

Ah, there it is. She discovers by the haze of the night light the half-full bottle of red wine behind the bowl of overripe fruit in the corner of the kitchen counter. As she takes a wine glass from the cabinet, it tinks lightly against the rim of an adjacent glass. She pulls the cork - similar to the size of an e-vial - from the dark green bottle with her fingers, sniffs and smiles. *The bouquet.* She pours herself a healthy dose of the deep purple fruit of the vine. She takes a deep swig and lets it linger on her tongue. The swinging door continues to swing as she makes a beeline for her wingback chair in the living room. She pauses. The cilia on the back of her neck stand at attention.

"What was that?" She whispers and looks toward the hallway. Glowing more than the usual nightlight, like a lantern… from the end of the hall. Lila grips the stem of the wineglass tightly in her fist as she tip-toes toward the bedroom.

Wearing the navy blazer that he borrowed from Cleve's closet, Bruce presses the brass thumb buttons of the briefcase. He flips it open onto the wedding ring quilt with a 'thump'.

Maybe Pam and Earl are back. She rounds the corner to enter the master bedroom. "Pam? Earl?" Trying to convince herself that they are home. This is the Cleveland home. Safety. No fear.

Meanwhile, Detective Brown is parked outside the Coach's house. Surveillance. Lights are 'on' in the front room of the house, but there's no movement.

I'll be glad when lights are out and he's in bed. The clock on his car's dash glows *10:00.* Another hour and Coach should be tucked in for the night *–and I can go home.* He slides down low in his seat and continues reading his e-book, a classic Arthur Conan Doyle story, *The Adventure of the Empty House.*

The timer clicks the light off at eleven o'clock. All is quiet.
Sunday, my day off –thank God! Detective Brown drives away from the quiet, *empty* house.

59.

No fear. Lila sees the back of the man wearing Cleve's navy blazer, the one with the polished brass buttons. *Cleve?* For an instant she imagines Cleve back home from a business trip, suitcase opened on the bed –home. In her delusion Lila says softly, hopefully, "Cleve?" He turns to face her. She loses her grip, and the glass of sweet red muscadine wine splays across the carpet. Fear.

"No, Lila, it's not Cleve. The better man has come to conquer the Cleveland house." Bruce grins like a possum, wild, crazed eyes and disheveled gray hair - just before being hit by a truck.

"Bruce!" She muffles a shout as if the children are sleeping in the next room. "What are you doing here?" The briefcase lay open on the bed.

His evil eyes are burning. "Where is it?"

"What?" Lila lowers her voice. Bruce undoes the brass buttons on the front of Cleve's blazer.

"You know what was here, Lila." He points to the briefcase. It still contains sundry papers, folders, notebooks, and a kno-pad. "Lila, I know you know," says Bruce, full of sugar.

"Really, Bruce, I don't know what you're talking about." She adamantly denies.

He pulls a vial from his pants pocket. "This!" Bruce barks. "A whole sleeve of these is missing." He holds out his fist and unfolds his palm.

"What?" Lila asks.

"E-cigars, e-gars," says Bruce.

"E-gars? Why would I want those?"

"You know, Lila. Trying to protect me, my love?"

"Protect you –from what?"

"From the truth, from what *I did*!" Bruce shouts.

"What *you did*? What did you *do*, Bruce?"

"I did *it*, what you didn't but could have," he answers vaguely.

"I don't understand, Bruce –did what?"

"Helped Cleve die, Lila!" Bruce yells, slamming the briefcase. Papers fly and flutter around the bed, falling shot birds.

"You..." Lila fades, starting to understand.

"*I killed him*! Yes, Lila, you *knew* that!"

"No! But he..." Lila halts, confused.

"*Natural causes*, yes, so natural..." Bruce starts.

"You killed Cleve? You *killed* him -you bastard!"

"You killed him, too. *We* did it, and you're glad, aren't you?" Bruce smiles, the devil.

"No, no, no!" Lila stomps around the foot of the bed, her face red and fists clinched.

Bruce grabs both her wrists and shakes her. "You would have done it, woman, if I hadn't!" he snarls, jaw clinched.

"No, I couldn't! Cleve was... father. Earl, Pam...Tina..." Lila starts to lose her grip.

"You *could* –and you *did*!" Hateful and cruel. "Tina! Remember Tina, that little girl –you killed her! You murderer!" Bruce stabs Lila with the words that the young mother hurled the day of the tragedy, the first Tina, the little girl who was no more.

"No, no, no!" Lila cries, shaking her head violently, closing her eyes to the horrors before her, behind her and within her.

He pushes her down onto the bed. She bounces off the end of the mattress like a child missing the mark on the trampoline and catapulting over the side. She crumbles onto the floor, curling up like a roly poly pill bug, but with no chitinous armor to shield her core. Papers from the briefcase fall around her like confetti.

"Get up! Face me, killer! You kill little girls, babies and of course your *beloved* husband!" Bruce pokes her again and again with his jagged words.

Lila remains curled up in her safety position at the foot of the bed, hyperventilating trying to re-wrap the package of tragic memories in her mind. *Did I really kill Tina?* The words unhinge the Pandora's box, so many years shut and locked.

Murderer, Murderer! The voice broke, the nightmare replaying in her head, seeing the golden strands, the crimson patches splayed on the pavement in front of her car. *You killed her, my Tina!* The hysterical mother yelled.

No, Tina's fine...with Ester...not...No! Lila attempts but the circuits in her brain won't connect.

Bruce stands shaking his head over the crumpled shell of Lila. He spreads Cleve's navy blazer across her back. He spits one final humiliation on the broken woman and crushes the e-vial beside her with the heel of his shoe. He lurches from the master bedroom, down the hall and out the front door.

The neighbor Anna opens the front door and looks up and down the street. Bette thought she'd heard some beating, muffled drum-like sounds from across the street, so Anna investigates. A van is parked a couple houses up the street. Across the way at the Cleveland's light flashes as the front door opens. A shadowy figure emerges, leaving the door ajar, a sliver of light cutting. The dark hulk retreats into the shadows between the Cleveland's and the Taylor's houses. Lila's car is in the driveway –but definitely not her silhouette leaving the house.

"Something doesn't look right, Bette. Should we go over and investigate?" Anna asks.

"No, no, we shouldn't get involved," Bette says.

"What are you talking about, Bette? We always have our noses out there, and we were at Cleve's visitation. I feel like we should be good neighbors and get involved."

"Then we should call someone, Anna."

"But who, the police?"

"No, too drastic. Remember that nice Reverend Arnold? Maybe he'd come check on Lila. He's a man of God," Bette says.

"That's what we'll do, get involved –beyond our noses," says Anna.

60.

Bruce lumbers through the Taylor's back yard, trying to evade the little bit of light emanating from the Cleveland house and the glare of the neighbors. He stumbles and falls like a dead, beetle-infested pine tree from a deluge of rain and with wind, enough to topple the hollow remains. He clambers, to his hands and knees, unconscious of his torn pants and bloody bitter strawberries on the heels of his hands. Going nowhere, but somewhere. That girl, Earl's girl, within walking or stumbling distance.

"Chuck!" Bruce yells alone in a raspy voice to the bug he intends to squash for breaking into his office, for stealing, *for "disrespecting me, the coach.* "You better come... back... or your friends, Earl... that girl, will pay...for...you, Chuck!" He shakes his fist at the darkening sky.
Onward... away from Lila... and her lies... payback... Chuck, that meddler!

Reverend Arnold sits at the desk in his church office processing words, and the Word, for tomorrow's sermon.
"Fear not, for Thou art with me. Thy rod and Thy staff they comfort..." he reads. The phone sounds. *Someone calling on a Saturday night. Something's wrong.*
"Yes?"
"Oh, yes, I remember you, of course. Lila? Her car's there?" *She should be at Ester's with Tina.*
"The front door? The light? What? Dark... shadow?" *A dark figure... should not be there.*
"I'm on my way. Thank you, good neighbors."
The Reverend runs out, leaving open the door - and the Word. "I shall fear no evil..." *Lila, He is with you. Fear not.*

61.

Philly finishes packing her mom's third shift 'lunch' –leftover homemade lasagna from the freezer and freshly prepared salad. Glenda comes into the kitchen barefoot, carrying her shoes and wearing her hospital scrubs, carrying her shoes. She sees the lunch bag on the table, drops her shoes by a chair. Philly is putting produce back into the fridge as Glenda reaches both arms around her in a big mama hug.

"You startled me, Mom!"

"Just showing the love to my wonderful daughter, the chef who prepares my gourmet lunches." Glenda loosens her hug.

"Mom," Philly sings, "I always make your lunches. It's no big deal."

"Whatever you do, Felicity, is a big deal to me –always."

"Shall I put your shoes on for you?" Philly notices her mom's bare feet.

"I'm a big girl –maybe you could strap them for me?" says Mom.

"Sure, Mom, not a big deal," Philly smiles, and they both sit down at the table.

"You miss Earl, Philly?" Mom asks, slipping her white socks on her pink feet.

"Well, I've been busy all day, but I think about him when I'm doing mindless chores like chopping veggies and cleaning," Philly says.

"That's sweet...that you think about him," Mom says, pushing her socked feet into her ugly but sensible work shoes. Philly squats and straps her mom's rubber shoes.

"Oh, Philly, you know I was kidding."

"You know I'd do anything for you, Mom."

"I know, I know. And 'I'll do anything for you, dear, anything'." Glenda sings the first verse of the song.

The house sure will seem lonesome tonight with Earl being off at college with Pam and Mom at work. She doesn't want her mom to worry. Philly's fended for herself for most of her young life –and takes care of her mom, too.

Sometimes Philly gets angry at her dad when she receives one of his sporadic letters or emails right in the middle of some hectic time when her mom is falling behind in her schoolwork, and Philly's getting behind in everything else, including taking care of her mom. *Who does he think he is, running away to find his dreams when Mom can hardly keep up with reality?*

Dreams? Philly dreams; her mom dreams. Sometimes, but rarely, have they had the luxury of just dreaming. Sleep is restless some nights. Dreams are remembered. Nightmares are hard to forget. Philly wonders if her dad ever has trouble sleeping or has nightmares amidst his realized dreams. She wonders. She is angry. Philly misses her dad. Where's the letter? Over a month, it's time for a letter –or email. Now she misses Dad, Mom and Earl.

"Philly," her mom says softly.

"Huh? Oh, yeah, Mom, got everything together for work?" Philly asks, shaken from her thought.

"Yes, Philly, thank you. You OK? You were zoning out. Remember: Miss him, but don't let pining distract you from taking care of Felicity, and don't let your caring for me push your dreams aside. You and your dreams –'I'd do anything for you, dear, anything for you'," Glenda sings the last part to lighten the heavy load.

"Maybe you should've been a singer on Broadway," Philly pokes, and kisses her mom on the cheek.

Glenda grabs her lunch and her school bag, lovingly pecks her daughter on the cheek, and bows as she heads out the door. "Anything, dear," she sings as she exits stage left.

"Encore, encore!" Philly applauds and whistles loudly through her teeth as if calling her pony from pasture.

62.

Meanwhile at Viceroy college.

I wonder if she misses me. Earl thinks as he sits on the edge of the twin bed in Pam's dorm room.

"You alright now, Earl?" Sally asks. She sits on the floor in front of Earl, wrapping her ankle with a spandex bandage.

"Yeah, my stomach's pretty bruised, but nothing vital."

"That was a pretty cheap shot Joey gave you. There was nothing you could have done," Sally comforts.

Earl rests his forehead in the palms of his hands, elbows on his knees. "I shouldn't have been here."

"You miss her, don't you, Earl?"

"Yeah, Philly's been my friend for a long time and now that she's my girlfriend..." he trails off.

"You miss your girlfriend. I know. Sounds like you have a good thing going –much better than I had with that meat head Joey."

"You deserve a lot better than him," Earl says.

"I guess that's why I like you, Earl. You're a good guy, and I'm not used to good guys."

"I like you, too, Sally, but..."

"But she –Philly's her name, right? –got you first," Sally says.

I really need Philly. She was there at just the right moment when I lost Dad and I felt like I was on the edge of losing it all. The fire in the woods, salt poured in the wound after the sudden death of Dad - Philly came to me that day. Earl knew. He had carelessly ignited that flame at the fort and it burned a hole in the heart of a little boy whose father had helped overcome his fear. Even though his girlfriend history was short, his friendship with Philly had helped him through the most trying time of his sixteen years. Sally looks up at Earl, admiring and respecting one almost four years her junior, sensing the intensity of his thoughts. He had experienced loss which she had not. *Have I always felt that loss, since my father was always absent, never was a daddy, only a one-night stand for Mama, a teenage mistake?* Maybe she liked Earl because Pam had told her about her dad, Cleve, and the strength he sustained through the years with a mother who was 'not all there'. Sally wanted to have a father like Cleve – like Earl. She wanted to be a mother to the little boy inside who longed for love. She was so conflicted: Daddy and daughter; little boy and mother. Where was she left?

Pam also told Sally the story of Philly who had known a dad but had lost him. Where was he? *Philly has found someone who can ease her burden, help her get up, hold her when she cries, carry her on his shoulders and make her laugh. But I know I can never be Earl's girl. You're a lucky girl, Philly.*

Sally gets up from the floor and sits beside Earl on the bed. His athletic shoulders tremble, his face concealed by his hands.

"It'll be alright, Earl." Sally puts her arm around his shoulders. Earl flinches then relaxes as Sally strokes and smoothes his tousled dirty blond hair.

Chuck rattles the railings as he pursues Pam up the stairs, half flight ahead of him.

"Hold on to your toga! Pam shouts and laughs, echoing through the stairwell.

"You won't get away with that!" shouts Chuck, panting and laughing.

Pam had unclasped the safety pin from the side of Chuck's toga, leaving him vulnerable to drafts from the rear, like wearing an open backed hospital gown. She ran with the pin and headed up the stairs before Chuck discovered his sheet dilemma.

"I already got away with it, Charles!"

Pam reaches the third-floor door, quickly enters the hall and holds the door shut. Chuck reaches the door seconds too late and tugs on the handle –doesn't budge. Pam smooches her face against the wire-reinforced glass, puckering her lips.

"Come on, Pam!" Chuck bays like a hound dog.

"What's the password, Charles?" Pam's muffled voice comes from the other side.

"I'm going to get you, Pam!" Chuck enjoys the game.

"That's it! That's the password!" Pam shouts as she releases the door handle and makes a break toward her dorm room down the hall, her toga hem flapping.

"I'm coming, Pam!" Chuck shouts. Pam cracks the door and peeks out.

"Shh!" Pam shushes Chuck loudly, her index finger held to her lips.

"What?" he whispers back.

Pam shushes, softer this time and opens the wooden door slowly letting the fluorescent light from the hallway slip into the room. The light illuminates the white clad figures spooning peacefully on the bed. Sally lay behind the lanky overgrown cherub, Earl, bare feet extending into the soft light -a masterpiece, Madonna and Child. Pam smiles, takes Chuck's hand gently and leads him into the room to sleep peacefully in her neatly made twin bed.

The dawning *red sky in morning* comes as Rae and Charlie sit on the igneous edge of Sauertown Mountain, cool damp air creeping around the warmth of her in his arms. They share the cup of sweet muscadine wine.

63.

Bruce lurks in Philly's backyard, huddled in the darkest corner, puffing an e-nhancer to lift his dragging ass. The chemicals absorb quickly into his lungs, giving a boost. He rebounds but can barely muster wits to restrain his wound-up-tight body from breaking down the door. He'll slither up like a python to squeeze Chuck's little friend. *What's her name? Pony? Sissy? No matter. Chuck... stand down, keep your mouth shut.*

A rare roast beef sandwich will give her stomach just what it needs to drain the blood from her brain and digest her restlessness. Philly gets fresh bread, Swiss cheese and roast beef from the refrigerator to make a sandwich. Her mom left for work at ten thirty. She gets hungry late at night when her mom works and has difficulty going to sleep sometimes.

A sound out back, maybe a deer. She looks through the glass and sees a flash in the farthest corner of the yard. *Too dark to make out. The glowing eyes of maybe a fox, raccoon or a possum?*

She continues her sandwich creation, carving the rare roast beef with her favorite butcher's knife.

A scuffing sound behind her.

She turns. *Coach!* Almost unrecognizable in his soiled, torn clothes, disheveled hair and beet red face, grinning.

"Hello –Pony, right?" Coach asks, casually as if he's supposed to be here.

Philly remains calm but tentative. "My name is Philly –and this is my house. Please, leave."

"Oh, sorry –Philly. I'm looking for Chuck."

"He isn't here; you know where he lives," Philly continues, firm and terse.

"He's not home, but you are. I'm here to see you, little pony." Coach ogles her, from her stoic, unemotional façade, down her budding body to her bare feet. He takes a step closer to Philly, on the opposite side of the table.

"I know what Chuck knows," she says, full of false bravado.

"So, Chuck knows for sure, huh?" Coach scowls. "He despises me. I was guilty in his eyes all along."

"All he wants is to be on the team –with Earl. He will never be on *your* team. It's *not* your team, more like *Earl's team* - and you're dead weight." Philly taunts. She fears but knows not to show it.

"Earl's nothing without me and his dad. I took his dad away –and Lila, his mom, too. They took mine, and I took theirs. Cleve's nothing. Chuck's nothing. And now Earl's nothing – and you either," he growls.

"Get out of my house!" Philly snaps. "Mom will be home soon."

"You lie –you all lie! I know she's on third shift and left her little girl alone –again. And, where's your daddy? Ran off on you girls, eh?" He taunts her.

He strikes a nerve. "You shut up! You're no coach –and never could be a daddy! Now get out!" Louder, angrier Philly starts shaking.

Her back is to the kitchen counter where she had been carving the roast beef, its red juices puddled on the dark wood cutting board. Philly holds her right arm straight by her side, tightly gripping the solid oak knife handle. "Leave my house!" She points with her left hand, a distraction from her armed hand.

"I'll show you a *daddy*!" Bruce stumbles on the metal chair as he lunges for Philly. "Come here! I'm gonna break you, little pony!" Bruce regains footing and flings the chair against the cabinet.

He lashes out with his filthy claws, grinning like a possum - but not playing. Philly stumbles back as the table skids and squeals across the tile floor toward her. She raises her right arm, flashing cold steel. The blade sears across his meaty arm. Thunder rolls off his tongue. His split left arm reveals white ligaments like splintered wood in the blood flow. Bruce's face pales. His demon rises to the surface, exercised by the girl's spirit.

A warrior prepared for more battle, Philly holds the knife point up, standing her home ground. Bruce looks at the wound, stupefied that the tide has turned blood red; he grips the useless arm just above the fresh gash, damming the flood. *He* is terrified. The one who was his victim, now his conqueror. With less than the ounce of compassion that she would have for an injured animal, Philly tosses the smeared bar towel to Bruce. He grabs the white cotton terry and wraps it around his gaping wound. The towel quickly soaks up the life blood, turning litmus red.

"Get out! Out of my house!" Philly yells primally, the predator, no longer the prey.

Bruce stumbles over the chair, slowly regains his footing and bursts out the kitchen door. He disappears as a specter, back to the other side.

The owl screeches overhead, and the rabbit scampers into the wild out back, leaving a piddling of droppings along the trickling blood trail.

Philly stands statuesque, her knife pointing heavenward, a Joan of Arc. She begins to shiver. Blood, puddled and smeared across the black and white tiles, ends in a handprint on the white metal storm door, a red tail, a child's finger painting of a kite and a girl, the stick figure holding the string. The knife slips from her hand with a metallic clink on the bloody ceramic floor. Philly drops to her knees and vomits onto the black, white and red pallet.

64.

Reverend Arnold approaches the Cleveland's open front door and calls, "Lila? Lila, are you home?" No answer.

He steps inside the foyer, scans the living room, dining room and down the hall.

"Lila? Are you home, Lila? It's Reverend Arnold."

He hears a bump from the master bedroom down and creeps slowly down the hall, like a burglar. He approaches the lighted bedroom and peeks around the door casing. A tousled bed? Unlike Lila to leave in disarray.

A series of muffled murmured hums rise from the foot of the bed, like a mother would sing rocking her baby.

Papers are scattered all over. A toppled briefcase lies on the floor beside the figure, draped with a navy blazer, in fetal position, rocking and humming in rhythm of sorrow. He kneels down beside her.

"Lila?"

Humming and rocking continue, as if she doesn't hear the Reverend's voice. He calls 911.

"They'll be here soon, Lila. I'm here, with you. God's with you, child," the Reverend says softly, fatherly.

Lila hears a voice, but doesn't recognize from whom, or from where -sounds far away. *God, that you*? Holding her first baby Tina in her arms, Lila hums an old spiritual, This Little Light of Mine; light shines off the perfect child's golden hair. She rocks.

The Reverend puts his hand on Lila's head, smoothing her hair. Lila feels Cleve's hand, not the Reverend's, on her head and smiles, continuing to rock.

"It's going to be alright, Lila." She hears Cleve.

Reverend Arnold calls Detective Brown. The call goes to voicemail. The Reverend fusses with his earwig. Detective Brown interrupts. "Reverend Arnold? I'm almost home –what's up?"

"Bruce is what's up. He's been to the Cleveland house –hurt Lila."

"Bruce? What's Bruce doing there? I just left his house –lights were out! And what's Lila doing at her house? I thought she was with Cleve's mother and the little girl," Brown says.

"No matter why. She's here on the floor –I called 911. Can't see any physical wounds, but she's real messed up in the head. She's humming and rocking, unresponsive to me," the Reverend says.

"Any sign of that bastard –excuse me, Reverend –that Bruce, son of a b...," He cusses.

"No, just Cleve's briefcase ransacked -papers everywhere."

"Yeah, I know what he was searching for," Brown says.

"Just get over here. He may still be nearby," the Reverend says.

"Hold on, Reverend, I've got another call coming in."

Philly slips in the putrid mess and pulls herself up by the chrome edge of the table. She pushes the pepper mill aside and takes the business card in her fingers: 'Detective Brown'. Chuck had shared this with her before he and the guys left town, knowing she'd be alone part of the weekend. She's alone now; Bruce has been gone for ten minutes –or longer. Time suspended briefly for Philly. She makes the call.

"Detective Brown," he answers on the third ring.

Philly, in shock, doesn't speak.

"Philly, is this you?" he asks, knowing that the call is from her – caller ID.

"He was here," Philly says in a raspy voice.

"Philly, are you OK? Are you hurt?"

"No –I cut him...bad...blood all over..."

"Is he still there?"

"No, gone...blood everywhere...ran out..."

"You sure you're alright, not hurt?"

"Not all right -but not hurt."

"How badly is Bruce cut, Philly?"

"...cut his arm...deep...carving knife...lots of blood..."

"Stay calm –try, OK? Police will be there shortly." Detective Brown tries to reassure.

"Mess...big bloody mess...got to clean it up..."

"Don't worry about that, Philly. We have people who will do that. Just get away from the blood –and stay calm. I'll be there real soon."

"OK," Philly fades. She stamps a trail of bloody barefoot prints as she leaves the kitchen.

"Reverend, stay there with Lila, and call Philly's mom. Philly needs someone there."

"Will do, detective."

Detective Brown turns around, almost home, and heads toward Philly's. He calls for backup to come with the old reliable Plott hound for tracking Bruce.

The neighbors from across the street enter the front door of the Cleveland house calling, "Reverend? Reverend Arnold, it's us!"

He recognizes the ladies' voices. "Ladies! Back here!"

They hurry down the hall and see the Reverend kneeling over Lila. "Is she hurt, Reverend?" Anna asks.

"Doesn't look like anything physical –that I can tell –but she's in a bad way, mentally," he says.

"Can we do anything, Reverend?" Bette asks.

"Well, there is something you could do."

"Anything for our neighbors," Anna says, more than their reputable nosiness.

"You know Earl's girlfriend, right?" the Reverend asks.

"Of course –a lovely girl. What can we do?" Bette asks.

"She's by herself. The same brute that came to Lila went after Philly, too."

"Say no more, we'll go. Is she hurt?" Anna asks.

"Like Lila, not physically hurt, but real shook up. And, to warn you, she cut the intruder, so there's blood everywhere," the Reverend says.

"I hope the bastard bled out!" Bette growls.

"Bette, let's try to be civil," Anna says.

"He'll get what's coming to him," Bette says.

"Ladies, he got away, so far, but he's still around somewhere. Detective Brown has people coming. They'll get him, but just be aware –be careful."

"We'll be careful, Reverend," Anna says.

Bette says under her breath, "Careful –and armed and dangerous." She clutches her purse tightly to her bosom.

Reverend Arnold calls the hospital. "Yes, I know, but there's an emergency." He tells the call designator for on-duty medical staff. "Let me speak to her first." He pleads. "No, don't alarm her, please."

He sits at the head of the hospital bed. Lila is curled up in fetal position, rocking and humming. He uses his mother's antique embroidered handkerchief from his breast pocket and wipes Lila's damp forehead.

She smiles, *Cleve*, rocking in rhythm with her hum song.

"This is Glenda."

"Glenda, this is Reverend Arnold."

"What's happened? What's wrong? Philly?"

275

"Philly's OK; she's not hurt."

"Tell me –what is it?" Glenda gets panicky. "I know something's wrong. They wouldn't call me up - unless it's an emergency."

"Like I said, Philly's not hurt, but –" he pauses, and then spurts out the news, "the coach broke in your house –Philly's OK –she stood up to him, so he got his due from her, but he got away."

"Coach...broke in?" Glenda starts shaking, fear and rage.

"Philly's going to be fine. She cut *him*... with a kitchen knife...hurt him *bad*. She's shook up, needs her mom," the Reverend says, as calmly as he can.

"I'm on my way."

The Reverend catches her before she hangs up. "Oh, just to forewarn you, Coach shed a lot of blood, so try not to be shocked. Philly's holding up, considering the circumstances."

"Oh, God!" She slams down the.

When Glenda gets home, she is expecting to see blood everywhere, but the shocking sight is the two neighbors sitting on the couch on either side of Philly, each holding a hand. Philly sees her mom and springs from the couch. Glenda gasps when she sees the blood splatters and smears on Philly's pants. Philly falls into her mother's embrace like a lost child, found.

"Mom, I was so scared!"

"But she stood up to that monster," Bette says.

"She's a brave soldier." Anna praises. "I want her on my side."

Glenda holds her daughter by the shoulders and studies her face from arm's length. "My little Philly," she hugs her again.

"But she kicks like a horse –don't mess with this young woman!" Bette offers accolades.

"Come on, Philly, let's get you cleaned up. Excuse us, ladies." Glenda escorts her daughter down the hall.

"Our work here is done," Anna says. "Shall we go?"

"Yes, but just in case," Bette pats her purse, "I'm packing heat."

Reverend Arnold rides in the ambulance beside Lila. She continues to rock, strapped to the gurney. The EMT tells him that Lila has severe trauma and bruising on her abdomen and possibly some broken ribs. They've her back and abdomen with ACE bandages. Holding Lila's right hand between his soft, pastoral hands, he asks her if he can pray with her. She gives no response, just rocking and persistent humming.

"Dear Lord, Father God, be with your daughter Lila, in this time of turmoil and pain. Lord, You know she is suffering now, and has suffered in the past in body, mind and spirit. Only You know where she is right now, Lord; though she be here in body, her mind and spirit are elsewhere. Comfort her, hold her in Your bosom and let her know that she is loved, and You will see her through this dark valley. Be with her children; help me to convey the love and care that their mother is receiving at this time, and forward. And, Father, I pray, though - forgive my reluctance to ask - for the lost soul of the brute who has brought such pain on Your children. I pray for the strength and courage for those who work for right and good and healing. Thank You for Lila –and Your little child Philly, so brave, so scared –comfort and protect, watch over us in these trying times. In Jesus' name I pray, Amen."

Lila begins relaxing her tense, rocking muscles as the injection infuses warmth and comfort through her vessels. Her mind continues to rock the baby Tina and hum lullabies that only they can hear.

Seven in the morning and the cleaning crew begins the wet-vac, scrub, wipe and sanitization process to remove the bloody mess left in the kitchen by the attacker. Philly is clean and curled up in her mother's bed, nestled close inside the safety and love. Glenda has not slept all night, but held her baby in her arms, rocking and humming her to sleep. Listening to the sounds of sloshing mop water and scrubbing, Glenda vows not to leave her sweet Felicity's side until 'he' is caught –or killed. She mulls the scene over and over in her mind. She would not have stopped with slicing his arm.

"I'll do anything for you, dear, anything…" Glenda sings softly, stroking Philly's fine, damp baby-shampooed hair.

65.

Pam's earwig tickles her left ear. She lies behind Chuck, spooning for the last few hours of sleep. Pam touches his rosy cheek and kisses him lightly on the crown of his head. He breathes easily, smiles sweetly and continues sleeping as Pam answers the call.

"Hello?" She flinches and sits up straight in bed. "Reverend Arnold?"

Chuck moans. "Hmm...what?"

"Shh!" Pam shushes Chuck. "Oh, not you, Rev...No, not at all – never too early or late.

What? What! Is she alright?

How? What's going on?

No! Not that bast... Oh, sorry.

No, no excuse for language.

Yes, thank you, Reverend. So, you'll stay with her?

Called Emaw?

OK, we'll be there around 11.

...and bless you, too, Reverend Arnold."

Chuck's feet hit the floor, and he's pulling and tucking at his wrinkled toga, trying to stay covered and decent. Earl is asleep on the outside edge of the other twin bed, feet hanging over the footboard. Sally is pressed against his back, one arm flung across Earl, his arm clamped over hers.

"Earl, wake up!" Pam whisper-shouts.

He moans. "Pam, leave me alone. It's too early." Suddenly his eyes open, and he sits up like he's been stung. Sally is stretching and yawning; her toga has slipped off her shoulder, exposing her breast. Earl quickly averts his eyes.

"I didn't...we were just...fell asleep...I didn't do..." Earl panics.

Sally sits up, her injured ankle wrapped and held straight out in front of her.

"Sally!" Pam signals the 'revealing' situation, placing her hand over her breast.

Sally puts her hand on her chest, feels the cool bare skin, and quickly covers herself.

"Oops, sorry," Sally says nonchalantly. She sees Earl's back turned to her and says, "Sorry, Earl, you can turn around now."

Earl turns slowly. "You won't tell Philly, will you? I didn't…"

"Earl, it's OK. You –we –didn't do anything - real cozy, but just sleep," says Sally.

"But…I…you…your…No, I didn't -"

"I know you didn't, Earl. It just popped out; they do that sometimes," says Sally. Earl's face turns beet red.

"Sally, he's embarrassed enough," Pam says. "I won't mention this to Philly."

"You're the perfect gentleman, Earl," Sally says.

"Yeah, yeah –gentleman," Chuck chimes in.

"I don't know about you, Chuck," Pam teases.

"I didn't…you said…" Chuck tries to explain –something.

"You're a gentleman, too, Chuck. I pulled you into my bed. I'm the harlot!" Pam confesses.

"Oh, stop it, Pam. You're a lady, and we all know it," Sally says.

"By the way, why are we up at seven in the morning?" Earl asks.

"God, I'm such an idiot! All this chit-chat. We've got to go, asap!" Pam says.

"What?" Earl asks.

"Reverend Arnold says that bastard-son-of-a-bitch… the coach broke in the house and hurt Mom –scared mostly –but she's in a bad way in her head –again. The Reverend went with her to the hospital." Pam explains, somewhat.

"We gotta go!" Earl says. "Did he mention Philly? Is Philly alright? We gotta check on Philly!"

"The Reverend didn't mention anything else, so she should be OK. Just wait, Earl, and call her on the way home. I'm sure she's fine," Pam reassures.

Sally sees the worried expression on Earl's face; she gets off the bed and faces him. "I can tell that you care a lot about Philly." She grabs his hand and touches the back of it to her lips. "You're quite a gentleman, Earl." She smiles into his eyes. "Now, get your clothes on, the toga party's over."

66.

Bruce's arm is seeping blood through the bar towel, leaving a trail of drops all the way to the school micro-van parked by the curb. He smears red across the back of the seat as he retrieves a roll of gray duct tape from the glove box. He wraps the 1½ inch tape around the towel on his arm, like wrapping pipe insulation. Tighter, tighter. The blood stops. His forearm and hand, cinched by the duct tape tourniquet, numb and turn from pale to dark red.

He is weakened from the hike from Philly's back yard to the van, parked just up the block from the Cleveland house. "Gotta go to the gym - need a boost. E-nhancer…must not stop…home…No." He does a U-turn. "They'll be here…soon."

Disoriented and diminishing, Bruce hits the curb several times en route to the school. He runs over a driveway marker at the gym parking lot and drives around back to his office.

"Security guy's gone. Good. Key. Where's my key?"

Bruce finds the key in his left pants pocket with difficulty, using his good hand. He feels a throbbing sensation in his left hand, but no pain.

"That little bitch! He curses.

Detective Brown stands at the curb as the dawning sky brightens. The K9 handler has the large floppy eared Plott hound's leash tethered to his wrist; the dog sniffs in circles. It had lost the trail.

Detective Brown says, "So they tracked him from the Cleveland house, out back, all the way to Glenda and Philly's, then back down the street to here."

"Detective Brown?" The neighbors approach.

"Ladies, what can I do for you?"

"What we can do for you, we hope, is help solve this crime. We saw a van," Anna says.

"Yes, a van, right here," Bette agrees.

"What type of van?" Brown asks.

"Small, white, some logo on the side…" Anna says.

"Could you tell what the logo was?" Brown asks.

"No, just a round logo," says Bette.

"Anything else, ladies?"

"Just a shadowy figure running out of the Cleveland's front door…left the door open…couldn't see his face," Anna says.

"We know who he is," Brown informs.

"So do we." Bette pats her loaded purse.

"Just keep your eyes open, ladies. Thanks for helping."

"It's what we do," Anna says.

"Philly? It's me," Earl speaks and listens through his earwig. Pam drives him and Chuck closer to home.

"Earl!" Philly begins to cry.

"Philly, you alright?"

"Um…I'm not hurt." Philly sniffs. "I'm OK."

"Is your mom there? We'll be there in less than an hour. I miss you, Philly," Earl says.

"Miss you, too, Earl. I'll be glad when you get here," Philly says, with a little stronger voice.

"Soon –did they catch him?" Earl asks.

"Not yet, but I…" Philly starts.

"But what, Philly?"

"I cut him, Earl!" Philly starts to break down. "I cut him bad!"

"I'm glad you did, Philly. Don't cry. You had to do it, or…"

"Or I might be dead," she lowers her voice.

"But you're alright. You had to do it! He's a bad man, Philly, we all know it," he reassures.

"Just come home. I…love you," Philly says.

"I…love…you…too." Earl hesitates, feeling guilty about last night, though innocent, with Sally. He was partying and scuffling at a frat party while Philly was fighting for her life.

Earl thinks. *Coach attacked Mom -and Philly? What's up? Why would he? Dad's gone; Chuck had his hunches. Pam, Philly and I are Chuck's friends. Dad, what happened to Dad? He had seen the coach…the day before he…died. He was healthy, happy that morning. What? How? Why?*

And Chuck thinks. *I should have been there, but I was partying with Pam and Earl.* He feels guilty. He knew. He gave Detective Brown the evidence. *Got to find Bruce, got to…*

"Earl, I'm dropping you off at Philly's. Chuck, you want to hang with me? I'm going to Emaw's and then to the hospital to see Mom," Pam says as they pass the high school and head down their street.

"I'd better check in with Mom and Dad. They probably got back a little while ago," says Chuck.

Earl grabs his bag and gets out at Philly's.

"Later, sis –thanks. See you, Chuck."

"Later, bro….and remember, 'nothing happened', OK?" Pam knows that he's fretting over the 'Sally affair'.

Earl walks away from the car, hanging his head. Pam catches Chuck's eye in the rearview mirror.

"You know you're my hero, don't you, Chuck?"

"Right -and you're mine."

"Am I...*yours*, Chuck?"

"What? Uh, if you want; if you say so, Pam."

"Yes," Pam says as she pulls to the curb at the Taylor's.

Chuck squeezes out of the back seat, grabs his bag and comes to the driver's side window.

"What?" Pam asks.

"This," says Chuck as he reaches in, palms the back of Pam's head and leans in for a long kiss.

"Yeah." Pam holds his hand until he is away from the car. She kisses the air and Chuck catches it with his hand.

Glenda greets Earl at the front door with a big hug.

"Hey, Earl, I'm so glad you're here. Philly's asleep again –she needs it after all she's been through," Glenda says. "Drop your bag and come on to the kitchen; we can talk."

When they get to the kitchen, Glenda stops short and stares. The clean black and white tiles and spotless countertop seem to be covering some lie, some false sense of security. She finally moves forward and sits in the chair.

"This is where it happened, Earl, where Bruce tried to attack our girl. Philly hasn't been back in here since then, and I can't blame her. She's getting back to herself after the shock, but she needs us."

"I'm here. What can I do?" Earl asks.

"Be patient." She takes his hand. "Comfort her. Love her."

"I'll do that. It sounds worse than Philly said on the phone. She said she 'cut him'."

"He was coming at her, Earl. She'd been fixing a sandwich, carving roast beef when he came in the back door, filthy -like a wild animal. Philly just reacted –reflexes -and cut a deep gash in his forearm. There was so much blood, Earl. She feels badly that she hurt him! Can you believe that girl 'feels badly'? She's such a good girl, not wanting to hurt anyone. I'd have sliced him to pieces if I'd been here!"

"God, Glenda, if I'd only stayed here and not..." Earl starts to say. He still feels guilty for –what? They said, 'nothing happened.' If he'd been here instead of there, nothing would have happened there –but here?

"If you and Chuck had been here, you all might be hurt –or dead. The monster left a trail of blood, but even the tracking dog came up cold," says Glenda. "The police couldn't find him. By the way, where is Chuck?"

"Went home."

67.

Bruce chain-puffs e-nhancers, getting more and more hyped –and delusional that he's better. Adrenalin pumps him up tighter and higher. A loud metallic click from the door closing at the other end of the long corridor uncoils the coach's taut spring. He bounds to his office door, paranoid, listening. Steady dribbling of a basketball off the hardwood floors of the hollow, empty gym sounds like war drums calling.

Chuck bounces the ball consistently three times, sets and shoots from the free throw line. Swish! Again. Swish! He dribbles to the corner, turns, pump-fakes and shoots. Swish! The steel door opens at the opposite end of the court

"Hey, Coach, I've come to play," he says coldly. "Put me in?" *I've come for 'the game', for the championship.*

"Put you...in your place, boy!" Bruce's whisky baritone voice, reverberating through the metal rafters, echoes off the concrete block walls. He laughs hysterically like a wild hyena at his own 'joke', then cackles like a doomed rooster caught for the chopping block. His hair is mottled, and once-neat khakis are filthy, blood-stained from Philly's saber slash.

Chuck dribbles to the free throw line; slowly, methodically, he stops, bounces to his own rhythm three times, shoots –swish! The leathery orange globe returns to his hands. He turns to face the coach standing in the lane at the opposite end of the court. Dark coagulating blood oozes between the gray duct tape wrapped tightly around his atrophied arm, mottling the glossy wooden gym floor like oil leaking from the cracked engine block of his old Mustang.

"Throw me the ball, Chuck. I'll show you how it's done," Coach says, slurring and slow.

"Come on, Coach, how 'bout we play a game of one-on-one," Chuck taunts.

"One-on-none!" Bruce scoffs. Dead humor.

Chuck dribbles, dribbles. Hook shot. Swish! "Two points!"

"Very good, Chuck, one-on-one equals two –genius!"

Chuck lowers his stance and starts dribbling, playing offensively, back and forth across the width of the court, going through mock practice drills.

"Show me some defense, Coach," Chuck says, strongly offensive.

"You ain't got nearly enough for me, baggy boy!" Coach digresses, attacking the Chuck who used to wear droopy jeans, too low and large.

Today Chuck wears the jeans that Pam said, *'fit just right'*. He feels comfortable in his new skin.

He offers Coach a sinister jackal grin and dribbles steadily, rhythmically in offensive stance, ready to the play -the game.

'You're my hero, Chuck,' Pam had said.

I am? Yes, Pam, I am.

Coach assumes a defensive position, offensive to Chuck, blood puddling beneath his feet. His heart races, blood pressure rises but eager to fall, e-nhanced far beyond his capabilities.

"Be ready, baggy boy!" Bruce the barbaric warrior roars.

Coach steps once; stops. He steps again. Quick-steps and he slips in his body's depleting gore. Two-steps. Falls to one knee, one good hand. He steps out of bounds, beyond the crimson boundary of the puddle of blood.

"Never on my team, boy!" Coach's arm throbs, head pounds, pressure like a vice, sweat beading on his forehead. Shock, fright, defeat and awe wave across his red face, and then the façade of peace replaces all expressions as he crumples to the court. Thud. Squeak of shoe on shined hardwood. Silence. Chuck drops the ball. It bounces, slowly down to quick dribbles, then rolls easily down the floor, finally inert by the body. Chuck averts his eyes, forward, past the object. No more fear.

68.

"She finally said a few words," the Reverend says to Ester standing by Lila's hospital bed.

"She remembers, doesn't she?" Ester asks.

"Yes. Bruce must have set it off. She said, 'Bruce... Tina... killed... Cleve.' He basically confessed to Lila that he killed Cleve, and tortured her with the memory of the tragedy, that little girl," says the Reverend.

"All that at one time was too much for her. At least her mind is starting to wrap around it," Ester says.

"She's going to Hope Harbor Hospital in a couple of days. It'll be intense for a few months, but she should be able to come home and be happy again –it's been so long since she's been happy," the Reverend says.

"I hope she'll agree to stay with Tina and me when she comes home. Tina needs her, and she needs Tina."

"Mm," Lila makes a little sound and smiles in her sleep. "Tina, mm."

"She's going to be fine," says the Reverend.

Pam enters the room and immediately hugs Ester and then Reverend Arnold.

"Mom, I'm here," Pam leans over the bed and kisses her mom's cheek."

"Mm," Lila smiles.

Out of the blue Pam announces "Emaw, I've made a decision about my life."

"Good for you, Pam." Ester puts her arm around her.

"I know you won't like it, but I've decided that I should take spring semester off. I know what you're thinking, but I *will* go back. Pam quickly fills in the blanks. "I'll take all my exams this semester and put everything on hold for spring and summer."

"You've always been a smart girl, Pam. Now you're a young woman. How did you come to this decision –about your life?" Ester asks.

"Earl and I got along so well this weekend, and I think maybe he needs his big sister –and I need my little brother. We can stay at home; Mom can stay with you and Tina, "says Pam.

"You seem to have it figured out, Pam." She turns to the Reverend. "What do you think?"

"I think this young lady can do anything, and with all this happening, her dad dying, Mom in the hospital, getting arrested –" the Reverend starts.

"Arrested? What?" Ester asks.

"How did you know, Reverend?" Pam asks.

"A little bird told me. Ester, don't worry, it was justifiable assault – uh, self-defense," the Reverend says.

"Assault?" Ester asks.

"Emaw, it's one of those stories that I will tell you later, and again and again and never live it down. It's alright," Pam says.

"I know Earl will be glad you're here, Pam," Ester says.

"And Chuck, too," the Reverend grins.

"What? How did you know?" Pam asks.

"Those little birds keep tweeting."

"I'm behind you 100%, young lady," says Ester.

"And so are we," says the Reverend, holding his worn black leather Bible to his chest.

Chuck rings the doorbell. Glenda greets him with a hug as he crosses the threshold.

"Come on in. How are you, Chuck? You look tired."

Chuck follows Glenda to the kitchen and sits facing her. She tells him the whole story, and how Philly is in shock from her guilt –and all the blood.

Chuck tells her the news.

"Is he dead?"

"No." Chuck pauses. "I went by the gym. He was there… all hyped up on e-nhancers. He just collapsed –natural causes."

"He could have hurt you, Chuck."

"And I could have let him die, but I didn't. I called 911."

"That's insanity." *Maybe you should have let him die*, she thinks.

Chuck shakes his head. "Philly broke him down. I just finished him off in a friendly game of one-on-one."

"I'm glad you're here, Chuck." She looks him in the eye. *You're a hero – Philly, too.* She places her hand on his and lets it linger. "Why don't you go back to Philly's room. Earl's back there."

Chuck goes down the hall and knocks on the door. He eases it open. "It's me."

"Come on in, Chuck," says Philly.

"What's up, Chuck?" Earl asks.

"The drama's over."

"I killed him!" Philly gasps, putting her hand over her mouth, and starts to cry.

Chuck kneels by the bed. "No, you did not!" He puts his hand on her shoulder. "He's alive enough to go to jail – after they save what's left of his life." Chuck stands. "The stuff I found in his office, the vials in your dad's briefcase, evidence for the police that Bruce *assisted* in your dad's death. I'm sorry, Earl." He places a hand on Earl's shoulder.

Earl looks down at the floor. Philly rests her head on his shoulder, her arms around him.

"It's over, Earl," she says softly. "He can't hurt anyone else."

"No fear." Chuck says.

"I'm not scared either." Philly agrees.

"No more."

Detective Brown arrives at the scene shortly after Chuck leaves the gym. As the EMT's roll the gurney out, he shakes his head and thinks, *It's a shame... all a shame.*

Sunday, his day off halfway over – and the case is resolved. The evidence, plus the testimony of Lila and Philly, will convict Bruce. *If only there wasn't all the red tape to file after this! My day off is a goner!*

Glenda sits at the kitchen table, letters from her runaway husband spread over the old Formica surface. With her daughter out of the house, she's got Sunday afternoon off to rest –and reply. Philly doesn't know that her dad has been sending letters to her mom sporadically. In her letters to him, Glenda writes mostly about Philly. This time it's all about Philly.

She's a good girl - a young woman. She has a boyfriend –a young man friend. She helped apprehend a criminal... cut him with a knife. Philly is a brave young woman.

Philly: brave, strong, independent, smart. If you want to come back into her life before it's too late, you had better come soon, because she's growing up fast. Philly and I are doing OK.

She ends the letter with unwritten 'love',
Glenda.

69.

Earl and Chuck tromp through the charred underbrush until they reach the fort. The perimeter is scorched, and the pine straw-covered ground is sooty black. The orange twenty-liter bucket rests on its side. Earl goes over and sets it downside up in the center of the clearing.

"It'll come back in the spring," Chuck says. He recalls all the green camouflage that had concealed them from the outer forest, from the world.

"Yeah." Earl sits on the bucket, elbows on his knees, hands under his jaws. *The Thinker.* "Don't know if it'll ever be the same."

"Maybe not the same, but good," Chuck says.

The little boy Earl sees Dad, in his mind's eye, just before he goes out of sight, into the woods.

Do you hear me, Earl?
Yes, Dad.
I'm still here, son.
I know, Dad.

Pam and Philly rustle through the singed laurels. Earl stands as Philly leaps up and flings her arms around his neck, almost toppling him over the bucket.

"Whatcha got there, Pam?" Chuck asks.

"A little communion wine complements of the Reverend," Pam announces. "He just doesn't know it's his complements —unless he inventories the wine safe at church. I left a *Thank You* note."

"Bless you," says Chuck.

"Oh, and I've got these Moravian Sugar Cookies that Pam brought back from Old Viceroy!" Philly says, with crumbs on her chin.

"Sweet!" says Earl.

Pam sets the two bottles of wine on the overturned bucket, in the center of their circle.

"No cups?" Chuck asks.

"No, but I brought a corkscrew," Pam says.

"Hey, Chuck, how about your special pipe —any tobacco?" Earl asks.

"Just enough for one smoke."

The quartet sits on the charred ground, crisscross applesauce like Tina learned in Sunday school. Earl uncorks the sacred wine. Chuck strikes a wooden match and lights the finger-packed tobacco.

Pam pops the cork. Earl passes the bottle to Philly for the first sip.

"*Virgin* to wine, huh, little Philly?" Pam asks.

"Yes." Philly wipes her lips with the back of her hand. "Pam?"

"Thanks." Pam takes a sip from the bottle. "And, no." She pats her lips with a lock of her hair. "Chuck?"

"Yes - and no," says Chuck. He takes a puff of the smooth aromatic tobacco and passes the pipe to Pam before taking a healthy swig of wine.

"Easy, boy!" says Earl. He takes the bottle from Chuck.

"I forgot the question." Earl takes a double dose of wine.

"Wo, boy! Pass it onward to your little Philly," Chuck says.

They pass the powder blue pipe around the circle, following the wine.

Philly puffs. Her face turns flush. She coughs. "Enough smoke for me." She leans over to Earl and gives him a smoky kiss.

Earl sets the half-empty bottle of communion wine on the overturned bucket. Pam breaks the seal on the tin of sweet thin Moravian cookies.

"Take. Eat." Pam passes the cookies.

"More wine, Philly?"

"Yes, please."

"But don't drink all of it, boys." Pam reminds them. "Remember your christening at the NUB? *Do* you remember?"

The four friends gather in the fort religiously as winter advances.
Love and friendship flourish even as the woods remain dormant.
In the spring when Philly and Earl, Pam and Chuck are blossoming,
tender grasses attract the young bucks and their dear ones.
Fern fiddleheads unfurl out of the scorched ground.
The laurel sheds brown scorched leaves.
Fresh clusters of pale pink blossoms open amid waxy new leaves.
And the orange bucket stands unscathed in the center of it all.

The End...

and the Beginning

CPSIA information can be obtained
at www.ICGtesting.com
Printed in the USA
FSHW010753050820
72681FS